Paradise & Back:
A Damfool Career

Paradise & Back:
A Damfool Career

J. L. C. Strang

JLCStrang

Mayland Graphics Limited
Essex

First published in 2003 by
Lawrie Plantation Services Limited
Wrotham Place
Wrotham
Sevenoaks
Kent TN15 7AE

ISBN 0 9546253 0 7

Typeset by Alan P. Carnell Printers, Chelmsford, Essex
Printed by Mayland Graphics Limited, Chelmsford, Essex

To my beloved wife,
without whose support and joy of living
the volumes of *Paradise & Back*
would probably never have been written.

Preface

This book is a memoir which, because it begins in 1947, required a reconstruction of actual events, stories, descriptions of life in north-east India, with characters speaking in the way of those times in dialogues which evince much more atmosphere and interest than the author could create without them. There are fictitious characters who are accredited with collected stories to reduce the long list of names; there are actual characters with fictitious names who would recognise themselves with approval and amusement. Planters, tribal people on or off the estates, the wildlife and the wonder of the Himalayan foothills are all the material of this book. The British planters continued working for three and a half decades or more after Independence, and the book will tell how they liked living in Assam.

Chapter XIII

The last traces of cloud had cleared away during the night. Telford and I arrived at the hangar together, and I asked if all had gone well with the meeting of his family. He said the train had been two hours late, both daughters had very bad sore throats, and they were all likely to stay in bed for the next six hours. I had done the daily inspection the previous evening, and was ready to go as the mist was clearing. As I called out the starting check I saw Telford turn his head, and then heard the sound of an approaching vehicle. It was Fraser's black Riley, and Telford made a noise like a curse or a surprised recall. 'We'd better wait for him,' he said. 'Switches off.' It turned out George Fraser was making a prearranged visit.

'Good morning gentlemen! By jove, MacStorm, this must be like old times for you flying off into the wild blue yonder, eh! Where are you off to?' Before I could comment Telford spoke.

'Fraser, I am sorry. I had a telegram last night telling me my wife and family were due to arrive at two this morning. They didn't actually arrive until after four. I forgot to send you a message. I forgot your visit, and I am sending MacStorm off to the North Bank on his own, to make his survey and report.'

When Fraser heard my arrangement to stay with Jonson his eyebrows shot up, and he asked Telford with a gust of laughter if he had warned me what to expect. He clearly thought the hard-drinking Jonson with his reputed unorthodox establishment might give me a bit of a shock. He turned to me. 'No polo over there, MacStorm, but marvellous fishing and shooting. You'll miss your polo this afternoon.' He looked at Telford, who seemed not to have heard him. When I had answered Fraser's question as to how long it would take me to reach Bogahilonia, I noticed Telford with one hand on the propeller, and climbed into the cockpit, grinning at Fraser's amazement at

1

the short time it was going to take. I went through the starting procedure, and after a short warm up taxied out, saw the two *chowkidars* in the mist wave flags to show the strip was clear, and took off. It was good to be flying alone, and breaking out of the thinning veil of mist into the brilliant sunshine I turned along the line of the river and climbed towards the great Dehing reserve, where I had been lost for three days, humiliated and taught a lesson. I saw the peninsula, noted the fallen tree had been swept away without trace, and observed the vast level expanse of luxuriant trees with a feeling of rueful respect. I turned to cross the Brahmaputra, thrilled with the wonderful view of the snows, and levelled off at 2,000 feet. Looking at the map I saw the 'inner line' boundary ran mostly along the low hills of undulating forest just before the steeper ridges suddenly thrust upwards like breakers about to break along the shore; but when the line came to the point about three miles north of Bogahilonia where the Subansiri river left its gorge for the plains of Assam, the inner line went up the Subansiri river for about seven miles, and then went twisting eastwards along a ridge about 3,500 feet high for about fifteen miles before descending into the bed of a smaller river called the Jiya Dhol, where it met the plains. I came closer to the mountains, and marvelled at the steepness of the ridges, the cover and size of the trees, the beautiful jade rivers embroidered with white rapids amongst dark boulders, and banks of ivory sands at bends. Approaching the Subansiri I climbed to 3,500 feet, and flew north to the ridge where the inner line ran. I flew along this ridge revelling that the line left free about a 105 square miles of primeval forested ridges as part of Assam: a wilderness for exploration some day. I flew on, gazing into the first high valley north of the ridge, and saw a green cultivated valley with a score or more long houses on piles. There were cattle, and I could see tiny figures in what seemed to be a perfect hidden paradise on a small river. I descended until I was about 200 feet above this village, and saw what looked like Abors, the men with their hair cut like inverted hemispheres, the women with plaited pigtails in tight chignons. Their skin gleamed like polished copper, and they waved happily, breaking off with scampering boys and girls to chase after their frightened cattle. I climbed to regain height, feeling rather ashamed to have made so much noise over such an enviable preserve of peace. I wondered just what such a place would be like during the monsoon. From high I saw the fantastic gorge of the Subansiri, into which I ultimately descended with half throttle, marvelling at the great cliffs of stone, and the steepness of the forest on either bank. There

2

were sandbanks on the insides of various bends, and I could see many tracks mainly of elephants, and others too small to identify. I came out of the gorge where the jade river split into three or four large beds, running between islands with boulder and sand shores, and stands of tall forest on each. I could smell a scent that was to stay with me all my life: a mixture of virgin forest, and the spume from the rapids of a snow river where large fish abounded, a scent of wilderness. I was once again caught, this time firmly, in the golden web of the North Bank. At 500 feet I steered for Bogahilonia, to announce by a gentle low 'buzz' over the bungalows and the office that I intended to land.

It took time for the truly rural cowherds to clear the many cattle from the airstrip, so that the estate jeep arrived before I was able to land. Two men stood beside the jeep, MacDonald and Jonson, the latter being even bigger than his assistant. When I landed I saw each had the look in his eyes of a lonely crofter of the highlands, proud and questing. There were strong handshakes and introductions, and when I told them what I was briefed to do, it was clear Jonson had heard nothing. He shook his head and lowered his brows, looking sideways at me, but he said he would certainly be happy to help as much as possible. Steve MacDonald asked if I had noticed how much of the strip had been eroded away since my last visit. I said I had not noticed, and we went to the upriver end of the strip where there was a long diagonal end, just as I had remembered it, but they said about twenty yards had been lost, and next monsoon more would certainly be cut, because the river had deposited most of its silt on the other beds to the east, and was bound to undercut the now vertical bank about fifteen feet above the water. Jonson explained it would be the early rains which would do the most damage, raising the water above the boulder layer, and washing the sandy, gravelly layers below the fertile brown soil. Jonson was tall, heavy, and broad-shouldered, with a head of thick, dark brown hair, and bushy eyebrows. I noticed he seldom met my glance when listening, but when he spoke, he fixed his eyes fiercely on mine until he had said his piece. He told me this airstrip was likely to disappear during this year's rains. 'This is the way it happens in this country, especially on the North Bank. Look at the profile of these layers we're standing on. About fifty years ago the river deposited these boulders, twelve feet down, and in fifty years it put silt back on top of them, and the forest put in the humus. I can show you places over there,' he swept an arm to the eastern foothills, 'where there are banks twice this height. It's all because of the fantastic rainfall in these mountains; landslides, huge trees coming down; look at them.'

I asked if there was level ground somewhere to make a landing strip which would be safe from river erosion, and heard a burst of laughter from MacDonald. Jonson didn't laugh, and staring at me asked who the hell was it who wanted landing strips all over the place. 'We are quite happy with one visitor from London and one from Calcutta in the year, in January and February, preferably February when the fishing is not so good.' He was about thirty-five, and had been in the navy during the war. I came to know this when I explained, as I was sure MacDonald had explained, the idea of an aeroplane being available once a week for serious medical cases. He caustically described how they had managed well enough in a destroyer, hundreds of miles away from friendly land, with a doctor who was always seasick, and nothing worse than chronic constipation for the whole crew. 'If MacDonald gets married and puts his girl in the family way he can send her to the South Bank a month before she's due, and feel happy she'll be looked after; but I'd bet she'll be no better off there than here. We don't want intruders, busybodies and holidaymakers, spoiling this cold weather paradise of ours.' Pausing a little he began to smile as if contemplating mischief. 'They're all welcome any time during the rains; once will be enough for them.' He spoke quietly, sweeping his eyes over the river, 'but we don't want the kind of people that drove all the way from Jorhat in a car followed by a lorry with all their gear and, believe it or not, uniformed servants. Spent all their time trawling in a big dugout propelled by incredulous Miris.' I followed his gaze to where the various rapids thrust up their white plumes, and gave a background of soothing low sound; the great forest receded towards the whole horizon of blue ridges, rising into the distant high range. I told him I understood what he meant. He put two men to protect the Auster, and we went to his bungalow 'for a drink'. He seemed almost offended when I said I would prefer tea to beer or whisky, although it was hardly ten-thirty. After a long draught of beer he licked his lips and said it needed a bit of thought, and eventually began to speak, punctuating again with one index finger poking the palm of his other hand. 'Maybe the other managers nearer to the town have had a telegram, and even if they have not, the best thing to do is to drive in to the club; they'll all be there by five-thirty to six. You coming with us, Mac?'

'No bloody thanks!' MacDonald turned to me with a slight flush on his cheeks. 'You ought to get it straight before you bump into that lot. You and I, never mind what the hell we were during the war, we are the lowest form of animal life in Assam, chum, and they protect their marvellous social life mostly for themselves. Once a year, once a bloody year they invite each other to dinner, the ones that can stand each other, only during the cold weather when the roads are open. One thing about this godforsaken place is having a manager who was in the second war, and actually talks to his assistant.' They laughed at each other.

'The only thing wrong with him,' said Jonson loftily, 'is he can't stand being treated with the disdain of a manager who was in the senior service. The other thing is being besotted with a girl in England and frightened stiff to bring her out to a place like this. But he's right, you know. Just before the war there were eight of us in the club after playing tennis in the April heat. His highness George Fraser walks into the bar, where we were all drinking, in his dove grey gabardine suit and silk tie. He looks around like Lord Muck and says "Well I'll be damned! Nobody here! I might just as well go home. There's lightning flashing down west; they must have guessed rain's coming; scared of the bridges going. Hah!" and he goes out and drives off home, taking his lovely wife with him, much to our disappointment.'

I said Fraser seemed to be paternally friendly with those of us who were in the services, and had spoken a lot to me; even this morning he said he was sorry I would be missing polo this afternoon. Jonson said he wasn't a bad old codger: a damn fine manager; no nonsense about getting things done. His only trouble was carrying on as if we were all acting out some great drama. He laughed, and said George's wife, a real peach, once told him when he was chairing a club committee meeting he should wear a toga when he made such serious speeches. 'A helluva shame,' Jonson said with feeling, 'they couldn't produce children. She's meant to be a bloody fine mother, that one.' He finished his beer in a couple of huge gulps, and looked at his watch. 'Right! We'll grab some tackle and drive up to Dulung Mukh for about an hour or so of fishing. Back to lunch; then we'll leave for the club about four-thirty. We don't want to be late back and having to wait for the elephants to get off the road. It's slacks and ties for the club.' When I said I hadn't brought a jacket he said a thick pullover would do as long as we went no further than the bar.

The drive up went north through the estate to where the small foothill river Dulung met the Subansiri. On the estate, pruning was well under way.

The *sirdars* were mostly old, and venerable looking, and the labour seemed to me to be leaner, less handsome than in Medeloabam, and when I said so Jonson said life over here was much more difficult for everyone. There was no railway, and in contrast to the South Bank, where all kinds of food came from the far south, here it was a matter of living mostly on what people grew locally. He told me the Assamese didn't go much into the business of raising money from their own crops, but the Bengalis, Oriyas, Biharis and Nepalis all offered their surpluses at local bazaars. The trouble was there were not very many of these outsiders around these parts. Leaving the estate we drove through tall forest on a clean leafy track, catching an occasional glance to our right of the great riverscape. Eventually we emerged into the bright sunshine, and stopped near a small bungalow on stilts, about thirty yards from the small river. Its water was crystal clear, not more than four feet deep, until it swirled into an eddy pool where its current met the jade snow water from the Himalayas, all the way from Tibet. The mountains were huge, the first ridges being hardly more than a mile away. They rose suddenly from the low forested rises beyond the Dulung, like gigantic petrified breakers, with here and there a cliff face, and their colour was heightened by the blue alpine shadows on every tree. Range after range rose, fading with distance into delicate tones, and the most distant high tops around 10,000 feet were now almost obscured by our closeness to the magic 'inner line'. The noise of the rapids was here much louder, the water faster between successive pools, and the spume rising mingled its scent with that of the primeval forest: a scent seeming to raise dim memories of something dreamed or inherited. The benevolent sun warmed and gilded the scene. I felt almost breathless with elation; everything seemed in harmony. There were no humans in sight except the three of us.

Jonson explained the bungalow had been built several decades ago as a forest fishing lodge for use by the Viceroy of India. During the second world war it was used as a rehabilitation rest house for Allied soldiers and airmen who had been badly injured or debilitated. The airstrip where I had landed was built so that deserving cases could comfortably be brought during the cold weather. It had not been used since the war. Our shirts came off, and Jonson gave me a rod with advice to cast high so that the bait dropped where the clear Dulung water ran alongside the fast green snow water, and sank flickering like a small fish in trouble, which was what could bring the lunging mahseer to attack. After half an hour Jonson had taken out a ten-

6

pound fish, and MacDonald suggested we had a swim. We stripped off, and after listening to Jonson on safety precautions, which he delivered scratching his hairy and slightly adipose belly, we plunged into the Dulung water. It was pleasantly warm, but in the eddies came now and then the shock of a wild vortex of snow water, spurring us to speed back to the warm shallows. We came out breathless and tingling, and sat to dry on a smooth trunk of some ancient forest giant, as pale as ivory, polished by the silt-filled water of the monsoon torrents. We walked a few hundred yards along the sandy shore of the Dulung, examining tracks galore of all creatures except men. There was one tiger track of terrifying size, the forepad being over six inches broad. I had my first sight of the beautiful pointed tracks of the gaur, or Indian bison, a kind of wild ox, the bulls of which grew to a great size; they were extremely shy, and very careful in their movements. Their colour was dark brown, with mature males almost black, and all had white stockings. Jonson said there were one or two salt licks up some of the streams which fed the Dulung where, if one could find them and spare the time, one could see all kinds of game. He had done it once with a Miri *shikari*, but saw only porcupines and imperial pigeons, although there were tracks of everything. It was all open to explore, and outsiders never came. The only paths were those made mainly by elephants, utilised preferably by prowling tigers. As we drove back I had to shake off the trance of that unique scene, rather like when as a child I had heard a great symphony for the first time; I felt it had somehow been lying in wait in the unexplored hinterland of my being, waiting for this day of glorious discovery. Now I knew the light in the eyes of that colonel in Allahabad had not been a false delusion, because I had now seen what had kindled it, and felt a great relief. I need not any longer feel bound to stick to this way of life by sheer discipline, almost punishing myself for the kind of romanticism which drove young men to fly in wars. The light I saw in that man's eyes had kindled something which I had not really recognised until I had walked into the Calcutta tea office, when the whole thing caught fire. It was as well that after the serious disappointments of finding an Assam so different from what I had dreamed it to be, and the prospects of a career in India threatened by the imminent possibilities of violent civil war, my morale had fortuitously been improved by Constable and his Piper Cub, polo, and the remarkable change of scene with the coming of Independence at Medeloabam; but none of these had taken as great an effect as the sight of the Subansiri from Dulung Mukh. What I had dreamed of was, in its wild beauty, actually there, waiting to be explored and experienced: a part of the world as it might have been long before men appeared on earth.

Jonson took me to the club that evening. MacDonald refused to go, and told me to beware of those senior managers, who, no matter what your war record might have been, would treat you as the lowest form of animal life in Assam. At the club I was impressed with Jonson's willing help, and the way he left me with one manager whilst briefing the others on what I had been sent to find out. I found them less forbidding and supercilious than MacDonald had implied, although it was quite surprising to find how only two of the managers present showed any sign of welcoming the idea of making airstrips for a 'company' aeroplane. I think it was fortunate I told each one, interviewed separately, I had no intention of becoming a company 'air taxi' driver, preferring to become eventually an estate manager with flying as an enjoyable hobby. I enjoyed meeting them, three ex-first war, and three ex-second war. Melville Gordon MC and 'Isaac' Newton, ex-Royal Flying Corps, were frankly much against improving communications with Calcutta, saying their profits record put most of the South Bank estates to shame. They each said they treated Calcutta correspondence as Nelson treated his signals at Trafalgar: they turned a blind eye, and did what they knew was best for the company, always prepared to take the blame if anything went wrong, which it never did. They did not want interference by visiting accountants or engineers who had the habit of saying the North Bank was twenty-five years behind the South. They would become a terrible nuisance if they could hop into an aeroplane and land over here whenever they needed to impress London with their wonderful efforts to rescue the estates from the hopeless bungling of their uncooperative managers. I was impressed by their very positive attitudes, accepting the legitimate pride in their results, even aiming off for a certain amount of 'wilderness effect'.

We returned from the club after having made arrangements to land at three places, and visit one other over the next two days, which was all I needed to do, making five places including Bogahilonia. I rose early on Sunday morning, and completed the daily inspection helped by MacDonald. He told me Jonson was a good manager to have, but he had some annoying habits. He was fed up with him coming to wake him at five in the morning after a very late night of drinking. He said he was one of those ancient mariners with hollow legs: showing no sign of the effects of alcohol. He was not an alcoholic, but he seemed to burn it all off by working long hours, talking long hours, and not leaving him in peace. He was so friendly it was difficult to make him believe he was such a 'bloody nuisance'. To me it seemed this was something to do with living in such an isolated place; and when I hinted that Jonson, despite being a strong character, might simply be lonely, Mac laughed like a drain, and said I should see what actually saved him from being lonely. I thought a test flight would be in order, and we took off for a circuit and landing, with Mac on the controls. He flew well; after all, he had flown Mosquitoes. The visits were all successful. When I landed on the slightly limited sports field at Bandarjili, I thought something had gone wrong. Gordon came up to the Auster as I climbed out and said, 'You just don't know what you've done, do you?' I swung round, looking for perhaps an aerial snapped by my wheels on the approach, or a dog hit whilst landing. He said, 'You've destroyed our sanctuary, our treasured isolation, for ever. It's not your fault. This is my wife, Catriona.' I apologised, saying I thought I knew what it must be like. The more I saw of their situation, the more I thought there was no such thing as a perfect place to live; one would always have to accept flaws in order to enjoy beauty. It made me think I should be ready to make compromises, and I remember feeling hopelessly ill equipped to do this without learning the hard way. They took me to their beautiful house, plinth built, situated in a garden frothing with flowering trees and shrubs, on a plateau above a splendid river, facing the innumerable ridges and great forests to the north and west. There they gave me tea to drink which was the finest, delicate flavour I had ever tasted. It was a memorable experience. I found later Bandarjili was top of the Assam Lothian group for prices, and had been so since Gordon had brought it up from near the bottom when he became manager about fifteen years ago.

After tiffin on Monday afternoon I wrote my report in pencil on a foolscap pad which Jonson let me have. We took a picnic tea up to Dulung Mukh and, whilst Jonson fished, MacDonald and I walked barefoot up the Dulung, looking at new tracks. Every night the strong katabatic winds blew sand over the previous day's tracks, and it was fascinating to see how much recent movement of so many different animals there was. MacDonald said one of the old *shikaris* had told him, when there was a full moon in April and May, and cloud over the mountains, there would be no breeze, and animals would come out of the hot forest to the cool, wide river bed; he had never tried it, but if one hid on one of the wide bends they say you can see all kinds of game.

Before we left to drive back, we put on our sweaters and watched the ranges change through dark blue to purple against the western end of the ranges, and we saw Venus, brilliant in the afterglow like a piercing white flame.

Supper was late, and before supper Jonson insisted on having beer with MacDonald, whilst I drank salted lime juice from huge green limes grown on the estate. By the third pair of beers Jonson called for Kanasundri, who seemed to have been waiting not far away and entered the sitting room to stand by Jonson's easy chair. She was tall for a local girl, and beautiful, well built in a definitely voluptuous way. She had only one eye, the result of some infection when she was a small child, and Jonson explained he had been offered the girl by her parents who said they could not marry her off with only one eye. Both eyelids had long black lashes, and she had a permanent smile, with the mouth on the blind side drooping a little, just enough to form a sad but attractive appearance. Jonson said he made an arrangement to keep her for three years, paying her a monthly 'salary', his idea being he would next year return to Britain for six months and find a wife; but he laughed self-consciously, and confessed he found himself so fond of her that he couldn't bring himself to push her out. I wanted to know an awful lot about such things as having babies or not having babies, marrying or not marrying, growing old with a native mistress and so on, but I felt such questions were probably unwelcome. When dinner was eventually announced, and Kanasundri walked from the room like a satisfied tiger with perfect natural grace, I felt my head swirl a little. Was it so easy to help oneself to temporary fulfilment of the strongest natural urge? I seemed to hear warning bells toll, somewhere deep in the innermost but unidentified conscience, of a man striving to find his way, like an eel from the Sargasso Sea, bound for its inherited destiny in some unseen and distant river.

The following morning I flew back to Medeloabam, arriving at nine-forty-five, where it was clear enough to land. Between the hangar and Telford's bungalow there were five cars parked under the trees, Fraser's black Riley among them. Nunoo appeared magically, to take my bag from me as I unloaded it. After filling the tank with petrol, and checking the oil level, I walked through the tea to Telford's office, and gave the head clerk my report for typing. It began with a general appraisal, in which I wrote there were some who were not keen on the idea of airstrips on their estates, as well as others who were quite keen. Under the name of each estate I wrote a description of length, width, surface, approaches and proximity to buildings.

I said I had suggested estimates of time and cost might be made in order to give some idea of what was involved. I wrote a note on the availability of Lilabari as a pick-up point, describing its usable state. I learned from the head clerk there was a senior men's conference being held in Mr Telford's bungalow. I said I would go to my bungalow to change into working clothes, and return to the office to check the typed report of three pages, so that it could be sent in to Mr Telford. When I reached my bungalow there were three letters addressed to me in Telford's writing. One was a note to point out I had failed to attend the field office on Saturday morning to discuss and issue work orders for that day: 'something that must be done even if you are leaving early to fly, as you probably will be doing now and then as time goes on'. The second was a letter telling me to be ready within twenty-four hours of my return from the North Bank to accommodate Mr and Mrs Field in my bungalow for at least a week. Crockery and any other necessary requirements can be borrowed from Mrs Telford. The third letter said I should report to Telford to discuss a road trip to the Tea Research Association as soon as possible after my return. I found it odd, and a little disturbing, to find these things notified by letter, instead of by word of mouth. I asked the servants if they knew about a *sahib* and *memsahib* coming to stay, wanting to know who they were, but they looked blankly at me, declaring complete ignorance. I changed and returned to the office, where I asked the head clerk if he knew Mr and Mrs Field and why they were coming to stay with me. He was rather uncomfortable when he said he had once seen Mr Field but did not know him. He said he thought there had been some trouble but did not know any details. 'Perhaps this is being discussed in the conference,' he said. I thought twenty-four hours didn't leave me much time to prepare for these people and decided to write a note to Mrs Telford, asking when I might meet her to ask for help with two mattresses and two blankets for the Fields. I said I would be grateful for extra milk if available. I sent this note by the office *chowkidar* with instructions to tell the servants to ensure it was delivered to the *memsahib*. I cycled quickly back to my bungalow to give the servants money enough to buy eggs, chickens and potatoes for the people who were coming. The horror on the face of the cook, and the doubt on the faces of Maneklal and Nunoo, did nothing to cure my sinking feeling after the enjoyable North Bank trip. When I arrived back at the office, the *chowkidar* said the *memsahib* would meet me at the stables, now, and I went in haste. Mrs Telford was coming from her garden, accompanied by her two daughters and her son. The daughters were seventeen and twelve, both as good looking as their mother, the younger perhaps even better; the son was seven, very shy, and very like his father with panther eyes. In her rather nasal drawl Mrs Telford introduced Lucy, Linda, and Martin, the girls pleasantly smiling and shy, and Martin reluctant to offer his hand, looking at me with suspicion, rather like father, who seemed to look at everyone that way.

'Well, you can see what I have to cope with now,' Mrs Telford said with a faint smile, 'three extra people. I'm not sure whether we are going to have visitors this coming weekend, so I'll have to speak to my husband. I presume he told you to ask for help?' I said he had sent me a note, and he seemed to be busy at the moment. 'You haven't been here a year yet, have you?' she asked. 'It's a bit much expecting you to put up that pair. I don't suppose you have met them yet?' I said I hadn't even heard their name until today, and admitted I was virtually unprepared for anything more than a Catholic padre, about which Mr Foyle had warned me. 'Yes, and you are still paying off the cost of Jet, aren't you?' This shook me, and was a sign that the jungle telegraph was in action. 'You had very bad luck with that racehorse. Look, this conference will finish before noon. I've sent in tea and biscuits, and they'll all go home for their own lunches.' At this point Linda, the younger daughter, spoke.

'Thank you very much for lending me Rani, Mr MacStorm! She's huge, but she's lovely to ride. I'd love to see you play polo on her.' She blushed, and her mother spoke again.

'See my husband at the office about one-thirty; or, if your servants watch when the cars all go away, come one hour after that, would you?' I said I would do that, wondering what would transpire. Lucy kept watching me, but switched her eyes away if I looked at her. I smiled, thinking she was little more than a child: seventeen!

I cycled out to the men's pruning, and began to go through the work, taking a knife now and then to see how my hands had profited from the rest they had been given. The Assamese head overseer met me, and when we walked back to our cycles he said it was a very bad thing which had happened at Soomoni, an outgarden of one of the estates the other side of Panitola. I asked him to tell me what had happened, and he said some of the pruning men had objected to the raising of tasks, and had eventually thrown stones at Mr Field, who fled to take refuge. He said Mr Field was a man who had been employed during the war during the shortage of senior staff. He had been sacked by a company in the Bengal Dooars, and worked for an engineering firm in Tinsukia. 'He was not really a *pukka sahib*: he is using bad language at the labour the whole time, and taking drink even from breakfast time. His wife is very unwell, very thin.' The trouble had happened yesterday, and the news had travelled all the way to Medeloabam, just like that. When I cycled back for lunch I saw Telford leaving his office. He put up his hand and beckoned. His first words were, 'How long is it before you finish paying for your horse?' I told him my last payment would be in February, and he gave a single nod. 'Thank you for the report,' he said. 'I didn't expect you back so soon, but it seems you were lucky enlisting Jonson's help. We'll talk about it.' He put his head down in one of his concentrated thinking postures. 'Walk with me to the stables. I think the Fields will be bringing their own mattresses and bedding when they come. They are bringing their own two servants: cook and bearer, so they will be able to look after themselves, more or less. He's not going to work here, thank goodness! The trouble is he was given a new contract which doesn't end for another eight months, and he won't take cash in lieu of those eight months' pay. He's got nowhere to go, been in this country since he jumped his cargo boat in Calcutta when he heard war was declared. He was too old for the services, older than me, and Calcutta took him on believing he was a ship's engineer. He's been nothing but trouble since then: a complete rummy, married an Anglo-Indian hospital nurse; the poor woman seems to adore him, but she's suffering from chronic liver trouble, thin as a rake. We've recommended to Calcutta that he be given a one-way ticket to the UK; he's not entitled to it, being taken on in this country on a temporary contract, but no-one in Assam wants him the way he is. A real problem.' I was impressed at what seemed to be his charitable view, but could find nothing to say.

'Do you have any alcohol in your bungalow?' he asked, and when I said none, he went on. 'You have to explain to your servants that Field is a raving drunk at times. They should keep out of his way, politely, if you know what I mean. If he starts shouting they should stay silent, or send for his servants. I hear you are speaking the language well. How would you say all this to them?' This caught me guessing, and I tried my best, which made him nod and smile. 'I would never have dreamed of saying it that way,' he said, 'but they won't be in any doubt about that. I know you haven't got a sleeping dictionary. I would know within a day if you had started that; but if you let strangers hear you speak that way they will feel quite sure they know what you are up to.' He also was warning me, more or less as Foyle had done, that there were voice prints which told tales of sexual relationships. I had obviously mused a few seconds too long because Telford did one of his sudden changes of subject. 'I sent you several notes this morning. I didn't know when you would arrive back. I have to do this because, as you will find, there is so much to remember about everything in this job that one must put it down quickly. Do the same and you will find it pays.' I nodded, relieved there was nothing more than that. Then I did a quick change of subject.

'None of the managers had received a telegram on the North Bank about airstrips,' I said. 'When I said what was required of me they seemed to think there must be some official explanation on the way; either from you or from Fraser.'

'There was no sign of any difficulty in your report, not on that account.'

'There wasn't. I had expected them to be very stand-offish but they were in fact helpful.'

'Good! I sent nothing, and obviously George sent nothing. It was up to Calcutta; they were the ones who actually sent George the word that a report was required. They will probably have written letters to them all which will take at least a week to ten days to arrive. None of us has a telephone, and the mail comes by rail. The North Bank mail gets as far as Tezpur, and then has to travel 150 miles by road to North Lakhimpur; and from there it depends how long it takes them to sort it out so that the estates' *dakwallas* can collect it by bicycle.' We stood fondling horses' heads, and he went on. 'You can see there is a case for sending all the estate mail to Hiloibhanga or Panitola, from where it could be flown to points north and south say twice a week.' I smiled and said there was a view over there that improvement of communications would ruin their relatively independent and successful efficiency, and I could appreciate their point. There was a pause whilst he examined Rani's mouth.

'From tomorrow, when you go for your ride at five-thirty, please take Linda. She'll ride Conker; I don't want her riding too fast yet. My wife and Lucy won't be riding early,' he smiled, 'they say a few months in England have made them lazy.' He looked at his watch and said we had better go for tiffin. 'Once the Fields are fixed up so that they can look after themselves, we'll arrange a date to drive down to Tocklai to see the Tea Research Association. We want to go into the problem of red spider, and see the latest developments on growing tea from selected cuttings. I'll send you some papers on that and we'll discuss it soon. Oh! By the way, Calcutta has taken on our first Assamese trainee planter. He has a degree in economics, and is going somewhere in the Hiloibhanga group; someone called Bhupendra Sarma. I'll take Linda riding this afternoon. There's a tricky case for you to deal with at three-thirty this afternoon. It will put a strain on your language. Bhose is very worried about it: Gonds.'

I was beginning to see his style of conversation: if one said something he had not expected, or which presented a new subject for consideration, he would shift it to his 'holding' file, so to speak, until he had time to think it over. I was fairly sure he would only induce conversation on a particular subject when he had exhaustively examined or researched it. I was bursting to talk about the airstrips, the flying, the beauty of the North Bank scene, but I saw I would have to wait, not only for that but for what was to happen to the South Bank air service. I began to make notes of everything he said, and before going out to the field work that afternoon went through the book where the work plans were written. The *jemadar babu* had written them in my absence, no doubt with the manager's prompting.

At three-thirty I arrived at the space on the office verandah where the table of audience was in place, and found about twenty Gond men, all wearing their ample turbans and blankets. They all saluted, looking grave, but with their gravity plainly worn like a mask, which set my mind seeking an explanation of their mood. There were several Gond women in their richly coloured saris and silver ornaments, standing more than twenty-five yards away, Sukhwaria being prominent among them, stressing some point with a mobile hand. Even at that range she put both hands together in greeting, followed in this by her companions. The welfare *babu* was nervous, and I asked him in English what matters there were for hearing. He said 'these people' were very difficult, raising most unusual matters which they should settle themselves, not embarrassing other people with unpleasant things. I sat at the table with him at the end on my right with the 'Domesday book', as Foyle had called it, where proceedings, findings and agreements were written, signed, and thumb printed appropriately. I asked him to tell me roughly what the problem was. He said it was very difficult for him to explain, because these were peculiar people. He said they should speak, and he would try to translate what they said. Now these Gonds, said by Foyle to have been a tribe of hunters similar to the Koyas, had somehow converted to

Hinduism, and were – or considered themselves to be – quite a cut above most other converts, and when they spoke formally they did so through their noses using a kind of Hindi which certainly sounded very formal indeed, but was difficult for me to follow. It transpired that a young bachelor who looked about twenty, said by Bhose to be slightly 'crecked', had not been able to marry because he was an idiot. He looked as if drugged, a good looking youth of clear complexion, whose eyes were large and black, heavily lidded. He spoke slowly and clearly, too slowly for normal conversation, and in a way which seemed to prove he was mentally deficient. The spokesman of the Gonds was an assistant *sirdar*, and Bhose asked him tersely to explain the complaint to the *sahib*, and to be careful not to use unclean language. There was no sign of the anger or unhappiness usual when complaints arose; one saw only the masks of gravity, with perhaps a smirk in the background. My interest was whetted, and my resolve to deal wisely strengthened, as I tried to draw the man to clarify for me what he was trying to say. This young man, Babulall, had been seen late at night, when people should have been sleeping, to enter the line cow shelter. Bhansilall *bura* saw him, because he was watching to see who might be stealing milk from his large white cow. When he saw what was happening he crept to Tilsai *chowkidar*'s house and brought him quietly to witness. To witness what? I looked at Bhose who frowned and turned pages in the book. I asked the spokesman to explain, and looking at Bhose, he murmured something in the Gonds' own tribal patois for the benefit of his own people, whereupon one old Gond with white eyebrows and moustache stepped forward, salaamed deeply, and said in good Hindustani that this Babulall was behaving to the young spotted heifer of Sukhuaro, the sister of Sukhwaria, as if it were his wife. Bhose slapped the book shut, and began to speak.

'There you are! That is the way to tell it properly to the *sahib*.' He glowered at the spokesman, who frowned and looked sideways at the older man. 'Now it is understood, and there is no need to say any more about this unclean business.' He turned to me and said, 'Sir, you see, these people!' But the spokesman began to speak again, explaining that the womenfolk were very angry about this. It is true Babulall is mad; not too mad to work and look after himself. He is not a wicked boy. He cannot help being...being mad. Everyone nodded. I then asked, looking from him to Bhose, what then is to be done? The spokesman began to speak with what must to him have been his special legal voice, only to be interrupted by the white moustached elder,

16

who explained in his slow, clear Hindustani that the owner of the heifer, a beautiful heifer of great promise as a milker, could never do anything but get rid of it, so far away that it could be sold without people knowing what had happened, for a sum...but here there was interruption from several of the men, one of whom asked me if he could call Sukhuaro, the person suffering this crime on her property. I said she should come and speak, and like a closely packed scrum of warriors in silver and brightly coloured silk, eight Gond matrons, eyes wider open than usual, with lowered brows, swept into the office compound led by Sukhwaria and her sister. The men receded, making way for them with frowning brows and smiles below their moustaches. Sukhwaria, wagging an index finger in Babulall's direction, began in nasal tones with curious enunciation to warn us all of the dangers of allowing even a mad one to behave in a way that was not only repulsive but shameful to our community of the Gond brotherhood. The elder speaker, obviously respected for his age and calm speech, motioned with his hand for her to be patient and listen. He said Sukhuaro demanded a bride price from Babulall of not less than 130 rupees. After he pays this he must take the heifer and go, just go away and not come back. There were murmurs from the men, and loud noises of assent from the women, which were abated by the elder's patient gesture. He said to me it was not right to send this idiot young man away with the heifer. He could not protect himself from the many wicked people who would steal the heifer, steal his money, and make him work for almost nothing. We can see he has been well fed; he works well with his fellows under their instruction and discipline. He cannot live without it. Even the women nodded at this. Babulall, he said, has nearly 800 rupees saved over three years, deposited in the office and written by the second clerk in his saving book, signed by the manager *sahib*. I looked at Bhose, who said quietly Mr Telford had been encouraging this for many years; I was impressed. The elder went on to say he knew Vikram and his family would be travelling back to Bilaspur in January. Babulall is a nephew of Vikram; he should take him back to his own village. He can pay the bride price to Sukhuaro, and they can walk to Dibrugarh to take the train, and on the way they can sell the heifer. He smiled at me, showing the upturned palms of both hands, and looked at Bhose, the women, and the men. One of the men stepped forward and saluted, saying he was Vikram, and he was willing to take Babulall; but he wanted it made clear if he could sell the heifer for more than the bride price, he would be able to pay Babulall his bride price back and take the profit for his family who, after all, would have the trouble of looking after Babulall all the long way to their village beyond Bilaspur. Sukhuaro came forward with one hand on her hip and an expression of incredulity. She demanded one condition before she agreed to that arrangement: if the heifer sold for less than the bride price, Vikram would make the difference up to Babulall. There were loud cries from men and women, and Vikram began to scowl; but when Sukhwaria wagged her finger at him and, looking at me, said she would not trust a greedy man like him with such a beautiful heifer, not at any price, the women screeched with ribald laughter, the men hooted and hid their mouths, and Vikram began to laugh, punching his neighbours on their arms. Bhose shouted for order, and trying to look stern with his mouth twitching into spasmodic half smiles, began calling out what, although he was writing it in English, was being put into the *burra kitab*. I asked if that was all, and standing before anyone could think of any other angle, I said I would go into the field office and get on with writing tomorrow's work plan. I moved swiftly and quietly along the verandah, surprising the huddle of clerks who had been listening behind the field office door to the proceedings. The Assamese third clerk who had been teaching me the language gave a broad smile and said, 'Sir, you have brought a very wise judgement. It was a very difficult case.' I nodded, trying to work out whether I had done any more than listen and learn the strange ways of my fellow men, and sat down to the business of tomorrow's work plan. The line watchmen, who fulfilled the ancient duties of estate criers, appeared from behind the office building, where they had positioned themselves at the other end where they could hear the '*bichar*', and prepared to listen to what would be called out amongst the houses of the lines and villages at sunset and sunrise. When I returned for the signing and thumb printing I was pleased with Bhose's account of the proceedings, and said so. He thanked me with a relieved smile, and said Rambilash, the elder, used to be a *sirdar*, and was demoted by Mr Telford for seducing a girl of about sixteen, many years ago. He is a very wise man, living in hope of being forgiven; but Mr Telford will not forgive him, because he already had two wives, which he brought from his country when he first came. The book was shown to the manager every morning, and I sat by as Telford read it, waiting for comments which never came. When I said Rambilash made a commendable contribution to the settlement, he said he had probably spent many hours for the past week arguing until they thrashed it all out. He took

18

some papers from his desk and gave them to me. The title was 'The Vegetative Propagation of Tea From Selected Quality Bushes'. He said I should read it all carefully because he thought there was something promising in it. I thanked him and rose to go.

'It seems you had a long chat with Linda on this morning's ride. She's quite a chatterbox. I believe she asked you if you would take her for a "flip" in the aeroplane.' I laughed, and said I had told her she would 'have to ask you, because it's your aeroplane'.

I went on: 'She did say you wouldn't take her until you had had much more practice, and I said it wouldn't be long to wait.'

'I could take her now, but one does attach a lot of value to one's children, one's wife.'

'I understand that, but they wouldn't have given you your licence unless they rated you safe.' His eyes seemed to smoulder as he looked at me. 'Please let me know if I may help, let me support you in frequent practice: it's good for both of us.' He nodded, and murmured we should try to fit it in some time.

Chapter XIV

Within the first year after Independence, apart from the departures from all over India of the hitherto dedicated civil servants, earlier described as the cream of Britain's best universities, there was an exodus from the tea districts of Assam and Bengal of Europeans who were convinced the continuation of life as it was between the wars would not be possible. They were those who had become so immersed in the role of *'pukka sahibs'*, enjoying the ambience of a quasi-aristocracy in which they enjoyed being above criticism or argument, their word being law within such isolated fiefs as tea estates. Although most were reasonably just and well respected, their disappearance in most cases was regretted mainly by servants, local 'unexportable' mistresses, and others who had been dependent upon them for a livelihood. They were in fact a very small minority, much to the disappointment of those remaining who were anxious for promotion.

Rodney Field was a slightly different case, as Telford had pointed out. He certainly was arrogant, and it was to take ten more days before he would know what was to happen to him and his wife. Their stay in my bungalow began well, but eventually erupted into the first really unpleasant episode I had experienced since arriving in India. The Fields' two servants gave the impression of being terrified of him, and I heard later from Maneklal and Nunoo, who had been able to talk to them behind the scenes, that the *sahib* was in fact mad from drinking too much alcohol. His servants had not been beaten, but they were obviously frightened of him, and were sorry for the *memsahib*, who seemed more traumatised than they were. On the first night I found the Fields quiet, friendly, and grateful for being able to stay in my bungalow. He drank and talked a lot, and one evening gradually came to the point where he spoke in a hoarse whisper, warning there was no future for me in this country. 'It hasn't hit them yet, you see! They can't believe the

British have handed over power; but it won't take long before they test it, and when they discover they can do what they like they will go on the rampage. They'll help themselves to whatever they know you have! Who's going to stop them? It's time to get out, sonny boy, before they find out. They'll be like rogue elephants! Once a trained elephant discovers his *mahout* is just a puny creature with a sharp spike, he kills him. It takes a long time before he breaks out of the power of man, but when it happens he wreaks his vengeance with his new found power.' Mrs Field spoke almost not at all, sitting with her petit point embroidery on which she concentrated through large spectacles, hands tremulous, smiling nervously now and then, signing to the servants who seemed to know what she wished to be done. Field gulped at his whisky and water, brows lowered and a grimace that was meant to be a grin on his large mouth. He spoke with a south coast accent, somewhere between Southampton and Dorset. 'Have you never thought how thinly spread you are in this place? Not a problem when the British Raj was ready to descend swiftly if trouble began to brew somewhere; but without it any bunch of looters could pick off the lonely planters, bungalow by bungalow, estate by estate; and not only would it not be dealt with as a breach of the peace, but others would see and follow suit, help themselves. Guns, drink, jeeps, everything that could be worn or sold. God knows what would happen to the British planters.' Mrs Field raised a trembling hand to her mouth and whispered his name. I saw he was trembling himself, and I spent some time trying to subdue both of them.

By the fourth or fifth day, all having been quiet and peaceful, there came an evening when Field seemed broody and stared in silence at the fire. I rose to excuse myself, saying I would take my evening meal as usual. This was an arrangement I had made on discovering the Fields wouldn't eat until at least nine o'clock which was my bedtime, based on a tendency to fall asleep over my book at that hour, having risen at five-thirty. They had agreed to this pleasantly, he with cynical amusement, and she with a large-eyed smile and a few words of approval. She was thin, almost haggard, with very dark shadows under her eyes. She still showed signs of some beauty, with heavy dark eyelids, large eyelashes, and heavy lips over large but excellent teeth; but she was very self-conscious and clearly rendered virtually speechless in her husband's company. Having had two large whiskies, Field rose from his chair and said it was time I had a drink with him. 'I know you always say you don't drink, but I know you air force types, you always had a stiff drink before you took off for a difficult show.' I smiled and shook my head, telling him I simply didn't like the stuff, and never mixed booze with petrol. He laughed, clapped his hands and said, 'You'd better get used to the odd tot of whisky, sonny. You're going to need it if you insist on trying to control this bunch of bastards.' His bearer appeared at the sitting room door and salaamed. 'A double peg for the *chota sahib, jaldi*!' Field raised his voice like a sergeant major giving orders. The bearer looked at me with wide eyes, and I held up my hand, palm towards him, rocking it to signify disinclination. Having his back to me, Field did not see. The bearer gave a sickly smile and said in a voice like a six-year-old that the *chota sahib* did not drink whisky, and Mrs Field murmured timidly that Mr MacStorm didn't really want to drink, he was going to eat. At this Field became rigid, arms stiffened and held like the wings of a fighting cock. He began roaring in 'kitchen' Hindustani at the top of his voice, with spittle flying from his mouth. After about a minute of nasty name-calling, which reduced the bearer to a wide-eyed and quivering state of fear, Field turned to me, still roaring, his faded blue eyes bulging from his red face. 'You see what you are up against!' he screamed. 'They'd never have done this before. Putting me right! Putting me bloody well right!' He swung back to face the bearer who was now pale under his dark skin, still quivering like a terrified animal unable to escape or attack. 'You people think you can treat me like this! You are not fit to talk like this to a dog, a pig. Have the *babus* told you you can behave like this? Do you know what the *babus* are going to do to you once we have gone? You'll cry yourselves to death, all of you. You'll be screaming for us, but we won't be here to help you. You bastards, thieves, you...' He began to use obscenities, and his wife, who had been trying to attract his attention, burst into tears and stumbled into their bedroom, crossing herself as she went, with Field paying no attention at all. He ranted more obscene nonsense at his bearer, who for want of something to ease the tension raised his trembling hand to his forehead and tried to speak against the torrent of abuse. Field took a sudden step forward, leading me to think he might go too far and assault the bearer, or push him down the stairs.

'Field,' I said, stepping forward, 'would you be so kind as to ask your bearer to tell my chaps to bring my food up. I'd be grateful if you'd do it before you reduce him to a nervous collapse.' I hardened my voice. 'I don't like you shouting like this. People might think you are drunk, having a row with me in my bungalow.' He swung to face me, eyes blazing, and I shook my head, smiling. 'I'm quite peckish, you know, and I really don't want a drink.' His face softened into a mild smile, and he turned to the bearer.

'Tell the *sahib*'s servants to bring his food. He doesn't want a drink.' The bearer bowed, salaaming to each of us in turn, and went downstairs speaking to the others who had been waiting at the foot of the stairs. I heard a rapid slapping of Maneklal's bare feet as he pounded the twenty yards to the kitchen, and thanked Field. I sat in my easy chair and he, after gazing at his wife's empty chair and the bedroom door, sat in his place, clasped his hands before him, and spoke in a soft undertone. 'That poor girl. This whole business has really run her down. She's frightened of Indians; they know she's Anglo, and they all take it out on her. About four years ago when I found she was pregnant I married her. She had a miscarriage and nearly died. I wish to God the company would make up its mind and either sack me or send me to somewhere else in the world. I can't get back into the merchant navy after jumping my ship, and even if I could I wouldn't be able to leave her on her own for months on end. There's some talk of sending us to the UK, but the English will be just as nasty to her just because she's an Anglo. I've heard there's terrible unemployment there, and I haven't got much to live on. Maybe I should try for New Zealand.' He put his head in his hands and wept. I heard Maneklal bringing my food up the stairs, and so I stood, went forward and put my hand on Field's shoulder, patting firmly, at a loss for something to say. He dropped his hands and looked up at me, pointing at the bedroom door. 'I've upset her, haven't I? I do it too often. She's a marvellous kid you know, marvellous.' I was about to say something about cutting down the booze when he gazed up at me with his eyes full of tears. 'I keep trying to get off the bloody whisky, you know, but as soon as I am sober I just can't face anything. I don't know why. You're a good bloke, you are. Sympathetic. Not like some of these bastards: black or white; bastards. Look down their noses because I jumped my ship, scared of the war, married an Anglo, a drunken sod. She's a Catholic, wants me to convert. I wish I could.' I took hold of both his shoulders and bent close to his face.

'You've told me enough to show how loyal you are to your wife. It's great. It means you can cure yourself of the booze, you know. It's only people who don't have that kind of commitment who can't shake it off. You'll do it, take it from me, but it'll be hard.' For want of a better way to conclude our conversation so that I could go into the dining room at the door of which Maneklal stood, his eyes wide open, waiting for me to enter, I said, 'There

23

we are. Shake on it. There's a long and worthwhile future waiting for you, both of you.' As we clasped hands staring at each other in a heavy miasma of whisky, I heard the bedroom door open, and Mrs Field came out, short-sighted without her spectacles, holding a napkin under her chin.

'Oh Mr MacStorm. You are very kind. My husband is suffering from strain. All kinds of difficulties. Come Field, let me tidy up your face.' She came forward as he stood up, and they went off into the bedroom in silence. About a week later news arrived that the company had booked a passage by Anchor Line for the Fields to travel to Britain, finishing his contract permanently. They went to the club for the first time two days later where Field, obviously not yet having managed to summon enough willpower to curtail his drinking, spoke loudly and bitterly about the company sacking him for standing up to his staff and labour who thought they could treat him with the insolence granted them with their new freedom. I was not there, but George Fraser was, and it was said he went up to Field and told him very quietly if he did not moderate his tone he would find himself stranded in India without a free passage to England. 'For the sake of your poor wife,' he is reported as saying, 'stop talking such absolute nonsense and consider yourself lucky the company is dealing so kindly with you.' Not more than a week later Telford told me the Staplefords were leaving on resignation. I didn't see them again, and found Telford had bought their two rather good horses.

Telford took me in his jeep to visit the Tea Research Association near Jorhat, eighty miles or so from Medeloabam. It was a pleasure to drive on the 'trunk' road, metalled with shingle most of the way through forests, villages, and large areas of rice fields where the paddy was ripening in all shades of pale green, buff, ochre and gold, with harvesting in progress. Once the mists cleared the whole landscape was brilliant with colour, the forest-covered Naga Hills to the south being blue-grey against the sun, and the Himalayas more than a hundred miles to the north showing pale cobalt ridges with the delicate crystalline snow ranges spreading into the distance towards the south-west. We saw many happy Assamese on the road: men with bamboo yokes, women and girls with sickles and cloths containing picnic meals for the fields. Many of them carrying large pale yellow pomelos, which Telford explained were for slaking their thirst through the day. They seemed full of joy to be tackling their harvest, all of which would be cut by hand and carried mainly by the men on their shoulder yokes. They glowed with good health, white teeth gleaming in the rosy copper of their skins. Older people were wrinkled, some bent from many years of arduous planting and harvesting which entailed many hours of bending deeply. The women all had strong arms, broad shoulders, and thick long black hair. They bubbled with good spirits, and gave me a feeling of mixed admiration and envy. We stopped to have a picnic breakfast at an ancient Ahom ruin in a place called Sibsagar, once a capital of the Ahom kingdom. We marvelled at the huge building which was said to be used for elephant fights, having high galleries for the court spectators. There were many reservoirs built by the Ahoms in the fifteenth, or sixteenth, century. They used bricks or tiles, cemented with a mixture of lentils, fishbones, white of egg and clay. When we climbed the embankment of one of these to see the contents, flocks of assorted duck, teal, and moorhens totalling about 500 rose with the exciting gasp of a thousand or more wings. Although the Assam plains would have between 80 and 120 inches of rain during the five months of the monsoon season, there would seldom be more than an inch or so during the other seven months of the cool, clear season, and the Ahom invaders, coming from the Shan regions which merged with Thailand and used to plentiful rainfall, made sure they would enjoy adequate supplies when all but the large rivers would dry up, and armed campaigns would be based upon access to drinking water.

The visit to the tea research centre at Tocklai was for me a highly beneficial change of scene. I met several of the scientists, some botanists, plant pathologists, entomologists, horticulturalists and biochemists. I listened as Telford spoke to them, and was amazed at how complicated and fascinating the whole business of growing and manufacturing tea was turning out to be. Fortunately I had absorbed enough from MacFortune, Foyle and Telford to be able to understand, and to be stimulated by what I can only call the sheer romance of tea culture, and most of those we met seemed not only to be expert in their knowledge of tea, but enthusiastic in an infectious way. I met Dr Wight, of whom Telford had told me a lot. He was a rugged man, with a chin like T. E. Lawrence, bushy eyebrows, and a pleasant outdoor face with wrinkles about the eyes showing a mixture of humour and concentration. He had an amusing facial expression which nearly always followed his descriptions of experimental results or unexpected discoveries. After a concentrated monologue which ended in revealing the successful climax, he would suddenly transform his serious features into those of a mischievous schoolboy, sticking his tongue well out from his broadly smiling mouth.

I was yet to find how conservative planters were about changing the way they grew and made their tea: it seemed those who showed no confidence in adopting what scientists or other planters had found to be promising new methods, eventually turned out to be those who extolled the new method, usually explaining how they adapted it so that it turned out to be really successful. Dr Wight was the person who had advised, following long experiments and teamwork, that after pruning the mature tea bushes at the end of the harvest season the planter should allow new stems to grow next spring until five leaves emerged on them, beginning to pluck only when leaf grew above this measure. The shoots growing from the axils of these five leaves would only be plucked when they in turn reached the level at which the first stem had been plucked, and this would put the bush in a position to continue producing leaf with far greater abundance throughout the season. At the end of the season, when growth slowed down drastically because of lack of rain and lower temperatures, bushes would be pruned level, leaving half an inch of the past season's now woody stems, and all the growth of twigs and leaf which had emerged from the original stems below the plucking level would be returned to the soil in situ. When I heard that this produced six tons of organic matter to be returned to the soil in which the tea was growing I was filled with a warm delight, and this because I remembered speaking with a splendid farmer near one of the airfields from which I flew, I think Chamberlain was his name, who told some of us how he was producing record yields of wheat and barley by using green-cropping techniques. He had explained enough about it for me to understand what this all meant, and when I told Dr Wight of this he was delighted, saying that tea planters could now put fertiliser on, happily aware that a lot of the fertiliser would be converted to what he called an 'auto-green-crop', a bulk of organic matter which was already beginning to restitute tea soils which had been cropped for nearly sixty years with inadequate replacement of what had been removed from the soil. Application of organic fertiliser was hopelessly inefficient and, because of the expansion of tea estates, could not be grown in sufficient quantity. He asked me to imagine trying to apply six tons of organic matter to every acre of our estate, with people carrying about thirty pounds of it at a time in baskets on their heads, struggling through bushes which, in order to suppress weed, were cultivated and pruned to cover the ground, thus making rapid progress not only difficult but tiring, as well as destructive of clothes. Everything was against it. The shade trees had been of great value in producing organic matter from atmospheric nitrogen, through their root nodules, but this was simply insufficient to keep the soil permanently fertile.

This first visit to Tocklai was rather like what I had experienced when, still a serving officer after the war, I visited several university colleges, invited by ex-pilot friends Tommy, Nick, Peter, Hugh and Wilfred. Their 'professors' were all mad keen to impart knowledge, and stimulate interest. These tea scientists certainly alleviated the sadness which often descended on me when I read the books I had brought with me to 'improve my mind' and thought how I was missing the gifts of those dedicated tutors. We enjoyed a good lunch with them, during which the biochemist made it clear that one of the drawbacks of making good flavoury tea was that mostly such tea came from bushes which suffered cold, shortage of nitrogen, and too much altitude, all of which depressed yields, Darjeeling being a typical case. Attractive flavour was known to be associated, until now, mainly with low yields. He said this made it all the more important to find and propagate bushes which, we hoped, would give high yields of good quality tea even with a lot of rain and fertiliser. Arguments followed on the future demand for tea, and a young visiting economist gave his unusual opinion that Indians loved tea, but most of them couldn't afford to buy it, and tea stealing was beginning to be a problem. As there were more than 350 million people in India, and they were really beginning to multiply, the demand for tea could increase exponentially. If India could somehow industrialise, as Nehru kept insisting (much to Gandhi's horror), and workers' wages be increased, drawing the autochthonous small-holder peasants away from their depleted lands, and if even only half the population drank but one cup of tea per day, there would be tremendous demand, virtually for ever more. I think I understood what he said, and was made dizzy by his forceful delivery of such exhilarating facts.

After lunch Dr Wight took us to see his work on selection and propagation by cuttings. Thick books could be written on this subject, and to condense it enough only to give an idea of how it captured my interest and subsequently affected my attitudes is bound to result in the loss of much which would explain my huge enthusiasm. One learns from bitter experience that enthusiasts tend mostly to be bores, and only those who are gifted have a

27

hope of communicating their valuable messages without inflicting boredom on their listeners (or readers). Dr Wight began by explaining how he selected one-acre plots, not only at the research estate, but on estates where good yields and good liquors were being achieved. (Liquors are the fluid infused from tea, before adding milk, sugar, or lemon.) Beginning several years ago teams were organised to take samples from every bush in each chosen acre (generally about 2,722 bushes per acre), all through the harvest season, recording the weight of individual bush yields. It was found after several years that these yields varied consistently by large amounts. This shook people like me, but not the practical field scientists. It was established through many separate trials that the yields of individual bushes in a single acre were in some cases nearly twice that of the average for the acre, and others were just above half the average. I remember my pulse racing with the excitement of sudden obsession with the implications. Once a consistent pattern emerged showing positive characteristics of yield, the high yielders were staked, and experiments were begun to manufacture each high-yielding bush separately, so that expert tasters could evaluate the liquors, every week throughout the season. The fact that tea liquors varied throughout each season had been known since early times in China. In the plains of Assam the first twelve weeks or so of plucking produced poor colours and character; from mid-June to mid-July produced bright colours, excellent flavour and strength from a rising crop. Once the bushes began with copious rain to produce more and more leaf each week, quality fell, although increasing daily harvests began to stretch factories into more than one shift. This continued until November, when rainfall ceased, temperatures fell, yields declined and liquors improved again, showing better flavour. The search continued for bushes which showed less deterioration of liquor quality during the high cropping period, when a few pence improvement on a massive crop would be worth having. He had found some promising bushes, and had liquor samples prepared for us to taste. The bright colour and strength of one seemed remarkable, and others showed very attractive flavour but less strength. He then took us to see the system of miniature manufacture, suitable for dealing with the very small amounts of leaf from single bushes, and I made notes on what I saw of both manual and machine methods. We then went to nurseries where single leaf cuttings had been taken from selected bushes which, once weighments and tasting had shown them to have promising potential, had been allowed to grow without plucking for about eighteen inches. These cuttings were being closely planted in what he called 'striking' nurseries from which, once they had begun to form roots, they were lifted and put into raising nurseries from which they would be transplanted into the field in plots of identical plants henceforth identified as clones, with letters and numbers showing their origin. He emphasised the necessity of testing clonal blocks under full commercial conditions to see how they grew by comparison with bushes propagated from seed. When we returned to Dr Wight's office, joined by the director of the research outfit, we sat and talked a long time about the feasibility of selection and vegetative propagation: whereas bushes grown from seed produced bushes of a closely similar appearance, every bush was genetically different, and therefore relatively safe from the various pests and diseases of tea. Clonal plants would all be from the same parent bush, and would therefore probably be in danger of serious, rapidly spreading diseases and insect pests. This was what frightened many planters, but the scientists pointed to the possibility of finding certain clones which, as in fruit propagation, would display an ability to resist the worst diseases and pests. There were many such questions: would bushes grown from cuttings be able to develop roots which would sustain them in the occasional drought periods of an Assam spring? Would clonal plants follow growth periods in unison, unlike seed plants which were naturally out of step with each other, and therefore more convenient for field management which tried to reduce moderate growth peaks and dormancy? Many questions like these were discussed and explained, but Dr Wight was quite emphatic that one of the tea industry's most serious blights was sheer conservatism. Too many had said they would wait and see how the trial project turned out. He said to Telford he was lucky to have the essential ingredients for success: keenness and adventure. He pointed at me and said, 'Look how his eyes are shining. Just face him in the right direction and he will charge with vigour into the search for treasure on your estate.' I would never forget how he said with shining eyes that on many of the tea estates of Assam there must be 'golden bushes' waiting to be discovered, with potential for high yield and attractive liquors. 'But even if you have fire in your belly and a light in your eye: selection and testing is very hard work, and will need tremendous effort.' His red tongue protruded through his teeth, and he grinned brightly, twisting his head in encouragement.

We drove back talking about the whole thing, and it was agreed I should make a start with selecting from our highest yielding fields, and with the development of cuttings nurseries. The sun sank behind us as we neared Sibsagar, illuminating everything and everybody with the rose-gold colour of nature's evening theatre. The harvesters were bound home, the men with heavy loads of golden paddy on their shoulder yokes, and the women and girls carrying sheaves on their heads. Their carriage was magnificent, and their beauty most impressive. Telford said the Ahom women of Sibsagar were the most beautiful in Assam, according to the Assamese men, and I thought it had to be true. It was a terrible wistfulness being so impressed, being desperate for a mate, a lover, a wife, with very little prospect of fulfilling such a strong and natural yearning for who knows how many years to come.

This was late 1947, and I had not yet completed a year in Assam. My entry into tea was at last made smooth and positive by that visit, and the sudden falling into place of all my random and uncertain observations took place with the growing realisation that there was a future. Dr Wight and Telford gave the magic impetus: a clear perspective of what tea was all about, and the thrill of seeing a way to participate in something relatively new to everyone, particularly to me, so far unaffected by canny conservatism, so pitifully ignorant of so much which yet had to be learned. Here was something just beginning to happen which I could understand and treat as one of my main interests: pioneering in the field. The cold weather season was wonderful. Work began less early, but finished by two-thirty or three. Polo was a delight. Telford had me make plans on how to set up the selection and propagation project, and was helpful, reminding me it would entail much work after normal estate work finished during the harvest season, saying there would be an increasing amount of flying as time went on; I remembered him telling me, but I treated everything as something to deal with when the time arrived. Once or twice a week I was invited to join the Telford family in river picnics. We would travel by jeep to the Brahmaputra, embark in a large one-piece dugout canoe, made from camphor wood, with a 20 h.p. outboard engine (ex-military surplus), which took us out to find a large backwater of clear water which had warmed in the sun. There we swam, fished, and had tea with excellent sandwiches and cake made by Mrs Telford's expert cook. Lucy, the older daughter, was beautifully built; Linda, with whom I rode most mornings, was still lanky, with a long blonde pigtail down her back. The main streams were very cold, too cold to swim for more than a few minutes, and it was a pleasure to swim the crawl in the huge backwaters, and run on the white sandy beaches. I would run for the sheer joy of running, along the shore of the receding river, and this attracted attention. I said although I had done some competition running of the quarter-mile at school and in the air force, I really ran for the joy of it, mostly by myself. On one of these picnics we were joined by several guests invited by the Telfords, a couple with a teenage daughter who was friendly with Lucy, and their assistant, a strongly built man, ex-army and very military in style, almost to the point of deliberate mimicry. I caught Lucy laughing furtively into her raised shoulder when this man described himself on introduction as 'ex-captain John Butterworth, umpteenth Hussars. Do call me John!' This to Mrs Telford, who simply said 'Ah! Yes, I see,' and looked for her husband with one eyebrow raised. After we had swum Mrs Telford said there would be a race between Mr Butterworth and me, since we were both said to be very fast runners. He was a sprinter, and I by preference a quarter-miler, and so we paced out 300 yards. Telford said he would start us, and the ladies were to judge the finish. I think we were both rather embarrassed, neither knowing the other personally, and not knowing what to expect from a race. He said he was badly out of training, and I said cycling at work and riding at polo, plus swimming, had changed all my running muscles dramatically. We ran, and I won by about ten yards; but everyone said it looked as if I wasn't even trying – running, as Telford said, with a lazy long stride. I think we both felt rather as if we had been made to perform, not so much for the amusement of our hosts, but to enable them to place us, so to speak.

The Telfords invited many guests, and went to visit them in turn. It was good for me to be invited now and then to dinner on a Sunday evening when I had the pleasure of meeting the many diverse types who worked in Assam. So far I had met only the 'polo playing crowd', of which I was the only new member, and the youngest at that, and it was only the Telfords and Constable who invited their friends and invited me to meet them. This meant I was only meeting rather senior people. George Fraser frequently told me I should go more to the club, meet the other young chaps, have a relaxing time. He said it was important not to become interested only in the job; one needed to discuss things with others. I met some fascinating people at the Telfords' excellent table, and I say that in the sense of finding some of them unbelievably pompous, some vainly dogmatic, and some reminding me of

31

Belloc's 'stern, indomitable men', with little humour and much fierce conviction on the hopeless future for a free India. A typical illustration of an arch-type was the visit of a top superintendent from a company in the Jorhat area. He and his wife came for a weekend, and I saw him at polo, where he sat well on a beautiful, strong horse, which managed to carry his fourteen stone for two chukkas. I did not meet him or his wife, but had been invited to Sunday dinner with them. I had to dress in the only suit I had, which was a double-breasted grey flannel two-piece. I was introduced when I arrived at seven-thirty, shaking hands with the sun-dried duchessy kind of lady who made a flicker of a smile before resuming her conversation with Lucy. Her husband shook hands with a stern expression, not looking me in the eyes but glowering at my head.

'Blond, Telford! Those people in London simply don't know what they are doing, selecting young men with fair hair for a job in this part of the world.' He turned away without speaking to me, and continued to pour scorn on the London offices of Assam's tea companies. I heard no subjects of interest whilst drinks were served except to hear him say with a counterfeit smile to Telford, having noted my preference for orange juice, 'You see, Telford, I was right: fair hair, and teetotal. They all learn if they survive long enough. One or two chota pegs of whisky a day is the only way to survive.' The conversation reverted to criticism of planters in his district whose many faults attracted his scorn. I was sorry when Linda and Lucy, hearing dinner announced, excused themselves and left. Although I had found it impossible to participate in the general conversation, both daughters had begun to talk to their lady guest, telling her something about me. Linda mentioned I was a pilot and hoped I would take her for a 'flip' (as it was called in those days). The duchess, without looking at me, said she hated the very idea of flying, and would never fly, never. At dinner I sat beside her, and tried unsuccessfully to stimulate a conversation. Being a lone bachelor, so much involved with work, riding and books, I paid little attention to the preparation of my own food, and being on my stringent vegetarian meals I must always have been hungry, so that when Mrs Telford, noticing how quickly I had cleared my plate, asked if I would have more. It was a beautiful dish of Muscovy duck, with tinned mushrooms and Medeloabam asparagus, and I gratefully accepted another helping. Mrs Telford, aware I was finding the company hard going, said with a smile when I was nearly finished that it was good to see I had a healthy appetite. The duchess, whose nose was rather like Edith Sitwell's, looked down it in my direction.

'He certainly has eaten a huge amount,' she said, and looking me up and down with drooping eyelids went on. 'But he doesn't seem to have anything to show for it.'

This sort of comment was familiar to me, and I smiled as I ate on; but Mrs Telford, I am sure in sympathy for my feelings, came out in breezy support.

'Ah! You need to see him without his clothes on; he looks really well built.'

Telford dropped his knife on his plate, and stared with wide open eyes at his wife, who raised her napkin to her lips, her eyebrows rising first querulously, then forming a circumflex of dismay as she realised why he was staring. She blushed. The duchess put her knife and fork together and looked sourly at her husband, who had paused with a forkful of food a few inches from his mouth, staring at Telford.

I wanted to burst out laughing, and felt it might have triggered laughter from Telford; but all I could do to break the embarrassing hush was to dab my lips and say to my neighbour, 'We have been having wonderful swimming picnics on the river. Mr and Mrs Telford are very kind inviting me to go with them in the outboard canoe. There are some beautiful places where the water is crystal clear, and warm enough to swim.' It helped a little, but I noticed both the Telfords were pale, and felt sorry their guests not only did nothing to relieve the tension, but seemed to stiffen their resolve to demonstrate how one rode through difficult situations simply pretending they did not exist, in this case presuming it safer to be thought virtuous rather than vulgar. I boiled with contempt.

With the departure of the Fields I returned to my usual routine in the evenings. It was now cold enough for a large log fire, and after my evening meal I was happy to sit and read, with one standard lamp beside my chair. One evening at Medeloabam after drinking more strong tea than usual I opened no book, but sat staring at the burning logs and the red caves in the embers, turning my mind loose, and wondered at how things had changed dramatically since the day we, the damfools, boarded the ship bound for a career in India. The astonishing acceleration of Independence happened with so little time for any of us to grasp what was likely to happen, that looking back one could say it was a kind of shock therapy. Even now it was as uncertain as life had been in the war: no future to depend on, no certain career, no sensible reason for not breaking away for something more

33

reliable. No sensible reason. Where now the training that had been dinned into us? 'So train yourselves that when the time arises when you haven't either time or detachment to think reasonably, you allow your accumulated repetition, your drills, procedures, your instincts, to take over and save you.' Ah! But this is different; and if it's instincts that should save us, well here it is a case of real instincts stopping us from thinking sensibly. The marvel of the cold weather; the incredible proliferation of birds of all kinds, the intense sexual consciousness pervading life as a natural phenomenon, in stark contrast to our Calvinistic inhibitions; the grace of the boniest woman, carrying a pot of water from the river on her head. There is too much which cannot be named, holding us here in what for me is a curious mixture of austerity and joy, work and romance. How would I be had I not been able to fly any more? Lord give me the ability to set my thoughts in order. I am thankful to be really enthusiastic about continuing in tea as a career. I fell asleep before the fire, the first time I had ever done so, and crept into bed very late, glad to be under two blankets. I went to sleep wondering if the Telfords had somehow been upset with something I had said at that last dinner party. On the following day, right out of the blue between a comment on the beginning of clearing the airfield drainage and saying the Christmas rain might arrive this year, he said one never spoke to anyone about what was said at a dinner party, and I said that had always been my understanding, and as his tone had suggested there was more to say on the subject I waited, but found Christmas rain had become important. Linda said a few days later when we rode out in the beautiful cold dawn, with the sun rising in a cloudless sky, that Father was grumpy with everyone. She said he was often like that. I made no comment.

One afternoon when I called for tea and toast Maneklal said the Field *memsahib* had left many jars of marmalade and jam, and asked if I wanted to use it. I said I would have marmalade with breakfast, and jam for tea, and asked what kind of jam it was. He said their bearer had said it was mulberry, and went off to open a jar. After some time he came to the verandah holding a screw-topped jar with a very rusty lid. He told me it was impossible to unscrew it; what to do? I took it and tried hard to move the top, without success. He said they had put it into a pot of hot water, but it hadn't helped. I said he should try to open it with a tin opener. He went away with a thoughtful look on his face. After five minutes he returned with the jar and the tin opener, and with an obviously suppressed smile suggested it would be best if I opened it. This I could not quite understand, but I told him to take it down to the kitchen house and I would follow. The kitchen had been whitewashed, and the dark stains of woodsmoke had been well covered on the roof and walls above the stove. The jar stood on the robust kitchen table, tin opener beside it, and the four servants greeted me, the cook indicating with his hand that all was ready for my technical expertise. I went forward and began to examine the lid, and found it was remarkably robust. I said aloud it would be difficult to puncture it with the rather ancient tin opener, and held out my hand for the sharp-pointed kitchen knife, saying that would be better. No knife appeared, and when I turned with an open hand I saw there was nobody in the kitchen except myself. They had disappeared silently, and craning to see through the window I saw them standing in the warm sun close to the bungalow, whispering. The old cook looked worried, but the others were bright-eyed and expectant. Although I was vaguely suspicious I did not form any definite idea to explain why I was left alone, and attacked the jar lid with the sharp knife. I found it impossible to penetrate near the edge, where I could insert the tin opener in order to cut out a small disc; the jar kept tending to fall over, and whilst using one hand to grasp the knife and the other to hit the end of the handle, I simply could not prevent it toppling. I moved the knife point nearer to the middle and, becoming annoyed at how long it was taking the prestigious pilot *sahib* to demonstrate his speedy efficiency, I pounded hard on the handle. On the third stroke, which hurt my hand, the point stabbed in. There was a sudden piercing hiss, and a powerful jet of carmine fluid shot past my right ear and hit the roof, spraying me with a fine purple rain. I dropped the knife and the jar, and jumped backwards to escape the fall-out, only to see the jar behave like a living creature, spinning, rolling, and rocketing all over the purple slime on the table with tremendous speed, blasting me several times with the purple jet of fluid and gobbets of mulberry: shirt, shorts, hair, face and limbs being attacked without mercy. I suddenly realised the kitchen was filled with a very strong aroma of alcoholic spirits, strangely pleasant; but I lunged forward to catch the jar just before it fell from the table, realising as I did so there was not much hope of saving any jam, as there seemed to have been about a gallon of spirituous emission all over me and the kitchen. I roared curses and abuse at the carmine creature as I tried unsuccessfully to field the scooting jar. I reflected grimly how strong the jar must have been to withstand such pent-up pressure. No doubt thinking my expostulations were

35

cries for help Maneklal pounded to my aid, and entered the kitchen with wide eyes. He gasped, saying he had seen blood splashing on the window, and had to come and help. I could only laugh, and was able to say we should have waited for the Fagua spring *puja*, when spraying people with red fluid would have fitted in without special notice. I walked out to the bungalow, peeling off my shirt and stockings. The other servants, with faces registering earnest concern, put both hands to their cheeks and made comforting noises, but seeing me laughing they wagged their heads and busied themselves with the problems of cleaning up. Nunoo later asked if he could tell someone to come and take the alcoholic jars away; the marmalade ones were in fact easy to open, but the mulberry ones would come in useful for a birth ceremony. The purple stains on my clothes never came out and I gave them away. The stains on the kitchen walls continued to show through the repeated coats of whitewash for the next few years, and the incident became one more of the legends attached to the name of one of Medeloabam's *chota sahibs*.

Life became increasingly busy and absorbing as Christmas drew near, much of it to do with seeking the 'golden bushes'. Although Telford had been the prime mover of my introduction to the subject, he left me to adopt it as my obvious passion. My interest and dedication to the project led to much frustration and confusion when various other responsibilities arose. One of the most annoying of these was, strangely enough, my commitment to help the development of a company air service by flying the Auster as and when appropriate needs arose. Telford dealt with the business of deciding which needs qualified, and Fraser, the Calcutta office, and London gradually became more and more involved and impressed with the convenience of having an aircraft 'on call'. The problem was that although I had worked out my own work priorities for the exciting search for super bushes, as well as the routine field programmes for the estate in general, Telford, whose dedication to estate efficiency seemed to be second to none, gave my flying duties top priority. This soon proved to be far more demanding than I had surmised when I assured the company I did not want to become a pilot at the expense of my career as a planter. I had never contemplated, even after reading the books of Antoine de Saint Exupery, taking up a career in commercial aviation, and although I always enjoyed flying over the wild areas of Assam, the thought of being an airborne taxi or lorry driver made me shudder.

It took me by surprise when, on one of Fraser's visits to Medeloabam, he and Telford told me I would qualify for two weeks' annual leave. Fraser said perhaps Shillong or Darjeeling would be a good change for me, preferably if I found another assistant of my own seniority. 'Shillong is a delightful place, especially when the Assam plains begin to heat up. The girls are delightful, eh, Telford? But I believe there has been an awful lot of venereal disease brought in by troops during the war from other parts of India. Used to be a good place for young chaps to let their hair down a bit without dirtying their own doorstep, sort of thing. One just has to be very careful.' Later I said to Telford I would rather do a trek from due north of Medeloabam up to the foothills, and thence along the Inner Line to the Subansiri, and across to Bogahilonia, preferably in late January; for me that would be a real holiday. He looked at me with his head tilted forward and to one side. 'It probably looks easy from the air. I can understand you wanting to do something like that. No-one has ever done it as far as I know, but after the Jiya Dhol there are no paths or tracks except a long way further south, only elephant paths. You would need a compass.' He paused, thinking, and eventually went on. 'It would do you good to try Shillong, you know, or Darjeeling, round about March or April. We should think about it.' The subject was then changed, and I doubt if he realised how much more determined it made me, after saying how difficult that untrodden trek would be, to suggest it were better for me to go to Shillong or Darjeeling. A few days later I chose an opportune moment, when we were discussing methods of dropping and picking up written messages from places without airstrips, to ask if he would think it a good idea to give me an air drop of food just outside the gorge of the Jiya Dhol; it would be a worthwhile exercise for our air service. His reaction was caustic, with a hint of humour, pointing out how those of us who had 'served' in the forces had got into the habit of being served. To contemplate the possibility of arranging an air drop was typical; however, it was an interesting suggestion as far as a company air service was concerned, and we should develop it.

As Christmas approached Telford told me he and his family would be spending five days camping at the gorge of the Simen river on the North Bank. There had been no talk of using the sandbank for landing the Auster, although the Telfords had been there twice since the end of the monsoon. He said I would have to remain on Medeloabam over Christmas, where only the small Christian communities of Mundas and Oraons would have two days' 'festival' holiday. At the weekend I need only be back by ten in the evening, wherever else I wanted to go. In fact, Bobby Constable invited me for some flying, and an earlyish Christmas dinner. We had lunch with another contemporary of his, and three other bachelors. There were five ladies present, all Christians: one Lushai (Mizo), one Khasi, two Nagas, and one Assamese. They were all very attractive, two strikingly beautiful, paramours of Constable and his friends. They sat mainly together, laughing happily as they chatted, whilst we talked about flying and planting. They were amused that I was an unattached bachelor, and shrieked with delight when the Assamese beauty commented my Assamese was so good for less than a year in Assam that she suspected I was hiding something. When the time came for me to return to Medeloabam, Constable was furious to find his Christian driver was dead drunk, and none of the other four drivers could be found. He finally decided to drive me himself, and said he would drive me there, but he wanted a Christmas drink at my bungalow, and we set course with his assistant, who was teetotal like me and would drive him back. Pete sat in the back, Constable's Assamese beauty on one side, and his effervescent Naga girl on the other. For about fifteen minutes my leg was pulled by the girls, for living like a '*sadhu*' without even a girlfriend. When the Naga girl said she had a beautiful younger sister, and would bring her down next February, I could then see her, and I would not be able to resist such beauty, I made noises showing interest, but Bobby all at once barked for silence. 'No more nonsense like that! And as for you, Hamish, you are the marrying type. Don't make any mistake. If you do, I'll never speak to you again.'

Chapter XV

Having judged Telford was not a person who would yield to an importunate junior, I chose a more subtle way to achieve my strong desire to make my first trek. I gave no hint of wanting ultimately to follow the Inner Line which on the map swung north-north-east into the mountains and then west along the 3,000-foot ridge until it descended steeply to the Subansiri. Indeed, from the look of that route from the air it was sure to be difficult, and the ridge being covered with tall, dense forest meant I would have to gain much experience before attempting such an exploration, particularly in making the acquaintance of the hill tribals, whose help would probably be necessary in finding a route through hills too steep for there to be any tribal villages within fifteen miles of the tract between the Jiya Dhol and the Subansiri. The idea of having to take two men with me was unattractive, and thanking Telford for being so concerned for my safety, I assured him although I was relatively new to Assam I was not inclined to take foolhardy chances, and what I really wanted was to enjoy the atmosphere of the uninhabited wilderness on my own, with no shooting, perhaps photographs, and no dangerous climbing. He said he was responsible for ensuring I came to no harm or difficulty, and although I had done well to learn Assamese, there were people living over there who might not be able to speak enough of it to understand who I was, and what I was doing over there, especially if I was on my own; they are all what some people call very jungly, which in fact means they are shy, and jealous of their territory. Once one is experienced, and people like the Miris become accustomed to seeing one, they are happy enough. With an unusual and unaccustomed smile he said he remembered well his early days as a young man in Assam, and whatever I had said about not being foolhardy, he remembered having protested in a similar way when his father, who was a planter, warned him to be careful about what he called

39

'solo peregrinations' in the hills above Mirijuli on the North Bank. One Sunday in June he had decided to climb one of the forested peaks about 4,000 feet high, some five miles from the estate. He had almost made it when he saw a huge wall of torrential rain approaching from the south. Being able to see the river close below him, he scrambled at speed down towards it, realising the heavy rain would make it impossible to walk or run along the sandy marges; and so he quickly made a raft from banana tree trunks, which were easy to cut, and with sharp stakes made a raft about seven feet long and three feet wide. He finished just in time to float the raft on the rising flood, and with a ten foot pole he set off, aiming to negotiate the several not-too-violent rapids in the way he had learned from the Miris; they steered their dugouts straight into the fastest spill between the rocks. The trouble for him was the hopeless steering of the raft in the turbulence of the river. He couldn't stop it from turning, and it hit one of the boulders, tipped him off, and he nearly drowned when he grabbed at the raft and it turned over on top of him. He eventually managed to crawl ashore like a half-drowned rat; but there were some of the Mundas above the rapid, and when they saw him in trouble they ran down the bank, one of them diverting across to the estate to warn his father what was happening. The trouble was that with the other Mundas he went through the tall scrub across country to his bungalow near the factory. It was still lashing down with heavy rain. His father and the other Munda went to the river and found no trace of him, and kept searching further down the river before the Munda said it was possible he had gone home. Next morning at the office his father gave him the harshest dressing down he'd ever had, in front of the staff and the sirdars, and told him for the next year he must not ever go alone into the hills; if he did he would sack him.

Returning to the subject of my trek he said he always took plenty of anti-malarial drugs, sulphanilamide, friar's balsam, chlorodyne, and plenty of salt and tea; these were all things which were very useful for people living in conditions said to be like the bronze age, without any more medical facilities than the odd Bhotiya or a tribal shaman. I asked if he had a bird book I might borrow, as I was already seeing birds locally which I could not identify, let alone the shy forest birds of which he often spoke. He was very keen on birds and helped me a lot on the subject. When he offered me two books to study I felt optimistic.

On the second day of January I began my trek, taking Krishna Gatwar, a robust and very dark but handsome father of five children, and Somroo Parja, nick-named 'Dopey' by the Telford daughters, as he seemed unable to understand when they spoke to him whilst he occasionally helped in their kitchen garden; but Telford told me whereas Krishna was an excellent fisherman with a throwing net, Somroo was a forest naturalist of amazing knowledge, able to follow tracks, identify edible plants, find birds' eggs, imitate the calls of the wild, and he could shoot with his bow and arrows like Robin Hood; he also played a Parja flute, which I should, he said, ask him to play by the campfire at night. Telford insisted we carry a couple of small tarpaulins which, after cutting a framework of wild bamboos, could be draped as a shelter, useful if it rained, and necessary when the night winds swept down from the Himalayas. An estate lorry dropped us at the North Bank ferry near Dibrugarh, on which we made the long, slow crossing of the Brahmaputra. It was still misty when we began the complicated meandering course through the interweaving large streams of the huge river, and after half an hour a cheer went up as 150 or more bar-headed geese rose from a vast sandy island on our port bow, the noise of the wings and the wild clangor rising above the wheezy throbbing of our thirty-foot ferry boat. Our fellow passengers, all huddled in blankets because of the early morning chill, were Miris, Daflas, Abors, Nepalis, and some forest rangers, all of whom were taking supplies of mustard oil, kerosene for lamps, rice and other food. The Daflas and Abors were taking cattle and young dogs with them, and I learned these were all meat on the hoof, so to speak. They were all highly curious about me, and when they heard whither we were bound they shook their heads, saying the stretch from Jiya Dhol to the Subansiri was, literally in Assamese, 'no-go'. An old Miri said that forest was haunted. Some Abors had fled from some kind of attack, and the *'plitical sahib'* had told them to make a temporary village south of the Inner Line, to live there until he was able to settle the cause of disruption. They did this, but nothing was ever heard of them again. The Miris never went anywhere near them because they were very hot-tempered people, and were afraid of attack. I saw this affected Krishna's morale, although Somroo showed no reaction at all. It was some time before I realised he was neither deaf nor dull, but in the beginning I inclined to think he was either deaf or unable to understand what was being said. As the mist cleared the blue mountains of the North Bank became visible, their eastern slopes dusted with the gold of the sun, and the lone peak of Namsha Barua hid its pale gold summit as we drew closer and closer to the northern shore. The thrill of new adventure was similar to that of soaring above the earth in a lone aircraft; but once we landed and were walking on the dusty earth road, each man carrying two bundles attached to a stoutly sprung bamboo shoulder yoke and I carrying a modest rucksack, we were firmly down to earth. Krishna began telling me he had been made responsible by the Telford *sahib* to see I was not exposed to danger, thus he was glad I had heard the warning of the Miri about the haunted area, which we must on no account enter.

We passed a few shanties and mud huts where a few Nepali buffalo graziers and a few thatch cutters stayed, and thereafter saw little sign of life until several hours later when we had been following the bank of the Sisi river. We came to a Miri village, with houses of bamboo and thatch built on timber pillars, situated a few hundred yards from the river on higher ground. Seeing us approach, the children ran under the huts whilst several dogs barked and came towards us growling and showing their teeth. Men appeared from the river's edge where their dugout canoes were just being drawn up. They had fish with them. Their eyes were fixed on us as they came slowly in a line to intercept us. They were bare to the waist, and carried daos (bushknives), and spoke softly to each other in their rising and falling Chinese-style tones. They stopped ahead of us, and each raised his right hand, palm exposed at head height, a gesture which I returned. I asked if they spoke Assamese, and the leader, a wiry but well-muscled man, said 'a little'. I said we were walking to the foothills, and would turn west to walk to the Jiya Dhol. He made a short noise, and Krishna, being cleverer than I thought, said we came from the Medeloabam *sahib*'s tea garden, upon which they all began smiling, and saluted again. They insisted we sat with them and took something to eat and drink, as it was a long way still to the foothills. They offered their own rice beer, which I had to refuse, but Somroo and Krishna enjoyed a dish each, saying it would help them with their heavy loads. All the women came out, full of laughter and chatter, and we managed to part within the hour, having eaten fresh grilled river fish, and shared some of our tea with them.

The trip was more difficult than I had anticipated, especially after the Jiya Dhol, the gorge of which was in fact rather grim and forbidding, and both sides were very steep. The Miris had confirmed the story of the haunted Abor village, adding their surmise that they had all died from some terrible disease. They said there was mainly thick forest between the gorge and the

Subansiri. It was a stretch which belonged to the elephants, rich in bananas, bamboos, with a certain amount of permanent marshland where they would congregate when their young were born, the mud and water protecting them from the many tigers hunting in an area rich in game. We camped several times where I explored small rivers coming out of the hills. Somroo was truly excellent at explaining tracks, noises, scents and all the complicated knowledge of the primeval wilderness where the tribal people were by choice dependent on their own skills and knowledge for survival. The two men cooked for themselves, and I made my own chupattis to eat with the small fish Krishna netted. He was a good teacher, and I began to develop the art of casting the weighted circular net so that it fell in a proper circle, centred on the place where, in the gloaming, Krishna had thrown a handful of cooked rice, attracting scores of small fry. The fish were as incredulous as Krishna and Somroo, the victims finding such a marvellous plenitude of rice, and us finding huge numbers of fish; they were delicious, even fried in mustard oil. We explored down the Jiya Dhol, finding four Miri villages where we were made welcome, the headman of the first saying I was the first white man they had seen for thirty years, when a forest officer had come once to shoot duck. Many of the younger people were fascinated by my appearance: blond hair, which to them was a sign of old age, incompatible with my youthful physique; and blue eyes, which attracted mostly the young women and girls who stared and stared as if hypnotised, whilst I sat on a deerskin and talked with the Miri men. These visits turned out to be significant with the passage of years. The general opinion was that I should not attempt the short route to the Subansiri, but there was no clear cut explanation, only tales of ghosts. When I told them I was not afraid of ghosts they said perhaps white men would be immune to the evils of jungle ghosts, but they weren't sure. It was clearly established: there was no chance of a guide to lead us through what was barely twelve miles.

After making a few trips with Somroo, and having seen a leopard taking the sun on the rocks of the gorge, heard many elephants, seen two different kinds of pheasant, and recorded tracks of almost all the fauna of Assam, I decided we would make signs on the sandbank outside the gorge, where on the following day Telford would come with the Auster and drop some bags of rice, rough wholemeal flour, and any mail that had arrived for me. I told Krishna and Somroo I was going to make the trip along below the foothills. If they didn't want to come they need not. Somroo, with his strange, slightly crazy grin, said he would not let me go alone; he would go with me, because he was interested. Krishna made frenzied gestures indicating I could beat him, cut his throat, but he had a large family and could not take such a risk. He was also afraid to go south alone, and round to the Subansiri by the longer route, and as he was in such a genuine state of depression I told Somroo he would have to go with Krishna. When Somroo looked glum I had the excellent idea of asking him to play his flute at the campfire that evening after we had eaten. The following day they would go downriver and aim for the ferry at Chauldhoa about ten miles south of the hills, and I would, with compass and my own food, find a way through the 'enchanted' forest. That night Somroo played his flute. I can only describe it as magic music, very similar to the Koyas' flute and fiddle music, played using a scale the same as bagpipes, but with a soft tone, and a mixture of light-hearted repetitive melodies and slow, vaguely weird 'snake charmer' music. Whilst he played a barking deer called, less than fifty yards from our camp. His call was taken up by another about 300 yards away, and from further and further, in both directions. The barking deer call was on the husky note of a Labrador, but twice as long, a single call every twenty seconds or so. It seemed the call was being taken up throughout the Himalayas, and staring at the fire I wondered if it would echo as far east as Manchuria, as far west as Persia: a wonderful wild call.

On the day of the air drop the sky was covered with cloud. Instead of dropping the food on the sand, where we had laid out arrows and a huge circle with small leafy branches as arranged, Telford decided it would be safer to drop it in the long stand of elephant grass alongside our signs, in case the packages burst on impact with the shingly sand. He flew at about 150 feet; the elephant grass was actually '*kaguri*' about twelve feet tall, with hard blades edged like a hacksaw. Of six small packages in jute wrapping we found only two: the rice. My mail was apparently four copies of the *Aeroplane* magazine, sent out from Britain, and a small book, the name of which I never discovered. That night rain fell, light rain but a bad sign when in the morning the cloud depth was so thick it was quite gloomy. I said with my kukri I would be able to make myself a shelter to sleep in, from banana leaves and thin bamboos; and so we parted, Krishna worried about rain at this time of the year, fearing no good would come of it. I let them keep the rice, as I preferred chupattis, and had a good supply still available. I thought within three days I would be through to the Subansiri, and wished them well.

They knew they were to meet me at the bungalow of the Jonson *sahib* at Bogahilonia. I had the Mauser rifle with me, with no intention of using it except if I frightened an animal which would react dangerously, or if I needed food. I had the Zeiss camera with me, and hoped to continue taking pictures of all that was new and interesting. I admit to feeling rather unsure of myself, mainly as the weather was so depressing and untypical, but thought a little adrenaline was what I needed to make me feel happy. I told them to ask the Miris how to reach Chauldhoa, the place where they would find a ferry to cross the Subansiri. The Jiya Dhol was a curious river which, beyond the Miri villages, eventually ended in a swamp. The swamp abounded in fish, which was why the Miris chose to live near it. Others would not try to settle there, as during the monsoon the swamp would expand, and the Miris could only move in their smaller canoes, and enjoyed their undisturbed peace in their houses on stilts, despite the rigours of providing all that they needed to keep them alive. Like many rivers in Assam, the Jiya Dhol often changed its course. There was an old river course diverging from it, mainly dry in the cold weather, called the Maria Dhol, Maria meaning dead, or extinct.

Krishna and Somroo went their way, Krishna admonishing me, calling his gods to protect me; and Somroo said there was going to be heavy rain for two days, but the third day would bring clear weather again. He was right. The cloud was thick and the rain began by about eight o'clock. The elephant tracks were many, and arranged like a maze in a network which confused a sense of direction. The sun would have been a great help in choosing which tracks to follow; but it was difficult to use the compass whilst carrying the Mauser and using the kukri to cut the many cruel thorny tendrils, easily brushed aside by the pachydermatous vegetarians, but unless cut would mean painful and bloody scratches on the skin of a vagrant human. It became apparent my progress was going to be painfully slow, both because of the need to hack so much, and also because it was proving difficult to use the compass to good effect. Many times I came to a place where a giant tree had fallen across the track I was using, which meant retreat to avoid what would have been nearly an hour of cutting. About three in the afternoon I came to a clear stream, and decided in spite of the rain that I should make tea and have some food. I had half a dozen chupattis which I could eat without cooking, and had some currants to taste. I gathered small dead branches, having learned they would always remain dry, even during the rains, and when the bark was stripped they could be kindled easily. I had plenty of old newspapers, and used two sheets of the *Calcutta Statesman* to start my fire. It took nearly an hour to boil the water in my small aluminium kettle, into which I put the tea leaf and some powdered milk mixed with sugar, stirring it desert-style until the colour looked right. It was refreshing, but I realised I had to move faster to find my first night stop and build a shelter for sleeping. Moving on I began to hear sounds through the noise of the relentless rain. Once there was a noise which I was to identify within seconds: it was a tremendously heavy thump on the ground, somewhere close. It set my heart thumping with its mysterious power, and I dropped the kukri and raised the rifle, just in case. I nearly jumped out of my skin when, for the first time, at very close range, a barking deer barked, so loudly that I jumped with shock. The undergrowth was too thick for me to see him, but he went away with tremendous leaps, making a noise like the clicking of teeth until he stopped again and barked. I laughed at myself, and wondered if I was really competent to be doing this kind of journey. By six that evening I had noticed the rain had lessened, and the forest was remarkably clear of undergrowth. Here I saw many signs of wild pig having fed, the rich soil of the forest floor having been churned as if well ploughed. I saw a sambar doe at about twenty yards range in the eerie twilight of the forest. She stood stock still until I moved towards her, then turned and moved away in a ludicrous and clumsy trot, freezing for a second at every change of foot, black tipped tail erect. I made fairly swift progress in a positive westerly direction until I came to an area of small bamboos, amongst which there were plenty of fairly fresh elephant droppings. I retreated for a hundred yards or so, and decided to make a shelter, but finished up moving north until I found sufficient wild banana trees for the making of a shelter. It was dark by the time I had cut a framework and covered it with banana leaves. It was not long enough for me to lie down, but somehow I thought it would be better to sit with my back against some stakes, and doze that way. I managed to build a good fire, hoping to dry my shorts and shirt, having changed into dry clothes. I gathered plenty of good logs, and placed them, boy scout style, like the spokes of a large wheel so that I could keep pushing them into the fire. The rain slowly increased, and it became miserably cold. The banana leaf roof leaked in several places, and after dozing off several times I found the fire was drying the leaves of the under layer, increasing the amount of leakage. At about two in the morning I stopped feeding the fire close to the shelter. I came to life at dawn, almost as wet as before I had changed, but the shirt and shorts I had hung to dry were ready to wear. The embers were still red under the ash, and I made another four chupattis, two for breakfast, two to carry. There was a lull in the rain, although the cloud was as thick as ever. I shaved in a small stream, and when I had finished I hung the camera on a sapling and began repacking the rucksack. I became aware of a swishing and crackling noise in the direction of the bamboo grove. I stood and listened, certain the noise was coming nearer. Suddenly there was a deep rumbling sound followed by staccato trumpeting, and then complete silence. This was elephant territory, and I was not sure what I should do except to do nothing to frighten or threaten an elephant. There was the gentlest of swishing noises, attracting my glance to west of my camp, and through the huge tree trunks I saw the dark shape of a huge elephant moving fast towards me. In panic I grabbed the Mauser, and using the small stream as my only aid to location, I began with no little noise to stride northwards along the stream, knowing if I lost it I would be in trouble. The elephant, probably ambling aimlessly and accidentally in my direction, let out a frantic trumpeting sound. I heard him crash through something, and I kept going, although it sounded as if he had turned away. After I had gone about 200 yards the stream was hidden under a dense tangle of creeper and thorn, and I had never felt so friendly as to that little brook, not wanting to risk circumventing the tangle and losing it. I waited, and listened hard. After about half an hour I heard movement, and what I took to be elephant conversation: rumbles and squeaks, somehow indicating there were several of them, and not in too bad a mood. After more than an hour I heard them move away, and when the cracking of branches receded into the distance I decided to risk a careful approach to my camp.

My camera hung safely on the sapling, but the shelter had been pulled to bits, my rucksack emptied, and my food supplies, except for two tins of milk, were trampled into the forest floor, mixed with my tube of shaving cream and wallet of medical supplies. My clothes were well besmirched with dark humus, and the rucksack was filthy but undamaged. I found the kukri and the spare rifle ammunition, with one of the three films I had brought. There was not a spoonful of my chupatti flour available for eating. Forty love to the elephants. I counted five different sized tracks. I packed the clothes as they were, rolled the camera in the cleanest shirt, gave up the search for the razor and blades, and having the compass in my pocket I took a deep breath and set course again. After I had been going for an hour I stopped dead in my tracks, realising I had not found the several boxes of matches, nor the kettle, nor the tea. As I had searched and searched, I decided it was better to press on. The rain decided to fall again, and although it was really heavy this time, I stopped worrying about getting wet; the main idea now was to keep going, and to find something to eat – uncooked. The day was grim in every way. The lovely dreams of the North Bank wilderness in the cold weather began to fade. The rain fell relentlessly, and although the forest was easier for steering west to begin with, after about four hours I came to a marsh. There were many dead trees standing with all small branches long gone, and there were signs of many duck; but descending the small slope from the forest I found there was deep, sticky, and evil smelling mud, clearly not negotiable on a westerly course. I surmised the best thing to do would be to divert to the north, where it seemed the marsh narrowed towards the foothills, although low cloud obscured the true lie of the land. I covered several miles before realising I had actually moved a long way south of the hills in the maze of forest. Eventually I came to a place where there seemed to be a series of small islands and peninsulas, with many tracks of deer, pig and a tiger leading to the nearest island where the track was resumed. I decided it must be possible to follow the track without going out of depth, and struck out, already beginning to feel cold and hungry. The water was only three feet deep, but the mud beneath was thick and sticky. In this way, with much exertion of pulling my legs out of the viscous bottom, I managed to reach what I thought was the dry land of the forest. The trees were there, and the land rose, but the shore was designed like a sophisticated security barrier. With only about fifteen yards to traverse I thrust into the bed of evil mud, but felt it react like quicksand. I struggled back and sought a less difficult crossing, but when I thought I had one, I was half way across when I felt myself sinking. In such cases one summons up resolve and energy, and I somehow kept going until almost exhausted, sinking only five yards from the dry land. The warm feeling of finding hard ground at the bottom of the mud was a great boost. I staggered up into the forest, both shoes lost, but now becoming more and more concentrated on the target, not wasting time on small nuisance. After another two hours of good game tracks, with no thorns to threaten my bare feet, I came to a clearing near a small river. There was an area of about three acres where reeds and thatch grew, with some seven- or eight-year-old saplings growing. Amongst the thatch I saw what looked like dark heads, four or five feet high, having the impression there were creatures watching me. There were many of them, but with no movement, and I moved towards the northern edge of the clearing with the rifle ready, watching carefully. It took time before I noticed the dark heads were from a new angle in rows, and moving through the lessening rain, rifle at the ready, I finally recognised they were sets of pillars, and concluded this was the once inhabited Abor village, the haunted one. There were many animal tracks, including those of the gaur, the giant wild cattle whose tracks I had seen at Dulung. There was no thought of camping in such a place, and I moved on. The rain stopped late in the afternoon, and birds began to call, all kinds of birds, and an hour or two before sunset the sun broke through, and I saw some blue sky in the south-west. I found another small stream with sufficient clear water in a pool for a bath and a drink. Seeing tracks of small deer near the pool I decided to withdraw into the undergrowth and hope for a shot at some food. I had no luck, and had to make do with making holes in a tin of milk, which I sucked slowly for my supper. It rained no more. Next morning I awoke, chilled stiff, but happy to see the sun about to rise in a clear sky. For some reason the elephant tracks were much more sympathetic to my course, running mostly east-west. Within three hours I found myself in forest where things were growing in rows. I found both tiger, and better, human tracks, and before long came to a small area of tea, with huts visible. I found a man who looked like a *sirdar*, and imagine he thought he had found a man who looked like nothing he had ever seen before, as I had to tell him not to flee but stand and talk to me. He looked wildly at me, but hearing my accent gave a vague salute. I told him I wanted to go to Bogahilonia to meet the Jonson *sahib*, and he relaxed, showing me the way to go to find the path along the Subansiri, south to where I would see Bogahilonia on the other side. He said there were Miri villages down there, and they would take me across in a '*naoka*'. I felt it was better to move, although I was feeling very much in need of a meal, and went on my way, thanking the man for his help. As I moved away he asked where I was from, and I said I had come from the Jiya Dhol. He put his hands on both cheeks, staring, then turned and ran.

As I went the dream of the North Bank cold weather came true again. The sound of the huge river, its smell, its beautiful colours of jade, the tall forested islands and, looking behind me, the wonderful backdrop of the mountains, clear and blue, restored my morale. What was more: I had defied the ghosts and done my trek, learning a great deal about the reality of the forest. It was clear there was a vast amount of wildlife there, but with rain, no man-made paths, and a debilitating hunger, one could not summon up food on the hoof; not until one had become much wiser in the ways of the wilderness. Dreaming thus I went barefoot along the river, and stopped, hearing what sounded either like an aeroplane or an outboard engine. Away downriver I saw a large (twenty-four-foot) dugout with white bow waves, coming up the river. It was about one and a half miles away. I guessed that it would not come beyond the large rapid I was passing, and quickened my pace. My hair was badly tousled, and I needed a shave. I had a shirt drying over the rucksack on my back, and a pair of shorts with the rifle barrel through one leg over my shoulder. It would be good to see MacDonald again. The arrangement was that I would stay with him for a few days before returning, and he had weeks ago said he would look forward to seeing me. I saw the boat beach on my bank about half a mile downstream. A man climbed out and hauled the canoe half out of the water. It was Jonson, and the brilliant red blanketed figure sitting in the boat was certainly not Mac. Jonson walked up the shore and turned on to the path through thatch and scrub, walking towards me. He had a walking stick and smoked a pipe, wearing shorts of white and a thick naval sweater. He was scanning the scene as he approached, and when he was ten yards away I stepped to one side of the path, and hardly looking at me he lifted his stick, took out his pipe and said 'Salaam, Thapa!', not altering his stride. I let him pass, unable to believe he had not seen me, and before he had gone far I called 'Salaam *sahib*! Hey *sahib*!' He stopped, turned his head, and I called to him, 'Fancy not recognising an officer and a gentleman.'

He swung round, and taking his pipe out walked slowly until he stood a few feet away from me.

'Well, I'll go to the bloody bottom!' he said. 'MacStorm, by God. What the hell is the disguise for?' Then he started laughing and slapping my shoulder, asking questions about the trip. 'By the way,' he said, 'MacDonald is in Calcutta. He's had trouble with one of his ankles, and the mission doctor said he should go down to see a surgeon. You're welcome to stay with me.'

And so it went. I told him I was weak for lack of food, explaining all that had happened. The red blanket was Kanasundri, who smiled sweetly with a queenly gesture. We were soon back in his bungalow where he ordered tea and toast, telling me I would have plenty to eat because he had invited old Julian Stafford to drinks and dinner. He fixed me up with razor and shaving soap, gave my muddied clothes to be washed, and organised clean clothes to wear meanwhile. I had hoped to eat about ten slices of toast and butter, but there was only enough for two slices each; the new bread would only arrive later in the evening when the lorry returned from North Lakhimpur. Julian Stafford had been a senior manager in one of the big companies of the Jorhat area, and had crossed swords with his high command, and had been relegated to one of the small estates further down on the North Bank. 'A real old fashioned gentleman,' Jonson said, 'whose wife left him after one year over here, since when he keeps a harem of three girls and enjoys his shooting, fishing, and a fair amount of drinking. He'll tell you great stories of when he was a cavalry officer with the Lancers in France, first world war.' Stafford arrived about six in the evening with a crate of beer and a basket with eight brace of snipe. He was a most amusing character, very caustic about Jorhat, where he said the planters were living in the early 1900s. I said I had met the fourteen-stone *sahib*, which led him to vituperate with relish on that man's character until his mouth frothed with rabid hate. He and Jonson seemed able to drink and drink, without showing any trace of inebriation. A few chips were brought, most of which I ate with my terrible hunger demanding sustenance. Jonson kept saying dinner any moment now, and eventually he poured a cold beer, telling me to drink it, as there was nothing better to line an empty stomach before a good meal, which was coming up soon. I had drunk beer before, but had never liked it enough to form the habit. Perhaps it was a reaction to the exertions, lack of sleep and food, but after the first gulp I felt it was what I needed to calm the ravenous hunger no-one seemed to recognise but myself. By the time food was served, well after midnight, I had finished three bottles of Heinekens, and felt decidedly dizzy. I fell asleep several times, and eventually asked to be excused, staggering uncertainly to my bedroom. I fell on the bed, my head now spinning, feeling the bed was beginning to spin with me. I undressed in the bathroom, and crawled naked into bed, leaving the dim bathroom light on. My stomach was feeling decidedly badly treated, and I felt vaguely nauseous. Suddenly someone switched my bedside light on. It was Kanasundri; I was horrified. She turned, and brought from behind her a girl of about sixteen, who opened a shawl she was wearing to show her pretty half-lemon breasts, her eyes wide with embarrassment or fear. Kanasundri said quietly the *sahib* would give her some present if she was a good girl. I sat upright, the nausea now asserting itself, and I said 'Go! I am unwell. I have fever.' And unable to wait I half fell out of bed, staggered into the bathroom, and began to vomit, roaring like a tiger, hanging on to the cistern pipe to stay on my feet. The ladies disappeared, and eventually I crept back to bed, shivering and wretched. Some time later Kanasundri came into the room and, ignoring my advice to leave me alone, held a glass for me to drink. I would not have it, but she explained it was very good medicine brought by the 'Istaffad' *sahib*. I sipped it, then swallowed it, and fell into a deep, drugged sleep. In the morning Jonson gave me a breakfast of several eggs, a brace of snipe, and a lot of hot and flavoury tea. He asked me to tell him when I had last eaten before we met on the river, and shook his head, apologising for not having registered the true situation. He said Kanasundri was very worried about me. 'I don't know what got into her. When she told me she had brought that Bairi Salmi Oraon girl for you I went for her; she's never done that before. She told me she was only trying to help the girl. She was born deaf just before her parents came here from their country, and they can't get her married. If you're feeling better I don't mind if you want to take her on, but I don't like the idea that anyone thinks this is a house of ill fame.' He laughed, and I told him I was definitely a marrying type, and meant to study how to find a suitable wife, first of all learning more about life out here. I was grateful for Constable's gift of that clear category: a marrying type, and hoped I would be able to honour it.

The next four days made up for the last three. I gave Krishna more money, and Jonson explained to them how they were to find the track to Sisi Bargaon, where they could get a lift on a lorry calling itself a bus to Sonarigaon, where they could cross the ferry to Dibrugarh and hoof it to Medeloabam across country. I sent them two days before I was due to be picked up either by Telford or Constable, as I wanted to be first to tell Telford exactly what had happened. I knew he was likely to react with disapproval to my wayward decision, but I thought I would be able to make it sound better than Krishna's hyperbolic style, which was bound to omit his refusal to follow the 'haunted' route. I went round the estate with Jonson, who was another mine of good information. We swam, and I caught my first mahseer on the Subansiri, where we explored all the pools and rapids, picnicked at Dulung Mukh, and sat before the fire each night talking of everything. He said I should not mention it to anyone, but MacDonald's fiancée had sent her engagement ring back; it was all over. He's badly hurt; she's going to marry one of his best friends. I remembered how I had offered to change places with Mac so that he could bring his new wife out to the South Bank. It sounded no longer necessary, and I wrote a letter of condolence, remembering how deeply it had affected some of my friends during the war: the Messpot treatment. He would arrive back after I had gone. When Jonson asked if I knew who would be acting for Telford when he went on home leave in April, I laughed and said Telford had been on home leave last year; Foyle had acted for him. Jonson grinned and said the jungle telegraph had said Telford goes on home leave again. Like most of the planters who had carried on from 1940 to 1946 without any home leave, he was due two home leaves, and this is the way it works out for him. He would have had nine years without any home leave, and the company has waited until people like MacDonald and myself settled in before knocking off the arrears. I was shocked to learn this, and asked him where he got it from, but he grinned and said, 'From my cook, where all pukka gen comes from in this country.' When I said it must have been a letter from MacDonald who picked it up from the Calcutta office, he laughed and said it took eight to ten days for a letter to come from Calcutta. I was disappointed at the news, having wanted some continuity under Telford who, for all his strange ways, was a man with his own ideas, and wanted to see progress made with the development of clonal tea.

It was Constable who arrived on Sunday morning, not in the Piper Cub, but in an Auster. When I saw it and heard it I took it for granted it was Telford, and hoped he would be all right on the eroding strip. When I saw the low level 'beat-up' meant to impress the cowherds of the necessity to clear the field of cattle, and saw the steep climbing turn, I was worried that Telford had suddenly acquired too much self-confidence. As the aircraft touched down in a good landing, having used no engine on the approach, I realised it was not the Telford Auster. The sound of the engine was different, and I saw it was Constable at the controls of what seemed to be a Gipsy Major-engined Auster used by the army during the war. He climbed out without stopping the engine, and beckoned me. After a quick handshake and a quick explanation of his intention to buy this aircraft, which he called the 'Monster', he said he wanted my opinion on its behaviour. I climbed in and checked everything. The extra power was impressive. I took off with a third flap in sixty yards or less, and soared away. I climbed to 3,000 feet and tested the stall, then dived to 800 feet to do several tight steep turns, and landed. We had lunch with Jonson before boarding for our return trip. Bobby asked me to fly the Monster to Medeloabam, and to climb to at least 5,000 feet, saying that after the rain the snows were magnificent. We flew at 1,000 feet over the route I had taken in the rain, and it looked like a model country scene, with green pastures I knew to be stinking marshes. We saw twelve elephants and about twenty wild buffalo at the southern edge of the marsh, and climbed away above the Miri villages we had visited on foot. It was cold at 5,000 feet, but the snow ranges were indeed a marvellous sight. We talked a lot about the Monster, and all I could suggest was that he should try to find larger tyres, as the heavier aircraft would tend to sink into sand or soft sward in the rains. Bobby was trading in his Piper Cub as part of the purchase, and I was sorry it was to go, it having been for me a kind of rescuing angel, ensuring contact with flying even in my damfool career.

I asked Bobby Constable if he had heard of Telford going on home leave again this year. He said he had not heard, but knew he had, like himself, been eight or nine years without home leave, and would surely be entitled to go. He said he was going on leave himself in April if the company managed to find someone competent to act for six months. He said he had met Telford recently, and he was 'moaning about you being on holiday' when there was so much demand for the Auster. 'It sounds as if you are going to be busy when you get back.' He knew my views on flying a company taxi, and said the big trouble was going to be finding experienced people who would be prepared to be part planters and part pilots. 'It won't work, you know. You might find new people coming prepared to do it on that basis, but they'll have very little flying experience, no knowledge of the Assam monsoon season, and no knowledge of what planting entails, and it'll be their managers who'll kick. I wouldn't have a man working for me who's liable to walk off to fly some four-eyed accountant fifty or sixty miles away to the North Bank, or Jorhat, leaving the field or the factory to look after itself. Assistants after all are supposed to be learning how to be managers, for God's sake. It won't work unless you have someone who just flies and does the aircraft maintenance, and even then there'll be a problem, because there won't always be enough for him to do, unless he knows how to be an internal auditor or something bureaucratic which can be turned on or off without interfering with essential work.' It was scathingly well put, and served only to depress me more; but I knew I had to be careful not to act contrary to the promise I had made in ignorance of what I had since discovered to be the exciting demands of the tea production business.

We landed at Medeloabam about three o'clock, and saw Telford's car driving to the end of the strip. Constable looked at his watch and said, 'If he asks me for a cup of tea I can just about spare the time.' The car had stopped where the road to the bungalow met the airstrip, and drawing across the front of the car Constable switched the engine off, and we climbed out to greet Telford.

'What on earth delayed you?' Telford glared at each of us in turn with no sign of a welcome on his tensely set face.

'We weren't delayed at all,' said Constable. 'I landed, I let MacStorm fly a circuit in the Monster; then we had lunch, and took off. Here we are! One flying assistant safely delivered as promised.'

I turned and thanked Constable for being so kind, sensing Telford was for some reason in a foul mood, and hoped Krishna and Somroo had not preceded me.

'But I told you clearly I wanted MacStorm back as early as possible because I wanted him to fly me over to the Simen fishing camp. Now it's too late to be worthwhile.'

'Jack, I remember you saying to me yesterday in the club you had been thinking if, when I brought MacStorm back there was time enough, you would ask him to fly you over and have a look at the Simen strip. You made it sound as if it was nothing more than that. It's just after three; there's plenty of time to go and have a look at it. I told you I would have lunch with Jonson and fly straight back.'

'The family's gone off for tennis with the McNallys. I've had a makeshift lunch; I've been waiting since eleven, picnic and fishing gear all ready to go. The loss of my day. I must say!'

Constable asked him what must he say, and said he should have told him clearly about his intended trip. 'It would have been easy to start early and deliver MacStorm back at eleven, but you have to spell out exactly what you want,' and noting Telford turning petulantly away he went on, 'it makes me unhappy to think of you having wasted a day, but you must know I am not the sort of person who would scorn your arrangements.' He then turned to me and asked if I would swing the propeller for him. By the time he had taken off, Telford had turned the car and driven back to his bungalow. I took my rucksack to my bungalow, and sat to write a note on my trek, explaining how I parted from the men for a couple of days, how the elephants demonstrated their displeasure at my camping in their territory, and that MacDonald's engagement had been terminated. I thanked him for the air drop, and explained the difficulty in searching for the packages. I said the trip was certainly as difficult as he said it might be, but I had learned a lot from it, especially from Somroo, whose flute music had been a truly enjoyable interlude. He and Krishna should be arriving either this evening or tomorrow. They both performed very well. I had hoped to be called to his bungalow, but it didn't happen.

Next morning I rode out on my own, and reported to Telford in his office. He told me to go and check the work plan for the day and come back in fifteen minutes, which I did. He said he would wait to hear what Krishna had to say before commenting on the trip report. It struck me that the quiet, very casual murmur he used when dealing with things which were causing him deep thought was a very English trait, a kind of understatement which sank lower as the importance or emergency of the matter increased. He was doing it now, and I was learning to identify from it that something was irritating him. He began on yesterday's delay, and was critical of the fact that Constable had volunteered to collect me simply because he wanted to show off this 'Monster' of his. 'You realise Constable has always got to have bigger and better than anyone else. He was so full of it he either completely misunderstood or deliberately sabotaged my arrangement. Didn't apologise! Never does! One of the most selfish people one could meet. You needn't fly with him any more now you have an Auster on your doorstep. You'll see, you can't trust him.' I was deeply disappointed to hear this talk coming from a man I was learning to respect, in spite of his strange attitudes. It seemed he was suffering from a kind of paranoia, making unreasonable judgements about a man who, as seemed to be the case with the planters I had so far met, had plenty of idiosyncrasies, but certainly no flaws in his clear, if sometime abrasive, communication. I insisted he was wrong to suspect Constable of deliberate disregard. He had perhaps a tendency to exhibitionism, but that was a harmless and probably amusing flaw. 'He's not good company for you, you know. He obviously defers to your flying ability, but you must know he consorts with native women. Not the best for your future nowadays.' I could not restrain my distaste at this remark. 'I am able to tell you, Telford, he is the one man who has come out loud and clear to warn that keeping a mistress is not for me, and would be a disaster. He said he knew very positively that I was the marrying type,' and as Telford made one of his grimaces more like a sneer than a grin, I followed on, 'and he warned me if I disregarded his advice and took a mistress he would never speak to me again.'

'There you see the conceit of the man. He warns you of the tragedy of him never speaking to you again; he thinks it really matters.'

'To me it seems a noble conceit that shows such concern for my protection. Like you, he is a man I would never want to cross, for reasons less of fear than of respect.'

From his breast pocket he produced a paper with a list of dates and names headed 'Copy for Mr MacStorm', and explained there were three flights this week, and three next week, one of which was to Gauhati, capital of Assam, to collect the Calcutta Visiting Agent. After three weeks on the South Bank he would have to be flown to the North Bank, and be picked up to fly back to the South Bank for the Senior Men's Conference. A new strip was being made north-east of Jorhat, being made to the draft specification MacDonald and I drew up, and I was to drive down to inspect and advise on it. 'That's about all, I think. Oh, yes! I shall be sailing from Bombay on April the 4th, with my family, for six months' due leave. I was told Delapere is to act for me, in spite of my protests. He will arrive in mid-March. We leave on the 22nd. You will move over to the old assistant's bungalow by March the 7th, with your servants.' When I asked if Delapere knew about my commitment to the flying, he said Fraser would look after that.

Chapter XVI

It took me time to use the wireless set to hear the news, and it was only when I waded through the various copies of the *Calcutta Statesman* that I came on the mention of Gandhi declaring another hunger strike because India was refusing to pay 550 million rupees to Pakistan as agreed by India in December 1947. It was something to do with the stalemate over Kashmir, and Gandhi declared India was wrong to break its promise to pay. The anti-Pakistan feeling was running high in India, and there was a public outcry against Gandhi's declaration, so violent that Gandhi decided he must try to hold India to its promise by going on a hunger strike. It seemed sad he had to resort to what must have been a dangerous course for a man who had put his physical well-being under such repeated risks for years past. I thought the euphoria of Independence, which had apparently survived through the terrible Hindu-Muslim massacres, was probably beginning to crack, portending a change throughout India which might even reach Assam. I received a note from Telford two days after my return, telling me details of the mail he had dropped. I never discovered what the small book was, or from whom it came; it bore an Indian stamp but no sender's address. Having promised, I began flying Telford's Auster on the trial of a company air service. As far as I could see, if it was company business Fraser had first to approve it, and give Telford the permission to arrange for me to do the flying involved. In offering to help prove the benefits of such a service, I had gradually modified my keenness to fly, finding myself increasingly motivated not only in exploring the possibilities of selection and propagation of 'golden' bushes, but by becoming more able to communicate with the men and women who worked on the estate at the many and changing tasks involved. Once the flying began I soon discovered I was using more time waiting for people to arrive and board than in the actual flying, and said so to Telford but he showed no reaction, probably pleased enough to have a growing demand for such a service.

I found it strange he should describe his acting manager in terms indicating scorn for his abilities and contempt for his way of life. Mrs Delapere had been a teacher, and had written books of which no-one had heard, and dressed in the style of the Bloomsbury set, completing the picture of sophistication by drinking and smoking as hard as her husband. Telford was emphatic that he was depending on me to see the estate was run in the way he had taught me, Delapere being incapable of managing his own life, let alone anything else. This contrasted oddly with his frequent reminders that it took at least ten years for anyone new like myself to learn the rudiments of tea sufficiently to be competent. It seemed therefore odd he should expect so much from someone with so little experience as myself, who would be liable to disappear on flying assignments from time to time, thus undermining the confidence of the acting manager in his 'part time' assistant. He was critical of the company for allowing too many hopelessly inefficient people to continue in service, using them mainly for acting managements and giving them very little promotion. I thought such people must have been very useful during the war when most of the young planters left to join the forces. However, I had seen very little of Delapere except for meetings in the club, and had to reserve judgement. My visits to the club were seldom and brief, mostly for a short while after polo and I was glad the Telfords were neither hard drinkers nor club socialites. George Fraser and his wife often buttonholed me with advice to mix more, but lack of transport made mixing difficult, and I found the idea inconvenient, as time to ride, explore, and read was decidedly precious.

One Saturday afternoon I was walking to the Telfords' bungalow when I heard the sound either of an aircraft or an outboard motor; it was neither. It was a motorcycle, ridden by a man round about my age, and he pulled up where I stood in the middle of the road. We shook hands and exchanged names. He was Roger Carrick, ex-armoured corps captain, who had seen the last months of the Burma campaign. His sandy hair was parted and his lower jaw hung long in T. E. Lawrence style. He wore slightly faded jungle green shirt and shorts, and was well burnt by the sun. I suggested he came to the club to see the polo, and perhaps consider taking it up, but he declined, saying he was not a horsey type. He asked the way to the Brahmaputra, and I told him where he could best reach it without too much cross-country riding. I invited him to call in for a cup of tea whenever he next passed, and waved as he went on his way. I didn't see him again for another two and a half years. There were several of us who were the same in preferring to avoid being caught up with others, whatever the reason, and I found myself thinking this attitude was probably caused by many like myself who, having been schoolboys in the thirties, had been captivated by the mystery and intrepidity of the extraordinary Lawrence of Arabia. We read the *Seven Pillars of Wisdom*, and steeped ourselves in the later legends which arose when he sought to hide himself as a ranker in his beloved air force. During the war one met so many people in the air force who told of meeting Lawrence, all of them holding him in high respect. His death before the second world war was surrounded by mystery, and when the second war led to many of the remarkable pastel portraits of fighting pilots, mainly by Rothenstein, there seemed to be a link with the same artist's first war portraits of Lawrence, Allenby, Feisal and others, and the charisma grew. There was certainly some deep-seated sympathy for Lawrence's disappointment and disillusion at the end of his own war in the desert, when the British and the French, seeming to ignore implicit promises used to encourage the Arabs to fight under Lawrence against the Turks. Were we trying to emulate Lawrence's wartime enthusiasm for leading the Bedouin and learning their language? Did we covertly feel so depressed by the second war ending, before we had personally achieved the glory of which we had dreamed, that we felt it necessary to withdraw to the wilderness, to revert to his kind of self-effacing 'karma', renouncing modern comforts and following the ancient wisdom of non-attachment? How many of us could explain even to ourselves why we were drawn to such ideas? Corders was certainly one who may justly claim some affinity by virtue of the common yoke of illegitimacy, but that did not apply to the rest of us, each in his own solo mode which seemed to forbid by its very nature the formation of a cult membership.

On the 30th of January, 1948, nearing the end of my first year in India, I arrived back at Medeloabam after a tiring day of which the flying, although the shortest part of the day, was all that I enjoyed, with one first landing on a new airstrip, two other landings on the North Bank to deliver supplies of the improved drugs now becoming available for things like septicaemia, and a last trip to deliver the wife of a North Bank second clerk to Dinjan; the poor woman was in the throes of what was seen to be a difficult delivery, and was brought over for a Caesarian operation. I managed to bring her mother in the rear seat, and having been delayed throughout the day, made a low pass over the surgeon's house to signify arrival, then landed at the tarmac strip to hand over the ladies to the ambulance. It took twenty minutes before the ambulance arrived, and I landed back home well after sunset having left soon after breakfast. Having been frustrated in my plans to supervise the construction of the new cuttings nursery, which was to entail a roof with light-permeable and controllable shade, I hurried to see the aeroplane refuelled, cleaned, and put safely into the hangar, and strode off briskly to see what progress had been made in my absence.

Irritated at finding my instructions for the building of the new cuttings nursery misunderstood or ignored, I walked back from the new nursery to my bungalow in the deepening twilight, looking forward to a cup of tea before having a bath. On the way I heard singing: male voices in chorus with someone playing a flute. The voices were in slow rhythm, with a melody which rose and fell in a kind of sad cadence, the words of the descending line being easy to identify as 'Ram, Si-ita Ram, Si-ita Ram, Sita Ram'. I diverted towards the group of about twelve men who sat cross-legged around a hurricane lamp, blankets round their shoulders, and their faces sad in the lamplight. I recognised the head clerk and several others. In the gathering darkness I made out quite a crowd of men standing at a distance beyond the singers, watching in silence. As I stood, well enough away to avoid disturbing their singing, a shadowy figure materialised at my side. It was Dr Pal, well muffled against the evening chill, who made a namaste sign, whispering 'Good evening, Sir. They are singing prayers for the Mahatma.' I nodded, saying quietly I was greatly relieved his hunger strike had been so successful, and hoped it would be the last time he would ever have to use such debilitating force. 'O Sir!' he gasped, then put both hands to his face, muffling what could only be a huge sob. I put my right hand on his shoulder and tried to comfort him in what seemed to be unusual grief. 'Sir, you have not heard!' And between sobs he told me Mahatma Gandhi had been shot that evening, a few hours ago, by a Hindu extremist. The sound of his sobbing penetrated the singing, and the men rose, coming to see who stood in the deepening darkness. The head clerk managed to speak. I apologised for disturbing the prayers, and said I was shocked that the Mahatma, who had brought freedom and peace to India, had not been allowed to live to enjoy his wonderful achievement. There was too much sorrow for anything more to be said, and I placed a clenched fist against my heart, leaving them grief-stricken. Back in my bungalow I was eventually to hear on the wireless the shocking news of how Mahatma Gandhi had been killed in Delhi. There had been massive public support all over India for his hunger strike, and the Indian government had yielded, agreeing to pay Pakistan what was promised. He was recovering his strength after ending the strike, only to be shot by an extremist who hated Gandhiji and the Muslims he had protected. It felt to me as if I had lost someone very close, and after tea, in a fit of sheer sorrow and disillusion, I went downstairs and stood on the lawn, staring up at the stars, asking just what the hell was wrong with us all, only to have my question answered when I suddenly felt a fury rise in my breast, igniting a murderous desire to ride forth with a flaming sword to kill, kill, kill the fanatics...with fanaticism.

The horror spread everywhere in Assam, and Gandhi's death was bitterly mourned. This was for me the first crack in the splendid picture I had created in my mind of India: a country where religion was so strong amongst its people, and kept them living peacefully in its millions of remote villages. Someone had killed the man who had used the most powerful weapon of non-violence to achieve freedom for India; the man who was prepared to die to save his fellow men from committing evil; a man who would eat no flesh and do evil to no-one. He preached the same simple but most difficult doctrine as Jesus Christ: non-violence; and like Jesus, he died for trying to save men from killing each other. In the days that followed there were many different voices, some blaming the British for being in too much of a hurry with the handover of power, but some blaming Gandhi himself for stopping the Hindus from settling their account by reciprocal massacre of the Muslims. This was an ugly twist in the ideal scene I had so naively pictured, but it seemed to be associated with extremists, of whom there were as far as one could see, very few to be seen or heard in Assam, and according to Telford and the staff were a tiny minority in the whole of India. However that may have been, from that time onwards there seemed to be a change in my outlook. Having read Gandhi's story of his life I had become deeply impressed with the moral strength of this unusual man, and regarded him quite positively as a good influence and a remarkable teacher. This made his death by murder all the more difficult to accept, and a small weed of bitterness began to grow in what was the more religious corner of my brain, amongst the sad flowers which had grown when I had realised as a rising boy that most of the wars, massacres and burnings throughout the western world had been caused by Christians fighting Christians, committed in the name of God, by fanatics unable or unwilling to understand how divine judgement would condemn their guilt and vanity.

Telford was quite clear in his understanding of what had happened to Gandhi. He had said before, it was fatal always to be right. Men who were wrong, or doers of wrong, would destroy those who were right. When I suggested by 'right' he actually meant 'good', he riposted by saying it was quite ineffective to use the word 'good' instead of 'right'. People would smile complacently about a man who was good, and meek and mild; but a man who was right was a man who was respected but not loved, which is better than being tolerated as good; and in India, he warned me, there is often not much difference between respect and hate. I was discovering his people respected him, tolerated his humourless hard discipline; and to me, doubtless aware I might repeat it, they said such strong discipline and control was vital for reasonable prosperity; but it seemed to me, as time went on, that he must have known fear leads to hate, and accepted it as better than any of the alternatives. He warned me, as did Foyle, that it was acceptable to promote happy friendliness, so long as there was a foundation of firm discipline, and an earning of respect. I was grateful for wise counsel, but it was too early for me to understand how to work out my own working philosophy. With the death of Gandhi we, the damfools, had almost stopped thinking in terms of an insecure future. It was a tragedy which involved most of us with the same sense of loss as those amongst whom we lived and worked. There was a polo meet at Moran not long after the assassination, attended by many planters, including the set of hard drinking damfools who insisted on celebrating the end of the war at every club night, changed only by the various post-war scars from turning turtle in their cars at two in the morning, returning from the club. At Moran there was much talk of the tragedy of Gandhi's assassination, and even those who had accused Gandhi of being a wily old political fox paid tribute to him as the nearest thing to a saint we had known in our lifetime.

The polo was some of the best I had ever known, with the bonus of a large gathering of spectators, club members and locals. I met several other damfools for the first time at the polo meet. It was embarrassing to be addressed as the intrepid bear slayer, tackling the killer on foot and so on, and my attempts to explain just what a foolish and supremely lucky episode it had been invoked protests at my modesty, and made me feel even smaller in my own mind. It was here that Telford introduced me to a Scottish estate manager who was having trouble from a family of tigers, and wanted someone who was keen and a good enough shot to help either to drive them away, or kill one or two of them. His estate was not too far from Medeloabam, not far from the great forest reserve where I had been lost. A few days later Telford let me take the jeep with Gerella to reconnoitre the area. We spoke with the villagers who had suffered serious losses of cattle, and they told us there was less trouble at the moment because many wild pig were coming from the reserve to raid their vegetable patches. There were several large boars, of whom even the tigers were afraid; but they said they would send word to Gerella if they had further cattle kills over which we could sit. It was Gerella who suggested I should tell the Koyas about the wild pig, because he pointed out to me an area of dense, overgrown tangle, impenetrable to men, where he thought the wild pig would remain in hiding during the day. The Koyas would be very good at driving the game from this tangle, using their small dogs, and it was fairly sure there would be some succulent pig to carry home for everyone.

About ten days later I managed to arrange for all twenty-six of the Koya men to set off across country with me to the area where the tigers had been causing trouble, in the hope of beating the long tongue of thick cover for pig and, the Koyas said, pointing to the tracks, barking deer, porcupine (which they loved to eat), and the unfairly named hog deer, which were beautiful creatures. The sun was well up when the beat started. The Koyas, wearing nothing but a necklace of large red beads and a very brief truss, lean and muscled like greyhounds, carried a bow with one steel-tipped arrow strung, and two other arrows stuck with one sharp barb hooked in the tight chignon of hair at the back of their heads, the feathered flights bouncing gently on their backs as they moved. They moved furtively, making no loud cries like the Mundas, but clicking their tongues and breaking twigs as they went. I stood at the outermost point at the end of the long tongue, prepared for a long wait. At my back there was an area of high reeds and thatch grass, for which any driven animal would aim, and I stood half way where I would have time for a safe shot. After about twenty minutes I heard the little hunting dogs give tongue: a high-pitched soft yelping which set my pulse bounding with anticipation. They were still about 400 yards away, and a Koya came bounding along the side towards me. By this time I knew the names of most of the animals, and when he said the dogs had sensed a tiger, I checked to see I had three bright new rounds at the top of my rifle magazine. He loped back again, and I watched him slow down beside one of the small dogs, 300 yards away. The dog was pointing, and the Koya suddenly crouched, drawing his bow. I saw the dog bounce to one side, and there sprang from the tangle a large, beautiful tiger, straight at the Koya. He had time to shoot, but the tiger landed on him, roaring with the pain of the arrow in his shoulder, and I saw the Koya fall limply as if dead under the weight of the great beast. The dogs then all started staccato barking, darting in and snapping at the tiger's heels, distracting its attention from the fallen man. I began running through the rough tussocks towards them, and saw about a dozen Koyas streaming from beyond the tiger at a sprint, arrows strung, more little dogs charging in a frenzy. There was no hope of a shot with the Koyas now advancing within twenty yards on the other side of the bellowing beast. By the time I was within twenty yards the tiger was in his death throes, and I went forward to put a bullet through his spine at the neck. There were forty arrows in the tiger's body. The Koya, Poyami Adma, who had been attacked by the tiger, stood up, smiling and nodding, and joined with the others, acting out their apologies and regrets to the tiger, wondering who could have done this to him, protesting their admiration for the black and red lords of the jungle. Adma had three small punctures behind one shoulder from the tiger's forepaw. When I looked at the forepaws, with the Koyas pressing the sheathed claws so that they emerged fully, I felt almost dizzy at what the result would be if one had the misfortune to be engaged in close combat with such a powerful opponent. I remembered holding a kitten by the neck, seeing the lightning thrusts of his hind paws, claws unsheathed, and felt myself sweat with horror. The villagers were delighted at the kill, and identified the tiger as the father of the cattle killing family. It would have been a magnificent skin but for the forty arrow holes. The Koyas presented me with three foreclaws, and for themselves took all the whiskers, and chunks of meat from which they said they would boil out the tiger fat, which was the best salve for aching joints or backs. It was the first time I came across the sad necessity of any Koya whose skin had been punctured by a carnivore, to leave his clan, his family, his friends, to go and find a new environment where no-one would know he had been attacked by a tiger. Once Adma's claw sores had been fully cured, he turned up one morning to say he was leaving. We gave him his fare back to Bastar, and he went away into loneliness like a hero. The reason for this was the strong belief of the Koyas (and other tribes of their part of India) that if a tiger drew a man's blood, that man would become a were-tiger, who would eventually, knowing human ways, kill and eat men or women. They would change their form for several days before and after the full moon, and they went far away from their own clan to be sure they would never kill and eat their own family.

Not long after this, one of the sites I had to visit during my work at Medeloabam was a place where beautiful sand was being dug by two men from under a large bank in an old, dry river bed. It was collected in baskets by four older women, and carried up on to the track where the estate lorry would collect it at the end of the day. One morning I said to the *sirdar* supervising the work he was undercutting too much, and pointed to the danger of the six feet or so of pale brown earth collapsing. I said he should make sure the men worked from one side to bring the earth down, then clear it away so that more sand could be safely extracted. I was telling Telford in the office what I had done when a youth arrived out of breath having run from the sand quarry, announcing in panic stricken tones the collapse of the bank on top of three people: two men and one woman. We drove at speed to the site where several men had arrived to dig frantically, but it was clear there would be no survivors under four or five feet of damp earth. The *sirdar* was in a terrible state, and told Telford how I had instructed him to put the men at one side, but they wouldn't listen to him. The surviving man began berating him, saying he was lying. He didn't tell the men to do what the *sahib* had said, and he had only survived because he wanted to go to the side, seeing the *sahib* was right about the danger of a collapse. There was great wailing and sorrow, and I felt deeply depressed at this black mark. On the way back to the office Telford stopped under a tree and said I was not going to like it but I was to blame for what had happened. I should have seen that they did what I had actually ordered. It was something I could not argue against, having seen the dead bodies with blood having streamed from their mouths and noses, and I said I had learned a bitter lesson. He drove on, and said he had received a complaint from the junior Assamese field supervisor that in front of the workers I had treated him angrily over the way he had bungled the building of the new cuttings nursery. I said I had spoken in English to him, and was angry because he said he would have done what I wanted if I had been to see the work early that day. Telford said he had given me this man on test, as he had not been performing very well; and as for speaking English to him it was most likely he did not understand what was said except that it was some kind of rebuke. 'I would advise you,' he said in his lazy drawl, 'to remember it is essential to make wrongdoers afraid of punishment, not afraid of you. Ask for explanations fairly; point out mistakes; punish slackness or dishonesty. To display anger directed at someone, and not to punish, is inviting trouble.' I nodded, resolving to think about it. 'Tell him he is to take over the drainage chalan: Mundas and Koyas. He won't like that because he's afraid of them. I suspect him of writing women's names in the weeding account, two of whom actually work on his home farm. Some of the settled men will probably cooperate with him, but not the Koyas or Mundas. See what happens.' Whatever I thought of his methods, I could see there was much more behind them than I would have dreamed, and I needed to digest it all. Foyle had said it took a long time to understand how the different tribes reacted to criticism, and if one upset them they would slide into a stony faced mood with little said except what translated as 'We will do what you want us to do; we have to earn our pay.' The only way out of that was to be patient, positive, and never lose compassion for anyone ill, bereaved or distraught by personal misfortune. It all took time, but one had to learn. It so happened that the supervisor who had complained of my anger, when told by me of his new assignment, said he would go straight to the office to complain to the manager of being victimised by me. Telford told him I had acted on his orders, as we needed someone strict to control the deepening of the drainage. The man went with bad grace to shout at the Mundas and Koyas, something even I, with a year's experience, knew was asking for trouble. One tall, well-built Munda called Ludroo, with a handsome face which always showed a saintly smile, became tired of the supervisor's bad-tempered abuse, and heaved himself out of the deep ditch, his muscled chest gleaming with sweat, and walked up to the supervisor, holding his heavy digging hoe before him, proffering it with the words 'We don't understand what you mean, but you can take this and show us, then we will do exactly what you do. Hey?' The supervisor walked off threatening to report Ludroo to the manager; but he went home, took some rice beer, wrote out his resignation and handed it in to the manager's office. Later that afternoon Telford showed me the letter and asked what had happened. Having spoken to the Munda's *sirdar* I was able to recount how they had all laughed at him when he had walked away, threatening them. At this point the junior supervisor appeared outside the office accompanied by a beautiful young Assamese lady, who held the hand of a small child of about three years. We went on to the office verandah, a foot above ground level, and the man came forward, his eyes bloodshot from drink. Putting his hands together he said in Assamese he had made a bad mistake, and waving his hand at the bright-eyed, honey-coloured young lady behind him said his wife had justly berated him strongly for being so stupid. She had insisted he come to retract his resignation forthwith, and to ask forgiveness for his bad temper. I must confess, being a bachelor hamstrung by the combined and complicated bonds of western social custom, caught in an oriental paradise where the serpent's subtle voice could not prevail against the hoarse Calvinistic voices of the Old Testament, I could not control another of my frequent surges of protest at seeing another splendidly attractive girl married to a man who seemed totally inadequate for her, and certainly not up to the standard of the average well-fed Assam youths. The junior supervisor was small, lean, with longish black hair and a straggly cluster of thin hairs on his upper lip which only indicated he lacked the masculine vigour to produce a sufficiently impressive moustache for his splendid mate. To be fair, I have to confess how, at the age of nineteen in the Western Desert, when water for shaving was in short supply, I decided to follow the older men by growing a beard. After two weeks my commanding officer put his face close to mine and said, 'It looks as if you haven't shaved this morning, young MacStorm.' One must be fair in one's criticisms, and sexual jealousy was probably my fault. Telford turned to me and said I should tell him his resignation had been accepted because it was better so for him, rather than to dismiss him for his faults. I think I managed to phrase this well enough, and hearing what I had said the man wrung his hands and looked at the ground. The girl left the small boy standing, and came forward, her eyes wide open, and her pink lips open in an expression of disbelief. In sweet tones and beautifully pronounced Assamese she spoke to us, alternating her glance from Telford to me in a hypnotic way that worked strongly on me, so that I expected Telford to show mercy and give the man another chance. To my disappointment, he deprived me of the strong desire to yield to this lovely advocate's brilliant plea for her miserable husband, and he said to her there was no hope of allowing withdrawal of the resignation. This silenced her, and she listened to him say he would rather not explain all the things her husband had done wrong in the past, because she would be shocked at all the times he had been forgiven just because when they were married we had hoped he would turn over a new leaf. The sweet advocate was transformed suddenly, and directing her strident tones at her husband she denounced him in embarrassing terms, describing some of his misdemeanours, the least of which was his drinking, and asking Vishnu to help her to make a good honest man out of such a dissolute rascal, for the sake of her children. She ordered him home, and as she went with her small boy she turned and said she would deal with him, but it would be hard. Afterwards I ventured a complaint that it had not been possible to give him another chance, to which Telford replied I had a lot to learn about real justice. 'You were quite overpowered by his beautiful wife, weren't you. She is the one who knows how to deal with justice and the moulding of her man. Assamese women are the real backbone of their society you know. They have humour, they are not affectedly shy like so many other Indians, and they are damned hard workers. It's a pity we can't employ them, but they would be too tough for the male staff.' It was the nearest to real humour I had ever seen him.

I had to dismantle the roof and pillars of the cuttings nursery and rebuild it with pillars high enough for us to walk about without crouching. The roof was of thin bamboo lathes, upon which loose thatch was strewn, so that as the cuttings grew the thatch could be thinned to allow more light. We would next prepare long beds into which we would plant the cuttings in late March and throughout April, when the tea would have produced enough growth to provide suitable stems for cutting. I kept several foolscap books on what was advised by Tocklai, and what we had done, with a third book of intended programmes. It was a good feeling to be launching this project on my own initiative, quietly encouraged by Telford, whose repeated advice was not to talk much about it outside except when I found someone who was keen on it. As it happened I spent time selecting vigorous-looking bushes, with multiplex healthy frames, which after the spring rain began to grow far ahead of the average stands in high yielding areas. We took cuttings from these so that we could test our efforts at propagation, and had enough to plant more than half of the new nursery. The men we chose to do this work were mostly **Mundas**, who were good cultivators, well known for their excellent vegetables, and they were becoming keen and intrigued with what we were trying to do. It was only about a week before the Telfords departed that one hot, dry Sunday at about eleven o'clock, an estate watchman came running to me with news that the new cuttings nursery was in flames. Most people were either away at a local bazaar, or off to the river to bathe and wash clothes. When I arrived the flames were almost finished. The bamboo pillars, being still green, had survived undamaged; it was the thatch which had caught fire. The cuttings were hardly affected. The watchman and others who had joined us at the scene were emphatic the fire was caused by '*badmashi*' (roguery), and were saying no person was being named, but it was not an accidental fire. When I told Telford about it he asked me what I was going to do about it, and I said I had decided to use green bamboo thinly split instead of thatch for shade, and was trying to work out a system of raising bands of the roof to the south-east when less shade was needed. He smiled and said that was all very interesting, so long as I checked with Tocklai; but what he wanted to know was what I was going to do about the junior supervisor who had resigned. I suggested if we could prove he had been responsible for the fire we would call the police. Telford said the supervisor had not ignited the fire; he had paid someone to do it for him, and I should patiently wait, and talk with reliable observers to find who had actually done it, and then tell the arsonist he was going to be handed over to the police. He will then 'spill the beans' and name the man who paid him to do it, and you will always examine suspects with plenty of reliable witnesses, so that you will then be able to visit the police in Dibrugarh and explain what has happened. He said after that it would not be necessary to do anything more, and it would be best to close the file and keep it in the safe.

Riding out with Linda for the last time before the Telfords departed on leave, I learned she and her brother would be staying at school in England, although her older sister Lucy would return with her parents to Assam, to live with them. She was near to tears at the prospect, and I comforted her by saying how lucky she was at being able to see her father much more frequently now that the war was over, to which she replied her memory of her father had almost gone by the time she met him again after six years, but she hated the idea of not seeing her mother for nearly a year after they left her at boarding school. I thought of the day when I would be married and have children, and felt it was not a pleasing prospect to have such separations; but it all seemed so far ahead, and I was but twenty-four.

One evening I had ridden to the river, and for a change turned north-east along the bank, returning by a way I had never taken before. There was a large expanse of open paddy fields, very dry in February, and I could see a small grove in the centre of the area which had paths converging from all points of the compass. I had often seen this from the air, and wondered at the unusual appearance, there being no sign of a farmstead in or near the grove. I decided to ride to the grove and continue beyond it back to Medeloabam, being able to see the trees of the estate well inland. It was a bright evening with the sun well above the horizon, and having cantered on the open turf near the river I held Rani to a brisk walk, although she always wanted to speed up for the evening feed at the stables. When we were about twenty yards from the grove, a small stand of one pipul tree and four or five other trees rising from evergreen scrub, Rani suddenly thudded her fore hooves, stopping abruptly with her ears focussing ahead on the grove. I could see nothing to cause her fear, but she began to tremble and become tense, trying to turn back the way we had come. I held her ahead, and as she was clearly afraid I steered her out so that we passed the grove on a radius of twenty yards or so. She was very agitated, and I felt the strain of holding her chin in as she breathed rapidly and hoarsely. I could see some kind of masonry, built from Ahom bricks, thin and flat like Roman bricks, but there was too much foliage for me to identify its shape. I thought there might have been a jackal or two lying up during the day, or a dead dog giving a scent which would frighten a horse, but there was no sign of any creature, alive or dead. Once beyond and striding for Medeloabam, Rani laid her ears back and tried to raise her head and flee. By the time she quietened down we had left the wide expanse of paddy fields and entered the scattered small farms with their clumps of bamboo, mango trees and bananas around the thatched houses, where cattle were being fed and children ran to wave at the passing horse and its rider.

One of the cultivators who sometimes worked for us came over to greet me, and I asked him if anything had died back there in the isolated grove. He said he thought not and looked askance. I said the horse had been badly frightened by something as we approached the island of pipul and other trees, and the man made a sound of understanding, half laughing, half commiserating. 'Ah! the Kali Than, *sahib*. There are spirits there, ghosts. Everyone knows. The cattle stay away from it. Before the war one of the *chota sahibs* was thrown from his horse and broke his arm. You shouldn't have come that way, *sahib*. The only time the priests come to the shrine is at the Fagua Puja, when the Assamese villagers have a large mela with marvellous drumming: at least forty drummers, and the girls dance the Bohog Bihu dances. They don't like other people attending. It is an old

Ahom puja. We like listening to the drumming at night; it is like magic music, and sometimes frightens the children.'

Later, when I met Gerella and asked about it, he said many of the Ahom Assamese like himself came at Bohog Bihu to the mela (gathering). It was an important puja. He described how it was a spring festival which asked the gods to ensure good fertility in the fields, the fruit trees, the cattle, and the bearing of strong children. When I said I had heard it was both famous and remarkable for the drumming and dancing, and that I would be very interested to see it, even from a discreet distance, he laughed in the way which showed he was embarrassed, turning in all directions as if to see who was listening. I told him how Rani had sensed something like wild spirits when we tried to pass the Kali Than, and it had made me think there was something important, powerful, in the grove, which made me feel I should learn about it. He said it was not safe to go too near the place, and said when Fagua came nearer he would think of something, but I should tell no-one, not even the Telford *sahib*, that I had discussed it with him. The weather became hotter and hazier, and the spring rain was enough to set the whole landscape exploding with delicate green shoots and scented blossoms of all kinds. The Fagua Puja approached, and from the previous year I remembered the general atmosphere of alcoholic euphoria, the spraying of red dye over people's clothes, the drumming and singing, every tribe having its own peculiar festival. Only the Christians made devoted attempts to celebrate Easter without reverting to bibulous revelry, a difficult task when the deep and strong tribal ties of such as Mundas, Karrias, Oraons and Parjas brought Christians and animists together in a festival which led even the abstemious to follow the ancient custom of imbibing rice beer, just during the Fagua festival. The European attitude was fairly clear: estates would give three days' holiday, and planters would arrange to disappear for camps or lonely fishing huts, there to enjoy peace, quiet, cold beer and good fishing, escaping the tiresome jollity of being sprayed red by staggering youths. One heard that in Calcutta it was crazy to venture out at all, the city crowds being less gentle in their mass spraying peregrinations.

Gerella did not forget my wish, and came to see me with an invitation, a week before Fagua, to investigate a tiger kill not far from the Kali Than. It was a buffalo which had been killed, and there was no suitable tree near it in which one could sit. He said it was seldom that a tiger would return to a kill if men had moved it. Under the pretext of following tracks he took me out into the treeless expanse, and finally explained what the general layout of the night celebration would be. All the paths, mostly bordered with reeds and ferns, with some eupatorium scrub, would be used by about three hundred people from the surrounding Assamese villages. The unmarried girls who were to dance would walk in single file leading their own families, singing and clapping in unison. People would carry lanterns, and everyone would be happy. He indicated with his chin a few knolls in the widest sector of the paddy fields, at least a furlong (a measurement widely used by the locals) from paths on either side. He also indicated where the drummers would stand in a crescent, where they would condition the watchers with an exhibition of expert drumming, after which the unmarried girls and youths would enter the area embraced by the drummers, singing at first, then dancing. All the watchers would be sitting, and if I were to sit behind one of the knolls I would be able to see, a furlong away, the drummers and dancers in action. There would be full moonlight and lanterns. I should cover myself with a red or light brown blanket, to be made scarcely visible in the moonlight. I should arrive only when I heard the mass drumming, and leave when I thought the dance was at its peak, so that no-one would notice I had been there. I was fortunate to have acquired one bright orange blanket, and wondering if it would be too easily visible in the moonlight, I tried it on a clear night when the servants had gone by spreading it on the lawn. When I looked down from the verandah I was amazed how difficult it was to detect it, and was thankful to have the wise Gerella to advise me on such things.

On the night of the mela I sat on the verandah when the servants had gone. The moon rose about seven-fifteen, a beautiful apricot colour to begin with as it ascended through the haze. The stars were bright above, but as the moon reached an altitude where the haze counted no more, its brilliance put the stars to shame, and tree shadows became inky black. By eight o'clock I heard first of all a distant soprano trill, followed by a chorus of almost highland Scottish whoops. I saw a line of lanterns passing through the stretch of tea and shade trees some 500 yards from the bungalow, and heard the singing of the girls, followed by rhythmic clapping of hands, and the trill-whoop at intervals. It was a wild, exultant sound, making me nostalgic for something I could not identify, and making me yearn for something Tennyson called a young man's fancy. Time after time I wondered if it was time to move under my orange blanket by the paths I had worked out where there was little likelihood of meeting anyone, and I went out to the dark edge of the expanse under tall trees, waiting for the sound of the drummers. I could see fires burning, and hear drummers testing the tension of their drum skins. I had to move when a village dog scented me and began barking dutifully until I changed my position by 100 yards. There came the sound of distant chanting, possibly from the priests, and at last a strong male voice sang something like a warriors' chant, ending it with a loud stroke on his drum. There started then a concert – I know no other way to describe it – of percussion in perfect unison, with broken and irregular beats interspersed with almost military rhythms. It somehow hypnotised me, probably in the way drums summoned up soldiers' blood at the point of war. I had to tell myself to relax, unclench my teeth, not because it was inciting to violence, but it positively stimulated an exciting and expectant feeling. After about an hour the dancers began to move forward to the rhythm of their singing and the drums, initially with slow grace, and sensing it was time, I too moved stealthily forward to the knolls. The girls wore pale gold homespun silken '*mekelas*', extending from the hips to the ankles, gathered and tucked at the waist, with a band of red pattern round the foot. They wore silken half-sleeved blouses of white, or pale blue, or green. Over one shoulder they wore white silken stoles, tucked with one corner in the front of the *mekela*, and another corner tucked in behind. There were border patterns of pale colours. This I could not distinguish in detail at a distance, but it was a dress I had seen often at close range. The youths wore knee-length white loin cloths, and headdresses resembling a turban, but more simply tied with a half knot over one ear, showing a red embroidered band of homespun cloth. Some of the male dancers had drums slung over their shoulders.

The slow, graceful dancing stopped, and the buzz of voices subsided. The powerful singer bellowed a kind of wild recitative, arms stretching moonwards, and silence fell, broken by a single crash of all the drums, which repeated the sound at decreasing intervals until it was beating a quick marching rhythm, with some of the drums adding intermediate thuds, until the speed of playing increased to an almost impossibly fast beat, when it suddenly stopped, with two quick loud crashes in unison. Then came screaming trills from dancers and crowd, and the drummers began their rhythmic beating to which the dancers responded with the strange, vigorous but graceful choreography which the Ahoms had brought with them from the Shan and Thai regions hundreds of years ago. I had spoken to Gerella, and the various Assamese staff about the Bihu dancing, and had found them shy

74

and reluctant to explain it; but now I was to understand. It was dancing which belonged to the category common to the Sikhs, the Russians, the highland Scots, the alpine people: strenuous, full of joy, demanding of exertion, and accompanied by trills and whoops of exultation. The girls had been trained by their mothers, and performed a dance which to me seemed to precede the garden of Eden. The sinuous writhing and hypnotic arm movement, all at vigorous and fast rhythm, performed in what puritans of most faiths would call a shameless, seductive fashion, was here being danced by virgin girls who, being brought up in the Vishnavite faith, would regard modern sexual licence with horror; and it was not done for married people to perform in this style. It was a beautiful experience to witness this spectacle, and to feel the strange excitement of what happened but once a year at the place where Rani, at least, had known there was something to fear. Being a celibate bachelor, I swallowed the yearning for the golden ages before man became vile; and although one would have expected the scene and the sound had captivated me enough to make me forget I should make an early departure – because truly my instinct was to go forward, to join all those to whom this was important and uplifting – I felt it was too much for me, too much emotion and too little understandable logic. A sadness descended on me, so that I wandered away, telling myself it was perhaps foolish to have fallen in love with a part of the world which by this occasion was proved so different, so seductive, and so hypnotic there was a danger in trying to embrace it all. The stars almost laughed at me as I sought their comfort on the way back, and I went to bed two hours after midnight, listening to the drumming until it subsided, and then heard the happy singing and hand-clapping as the villagers made their way home before dawn. I lay as if floating in a great sea of nostalgia, for a past I could only imagine, and faced the next day in a mixture of depression and daydreams, cured by Mozart's G minor Symphony.

There is a long, long period ahead of the damfool career, and there must be a change from the kind of detailed narrative which took this account through the coming of Independence. It is difficult to decide on the choice of episodes which will provide a fair cross-cut of the damfool life, of one damfool's life, remembering we were all different characters. One tends to become obsessed with the memory of events which, if one chooses to recount them, could well be a bore, or worse: pretentious fables to those with an appetite for real history, or tame stuff for those atrophied by the excessive sensation of modern entertainment. It is not fair to plead: bear with it; this is how it was! A damfool has to make it all presentable and credible, and be prepared for some saying: ah! But there is too much missed out, too much he hasn't told us. A damfool must by his very nature let his instinct form his presentation of what is fair, sincere, and as true as an ageing memory will permit.

The Telfords departed on home leave. Two weeks before they went I had to vacate my bungalow and move to the old smaller thatched bungalow well away from the others, with a garden neglected, a poorly polished floor. Like most bungalows there was nothing lockable. Maneklal, Nunoo, Mangal and Sitaram were very gloomy to begin with, but without much prompting began with great effort and dedication to polish the floors. Soon we were well settled in, and life changed significantly for me. After the first two weeks Maneklal and Nunoo reported with moist eyes and mournful expression they had been to see our previous bungalow. The servants were under orders to smear the beautifully polished timber floors with old engine oil. The Delaperes were disgruntled at having to live in an assistant's bungalow, and he kept prodding me to find out what large repairs were in progress, of which he could see no sign, preventing them from using the Telfords' bungalow. They kindly offered to take me into polo on Wednesdays and Saturdays when they wanted to do their shopping and visit the club; but after three afternoons of polo, following each of which we did not arrive home until between two-thirty and three in the morning, I decided I couldn't face such late hours, nor would I want to ride Rani home every time. Because of Delapere's early and understandable reaction to the inconvenience of having an assistant said by Telford to be capable of running the field operations himself, who was at unpredictable intervals away with the aeroplane, I found polo was in any case rather a luxury, and said I could try to play on Saturdays only, but saw it met with the club's disapproval, and I sadly gave it up. If anyone thought there was a streak of masochism in such behaviour he would be as suspicious as I was; but the idea of virtue in self-denial dies hard.

Chapter XVII

It took very little time to discover those traits of character in Delapere which had evoked the dismissive description by Telford. It was amazing to find someone as a tea planter, responsible for an estate of nearly 1,000 acres of planted tea, over 2,000 souls to care for, with all the plant and transport necessary for growing and making tea who had not the slightest sense of resolve or urgency to deal with it all. It made me feel dizzy just to think about it. He was an old public school boy whose father, realising his son had little academic talent and no ambition to tackle anything involving long years of study, had ultimately given up his hope to see him become a clergyman, and somehow managed to contact an old school friend whose uncle was on the board of a tea company. He had come to Assam in 1927, and was still not given the status of a permanent manager. He came one hour late to the office every morning except after club nights when he was even later. He loved to stand with his pipe, talking so much that I began to consider ways and means of absenting myself from the office on some essential visit before breakfast. He was strongly against cases and complaints being settled by the managerial staff, and told me I should not become involved with the *sirdars* and labour in the field. 'Deal with everything only through the *bahboos*', he kept saying, 'it always works much better, take my word for it.' His Hindustani was almost unintelligible, like some pidgin pronounced in what he seemed to think was an upper crust drawl. It was difficult for me at first to understand his speech, which was impeded by his pipe and a frothy foam of saliva from the corner of his mouth. He complained that Medeloabam was lacking in close and friendly neighbours, and seemed disappointed to find I was not a keen drinker, warning it was whisky which kept most planters going. He would not discuss anything to do with tea culture and manufacture, and after having made a habit of learning by asking people like MacFortune, Foyle and Telford it was disturbing to find myself in a kind of vacuum. Delapere's main objective was the avoidance of trouble: don't get too closely involved; don't ask too many questions; don't change anything; don't start anything new; don't keep putting your nose into work either in the field or the factory, leave them alone and all will run smoothly. It sounded like a recipe for disaster, and I began to be depressed about having to manage as Telford expected, realising I would have to do so mainly by stealth. Nevertheless, in spite of his negative advice, Delapere strongly disapproved of my repeated absence on flying mainly, I suspected, because he was in the habit of frequently 'having to drive into Dibrugarh' or somewhere else on business almost every other day, taking his wife, mostly before lunch. It happened that Fraser once arrived with a parcel of new fertiliser programmes which had come by rail from Calcutta, for me to take those intended for the North Bank estates by air. There were very few telephones on the South Bank and none on the North, so that communication was by letter or, from Calcutta, by telegram; it was the only flaw in the operation of the air service we had started. When I told Fraser that Delapere had driven into town on some business unknown to me, he wrote a note which he enclosed and asked me to hand to my manager when he returned. Thereafter it was expected that the manager would, if forced to leave the estate for any reason connected with company business, send a cycle messenger to the superintendent with a letter of explanation including timings. This limited Delapere's field of personal mobility, and he made no secret in the club of what a hopeless idea the aeroplane was, as he could not rely on only one assistant when there should have been two.

A message came from Fraser notifying Delapere he should arrange for transport to take me some fifty-five miles to Kagurijan tea estate to be shown by John Kerry, the manager, a new and dangerous fungus which was suspected of killing bushes, and had spread during the war years when pruning standards had deteriorated because of labour shortage. On the way there the transport was to pick up another assistant, in fact the first Indian assistant taken on in the history of the company, so that we could travel together. Delapere decided with some conviction that he also needed to see this strange fungus disease, and would drive Bhupendra Sarma and me up to Kagurijan, away beyond Doom Dooma. I said Telford always insisted one of us should be present on the estate whilst work was in progress; but Delapere waved his hand with an expression of benign authority, saying we would leave after seeing work started, and probably return just when it was ending; there was no problem. We set off at about nine, collected Sarma near Lahoal station, and drove on in Delapere's battered old Ford eight saloon. Sarma was a slim, well turned out fellow, who had been only a few months in tea. He had graduated in agricultural economy in Calcutta, and spoke good English very carefully. His family lived in Gauhati, and sounded quite rich with a fair amount of property. He was twenty-two, and very happy to have 'won a position in one of the best tea companies in Assam'. By the time we reached Kagurijan we were talking pleasantly together, and he struck me as very keen to pick up as much as possible about his new job. John Kerry was a southern Irishman bouncing with good spirits and full of enthusiasm. He had failed to join the army because of what he called a 'dicky heart', and impressed me with his full-throttle energy the whole time we were with him. He was an excellent raconteur and teacher, talking non-stop about his own estate and all the planters in the Assam Lothian group. We had tea with him about five-thirty, having heard him tell the story of how he was the first planter to have begun plucking all bushes level, instead of treating every shoot separately and trying to differentiate between shoots with such confusion that after the middle of the season when growth was vigorous and profuse, control was lost, and with it crop was lost. By the outbreak of war most planters had adopted the level system, with great benefits in control, plucking efficiency and yield. It was nearly six when we set off on the long way home, and when we neared the halfway point at Panitola, Delapere announced we would call in to the club, which would just be opening, to meet old friends and have a drink before continuing.

It transpired that we were not only still in the club at ten-thirty that night, Sarma and I sick of drinking over-sweet bottled orange juice, but we could see in the crowd at the bar how Delapere was excessively merry, drinking more than would allow him to steer a safe course to Medeloabam. Being on our best behaviour, I with a strong residue of air force discipline, and Sarma with instinctive deference for someone in the position of manager, we kept in the background until I decided it would be best for us all if I were to attract Delapere's attention discreetly, and tap my wrist watch with a pleasant smile and raised eyebrows. We were happy to see this worked, and after another fifteen minutes of farewells to the other well-lubricated boozers, Delapere waved to us and wove his way out, stumbling uncertainly down the steps into the darkness to look for the car. We led him to it, and I suggested since he had driven all the way up to Kagurijan, it would only be fair for me to offer to drive from here back home. To our horror he guffawed, telling us if we thought he was drunk he was dam'well going to show us how wrong we were. In a hoarsely confidential voice he leaned on the car door and told us it took long years of practice to drive with a bellyful of Scotch, and we should get in and stop worrying. Mistrustful but hopeful there might be some demonstrable truth in what he said, we climbed wearily – and hungrily – into the back, and put our fate in his hands. Instead of turning left through the tea in the direction of the trunk road, he turned right, and discovered after a mile or so he was in the wrong direction. It was agony turning the car about in the dark, and he became irritable with the car, the dark, and with us for our calls for caution when we nearly hit a bridge parapet or swerved on a tight turn. After some seven or eight miles we were lurching along at about twenty in top gear, and the continuous slurred invective of Delapere began to die into meaningless blurts, I saw his head drop, and the car began to swerve to the edge of the road, which was raised like most roads in Assam about six to eight feet above the borrowpits on either side. The road was about twelve feet wide of shingle with grassy margins of about five feet before the surface sloped down at forty-five degrees. Seeing disaster loom I threw myself forward and seized the wheel, throwing it round in time to save us from diving into the muddy pit, and immediately thereafter seized the handbrake and pulled on it with all my strength. The car engine stalled, and I got out, going swiftly round to the driver's door which I opened as Delapere came to his senses.

'Well, sir!' I said as heartily as I could manage, 'you need a rest. My turn to take the wheel. You have the back seat to yourself. Sarma and I will sit in front. Thanks for being so kind as to drive us so far. It's not much further now, we'll soon be there.' I reached forward to take the key, just in case, but not being familiar with its location I was astonished to feel Delapere lunge for it, and swing his arm roughly to push me away. Sarma had also got out, and having been shaken by our narrow escape we stood in embarrassed silence, wondering what to do now that my hearty and polite attempt had failed. 'Just what the hell do you think you are doing, Mac-bloody-Storm?' He struggled to get out of the car, and stood with one arm over the door to support him. 'I've never had an accident in my life, and if you think I'm too dangerous for you, you can bloody well walk. D'you hear me? Walk. I won't be insulted by whippersnappers like you.' His voice rose, and his speech was barely understandable.

'I think, sir, if you won't let me drive we shall have to walk. If I hadn't seized the wheel just now we'd have crashed into that *pukuri* (pit). If we walk we'll have to explain what happened, which wouldn't do anyone any good. Please understand I want to drive for the good of all of us. You need a rest. Please give me the key.' I went towards him and held out my hand, but he suddenly threw the key, roughly in my direction but over my shoulder, with some force, into the dark well beyond the dim rear lights.

'Take the bloody key then. I'm going to sleep in the car. We'll deal with this in the morning, by God! You'll be for the high jump, you will. Just wait.' He lurched round to find his way into the car, and having heard the key fall on gravel, Sarma and I went on our hands and knees for nearly half an hour before I found at last the single key, on a loop of bent wire. I thought the lights were so dim we might have trouble starting, and fortunately found the starting handle in the boot, so that we were able to start without depleting the battery enough to strand us. I dropped Sarma off where we saw his manager's jeep waiting on the road near Hiloibhanga, and I drove on to Medeloabam, where I coasted quietly and with great relief under Delapere's bungalow, switched off and got out stealthily to leave him asleep in the car; but his servants were waiting for him, and woke him before I was out of the lit area. Delapere called for me to wait, and wove and stumbled towards me, eventually insisting on accompanying me to my bungalow. It was past twelve-thirty, but Maneklal and Nunoo were still there waiting for me. Delapere gurgled and groaned, thanking me for having driven back, and went into the rigours and dangers of life in this country: the smallpox, the cholera, malaria, syphilis – especially after the war started – and now Independence. He went on and on, and would not let me go. He turned to Maneklal and asked them if my '*chokri*' (girl) was waiting for me, poor girl, and when they said there was no girl, Delapere turned to me full of concern and sympathy, telling me the girls on this estate were the best collection he had ever seen, and I should really pick a choice one. 'It's good for you. A healthy young man like you needs that sort of thing you know.' He gurgled, leering at Maneklal, saying to him he should arrange a good girl for me, to which Maneklal replied with a frown this was not his job, and if he were to do this people would despise him, and his father would beat him. The Telford *sahib* would beat him. He said I was a pilot *sahib* and a *shikari sahib*, and didn't play around with girls. I marvelled at the moral reputation awarded to pilot *sahibs*, and felt honoured at this early stage to be called a *shikari sahib*.

In English Delapere stifled a laugh, commenting on the threat of a beating by Telford. 'I wouldn't think a beating too much to suffer for some of these dusky damsels.' He groaned from his chest. 'Oh, to be young again. Oh, happy days!' Eventually he patted me on the back, and insisted on shaking hands. 'That's it, eh? No more about it. Don't want people talking. If my wife hears about it! Oh, my God! I'd go to jail rather than that.' He staggered erratically away, with Nunoo showing him the unaccustomed route in the dark. I had a little soup and half a chupatti, no longer hungry, and told the chaps I'd have a good breakfast tomorrow. When they went, they salaamed, and Maneklal said they had never seen a *sahib* as drunk as that, never.

One of the company's London tea brokers came on a visit, and I was requested to fly him to the North Bank, where I would leave him for three days, collecting him on the afternoon of the final day which was a Sunday. When I landed him at Mirijuli on the Friday morning, I met the manager, an austere ex-first world war infantry officer called West, nick-named Taffy by his few familiars, and his assistant Jake Vallance. Discussing when I should arrive on Sunday to fly the broker back to Dinjan, West introduced me to his assistant, and said Vallance had suggested I should come on Saturday and spend the night with him, so that I would be in a good position to take off any time on Sunday. In the end the broker, a charming man who enjoyed a good reputation amongst planters, said he would be sure to have finished by tea time on Sunday afternoon, and thought it fair to make that a firm date of departure. I thanked Vallance for his invitation, and said I would take Fraser's permission to arrive on Saturday if possible. Fraser wrote a reply to my request saying it would normally be the responsibility of the manager to decide who should remain on the estate, but he thought it a good idea for me to meet other assistants, especially on the North Bank, and said he had written to Delapere saying if I could be spared on Saturday afternoon he should let me fly to Mirijuli to stay the night there. It happened so, and I landed on the strip there which had been greatly improved, remembering Fraser's caution to have a good team of night watchmen around the aeroplane during the night to keep the elephants from damaging it out of sheer curiosity.

Vallance struck me at first as an ex-army officer, tall, strongly built, with moustache and accent decidedly military, and one leg very lame. I guessed he had probably been invalided out after a war injury, but it turned out he had suffered in childhood from infantile paralysis, not severely, but enough to prevent him from following his father, grandfather and brothers into the Indian army. He tried the air force, thinking flying would be possible as he had sufficient strength in his affected leg to work the rudder bar, but he was not accepted. It was a fascinating weekend for me. He took me up the beautiful river Daflanoi, running between Daflanoi estate and Mirijuli estate, above where the smaller Mirijuli river joined it. It was a good fishing river, but during the monsoon, when upwards of 200 inches of rainfall – never accurately measured in the mountainous area above it – fell sometimes at the rate of nine inches in one night, this caused unexpected erosion where it debouched, and serious floods on entering the plains. He showed me an amazing amount of elephant tracks and droppings on and around the estate, where the hills rising abruptly on the northern boundary of the tea were covered with dense, tall forest which held much game. The elephants had become so troublesome that cultivation around Mirijuli, Bankukurajan and Daflanoi was being abandoned as no longer worth while. The elephants emerged from the mountain forests during the night and helped themselves to the rice ripening in the paddy fields. Most of these lay in the embrace of forest-covered ridges, descending like sinuous peninsulas from the hills. There was plenty of food for the elephants all the year round, but they had their annual feeding programmes well preserved over countless centuries in their excellent memories, and liked to arrive in particular areas at the time they knew such delicacies as bamboo shoots, ripening bananas, newly emerging leaf shoots from especially tasty trees, and many other gourmet preferences were at their best. When early man began the cultivation of rice in larger and larger areas the wild elephants began to include it in their programmes, and the elephants' visits were worst when the rice ears had formed, and were filled with delicious white milk. Later when the grains hardened they still depredated extensively, and a herd would destroy by trampling at least twenty times more than they actually ate. The wild elephants were generally shy, timid enough to disappear like dim grey clouds in moonlight or starlight if the workers or villagers made a noise or waved flaming torches within twenty-five yards of them. In the last year or two there were reports of a tuskless rogue in the district, which had no fear of men and would not be frightened away easily; in fact it had been known to charge people, something the shy wild ones would only do if they felt they were being surrounded or driven into a blind corner. Three people had actually been killed in the area by this rogue, which was so clever that forestry people on elephants had been unable to track him down to shoot him. There were plenty of tigers about, but only occasional signs of leopard. Cattle killing was common, but there was so much cover for the tigers that shooting them from a tree or a hill was very difficult. There was a man-eater beginning to notch up a score. It had come from the south-west, and was old, wounded, and very clever, managing to elude all attempts. So far there had only been one man killed on Mirijuli, and people were careful never to go alone to gather firewood, and everyone was battened in his house before dusk fell. Vallance showed me the trees where the elephants rubbed themselves, and others where the tigers cleaned and strengthened their claws, in some places the marks being above seven feet at their highest gashes. At this time of the year the elephants often raided villages and estate workers' houses, breaking the bamboo-plaster walls to put their trunks in to find the huge close-woven bamboo basket receptacles in which the unhusked rice was stored, about four and a half feet in diameter, and the same measure tall, placed on platforms inside the houses to prevent rats or mice from access. Once the elephants found these baskets they would scoop the rice out with their trunks, and often broke the wall from top to bottom to spill the huge load of grain to the ground, where four or five of them would feed, making a noise of squeaks and deep grumbling roars which terrified the unfortunate inmates. Vallance said he was not steady enough on his feet either to shoot elephants or to run fast enough if any of them decided to chase him. His bungalow was not far from the Daflanoi and the confluence of the Mirijuli, on high ground a few hundred yards from the factory. We talked until well after midnight, after having dined on netted small fry which his men had taken from the river, and the talk was mostly of elephants and tigers, only later of aeroplanes and the air force. The following morning we walked up the Daflanoi river, following elephant tracks along the bank, where the forest was impressive for its wildness and lack of human signs. We passed several rapids and eventually came to a more open bend where the river was narrow and swift where it spilled from a large whirlpool, in the middle of which there rotated a collection of logs, branches and floating leaves. Mounting a rocky outcrop above the pool Jake Vallance showed me where seven or eight mahseer fish kept station in formation in an area of slack water just outside the foamy spill entering the pool from upriver. He said they were all twenty pounds or more, and although now and then one or two fish would lunge into the milky tail below the white plumes, as if after small fry, Vallance said it was a very poor place to fish except in October, when the water was clearing. We walked back, with Vallance naming many of the beautiful birds we saw at fairly close range, the noise of our approach being hidden by the thrash of the rapids. We saw langurs in the trees, and felt heat rising from fresh elephant droppings, and watched two otters play like kittens on a sandy beach. We walked the whole length of the airstrip, discussing possible improvements, and returned ready for the excellent curry at Vallance's bungalow. After tiffin he took me to the factory and showed me the huge turbine which was sufficient to run the whole factory once the monsoon rain filled the Daflanoi enough to bring a conduit from more than a mile away, where the main river was partially dammed to raise the water level enough to keep the turbine well supplied. The point of this was not simply economy, it was to provide power virtually on site during the time when the monsoon speeded the Brahmaputra current dramatically, making the 800 river miles transport of diesel oil from Calcutta painfully slow and extremely expensive. From the river transport quay to Mirijuli, lorries had a round trip of 104 miles by three-ton Austin lorry to bring barrels of oil and any other essential stores or spares. I marvelled at the audacity of the old Scots who dared to plant tea in such remote places, not only because of the transporting difficulties, but for the creation – still going on – of a remote and isolated municipality to raise the crop which was Britain's favourite and innocuous addiction. We sat on Vallance's verandah, watching the many families and groups of estate workers return from the weekly bazaar at Bankukurajan. He told me the cold weather here was much more appreciated than on the South Bank, because the monsoon was really hard going, against the steep hills with so much more rainfall, more 'flu', more malaria, and less bazaar food. Waiting for the sound of West's car on the road from the river, the talk switched to the planters who were in the district, and planters who had served in the past at Mirijuli: interesting stuff well recounted by Vallance, who had the gift of shameless but fascinating hyperbole. He drew a map for me showing the rough positions of the company's estates on the North Bank, naming the various people who worked there. The atmosphere was different from Bogahilonia, less open, closer to the forest clad mountains, with rivers smaller but beautiful, and tea planted on the rising plateaux which had been cast up a hundred feet or so by great cataclysms in the mountains hundreds of years ago, now covered by tea or forest, fertile beyond belief. Just before I took off with the broker, Vallance warned me never to come over to live on the North Bank until the company air service was properly established.

Delapere regarded the propagation of tea from cuttings and the selection of quality/yield bushes for such propagation as 'pie in the sky', one of his favourite sayings. He criticised the brick and corrugated metal roof houses for the labourers. Telford was one of the few planters who had gone ahead with an initial trial of ten houses per year of this type. It was true they were very hot, and those living in the first ten built did complain they were sometimes very hot indeed; but Telford had given thought to the layout of the new houses, providing plenty of land surrounding each house in which the occupants could raise vegetables and fruit, keep chickens, and had piped water laid on with two delivery points for the ten houses. At the end of each row he planned to have a tiger and thief-proof cowshed for about thirty beasts, a small byre for calves, and two brick-walled and roofed manure middens of equal size, one for the occupants and one for the company's use on the fields and nurseries. All of this was described by Delapere as interfering with the workers' traditional way of life: they would never be happy unless they had their thatched, village-type houses, dotted about the place like a real rural village. I repeated Telford's sensible ideas on building durable houses, with uniformly fenced vegetable gardens, but Delapere waved it all away, saying we mustn't make them change into what would turn out to be an industrial slum. 'They're all scruffs,' he kept saying, 'let them live as they please, and they'll be happy, mark my words.' It seemed to be a philosophy which worked well for himself. His shirts were all dark in colour, and bore unsightly stains where curry and custard had been spilled; his shorts, pockets bulging with a laden tobacco pouch, pipe knife and matches, were dark with oil and grease, causing people like Maneklal to ask me why he didn't change his clothes like other *sahibs*. His skin and complexion were unfortunate. His hair was crinkly reddish-brown, his small snub nose permanently red, and although his skin was very pale, he was covered with blotchy freckles. He always wore a hat like that of a cricket umpire, with a floppy brim, once white but now also freckled like his skin. His eyesight was poor, for which he wore spectacles, and whilst speaking he would tuck his chin into his neck, peering weakly over the very large rims. When one said something not to his liking he would stare through his thick lenses, which magnified his dark brown eyes so that they looked huge and black. One afternoon we were in his office when the head clerk brought the pay accounts and the prepared cheques for his signature, when we were disturbed by a Gond woman, distressed to the point of tears, who appeared at the office door and began explaining her problem in a loud but plaintive voice. Delapere looked at her with his chin high, and as she went on he turned to the head clerk and asked what she was complaining about. The head clerk looked at me expectantly, and I told Delapere there seemed to be an attempt by a twice married man to abduct this widow's fourteen-year-old daughter, her only remaining child. Delapere remained silent, and suspecting there were people on the office verandah listening to the widow I rose and went out, where I found two women, a girl, and a tall heavily built Gond whom I knew to be called Singrailal, a watchman of the bamboo plantation. He salaamed when I saw him, bending forward and raising his hand to his turban. I asked the widow if these people were involved, and she said this was her daughter and the man with his two wives. She begged they should not be allowed to register her daughter's name in the marriage book: she had been enticed by this man because her sisters have all produced several children. His wives have produced none, and just because she was a widow he was pushing her aside and trying to steal her daughter, whom she wanted to take back to their country to be married. I explained all this to Delapere, who gave me the full black-eyed stare whilst he fidgeted nervously with his pipe. Being amazed at the cheek of this man on whom the signs either of loose living or excess boozing, or both, were clear to see – perhaps through the filtered eyes of a grudging celibate – I sent for Bhose, the welfare officer, telling Delapere it would be as well to find out if Telford ever permitted such a thing as this man was proposing, which I very much doubted. Delapere concentrated on signing the cheques for the next day's pay, and when Bhose arrived I asked him to let the manager know what Mr Telford's attitude would be to this proposal. Bhose spoke very quietly in English, and said Singrailal was not a good character. He was a heavy drinker, and was always taking ganja. He had no children because he had had a very bad disease for a long time because of his bad behaviour. Mr Telford allowed him to take a second wife after.he had been married for five years without issue; but he would certainly not allow him to take Sandessia's daughter as he wanted, because she was too young.

Delapere asked to see the girl, who came forth holding her head high, but very nervous. I found it strange there were no other people around, and wondered why. The girl was well built, not beautiful but with the bloom of youth making her seem attractive enough to make any young man want to possess such a maid. Delapere asked her if she was happy to go to this man, pointing to Singrailal, who stood holding a heavy bamboo staff in his large fist. It struck me then how he resembled Frankenstein with his small weak eyes and large jaw. Not understanding Delapere's question the girl looked at me, then at Bhose, asking him, 'What does he say?' Bhose, eyes widening, looked at me, then at Delapere.

'Sir, Mr Telford disapproves very strongly of old men marrying young girls. She is too young to marry, sir, and her mother does not approve, sir. I do not like to ask her if she is happy to go with this man.'

'You, *bahboo*, are not trying this case. I did not ask you to give me your opinion. This is my responsibility. Do you understand?' Without waiting for an answer he turned superciliously to me. 'You seem to be the linguist. Ask her in a language she can understand.' I felt my blood rise as I watched the widow's agonised expression, and raised my chin slightly towards her, at which she put both hands together and came forward, bowed in an attitude of passionate entreaty.

'*Sahib*! My husband died last year. This is my last child whose marriage is my responsibility. She must marry a fine boy in our home village, and have children. It is our custom that no-one can arrange my daughter's marriage but me, or my brothers. This man is wicked. People are afraid of him because he gets drunk and threatens people with his staff. He used to be a police *sepahi*, and was put in jail for drunkenness and bad behaviour. Telford *sahib* gave him a job because he married Bhimlal *sirdar's* daughter. Where is Bhimlal *sirdar*, *sahib*?' She turned to me. 'He is afraid of this man because he accused him of being a *badmash* who was unfaithful to his daughter, and who threatened to kill him. My daughter doesn't understand. He has made her believe all kinds of wrong things; he has made his two wives swear that they want him to marry this sweet unripe girl. Don't let anyone ask her if she is happy to marry him. She is too young and silly to know what she is doing. He has given her all the silver bangles and necklaces belonging to his other wives. Look at them! Are they happy? They are afraid, *sahib*! Save me my daughter, *sahib*!' She went down on her knees, weeping bitterly, and reached to touch Delapere's feet. Turning to me she said she had been warned this man was coming to the office for a *bichar*, and she had run to catch up with them. 'No-one comes for a *bichar* at this time, *sahib*; everyone knows. All the Gond men went off with their nets to fish the

Chand Bil, which has dried out enough for them to wade in it; none of them knows this was going to happen, *sahib*.'

Delapere turned to me, his eyes like Guinness bottle bottoms. His hands fidgeted with his pipe, and his snub nose rose higher, affecting haughty outrage. 'You have not yet asked the girl. Ask her!' I looked at him trying not to let my nostrils dilate, which was a bad habit and damaging to any good cause. Quietly I said I would like, before questioning the girl, to speak to him privately, not in front of those present. Bhose, hearing this, immediately spread his arms and told everyone to move along to the welfare office whilst the *sahibs* had a discussion, and they moved, Sandessia retreating in the opposite direction, sobbing into her sari. I stood, thinking it wise for us to leave the office, but Delapere remained seated. He leaned back in his chair and pointed the stem of his pipe at me. 'Young man, I do not think it a good thing to give the impression there is something to be discussed between us that cannot be heard by the people who have asked for justice to be done.' His voice was raised in volume, which meant most of the clerks next door could hear him. I moved in front of his table and put my hands on it, leaning forward to speak as quietly as possible.

'It is my duty to advise on Medeloabam's customs as far as helping to settle *bichars* is concerned. Bhose is right: Telford would be furious if anything were settled without the Gonds being present, especially if he learned Sandessia did not want to give her daughter to that man.' In a loud drawl Delapere replied, jabbing his pipe stem at me again.

'You seem to have forgotten, MacStorm, that I am in charge of all that happens on this estate. I am responsible for doing the right thing, understand? You have been in tea for fewer months than I have been years; you know nothing about these people, yet you presume to advise me what I am to do. Is this the way the air force worked? Did you presume to advise your commanding officer? I advise you, MacStorm, to stand back and allow me to deal with my business. Understand?' He bit hard on his pipe and tugged at the brim of his floppy old hat. I could but take a deep breath and stand, my chest swelling with a ferment of anger and disgust.

I nodded. 'I understand you, Delapere.' As I moved to one side, reluctant to sit down, and beginning to turn more sour by realising the office staff had overheard what Delapere had meant them to hear, I stood facing the verandah door with arms folded and feet wide apart, in a posture which had in boyhood invoked warnings from parents and teachers mindful of my need for training. He called the head clerk who entered looking rather pale and worried, and told him to tell Bhose to bring the people back to this office. Banerjee looked nervously at each of us in turn.

'Sir, I think there will be a difficult disturbance in a few minutes. Gopal *babu* has just cycled from the Chand Bil, and has told us about fifteen Gond men are on their way here. They are very angry, sir.'

'Tell Bhose *bahboo* to send those people away and come back next Monday morning. Go on, tell him!' Banerjee looked at me questioningly, and I rotated my head slightly. Then we heard the noise of the approaching Gonds, and stepping on to the verandah I saw the string of men loping towards the office, from the opposite direction they would normally have come. Sandessia had moved towards them, obviously expecting their arrival, and as they crowded around her a hundred yards away she could be seen explaining what had been happening. The men wore their usual clean, full turbans, but were covered to the waist with thick mud. They came slowly, still panting, and as they drew nearer I heard several times the phrase: now let justice be done. I turned to Delapere and told him what was happening, and what the Gonds were saying, but he sat trying to write on a sheet of paper, his hand shaking, and ignored what I said. Along the verandah I saw Bhose shepherding Singrailal with his wives towards the gate, and I heard him call out 'Go! The *bichar* will be on Monday morning. Go!' Things began then to happen quickly. The Gond men arrived and crowded outside the gate. The two barren wives walked into the gate, and the men made way for them. Singrailal, staff on shoulder, beckoned the girl to follow him but Sandessia, having come through the gate near the manager's office, rushed and caught her daughter's wrist, preventing her from following Singrailal, who then strode with staff raised at the girl's mother, threatening to strike her retaining arm. Sandessia, being terrified, crouched with both arms around her face and head, and her shriek of fear and anguish made the blood of more than myself run cold and fast with hate. Men ran in through the gate, gesticulating and warning the bruiser of what would happen if he struck a woman. Seizing the staff in both hands Singrailal charged at the men, flailing wildly in a fit of violent temper, striking one of them on his lower ribs as he sought to turn and escape. The man went down in distress as the brute uttered the first sound I had heard him make since he had appeared. He roared and lunged at a second man who had fallen over the first, and something triggered me into action with speed and total disregard for anything but the disabling of the enemy. Hearing me coming he twisted, swinging his staff awkwardly, not balanced enough to work his will, and I collided with him in automatic unarmed combat style with one leg behind him and full weight forcing him to fall on his back. I was wearing tennis shoes, and stamped on the wrist holding the staff, which I jacked from his grip and threw to the men outside the gate. Thinking that was enough to restore the man's sanity I stood erect as he clumsily began to rise; but seeing his face, with teeth bared in a snarl indicating untamed fury, I dodged as he lunged like a wrestler. It flashed through my mind I should be careful in my position not to go too far, but the lightning circuits of the brain took over. Experience had taught me never again to use bunched fists: it hurt for a long time afterwards both striker and victim. Being fitter and far more nimble than the ex-policeman I managed to hit him so hard with swift full arm swings and open hands about face and head that he became stunned into a state of relative harmlessness, his turban lying unrolled on the ground. Twisting his arm easily behind his back I pushed him out of the gate, through the men, and told them to see him back to his house. One of the men picked up Singrailal's turban and gave it to him. Standing with his back to me he wound his turban carefully, and when he had finished he turned, nose bleeding and one eye swollen, to make a deep salaam. There was silence everywhere except for the weeping of the girl, led by Sandessia back home on the same path. The man who had suffered the blow on his ribs stood bent, with his hands on the point of the blow and his face contorted with pain. Bhose told the other men to take him to the hospital, where we could see Dr Pal watching with his compounder and midwife. I told Bhose to follow the victim and tell the doctor to give the manager a report on his condition. I went back to the office, to be told by Banerjee that the manager wanted to speak to me privately. He pointed to Delapere's figure, under a blue cloud of pipe smoke, half way to the stable.

'Sir,' Banerjee said, 'you have surely given the only justice which will cure that man. That is what Mr Telford would have done, but it would not have happened if the *bichar* had been correctly managed. Sir, I sincerely hope there will be no trouble; but he is an ex-policeman, very sly, and it might be troublesome. All the people are afraid of him.' That set my heart beating again, with no immediate hope of vigorous exercise to sop up the adrenaline. I went with a very guilty feeling to face Delapere, who was walking in a tight circle with his hands clasped behind his back, spewing clouds of smoke from his pipe.

'I've sent the injured man to the doctor. He'll send you a report after he's examined him. I don't think anything is broken; the lower ribs are well sprung, but he'll have a nasty bruise.' He stood still, facing me pipe in hand, his mouth moving as if unable to decide on words. He was pale behind his freckles, and big-eyed with distress. His words came out at last, almost in a whisper.

'Do you know what you have done, MacStorm? It's...it's...my God! It's incredible! You have disobeyed my orders; you have struck a man; you have interfered with my efforts to help these poor ignorant people to settle their affairs; you have lit a fuse leading to a serious explosion of trouble, terrible trouble, on my shoulders. You don't seem to realise there is no British Raj any more.' His voice became louder and hoarser. 'The days of that sort of thing when we could throw our weight about are gone, you understand! Gone! And I will be held responsible by the Indian government, by the company, and will finish up by losing my job, just because you, yes you, would not do as you were told.' I began to shake my head slowly, realising he was almost weeping with a mixture of anger and fear. 'Don't shake your h...' His voice broke and disappeared, and he shook both fists before him, distraught.

'I don't know what you mean by disobedience...' I began, but he interrupted.

'I told you to ask the girl if she was happy to go with that man, and you refused; you know you did. I should suspend you. I've a good mind to suspend you and tell Calcutta why, damn you!'

'When you asked me to ask her I had thoughts which I felt it necessary to discuss before doing so.' He stared at me. 'I knew she was probably too young to be cohabiting with any man, let alone that rascal, and felt if her mother made a complaint to the police it would lead to trouble if we had aided and abetted the seducer.'

'Who are you to lecture me on how things are done in this country? What do you know about these things?' I cut in sharply to tell him I had not disobeyed him but simply thought it wise to consider the law concerning minor girls. 'The law on minor girls!' He lifted his chin haughtily, pointing his pipe stem at me. 'Where I was educated boys were not taught that kind of disgusting business. You can keep that sort of thing to yourself. Look what you have done, for God's sake! If it hadn't been for you and your salacious education that girl would have gone happily to give that man and his childless wives a baby or two that would have given them something to live for; and there wouldn't have been any trouble at all.' He almost shouted the last words. 'You've never heard a mob coming with the ranting and yelling of threats, waving sticks. I've got a wife in that bungalow to think of. We're all alone now. If they want to rise against us now nothing will stop them. It needn't have happened if you had done what you were told. For God's sake get out of my sight!' He turned and went through the tea on a narrow path, towards his bungalow. I went back to the office to make sure the pay cheques were in order, then to my table where the *sirdars* stood waiting for me to write the next day's work plan. The atmosphere was very quiet, and I had to think carefully, asking a few questions of the head supervisor before writing everything down. Bhose, the welfare officer, came and stood until I had finished.

'Sir, please do not mind. I have taken the names of the willing witnesses of Singrailal's assault on Chotelal. He has no broken bones, only bad bruise and blood swelling. Here is Dr Pal's report. He recommends ten days' light work until his side is better. We are all witnesses, sir; and we are also witnesses to your action to restrain the miscreant.' There was a murmur of assent from members of the office staff who had quietly assembled behind me. The Assamese *jemadar babu*, a strongly built man, laughed loudly.

'Sir, how is it possible to knock that *badmash* down with slepping?' He said 'slapping' as Telford would say it. 'We always say slepping is for womenfolk, but your slepping was very strong; he will not forget it.' The head clerk waved a hand before him.

'We should be careful. Singrailal is a wicked person. He will try to cause trouble.' He spoke to me. 'Sir, it is better if the manager sends a complaint to the police about the assault, giving names of witnesses. We are all witnesses to the way you stopped the man from his attacks; but we should act quickly in case he goes first to the police or a lawyer.' I was fairly sure Delapere would report nothing to the police, and it turned out I was right. The next morning as I rode back to the office from the long road leading out of the estate I met Singrailal, formally dressed in the Gond style, with heavy leather shoes turned up in front like the prow of a canoe. He made a low salaam, neither speaking nor looking at me. His eye was still swollen and had turned blue, and there was still blood under his nose and on his chin: recorded evidence no doubt; he continued on his way to town. Late that afternoon when I returned from field work I saw a rather ancient Morris saloon outside the office. As I walked along the verandah the head clerk came out and told me a local Congress politician and a police inspector had been talking to the staff, having had a report from Singrailal, and now knew what had happened. He had told them the manager was about to send a report to the police but witnesses had gone to work. They had questioned Chotelal who had responded with much accusation of Singrailal as a drunk, ganja-wallah, and ill-behaved libertine. The visitors were in the manager's office, but Mr Delapere had not come. They would like to meet me. I went into the office, said 'Good afternoon, gentlemen,' and seeing the politician was Assamese asked if I was able to help. The effect was warming, as I was not sure how I would be received. He was delighted I spoke in Assamese, but broke into his educated English to say he found it very pleasing to find a young man who had wasted no time in learning the language of the province in which he lived. The police officer said Singrailal had reported I seized his staff and beat him with it, but it was clear from his injuries there was no such occurrence. 'He is known to us, you see! He is a *barra badmash* thrown out of the police in Jabalpur five years ago for extorting money from villagers, misbehaving with other men's wives; totally corrupt!' As we spoke I heard the sound of vehicles arriving, and moving out to the verandah saw George Fraser's car pull up, followed by Delapere's. I told the visitors the manager had arrived, and the Superintendent *sahib* had also come, and said I would invite them to join us. Fraser came towards me with a face like thunder. I greeted him and received a sharp 'MacStorm! What the hell have you been up to?' I said a police inspector and the local Congressman had come to meet the manager, and I murmured all was well as he would see. When he entered the Congressman rose, offering his hand and greeting him by name as an old friend. Fraser responded with happy dignity, and also shook hands with the police inspector, whom he obviously knew well. Delapere entered, nodding and puffing his pipe, asking Fraser to take his seat behind the manager's desk. The conversation was taken over by Horakanta Barua, the Congressman, who described the incident of the previous day in detail better than I could have done. He was supported by the inspector, who repeated his withering description of Singrailal, and added how well I had acted to prevent further injury by very clever methods. Fraser said he was pleased to hear the very lucid account of the affair, and glad to know how well Mr MacStorm had been able to deal with the situation. He laughed at Sri Barua and said MacStorm was a pilot in the air force, and must have learned how to deal with anyone starting a fight. The discussion ended, and the visitors drove away. Fraser said to Delapere he wanted me to take him for a flight over the Hiloibhanga group estates, for about an hour; it was approved by Calcutta. When we landed back Fraser thanked me for the marvellous experience. 'Don't forget to treat your manager as your commanding officer; and avoid physical combat except when saving others: I think you know that.' I spent much time going over the events since Delapere's arrival, adding much to my growing store of experience and paying with the odd sleepless night for failing to rearrange my mental programmes to suit my new life. I took furtive comfort from the signs of respect and approbation which had followed the last incident, well aware it was time to avoid the happy-go-lucky friendliness, and to learn how to induce willingness to follow a code of discipline meant for everyone's good. More difficult was to evolve a high level of respect without having to give a demonstration on the fortuitous emergence of a bad one like Singrailal, but it was something I would have to think about.

Chapter XVIII

There was an interesting sequel to the attempted abduction of Sandessia's daughter. Although the idea of repatriating Singrailal and his wives was sensible and popular, Bhimlal, whose daughter was the first wife of Singrailal, pleaded this should not be done, as she was the favourite and youngest child, and it would break his wife's heart to lose her; furthermore Sandessia was afraid to begin her journey to Jabalpur with her minor daughter if there was a risk of being intercepted by Singrailal. Delapere waved his hand, saying he should be sent away as soon as possible, and told me 'for God's sake' to do it carefully. I asked Bhimlal why his daughter should not refuse to travel with Singrailal if he was ordered to leave the estate. He answered that Singrailal would never return to his home village because no-one there wanted him back; he had been expelled from the police for a good reason, and was not trusted. He would insist on taking both his wives with him, and no-one would ever know where they would go. He would probably find work at an estate on the South Bank, or in the Dooars area of north Bengal. With two wives and no children he would be well off anywhere. Bhimlal was sure if his own daughter refused to travel with Singrailal he would refuse to go, and cause more trouble. I had a sudden inspiration, and asked Bhimlal if his daughter really wanted to carry on living with Singrailal; had she any true affection for him? He said she had become his wife because he was believed to be a widower and it was written thus in the book. I said since Singrailal had tried to procure Sandessia's daughter because neither of his wives had produced a child, it means to anyone with sense that he could have no claim on Bhimlal's daughter; and he could only keep her if she really wanted to stay with him. Bhimlal gazed at me with large, liquid eyes, and after a moment said all his other sons and daughters had produced children; his daughter weeps every weekend when

96

she comes to her mother to keep out of her drunken husband's way, weeps for the children she has never had; she was not happy with that *badmash*, and never will be. I told him to come next morning to see me, and meanwhile I spoke to Bhose, discussing if my plan could be made to work. Next morning the *chowkidars* called Singrailal, who was summoned when all other business was finished. I showed him a thick sheaf of papers, telling him here was the case against him for assaulting Chotelal, which was to be sent to the police in Dibrugarh, and as there are many witnesses he would probably be sent to jail again. The police have advised we should take security from him to ensure he will not abscond before the trial, and the security is to be Bhimlal's daughter taken into shelter by her parents, under the company's protection. Looking sternly at Singrailal I told him his marriage to Bhimlal's daughter was made invalid when, although all her three sisters have produced many children, she failed to do so. This now means the fault of barrenness falls on the inadequate husband, who could be tried for enticing a second and a third wife under false pretences. I gave him a letter suspending him without pay on a charge of gross misconduct. He took the letter without looking above the buckle on my belt, and walked away without any kind of salute or protest. I placed two Munda guards over Bhimlal's house that night, and a 'spy' over Singrailal's, and in the morning it was reported Singrailal had disappeared with his other wife. He was never seen again. Bhimlal's daughter, Rajputia, a handsome lady of around thirty, began to bloom as soon as Singrailal disappeared, and was married within three months to a Gond whose wife had died childless. The joyful tears of Rajputia and her parents when they came with her husband to announce she was truly pregnant gave me an unexpected and almost painful pleasure. Within a year she bore a bouncing son, said to be the image of Bhimlal.

The weather became very hot. The paradox of hot tea actually producing a truly cooling effect became important to me. Not having a refrigerator I was unable to try the effects of chilled water but, having tried an iced lime juice with the hospitable Foyles, and having suffered from a bad throat thereafter, I counted my blessings. I allowed myself an infantile envy after enjoying the delicious home made ice cream desserts of Mrs Telford and Mrs Foyle, made in wooden buckets and flavoured with fruit grown on the estate. Having paid off the loan which had helped me to buy Rani, my strong Australian mare, I found I had become used to my austere and frugal food, and as I seemed to flourish on it, reckoned it would be possible to begin saving three-quarters of what I had been paying off each month. I needed to buy another mattress, bedclothes, and curtains for the spare bedroom, in which I would have to put the various missionaries, engineers, and any guests of my own should any materialise. From MacFortune and Foyle I had learned it was possible through the local Indian bank to remit saved money to one's own bank in Britain. Having left £65 in an account which had been opened for me by the air force during the war when I was commissioned, I decided to write to my bank in London, informing them of my intention. The letter lay unfinished on my table for about a week, delayed by a combination of too much work in the early morning when it was relatively cool, and too much heat in the evenings causing so much dripping sweat from one's forearm and hand that the ink from my pen became a hairy blotch on the sweat-soaked paper. At the end of that week, pleased to have followed MacFortune's warnings on careful husbandry, I made pencil calculations of how much I could save, including annual salary increases, before going on my first home leave three years ahead, and took advantage of the cool wet Sunday morning to write to my London bank. Next day there arrived a letter from my bank which told me there had been an income tax demand from the inland revenue for £65, from my earnings in the air force. I managed to write another letter asking why it had taken nearly eighteen months to discover this deficit, asking them to re-check what sounded to me like a wrong assessment. After three more months their reply came with the welcome news that there had been confusion with some serving officer of closely similar name. Although I was highly sceptical, being sure there was no other pilot of my name or clan in the air force, I was so happy to be released from the mournful threat of further indigence that I let the matter rest, concentrating on adding my meagre savings to my rightly restored fortune of £65.

This second year, with none of the overhanging uncertainties of the first, and less of novelty, more of understanding and responsible commitment, was not so much an anticlimax as a disappointment. I found myself missing the support of Foyle, the challenge of Telford, the enthusiasm and the drive, all of which I tended to blame on the unfortunate Delapere until I realised the danger of becoming a despicable negative critic, allowing the shortcomings of someone suffering from fear and alcohol to drag me virtually into a closely similar state in which I substituted boredom for fear, and despite for alcohol. The flying was still a problem, with fewer visitors from London during the hot rainy period, and less time available for conferences or other meetings, but there were more emergency cases for surgery or medical attention. Although Delapere complained bitterly about my unpredictable absences on flying, I was myself suffering more, being distracted from my estate work, especially the optimistically planned selection of candidate bushes, which had to be carefully plucked every week, and after withering they had to be manufactured, rolling by hand, and 'fired' – or dried – by a very Heath-Robinson duct taking heat from the large drying machines. Supervised by one *sirdar*, this work was mostly done by a selected team of young ladies, selected by him with a view to pleasing me, with high standards of quality, appearance and efficiency. When I quipped that he had chosen a team of beauties, he assured me with a very earnest expression how beautiful girls were nearly always top class workers. My problem was in trying to organise the miniature manufacture as well as the selection of bushes and their propagation. This all meant my attention to the main work programme was less than it might have been, and I had to confide in the head supervisor that he was required both to control all field operations advising me on what his experience dictated, and keep in touch with the selection work without letting it distract him. The propagation nurseries were now doing so well that many people came, from staff and labour, to see the way plants were growing from just an inch and a half of stem and one leaf. We were all excited, and I tried to keep a log of success for each selected bush, with some showing very high, and others very low. The tasting of our manually made teas was laughed at by the factory staff, as the liquors were generally lacking colour and body. I told them less than a hundred years ago the British brought Chinese tea makers to show how tea was made, and all of it was done by hand, therefore we had to learn, with the staff's help, how to make better samples by emulating the full scale manufacture. It was complicated, and it seemed difficult to use the factory staff to supervise the timings and the standards involved in manufacturing relatively tiny amounts of leaf. Ultimately I managed to enlist an old factory *sirdar* who had retired two years previously; he was good with the girls, and well experienced in tea making, and after two days I was able to leave him in charge. When we tasted the first few days' experimental samples they were very disappointing, lacking in colour and pungency when compared with the run-of-the-factory teas. I decided to add each day a sample of tea picked from a rolling machine and put through the experimental programme, as a kind of control. I wrote a note on the limitations of the manual system, pending the introduction of a better one, and asked that the tasters should pick the teas which, within the group of manual samples only, were better than the others in colour, strength or character (flavour), which would possibly show up well when there were enough progeny bushes propagated to put through the usual bulk manufacture. After writing this I used Dr Wight's formula to work out how many years it would be before this could be done, and for fear of being ridiculed decided not to mention it. This was enclosed with the manager's letter covering the samples sent by post to Calcutta. Delapere came to one or two tastings and pronounced the liquors in his opinion as 'God-awful' and no use at all. Considering his day-long pipe smoking, his gin before lunch and whisky in the evenings, it seemed unlikely his palate was sensitive enough to identify anything unusually good under the mask of our rather primitive tea making. The first reports from Calcutta were very disappointing, the brokers' tasters reacting rather like Delapere, scorning the liquors and ignoring our hope they would be able to distinguish anything above average. This began to lower our confidence and enthusiasm, which had risen with the good results of the cuttings nursery. I missed Foyle very much, as he had taught me a lot about tasting tea and helped me to understand the various terms such as: briskness, body, nose, pungency, character, flavour, bakiness, flat, plain and many other peculiar descriptions. He preached it was important for anyone making tea to be able to taste it promptly on the day it was made, during manufacture, to detect faults soon enough to correct them. The trouble was that Calcutta not only discouraged planters from tasting, which they believed to be an esoteric art, and as a result there were too many managers who hadn't much clue about tasting and never tried to develop the art. They would send samples of each packed invoice to Calcutta by post, and were lucky if the tasters' report came back within a fortnight, in which time two hundred chests of tea or more could have been packed with a flaw not detected by the manager. Although I had learned the rudiments of tasting, I was under no illusion about the years of experience needed to reach the standards of Foyle or the Calcutta and London tea brokers. He would have been good at finding what we were after, and might have helped our morale, particularly my own, as my euphoric enthusiasm seemed to be evaporating fast. Without being able to identify the superior clones by tasting, there was little point in persisting with our visual selections and yield weighments, and this made me despondent and frustrated. I wrote to Dr Wight at Tocklai explaining the problem, but continued meanwhile to taste and send samples in the hope there would be somone who would understand what we needed; but I felt very low. I was, as a very junior person, delighted to receive a personal letter from him which gave great encouragement and good guidance. He stressed we should concentrate on 'pubescent' buds and bright copper fermentation, from which bushes we should propagate to find good growers, and this turned out to be advice which in the years to follow led all seekers in the right direction as scepticism faded and the methods of miniature manufacture improved.

It was becoming difficult for me to cope with everything and although there was less flying, whenever the need arose it made me very dissatisfied with the way it interfered with my work. After field work finished I would have to cycle out to the area plucked that day to look for the bushes selected by pluckers or *sirdars*, chosen for vigour and plentiful yield. It was seldom I finished this operation in time to make my relaxing evening ride on Rani after tea. In August the rain was heavy and persistent, and there began epidemics of measles, flu, and dysentery. The latter began with what Dr Pal called 'bowel trouble', then 'enteritis', the meanings of which were not clear to me; but once he began calling it dysentery there was no doubt about it. The simultaneous outbreak of measles shook me severely when I discovered how dangerous it was for children. We lost five children in six weeks. Delapere shrugged and said 'these people simply can't take that sort of thing like we can'. Dr Pal said it was always dangerous, some years worse than others, and there was little could be done unless diet could be improved for the children, who needed more protein which was always short during the rains. Patients with dysentery crowded the hospital, queuing to use the hospital latrines. I was horrified to discover I had been living in ignorance of what Dr Pal said was the real cause of the spread of dysentery: poor hygiene. The Europeans all used septic tank toilets and the Indian staff 'long-drop' bore hole latrines. Last year I had noticed bad smells in various parts of the estate, and was told by Telford these were defecating areas for the estate and some of the adjacent villages, where it was best not to go even when looking for clumps of ganja, as people would not use anything growing in these areas. The scrub was, I now realised, sufficiently tall for modesty, as there were no hidden closets or latrines, simply a kind of maze where people found their way to a suitable spot to void their bowels, generally demarcated in some traditional way so that males and females were never mixed. Dr Pal said there were very few latrines in the length and breadth of rural India. Only in towns like Calcutta was there an organised system of sewerage. In the villages and on some estates, the faeces were eaten by domestic pigs and some dogs. It was from such areas that things like dysentery and intestinal parasites – hookworm, roundworm – spread by people's feet on to their verandah floors where children crawled on all fours. It was sickening to contemplate all this, and when I asked why proper latrines were not made and used, Dr Pal explained latrines were thought to be filthy, and not to be suffered in or near houses. He said Indians were horrified at the way Europeans actually built toilets in their bungalows when flushing arrangements and septic tanks were brought in. He said there were still many planters' bungalows where there were no flushing toilets, which had only begun to be widespread in the 1930s. Another problem was if every worker's house had a bore hole latrine, it was likely there would be dangerous infection in the many wells normally dug, one for each house. It was a problem which was not solved, because estate workers were opposed to having a latrine within even thirty feet of their dwelling. He was very pleased with his own bore hole latrine; there was very little smell. Of course he would like a flushing toilet like the hospital latrines, but it would take time to make such improvements. We lost three people from dysentery, and the sight of the suffering people, not only at the hospital but being taken short on the village roads, filled me with revulsion and a sense of inadequacy. There were several local remedies of a kind, but if the infection had gone too far it was necessary to drip feed glucose and saline to keep people alive, and I could see the signs of fatigue on Dr Pal and his staff. With the overcrowded accommodation, the fetid smell, and the filthy mud everywhere because of the rains, everything appeared to be out of control, and I would dearly have liked to discuss with the enlightened Telford what to me was so depressing and backward.

The spread of flu, which seemed to be what one used to call a 'chill', was due to the incessant rain, and the impossibility of drying one's working clothes, a problem I suffered from myself, except for the flu. People were going to work in the rain wearing wet clothes from the day before, and whilst the rain fell it could be miserably cold. Day after day I went to the hospital to see who was there, and one day I was called from the hospital to take a message from Fraser, asking me to fly to Sirisbari to collect a woman having trouble from a difficult delivery. The cloud base was around 600 feet and the rain was heavy. I did not dare climb into the cloud whilst crossing the Brahmaputra, aware as I was that from 600 feet it was virtually impossible to glide, in the event of engine failure, to make a forced landing over a river as much as six miles wide at that time. I managed to find Sirisbari, took the poor woman on board who was suffering agony, and took off straight away for Panitola, wishing us luck as visibility in the torrential rain was poor. I was able to find Panitola, and saw the station wagon leave for Dinjan, where I landed to hand the poor woman over. The daylight was further darkened by the huge stack of cloud above us, and I decided to follow the main road westwards, helped by the headlights of lorries and a few cars. When I landed back at Medeloabam I learned that Nunoo, my second servant, was down with dysentery. Maneklal said he was very badly sick, and I went to the hospital with my umbrella to see how things were with him and the staff. It was a scene of dejection, fatigue, and misery. I began to feel I was in the wrong place; I was trying to cope without the power and knowledge which would point me in the right direction. I saw Dr Pal come wearily out of one of the small wards in the dusk, carrying a hurricane lamp. A moaning woman with a small child in her arms hurried to him, pleading, raising the child to him where he stopped in the shelter of the corrugated iron eaves along the side of the clinic. Dr Pal lifted the tiny arm of the woman's child, holding it as if feeling for a pulse. He put his stethoscope into his ears and bent over the child, listening. Two other children of about three and four, in soaking clothes, clutched the mother's wet sari, peered with large eyes at the doctor, who hung the stethoscope about his neck, placed his hands together, and said very gently that the child was no longer alive. The woman gave a great sob; she could not have been more than twenty-two, and hugging the dead child to her she raised her head into the rain and wailed with such terrible desolation and pain that the sound pierced to my heart like a dagger of ice. At such moments one reacts as if in fearful defence against the weird force of frightful misery, and in my case, because of my training for war, I found something smouldering in my chest which I must have encouraged to ignite like a rasping rocket, fulminating and spinning in my inadequate skull as if it would burst out in a fury of helplessness. I went over to Dr Pal, who was moving back to his clinic room. In the lamplight his eyes were huge and dark, glistening with the small flame in his moist eyes. I asked him how things were going, wanting to be careful not to show my angry depression. He smiled with effort and said he thought the worst was probably over. 'You are flying very late, sir,' he said. 'How can you see your way if it is becoming dark?' I told him of the difficult delivery case from Sirisbari, and the weather, and how I managed to find my way by following the roads. I did not tell him how lucky it was there was only one other aeroplane in our part of Assam and it would certainly, if I knew Constable, not be following the roads in the opposite direction. He told me he had sent Nunoo home with his sister where he would be given plenty of *bael phool*, a thick drink made from the fruit of the Bengal quince. His dysentery was comparatively mild, and the drink would work very well. He would be able to return to work after about three days. I thanked him, and asked how much rest he was able to have. He smiled and said he was managing just enough to keep going until things became better. Thoughtlessly I said I was shocked that such epidemics could happen with very little done to strengthen treatment facilities, and insufficient done to prevent dysentery in the first place. I said the hospital was too small, and needed electric light. In fact, I said, now seeing just how bad things were, I had come to the decision I could not continue working here. I could not expect after seeing the extent of suffering to order these people to strive to produce tea for people on the other side of the world. Such weather calls for something better than these people get in terms of earnings and enjoyment, and for a newcomer like myself so junior, very little could be done to improve things. I have enjoyed myself until recently, but I don't think I can stay any longer. I would go back to a flying career. Looking back it was clearly a case of the spoilt child, making a case for blaming my frustration and depression on the problems which others were not solving quick enough. I managed to pull myself up, realising Dr Pal's dedicated efforts under all these difficulties, and I complimented him on his excellent work. Dr Pal put his head on one side and smiled wearily.

'Sir, you kindly asked if I was taking enough rest. Please take kind advice from an old man. You are also in need of rest, sir. You rise very early; you are not taking the customary rest after your tiffin; you are flying in very bad weather, giving good service to suffering people. You are to take a good night's sleep, sir. Please do not mind.' I nodded, feeling ashamed, and walked through the rain to my bungalow, my head filled with little whirlpools of uncertainty: too much low cloud, low-flying in poor light; too much frustration at the measles and dysentery, and the inability to cope with it; lack of experience and teachers like Foyle and Telford. I changed after my shower into damp clothes, and after a light meal sat trying to read *Other*

Men's Flowers, unsuccessfully. I slept badly. After office I went to the hospital to see how things were, and found Dr Pal checking six drips of glucose and saline, with people beginning to queue at the four hospital latrines; after greeting me he spoke, not with his usual rather studied melodious politeness, but with a more detached and critical tone. I wondered if he had taken aspirin or some Collis Browne's chlorodyne.

'Sir, please forgive me, but there are things to be explained. Not many estates have hospitals like Medeloabam and Panitola. Not many managers are as progressive as Mr Telford; he is very strict, but he really wants to do what can be done to improve everything here, for everybody. And you, sir, you have been here for a very short time. Now you are working very hard, and you are doing wonderful service in flying patients from the North Bank estates who would probably die if you were not doing this. You want to leave us? We know you are a person of courage and intelligence, a person who wants to make things better. Please to remember, however distressful you find such a period as this with dysentery and measles, there are villages from here to Calcutta, from here to Delhi, to Madras, where medical facilities simply do not exist except in towns, where the problems are worse because they can never cope with such epidemics. If you leave us we would be disappointed, and think you selfish. It is a difficult life for you; but Mr Telford will be returning in about six weeks' time. You should wait, sir, and discuss your feelings with him.' I thanked him for what he had said, and felt as foolish and selfish as I probably was. For weeks after that incident I would flinch with horrified shame at the amazing vanity of my decision to walk out of a situation which didn't suit me, and I would lie awake in bed trying to explain to myself I had been suffering from giving up polo, lack of contact with people like Telford and Foyle, and the grudging celibacy of this particular life. The beautiful bloom of nubile wenches worked less during the monsoon. The excessively wet period passed, and there was scorching sunshine between drenching warm showers; but the greasy, sweat-soaked appearance of everyone, made more drawn, hollow eyed and tired by the long and heavy cropping days, abated the effects of sexual attraction. I did not sit down to the business of resigning, mainly because at last the reports, not from Calcutta but London, on the selected bush samples which were sent on to them, began to show there was someone over there who knew what we were after. Within weeks we were to find several bushes with possible superior character, and our morale began to rise again.

Mr and Mrs Telford with their daughter Lucy arrived back in mid-October, leaving Linda and Martin at boarding school in England. The simultaneous arrival of the cold weather transformed in its magic way the whole territory of Assam and the general outlook of Assam. It did not take long for the Delaperes to depart, and I said I was happy to remain in my old thatched bungalow. I showed Telford the work we had done on the clonal selection and propagation, and he was pleased enough with what he found. Delapere had obviously complained about my frequent and random absence on flying, so emphatically that Telford asked me to make a report on the flying part of my duties, with recommendations and comments on how to improve it. He had plenty of complaints and criticisms to make on the general state of Medeloabam, and said he had heard I had been working long hours, with little recreational riding and no polo. The polo I explained, which he understood and suggested I should start stick-and-ball practice straight away so that I could begin playing polo again. He said he was disappointed with the condition of his own horses, and was rather taken aback they had not been given more exercise, stressing to me how important it was not simply to tell people to give the horses exercise but to see that they actually did it. I had to apologise, but explained how the experimental work had demanded so much time. He asked me to check him out in the Auster, which I did. When I complimented him on how well he flew he told me he had done another fifteen hours at the flying club in England, mainly of short landing practice, and felt much better about trying more landings on the shorter strips and sandbanks of Assam. It was a delight to resume polo, but sad to notice how numbers had begun to dwindle. The shorter working days of the cold weather were a delight, and the transformation of everyone's mood and appearance was a great reward and reassurance. There were fishing and swimming picnics with the Telfords, and eventually Telford landed solo on his sandbank with some trepidation but reasonable success.

After he had read my report on flying operations we discussed what I had said about the service to the North Bank being seriously hampered by the lack of its communications with the South Bank. I said it seemed to make sense to station the Auster on one of the North Bank estates so that any medical emergencies could be transported with absolute minimum delay, and I suggested Mirijuli would be best. It came up in our discussions that I was unhappy about continuing too long in the business of proving the air service practical and beneficial, and still preferred to concentrate on learning to be a competent planter, involved as I was in the business of selection and propagation of superior quality/yield bushes. This was said several times, and was followed each time by a complete change of tack on to some other subject. One of these changes had switched to the incident involving Singrailal, and Telford thought although I had dealt with it reasonably and justly, he said it would not be long before some local politician of a different kind, eager to create an impression as a folk hero, entered such a scene with very difficult consequences involving the local press. He said more or less the same as Fraser had said, with less paternal concern and more disciplinary inference. The cold weather passed in a most enjoyable way. Twice I managed with Gerella to shoot wild pig which had been raiding the rice fields and sweet potato plantings, and with Telford's twelve bore I brought in a fair number of jungle fowl, large rufous turtle doves, and plenty of pintail snipe from the large scrubby islands on the Brahmaputra where buffalo were sent to graze. I flew several times with Bobby Constable over the holiday periods when Hindu festivals came, and enjoyed meeting more people again. At the end of February, I had somehow convinced myself I had come through a very bad period having learned more of my faults and vanities, but was now set to make progress working under Telford, a good teacher for all his odd characteristics. We were riding the boundaries one pleasant afternoon when we passed one of the scrub areas over which the faint but unpleasant miasma hung, unnoticeable only because it had become part of the permanent ambience; but I thought it an ideal time to come to terms with the problem of hygiene and sanitation and began to seek enlightenment. He listened without giving much sign of acknowledgement, and when I paused he surprised me by saying Dr Pal had told him how upset I was with the dysentery epidemic. I admitted I was, and he said he was amazed that I had told Dr Pal I was considering leaving my job in tea. Before I could justify myself by explaining about the incessant cold rain, the widespread flu, and the measles, and perhaps long hours of work, he reined his horse in and told me one should never be tempted to confide in junior staff about one's private feelings or intentions. His eyes smouldered with the light that showed extreme displeasure at my behaviour, and I felt a hot resentment that he had nursed his feelings on it for nearly four months. As calmly as I could I told him I had truly gone through a bad period, mainly because I had no-one with whom to discuss things. I thought the doctor was himself under serious strain, and as Delapere showed no interest at all in the general health difficulties I supposed I suffered from my inability to do anything about it all myself. We rode on in silence, which I ultimately broke by saying Dr Pal had convinced me I should not run away from things which upset me, especially as he and his staff colleagues could see I liked living in Assam. This evoked no response, and we rode back in silence. It took time to re-establish normal communications. I thought I had gone far enough to explain myself, and although I could see his annoyance at hearing of my threatened departure because of conditions I had criticised for which he was either responsible, or which he might himself have had plans to improve; but as he had apparently used my own indiscretion, in confiding my misgivings to Dr Pal, as a block to further discussion, even refusing to give me a 'rocket' like a tough squadron commander, I felt cheated and suspected he had perhaps been wounded by my implicit criticism. It was a pity, particularly as I found much later how much more enlightened and progressive he was compared with the average planter – if there ever was such a thing. I lived in hope of hearing his views on improving hygiene and sanitation, but ultimately made up my mind to leave it for a suitable opportunity. That year of 1948 went well. The rainy season was generally good. There were no epidemics of dysentery, but several cases of measles before the monsoon arrived. The propagation nurseries went from strength to strength, and we learned much about planting times and the control of shade over the beds. There were many visitors who were impressed with results but remained sceptical about the risks involved with large areas of completely identical clonal bushes. By the coming of the next cold weather in late '48 life seemed to be wonderful. Telford suggested I should take a holiday in somewhere like Shillong for a change, and not disappear again on the North Bank to explore places like Jamjing Bil. That place was a large marsh lake in the wild uninhabited country about ten miles from the Telfords' fishing camp. Flying over it one saw a network of tracks in the marsh, but never a sign of elephant or rhino. There were often wild buffalo on the eastern shallows, and Telford said the Abor and Miri tribals said there must be a *buru* or two there: creatures which sounded like carnivorous dragons to whom in living memory sacrifices were made by Dafla tribals in one of the high tarns to the west of the Subansiri. There were often thousands of duck to be seen there in the cold weather, and it sounded a good place to improve my growing knowledge of Assam birdlife. I told Telford I didn't like the sound of Shillong, although I would be keen to do a trek in the Khasi or Naga hills, preferably with someone who knew the lie of the land and the local languages. To this Telford said there were many such people about, most of them having chosen pretty mistresses from those hills; it was just a matter of spending time trying to make friends with trek companions.

'We know you haven't succumbed to the charms of such as Kumari, Belmoti, Rupni, and the other eligible young ladies of the labour force; I think you know every little conversation from horseback, every focussed glance at an unmarried nubile girl, reaches me through the reported observations of hundreds of curious people. They are complimentary in reporting your strict refusal to show interest in married women, and most are proud you should admire the girls; but you won't have noticed how the whole estate is on tenterhooks waiting to see which one you are going to choose. That is one good reason for your sake and the sake of Medeloabam, to make an arrangement with a hill girl. It is one of your problems that at your age such almost religious celibacy is likely to be misunderstood. You would become much less inclined to take life so seriously if you made a discreet and safe arrangement. You have a quick temper, you know, although you keep it so far under fairly good control. It's a sign of sexual frustration. A hill girl would be a very safe lightning conductor. Think about it.' Straightaway I must unwittingly have proved the point he was trying to make, for I told him I would prefer to make a trek to Jamjing in late January. When I said this he gave me a look which suggested there was a secret joke he had not told me, and I felt the involuntary spasms of my nostrils. 'I see,' he said. 'That needs thinking about, doesn't it.' The subject was changed, leaving me with the usual feeling of curious uncertainty. My initial thoughts were directed with a fierce pride to defend my own way of life, and I was pleased to remember how Constable, with an authority and, I like to think, a vision, pushed me vigorously to embrace what I was sure was a safe way to live: I was the marrying sort. It was true I enjoyed what he called conversations from the saddle; there was something universally acceptable about it to everyone concerned. I remembered Foyle's wise advice on neither making a favourite of any girl, nor making favourites, in the sense of promiscuity, of more than one. It annoyed me to be told that nothing could be hidden from Telford, and I drew comfort from having been told by Fraser, Constable and Foyle, never to believe furtive gossip on the estate or in the club. Hear it, remember it, but never believe it or act on it unless it begins to show signs of ripening truth.

I had been careful to change my rides on Rani so that I covered about six routes in a week, never in regular succession, and I made a point of exchanging words with old people and young, on the estate and in the villages, in order to show interest in more than pretty girls at the wells. In the cold weather evenings there would be horizontal skeins of blue wood smoke cutting the taller trees and bamboos in half, and over the lanes and tracks where the cattle were driven home from grazing there were skeins of dust, raised by the cattle, forming faint, flat veils as the heat from the ground radiated rapidly into the duck egg blue sky. The Assamese word for evening was in fact '*godhuli*', meaning cow dust, which to me remains as nostalgic as 'gloaming', the Scottish word for the later twilight. Even though it rapidly became cold as the sun neared the western horizon in golden glory, and no matter if my time of passing varied significantly, the fair maids of estate and village always seemed to be bathing. They would wear sarongs tucked high above breasts, and poured the very cold water over themselves with happy cries, not wetting their hair which was tied up safely and would be washed in the morning. One pleasant evening when I had seen Rani being groomed after a pleasant ride, Maneklal said he had something important to say. I told him to speak up as I took off my riding boots before undressing for my shower, and he went ahead in a quiet voice. He could not have been more than nineteen at that time, and I was impressed at what he had to say, knowing it had a lot to do with my general well-being, and was probably something which had been discussed by his father and his friends. He said Nunoo's mother was a widow, and would never have enough money to marry her daughter into her tribe. He said it would be good for her, and for me, if I were to take Nunoo's sister discreetly as a mistress. Everyone would be happy about that. My immediate reaction was to reject the suggestion. The girl was pretty, but she was very young, too young, and I would never want to spoil her chances of marrying. To this, Maneklal said the idea would be I should receive visits from the girl three times a month for two or three years and, being a *sahib,* I would not make her pregnant, so that her mother could then make an arrangement for her daughter to marry, and I would pay for the wedding: a matter of three or four hundred rupees. I was amazed and embarrassed, and said I would not take the girl on those terms, but would eventually pay for her wedding, as I knew the straits into which widowhood forced mothers with daughters. Maneklal said that was all very well, but that wouldn't do me any good at all; he said I needed a girl, and everyone knew.

110

It showed: I had fits of angry temper; I went riding to chat with the girls on the estate and in the local villages. It wasn't good to go on like that for too long. People are saying some of their girls are suffering heartache because of the young *sahib*'s glances, and it is not good for this to go on. Coming from him the wisdom of his words, which bore the sensitivity of the people amongst whom I lived, had strong impact on me. I was disturbed, and I said I understood. My butterfly behaviour I had allowed to continue with the comfortable theory that it was healthy and reasonably satisfying to allow my instincts to enjoy at least the pleasure of admiring what nature had designed me to admire, albeit as part of its plan for ultimate mating; but I knew that by trying to alter the plan by extending it, perhaps for too long, I was treading on new and dangerous ground, and Telford in his devious way had already tried to warn me of it.

Having told Maneklal I had understood what he said, and would take care to correct errors of understanding, I began to pull off my shirt. Manek stood his ground and said there was another thing I should know. Again it began with 'some people say...', and I asked him to go ahead. Speaking in a low voice, with an occasional glance towards the kitchen, where the lights had been switched on, he said all kinds of things were said, for instance someone from down there – pointing with his chin – said a shadowy figure in blanket and turban with a big staff had, well after midnight last Saturday, hidden in the bamboo clump near the house of Kumari and her mother. The man had made calls like a small owl, and a woman – or a girl – had come out covered with a dark sari, and one or two couples, wakened by their dogs barking, saw the couple walking bent like thieves in the starlight towards the centre of the estate. Who knows where? The dogs barked again when they went back before first cock-crow, and the turbaned man went back on his own. He didn't have a dog with him. People say all sorts of things. Manek said Kumari's mother was a Nepali woman called Hundli. She had been the mistress of the previous estate doctor, who was Assamese, married to a Bengali lady. There was a scandal and he had to leave the estate. The girl is beautiful, but her mother wants to find someone like a rich contractor to marry her. Hundli drinks too much, talks too much. Who knows, *sahib*? At this point I had to laugh and say I had a lot to learn, and I told him he had spoken with the wisdom of an old man, which was always good for someone new like me.

I remember not having slept well that night, with a dark cloud of uncertainty swirling across my thoughts. I felt it was like a mist on the mountain, and I would have to sit tight and wait for the mist to clear.

It happened in the following weeks as it had happened before with a familiar misleading euphoria: Telford and I seemed to have recovered our mutual confidence, and with his family I enjoyed picnics, sorties to their fishing camp, and plenty of polo. Flying duties were frequent, but the cold weather was less of a problem with shorter working hours and good weather. One day he took me with him to ride to Gerella's village, taking chocolates, cheese and cartridges as presents, where Gerella's oldest daughter was being betrothed. It was a happy ceremony, with everyone pleased at the well matched couple. As we rode back Telford remarked that Gerella had praised my Assamese, and said how well I could read and write. I said my reading and writing had a long way to go; I could read slowly the printed characters, but hardly understood Assamese handwriting at all. It was a beautiful evening, and as we crossed an open area approaching Medeloabam I commented on the beauty of the far Himalayas, deep blue, almost purple in the approaching sunset, and we halted to regard the marvellous sweep of landscape. 'You are still spellbound by the North Bank,' he said. 'Life is much more difficult over there in every way; bad communications; much heavier rains; and although beautiful girls are less common over there, girls are generally a worse temptation. The isolation sounds romantic, but for men of your age sojourns in the wilderness are generally bad medicine.' He said this almost mournfully, an unusual way of speech for him. After we had seen the horses stabled and their grooming begun I thought it fair to make sure he understood I was firmly rooted, and I told him how glad I was to be improving my understanding of the life in tea. I said I had begun to doubt the success of clonal selection and propagation, and couldn't wait to see, in some years' time, acre blocks of our own, and Tocklai's own clonal bushes. I said it had been depressing to find there was nothing of use to a keen young planter to come from Delapere, and I had suffered for it, but I hoped I could look forward to resuming my education for some time to come. With his back to the sinking sun Telford turned to face me.

'Tomorrow I'll give you a copy of Calcutta's letter about your posting. Your passion for the North Bank is to be fulfiled; you are posted to Mirijuli to work under West and Horsey. Vallance is going to Premalota up near Doom Dooma. I've booked you to leave Dibrugarh by river steamer, with your horse, ten days from now. The steamer will transfer you to a smaller feeder steamer which will off-load you at Bordutti where a lorry will take you the sixty-odd miles to Mirijuli. You'll spent the night on the big steamer and get in next evening. Ramjan will walk Rani from Bordutti to Mirijuli, but within a fortnight you'll have to get him to teach someone to look after Rani as I want him back here.' Looking at his watch he said, 'I must hurry. We're going to dinner with the Frasers. We'll talk more about it tomorrow. That was a good afternoon.' With the sun in my eyes my expression of incredulity would not have shown. Next morning, having slept poorly after hearing I was to leave Medeloabam, I went to the office with head and chest filled with a desire to make a strong case why I shouldn't be sent away from the place where I was so much involved with the experimental work of clonal selection and propagation, where I had learned more than 1,500 workers' names by heart, and where I had hoped to learn more from a competent manager. I simply couldn't understand why this was happening. When I finished my session with the *sirdars* and *chowkidars* I went to Telford's office hardly able to decide what attitude, what mood, I should have been developing during the troubled night in order to fight or acknowledge the shocking news of my posting. It must have been the air force training which won, because I wished Telford good morning and sat with a sigh to read the letter he had just handed across the table. It was brief, with a more human touch than the air force. 'Following discussions with your manager when he passed through Calcutta last year, and having on our records your request made in 1947 to exchange places with MacDonald of Bogahilonia, it has been decided to post you to Mirijuli in place of Vallance, who is to be transferred to the South Bank. MacDonald will be taking your place at Medeloabam.' There followed a paragraph informing me of the allowance I would receive for travel and transport to Mirijuli. The last paragraph read, 'We leave it to your superintendent and manager to communicate with Mirijuli to arrange the best date for everyone's convenience to proceed with the postings, subject to them being fulfiled before mid-January 1949.' I looked for the date of the letter and was surprised to see it was late November 1948. Telford busied himself with signing letters and cheques, the head clerk standing beside him giving and collecting what was necessary. Telford thanked him when the pile was finished.

'Mr MacStorm has just been reading the news of his posting to Mirijuli', he said. 'You should go ahead and settle his papers, his steamer bookings, and his account with the estate banker. He has no debts.' Banerjee looked at me with an expression of sad concern.

'We are all going to miss Mr MacStorm, sir,' he said. 'He is a very fine young gentleman. We are sorry we are losing him but very glad he is remaining with the company.' I saw he was trembling slightly, probably because he was not sure how Telford would take what he had said. I told him it was kind of him to have spoken thus, and I knew I was very lucky to have been posted to Medeloabam for my first spell in tea. I listened to myself speak as if I acted in a play, committing myself to a role I had accidentally fallen into. Telford smiled at Banerjee, and said he was sure I would learn less about tea where I was going, but more about people, including myself.

'He will be able to get the North Bank out of his system after a couple of years of it,' he said, looking at me with his wily half-smile. The news spread like wildfire, and as I went about my work the men and women expressed their sadness that I was to move away. Within two days I found the Munda men had given up their expressions of regret that the company was posting me high-handedly away. They seemed quiet and reluctant to speak in their normal way. When I asked the Munda *sirdar* if there was something worrying the men, he began with his big toe to draw pictures in the dust of the path, and eventually said they had complained to the Telford *sahib*, who had said I was being posted because I had told the company I wanted to work on the North Bank. I was shaken to hear this, and almost bit my tongue to prevent strident indiscretions in bitter words. As I spoke in normal tones the men drifted towards me to listen. I explained how MacDonald had wanted to marry, and thought his new wife would not want to stay on the North Bank and so, nearly two years ago, I offered to change places with him so that he could bring his wife to Medeloabam, where I had only arrived a few weeks before. I didn't want to leave now, but it was a case of 'Company *ka hukm hai*,' company orders, which no-one can disobey. They all nodded and murmured. Ludroo, with his broad smile, asked me when I was going to marry, to which I replied: when I find the right girl, not before. I told them MacDonald's marriage never happened after all; he would come here alone. Although I tried hard to be just, Telford's explanation to the Munda men was a clever but cruel deceit, difficult to forgive.

Chapter XIX

My passage was booked on the river steamer on the 28th of December 1948. The Telfords were going by boat to their fishing camp on the 24th, returning on the evening of the 27th. I was to stay in charge of the estate, ready to fly in emergency. Meanwhile I would pack my belongings, and be ready to depart early on the 28th. On the 21st I was working with the men who were finishing the medium pruning in the area where the height of the tea bushes had become too high to be plucked in comfort, and I was virtually learning how to wield the heavy pruning knife, cutting through tough wood about an inch thick, sometimes more, finishing up with a good level of all cuts, and feeling the strain on my unaccustomed wrist. Telford arrived in his jeep and signed for me to come out. He showed me several cardboard cases which had just arrived from Panitola, to be flown over to the North Bank. It was mostly things like sulfanilamide and precious penicillin, which the company had managed to procure for its estates. As we drove to his bungalow he told me the new Principal Medical Officer had brought these boxes with his wife, to introduce themselves and talk about the use of the company Auster. It was eleven o'clock, and he said I should meet Mr Napier FRCS and his wife now, and go straight away to take the boxes over to Mirijuli. I found them pleasant people, who said they were good friends of Bobby Constable; he had spoken highly of me which had impressed them, such praise being most unusual from him. Mrs Telford uttered a hum of subdued amazement, and I saw her flicker a glance at her husband, who said if I hurried I would be able to have lunch at Mirijuli, leave the boxes there for onward transmission, and return in time for him to fly his wife over to see the fishing camp from the air. It didn't take long for me to climb away from Medeloabam on course for Mirijuli, and I began to feel more settled, scanning the blue mountains, and the vast areas of forest and rivers, all the way to Mirijuli. I 'buzzed' the manager's bungalow and Vallance's bungalow before landing on what was the biggest and best airstrip in the group. West and presumably Horsey were beside a car as I taxied back to the road at the end, and I saw Vallance arrive on his bicycle as I unloaded the boxes. I suggested having lunch with Vallance, so that I could have a good look at the bungalow I was going to occupy later on, and this was agreed by Vallance with welcome alacrity. I was introduced to Horsey, who was posted as manager of Mirijuli; West was now superintendent of Mirijuli, Bankukurajan, Bogahilonia and Deoribam, the last being a small estate about twelve miles south of Bogahilonia, on the east bank of the Subansiri. West said once I was settled over here he wanted me to visit these other estates with him in order to plan airstrips, as during the rains it was very difficult reaching them in the terrible floods, often for months on end. Horsey smoked incessantly, having a drum of cigarettes in one hand, a walking stick in the other, and another drum of cigarettes in the pocket of his long, flapping shorts. There was nothing in his appearance to indicate he was a tough, rough-riding, hard working planter of the wilder hinterland; and had I seen him in the shoes of that colonel in Allahabad as a tea planter, I doubt if I would be where I was now. West was strongly built, flat-bellied, and vigorous in speech and manner. Constable, Foyle, MacFortune, all the polo players, the lithe Telford: all of them, with the curious exception of Delapere and now this Horsey, fitted the role of planters, even down to the typical air of challenge in their expression, and the mixture of irony and humour addressed to whomsoever they spoke. Shaking Horsey's thick, limp hand I felt a chilling sense that he was not going to be a good squadron commander, not the sort who, when taking over a new squadron, would give a fifteen-minute display of impressive aerobatics to impress his pilots right from the beginning. His brown, floppy brimmed trilby was so low on his brow he had to lift his chin to see one with his tiny dark brown eyes, which were close together on either side of a nose which began under his hat and drooped a long way down to find his swollen wet mouth. When we shook hands he spoke with an accent reminding me of Field, except for a broader southern twang which produced two or three sounds where only one vowel existed. I told myself to be fair and pass judgement only after learning more about him. He smiled with wet, swollen lips and said, 'MacStorm. I haowpe that doesn't mean you're stormy by nature,' and followed it with a throaty gurgle of coughed laughter. Vallance started giving instructions to the man responsible for the safety of the Auster, who started pushing small stakes into the ground in a rough circle round the aeroplane to which another man began tying a coconut rope, meant to keep people about fifteen feet away from the wings, tail and propeller. West took the boxes with me to the hospital, and then took me to Vallance's bungalow. He talked until Vallance arrived on his cycle, then drove back to collect Horsey. It took time before tiffin was made ready, and we chatted. I asked about Horsey, and Vallance raised his eyebrows and said he had never met him before, and couldn't really say what he would be like. His serious expression suddenly collapsed as he began laughing with great glee. He said my expression showed I wasn't very impressed, and he didn't blame me. His description of Horsey was unrepeatable. People said Horsey had been married before the war, but during the war she went off, being surprisingly attractive for such a man's wife, with a decorated captain in the armoured corps. I asked where Horsey would live, and he said I mustn't say anything about it, but he was going to live in the bungalow up in the middle of the estate, where he had once lived. It was haunted. No servants would stay after sunset. Elephants would rub their sides against the bungalow pillars; there were ghostly footsteps ascending the steps up to the verandah, and other uncanny noises. He had lain often on moonlit nights with his shotgun, covered with blankets on the verandah floor at the head of the steps, waiting for the footsteps, determined to shoot, whatever or whoever it was. He said there wasn't a hope in hell it would be a keen girl brave enough to creep all the lonely and spooky way for a welcome by a lonely young *sahib*; but the phantom footsteps never happened when he lay in wait. He didn't mind the elephants, which straight away shambled off silently whenever he roared at them. The time came when he developed serious malaria, and nearly died one night, unable to walk for help to West's bungalow, nearly a mile away. West was so shaken that he declared the bungalow unusable; but that was during the war when there was only one assistant. Last year four Indian engineers came to do the major overhaul on the 200 h.p. Blackstone diesel engine in the factory, and the only place to put them was in that bungalow. Next morning, by eight-thirty, there was no sign of them, and Vallance took a lorry up to collect them and bring them down to work. There was still no sign of them. He went upstairs and found the main door not only locked but barricaded. He hammered on it, and ultimately heard frightened shouts, saw frightened faces. He yelled at them to open up: there was work to do. They eventually opened up, loaded their belongings on the lorry, all of them grey-faced and staring like madmen; and when they climbed aboard and huddled close he drove down to the factory. They dismounted and began running, past this bungalow, across the river, and went all the twelve miles into town where they were said to have boarded a bus to Tezpur, without engaging in conversation with him or anyone else. He begged me for God's sake not to mention this to Horsey.

We had a good tiffin, with a chicken curry made with buffalo ghee, which he said was easy to obtain locally. He amazed me with the low cost of living over here. Food was limited unless one shot and fished, but my weekly bazaar bill was going to be half of what I had been paying on Medeloabam, where I had thought it was incredibly cheap. He told me the airfield *chowkidar* was called Holaram, a chap with a lovely wife and one kid. He lived in the old line, where the labour keep lots of pigs. He went out early one morning to the crapping ground well behind the housing area, and being still tipsy from a booze-up the night before, he was stupidly inattentive. The huge black domestic pigs would be out there, keen to feed on human excrement as they do all over non-Muslim rural India, excepting the Assamese villages, waiting before dawn like mounds of earth amongst the scrub, ready to be as competitive as hell against their fellows. Holaram didn't even have a stick. One of the boars, seeing what he thought was a delectable morsel issuing from the unsuspecting Holaram, rushed with sudden speed and yanked off the poor bastard's testicles, just like that. Vallance's eyes bulged as he swept his fist, clenching it swiftly across the table. I felt an awful nausea, and pushed my plate away. 'What a rotten shame!' I said, 'And his poor wife!' Vallance said it was wonderful how these people stood by each other; but as he spoke a cyclist arrived, shouting below as if something serious demanded attention. It was one of the field tally clerks, pale and distressed. He said he stood watching the plane when Holaram told some Koyas to keep the people from touching it while he went to the scrub on the other side of the airstrip to relieve himself. He said he saw Holaram wander into the '*germanhabbi*' (German weed, which when hoed down, always grew again worse than before), and was just about to mount his cycle when Holaram shouted in fear, turned to run back, only to be struck down from behind by a huge tiger, which then picked him up, fangs into his waist, and strode swiftly into a patch of tall scrub and creeper, about half an acre in size. Vallance told him to lend me his cycle, and we both pedalled furiously up the road to the airstrip. West and Horsey were already there, and about twelve Koyas had taken up positions round the half-acre patch where three of them had seen the tiger go to ground, and having run to the other side of it they were sure the man-eater was still lying there with his kill. Within the next half hour West and Vallance organised guns, an elephant, and a keen assistant from Bankukurajan called Coleman, who told me when we were introduced the Foyles sent their very best wishes. When I asked where he had met them, he said playing tennis at Panitola. Dierdre had a daughter about two months ago. It shook me how little I had been hearing any kind of news, and I said I would send them my very best wishes, and hoped to meet them perhaps before the new year. More Koyas and Saoras arrived with bows and arrows, and many other Oraons, Mundas and Santhals appeared with staffs and hockey sticks for the beat. Vallance and West explained there had recently been many people killed in the district, mostly close to the hills, and this was the fifth this year in the Mirijuli, Daflanoi and Bankukurajan area. It was an old male with plenty of wicked craft, too old to kill deer and pig in the forest, but taking toll of both young cattle and humans.

Eventually the beat began. The elephant turned out to be useless, probably panicking because it smelt blood. The Koyas typically showed amazing intrepidity in their quiet penetration of the thicket, strongly convinced the killer was hidden there. Eventually men with daos hacked every shrub to the ground, found Holaram's body, but there was absolutely no trace of the man-eater, who must have slithered like a fox, belly down, through the smaller scrub on the other side of the clump. Looking at my watch I begged to be excused, as I knew Telford wanted to use the aeroplane as soon as I returned. I had produced much adrenaline whilst creeping as a flank gun, sweaty hands on butt and trigger, and felt somehow the better for it. Taking special care to do my checks, I thanked Vallance and West, and took off at three-thirty to fly back. I thought to myself sunset would be around six-thirty, and if I landed back at five-past four, refuelled straight away, there would be more than an hour and a half of flying time for them to do their reconnaissance over the fishing camp. I climbed to 3,000 feet, and saw the pink snow ranges to the north before descending at speed to Medeloabam.

Telford's jeep was at the edge of the strip when I landed. Looking at the fuel gauge I saw there was still enough fuel for the fishing camp trip, and leaving the engine running I jumped out and ran round to tell him. He was stony faced and asked why the delay; but when I told him of the episode of the man-eater he simply said I should taxi to the hangar, fill the tank, fill the trip log, and close down. 'You've ruined our evening,' he said, and as I looked at my watch he went on: 'The air force hasn't taught you to get your priorities right, has it?' and he drove away, eyes watering with his own strange brand of fury.

I thought as I filled the tank I would one day treat the killing of people by man-eaters as unremarkable, and not allow such things to interfere with daily life; but I decided Telford was being surprisingly callous, remembering how I felt almost ill-mannered when I insisted on leaving Mirijuli where everyone from top to bottom had looked at me with sad eyes when I made haste to climb into the Auster. When I reached my bungalow and drank welcome cups of tea, watching the next hour or so of beautiful sunshine, I smiled to myself and confirmed I was not clever enough to have established a good relationship. It was not the way to ensure a successful career, and I resolved to try studying people more, learning to establish friendliness without sycophancy.

The Frasers invited me to their Boxing Day lunch party, telling me Constable would also be attending. A Christmas letter arrived from Jag, signed by Ted and Shag; the others had been dispersed by posting, reminding me I was being too sensitive about my banishment from Medeloabam. Jag said he had heard from Jackie Moss, DFC and bar, who had left the air force months before my departure, and was now a rubber planter under training in Malaya. He was an admirable character, a good pilot and popular member of the officers' mess; his only fault was on rare occasions, at parties thrown mainly for people leaving on demobilisation, he would suddenly be transformed from the heart and soul of the party into a raging menace, smashing glasses, driving someone's motorcycle through the anteroom and corridors, and pretending to be an aeroplane with arms spread for wings, roaring like an engine, eventually pretending to stall out of a steep turn and crash in a heap on the floor. He would then become quiet, smiling sweetly and apologising to the top brass and the wide-eyed WAAF lady officers. He was two years older than me, but seemed in his manner to be ten years older. I remembered him telling me it was a mistake to stay on in the air force just because I loved flying. He said it would cut me off from the outside world. I had to grin when I realised both he and I had left the air force, but had chosen callings which could not have been more cut off from the world; whatever that meant. Jag gave me his address, knowing we had been good friends, and I wrote forthwith, as well as writing aerogramme Christmas letters to the clan in Scotland, and the few others with whom I still had tenuous contact.

Try as I would, I was unable to understand Telford's peculiar way of wilfully and deviously refusing to communicate or discuss. I could not find by examining my own faults where I might have deserved the blind alleys and sudden calculated switches of conversation without any kind of mollifying reason, caution, or just remonstrance. I had never suffered this kind of thing before. I wondered if Telford's six or more war years of dealing with junior Indian staff had blunted his manner in dealing with people like me. At intervals I had decided I would take no initiative to attempt discussions, and simply answer questions or follow clear leads; but this had palled for me, although he seemed to find it comfortable. I came to the conclusion I needed to revise my knowledge of human nature; there must have been something I had, in my ignorance, done wrong in dealing with this extraordinary man. My efforts to gain his confidence had failed, and I found it difficult to reconcile my admiration for his many good points, and my gratitude for his family's kindness, with a resentment that was at first bewildering, but had now become bitter.

A few days after I received the letter of posting I rode a long way in the wonderful golden evening. The far Himalayas were deep cobalt blue, and I tried to tell myself life would be different over there. As I neared the estate, with Rani quickening her walking pace in anticipation of her food, I acknowledged the greetings of villagers and estate folk as I went until I became aware of the screams of a child, coming from a cluster of huts a few hundred yards away across rice fields and grazing land. I asked some passing men what was wrong, as the screaming cries sounded unusually serious. One man said it was a non-working Tanti man who seemed to be drunk, either frightening or beating the small girl. I saw the man holding the girl by her cotton dress, waving a stick but so drunk he was staggering and hardly able to keep his balance; but I saw one blow land, and hearing the girl cry I spurred Rani down off the road, into a gallop straight across towards the drunken fool. I roared at the top of my voice, appointing myself as a knight in shining armour charging to the rescue of a suffering child. There was a luxuriant green patch on the grazing land before us, and a slight swerve by Rani failed to register, and I kept her on the direct charge. How Rani didn't fall or injure herself I do not know, but she came to a very sudden halt, fore hooves two feet deep in thick, chocolate-coloured mud, and I, head up and calling something like 'Gregalach', went over Rani's head to land on my back, legs deeply sunk into the morass. I was plastered with the evil smelling mud all over except for head and shoulders. As I laboriously regained solid ground again, Rani did the same, and I was much relieved to note so far she was not lame or disabled. Men ran from all directions, many men, although I had seen probably six before I began to gallop. The girl had stopped screaming, and stood by her drunken father who, seeing me about fifty yards from him, dropped his stick and made a two-handed '*namaste*'. I told one of the men to go across and tell him if he ever had his daughter screaming like that again I would sink him in the mud and put a water buffalo to sit on him. The would-be shining knight walked the remaining three-quarters of a mile to the stables with as much dignity as his stinking mud allowed, saluting and smiling at the many people who lined the road to see the sight, the men and women making sympathetic noises, and the smaller children shrieking with delight at the sight of the chocolate *sahib*. Ramjan was appalled at Rani's filthy state, and I told him I would come back to the stables later to see if she had suffered injury. My own servants took my state very seriously, and when I stripped completely, they took everything to wash the filthy mud away. I was worried about my light polo boots, and told them not to soak them too much, fill them with dry newspapers, and not to put them before the fire. That episode cured my excessive introspection and almost wiped out my vain judgements on what had been happening. I say almost, because I awoke next morning at five with something very clear and significant in my mind: was Telford taking it for granted I, having recommended the Auster should be based on the North Bank, had done so not purely because it was a sensible idea but because I wanted to fly from there. Had he discussed this with me he would have found me repeating my desire not only to be released from what had been more than a year of voluntary flying, but to remain at Medeloabam, which was the only estate in the whole group involved in selection and vegetative propagation. If he wanted me to do this why had it not been discussed? If he had organised my posting as a kind of a trap which would catch me in a position of having to do it, despite having said for the sake of my career I didn't want to continue, then he had miscalculated. It would have been fair to ask me to fly the Auster for a year or less from the North Bank to see how it worked, and I would surely, if reluctantly, have been ready to cooperate.

I went to the Boxing Day party at the Frasers with misgivings, but by the end of it I was glad, not only to have been able to talk at length with each of the Frasers and separately with Bobby Constable, but to meet more people again. I met Bipin Sarma, still upset over our night journey with Delapere, but really enjoying very much working with a manager who was teaching him well and guiding him into the strange new protocol of life in tea. There were several of my polo friends, commiserating that there would be no more polo for me 'over there.' They pulled my leg, asking what I had been doing to deserve transportation to the penal settlement. I was glad I found conversation surprisingly easy in spite of the large gathering. Everyone said it was a shame I was moving to the North Bank, and it rather disturbed me, as they said unless I was going to be able to fly to the South Bank now and then I would lose touch with the real world. More than one of them told me the North Bank was in every way twenty-five years or more behind the South. Constable was the first I spoke with, and we were able to find a quiet spot for confidential conversation. I told him how I had failed to understand or cope with the strange behaviour of Telford, and had not been able to gain his confidence. He said it was usual to hear this from anyone who worked or dealt with him, and I shouldn't worry about it. He said I should be prepared for more of this oddness from the older planters, wherever I went. He said he had experienced the mysterious attitude of Telford, and knew why I criticised how he seldom spoke out clearly in explanation of what he wanted to happen; but he said he himself was, as I knew, a straight and even abrasive talker, making everything abundantly clear, and challenging argument or discussion from all ranks. He said it often happened one of his assistants couldn't stand such treatment, and wanted to be posted somewhere else. 'Human character is rather exaggerated amongst people who live out here, more so during and after the war. You won't like to hear it, but assistant managers are in fact just a damned nuisance to their managers.' He smiled at my petulant expression. 'During the war we all had to manage without assistants, and to begin with it was difficult; but within a year we had everything working beautifully, the reason being that the Indian staff very much liked receiving orders and trust direct from the manager, the *burra sahib*. They were totally dedicated to obeying orders, and enjoyed seeing how the estate ran well without the young *sahibs* who had gone to the war. Most companies paid their young planters something like half salary during the war, which was a marvellous thing, but the cost of running the estates without them was very much lower, and years of running like that accustomed all of us to a very efficient and relatively easy life. Never forget, Hamish,' he waved a finger at me, 'that assistant managers, although some of them can be a real pain in the neck, are all the time being trained to operate as managers, and that is why we have to put up with them.' He went on to say how life as a manager turned one into a kind of petty despot, and the coming of Independence has already shown that enlightened despots were making a success of their position. Those who were aghast at the prospect of losing their authority either had to develop ways of keeping it by earning respect, or disappear from the scene. He asked me who would be flying the Auster for the company once I was posted, and I said I didn't know. He said it all sounded like some highly secret operation, and couldn't think why, but he said he would fly over to see me at Mirijuli after I'd had time to settle down.

Later I spoke to George Fraser, again in a quiet corner. When he said I must be pleased to be posted at last to the North Bank I told him how I had taken the posting, which had come as a shock when I had somehow been convinced I would be staying for another year or two to deal with the selection and propagation project. It became apparent I was not the only one being kept in the dark, although George covered up very well; but when he patted my arm and said 'Never mind! You'll love it over there, and you'll still have your flying, which I know you love,' I told him I had been told nothing about what was to happen about the flying. Although I had recommended the Auster would be more valuable for the North Bank if it were kept over there, I had also said I didn't want to carry on with the flying as it had interfered too much with my prime duties as a planter under training. When I said my report had been given to Telford long before I had the slightest inkling of my impending posting to Mirijuli, Fraser stared at me, speechless, and then said he had seen my report weeks after he had sent the letter of my posting to Telford. Sensing the beginning of an unpleasant investigation I told Fraser I had become reconciled to my posting, realising I had attached too much importance to the work I was doing on vegetative propagation, and would go with good grace to the North Bank. I said I had told Telford when he returned from home leave in October I was unhappy to continue flying much longer, and since he has said nothing about me flying from the North Bank I have taken it to mean I can concentrate on planting. Fraser gave one of his mirthless orator's smiles and said, 'We who have been in the services do have trouble with those who lack the discipline of service communications. Misunderstandings; lack of clarity; no sense of teamwork. Never mind, MacStorm, leave it to me! You've done a magnificent job in proving the tremendous value of a company air service, and you are absolutely right in pointing out the Auster should be based on the North Bank. You are also absolutely right in sticking to your real target: to become a competent planter. I really respect that. Leave it to me!'

After the excellent buffet tiffin I had a long talk with Freda Fraser. She was flushed and bright eyed from the Chianti and claret which had flowed as part of the festivity, and took me to the same quiet spot where I had spoken with her husband.

'Bobby has been telling me what a splendid pilot you are,' she said. 'He tells me you really love flying. I am so glad to hear it.' I looked askance at her, wondering why she had expressed something like relief, and she resumed. 'Bobby loves taking people for flips, but he frightens the life out of them. His company is horrified at the idea of a company air force; but of course they don't have anything on the North Bank. I'm told you never frighten people. Do you ever do stunts? You know, looping the loop and all that sort of thing?' I explained the Auster could do a few such 'stunts', but as it belonged to Telford I would not dream of doing aerobatics unless he showed an interest himself. I had at his request done a loop with him. He didn't see much point in learning it. He said his wife would like to loop the loop just once, and I took her up to 5,000 feet and did one. I forgot to tell her to put her hands on the top of the instrument panel, and when we looped her head went down to her knees and she saw nothing of the earth falling away and coming up to meet us again. I apologised and said we should do it again properly, but she said once was enough: she had fulfiled her ambition to do a loop, and was quite satisfied.

'She's a grand character, you know. She told me she wanted to learn to fly, but he wouldn't let her. Strange, jealous man, her husband. Now what about Lucy? There's a girl who would love to be planter's wife.' I said I was nowhere near marrying yet. Lucy was very attractive, not as beautiful as her mother, but with a superb figure. Too young for someone like me who had to win his spurs as a planter before trying to support a wife. 'But you can't go on living like a monk, you silly idiot!' she said. 'It's totally unnatural.' I grinned ruefully.

'If we stick to our beliefs we seem to be required to understand that the Creator who organised nature allows all creatures to follow nature exclusively, except mankind.' Freda looked at me with one eyebrow raised, and I went on. 'I've learned from people like the Koyas, Saoras and Parjas, who have nothing to do with Christianity, Islam or Hinduism, that morals come before nature, although their morals are closer to nature than ours, I must say.' She giggled as if I had told her a funny story, and said she wondered how on earth I found out about such things, and I told her I had a lot of time and interest in trying to think these things out. She said I would be quite safe on the North Bank, saying she loved it over there: so wild and so close to real no-man's-land, not the wartime kind, but the true pre-Eden wilderness. We were joined by others, and the talk became difficult to co-ordinate, all about social happenings and possible scandals. When I arrived back at Medeloabam there was a note from Banerjee, inviting me to take tea with the Indian staff at their clubhouse near the office. I was just in time, reaching there at four-thirty as expected. It was for me a sad occasion, as I realised these were the first Indians I had come to know, whom I was now about to leave, to begin all over again. Banerjee presented me with a book by Swami Vivekananda, saying he hoped I would come to understand more about the Hindu religion and its deeper wisdom, which was less well known than the popular festivals. I thanked him for such a helpful gift, and parted after thanking everyone for having made my stay and my transition to India so interesting and easy.

On the 28th of December Ramjan left Medeloabam with Rani, who carried several days' fodder on her back, at two in the morning in order to reach the river steamer by seven a.m. I left with my possessions on the back of an Austin lorry, where Manek and Nunoo sat wound into their blankets, shivering in the cold, thick mist. The river steamer was huge, as far as I remember about ninety feet long, and half as wide. My overnight gear was carried upstairs to the cabin deck, and the remainder stowed below. The captain was a portly Muslim *serang*, bearded and wearing a woollen hat, who greeted me with 'Salaam aleikum' as I boarded. Poor Rani was nervous when Ramjan took her up the broad gangplank, and although our horses were never steel-shod in Assam, the sound of her first few steps on the thick sheet metal deck paralysed her in quivering terror, every small move of her foot clanging and booming throughout the ship. It took time and patience before the *serang* ordered many hessian sacks on which she could be walked to her bamboo fenced stall, and plenty of sacks as a kind of bedding made it possible for her to relax. Ramjan seemed to have been affected by all this, and gazed around, wide-eyed at the huge floating craft as if it was an invention of the devil. Maneklal and Nunoo accepted an extra fortnight's pay with embarrassment, and moist-eyed wished me well. I was sorry to see them go, and wondered what kind of servants I would find 'over there'. The steamer company travelling agent turned up when we were all settled in and introduced himself. He was a young man vaguely my age, perhaps a year or two older, and his wide, upward twirled blond moustache made it almost certain he was ex-air force, confirmed later when we were under way. At about nine a.m. the engine started, and soon we moved through the rising mists into the wide channel, steering west-south-west, away from Dibrugarh and the South Bank, for how long?

The agent told me the water was very low at this time of the year, especially in Upper Assam, and we must hope we wouldn't run aground, which could add a day or two to the journey. If all went well we would spend one night on the steamer, and transfer to the smaller feeder steamer around midday next day. Rani had not suffered much distress at the sound of the great diesel engine, now thudding away pleasantly below decks. Ramjan was well looked after by the mainly Muslim crew. The food was very good, and the sudden peace and quiet came as a delightful change, not foreseen. The mountains seemed closer, and looked splendid in the early sun, which gilded every eastern slope. We saw hundreds of bar-headed geese rising from the vast sandbanks, with flocks of golden plover skimming the grassy islands, and frequent pairs of ruddy sheldrake. There were red-wattled plover, common teal, spotbill duck, mallard, and pintail, mostly resting in the beautiful crystal backwaters. We saw several surfacings of the so-called blind dolphins of the Brahmaputra, and various birds of prey which at that stage of my Assam life I could not identify. The navigation of the steamer was intriguing: the *sarang* obviously knew his river, and followed courses designed to keep to the deep water being scoured by the flow of the faster currents in the sweeping bends. There were occasionally bamboos with cloth pennants, vibrating rhythmically under the swift current, planted by the steamer company launches which kept surveying for suitable channels. The water was coloured greyish with a hint of lovat green, caused by the silt being carried down from the Himalayas. Wherever the current slowed, the silt would tend to sink, building up shoals, and many years of experience had produced crews who knew what to look for. The agent said the river bed was like a living creature: the depths changed sometimes without warning. Our steamer carried a large cargo of tea chests, but because of engine problems was heading for Calcutta without the usual barges bound on side by side. I had heard of older planters who would take a holiday in the cold weather, travelling downstream for 800 miles to Calcutta to return to Assam by train. The food was good, and there was always plenty of beer. From Calcutta to Assam against the current was a trip seldom made by passengers, as it took a very long time, longer than the ancient method of travelling all the way by elephant. That night we talked of our time in the air force. He had flown Wellingtons and Lancasters, and like so many of us resented the war finishing before we had earned glory.

We lost about three hours next day by running aground within sight of the feeder steamer which waited to take us the short trip to Borduttighat, and it was fascinating to watch how, by moving all crew and passengers (except Rani) well aft to help lift the bows, the *serang* eventually managed to take us afloat again. The trip in the feeder steamer was fascinating, and I was amazed we were travelling up the Subansiri, about fifty river miles downstream from the magnificent gorge where it emerged from the Himalayas. The water was pale grey-brown in contrast to the upper reaches, coloured by the various marshes and backwaters where cattle and buffalo waded and wallowed in the cold weather. There were many people aboard: many tribals, Assamese and Miri villagers, bales of cloth, tins of oil, sacks of salt, and baskets of oranges from Shillong. There was no railway on the North Bank nearer than a hundred miles, at Tezpur, and the main road from Tezpur had four or five ferries, at this time of the year having timber and bamboo bridges. Anything coming to places like Mirijuli had to come either by steamer and country boat, or by lorry from Tezpur. It was a sobering thought, now I was about to live there. The Mirijuli lorry with its crew saluted me with broad grins from the river bank. When I stepped ashore they greeted me as the 'pilot *sahib*', having at some time or other seen me on the airstrip. The journey was proof I was entering a remote and very rural area. The people I saw seemed to treat the lorry as a special sight, and children would run fast to catch a glimpse of it. At a place where the lorry slowed down to negotiate an eroded gully in the very rough road, the little gathering of Miri women and girls who waved and called greetings caught sight of me sitting by the driver, turned and fled in a mixture of panic and delight, the girls uttering their high pitched trill when they stopped and turned to wave some twenty yards away. They seemed so fit and sturdy, their bare shoulders coloured like mauve-pink velvet, showing strong muscle and no sign of bones. It was more than two and a half hours of careful driving through some very bad surfaces, and across some rickety cold-weather bamboo bridges. There were stretches of forest, secluded villages, vast areas of rice fields, and birdlife abounded. At long last I entered Vallance's bungalow, with him still there rather like a guide for me in this relatively strange new situation. He gave me a good welcome and some good tea to clear the dust from my throat. He was staying until the 5th of January, which turned out to be of great value for me in learning the layout of the estate and surrounds, and the structure and customs of Mirijuli's estate work.

We cycled together everywhere. Mirijuli workers were some of the earliest starters in Assam. This was something started by the ebullient John Kerry, who Bipin Sarma and I had met at Kagurijan. We were up on the estate by a quarter to six every morning, by which time everyone was vigorously working at the pruning, weeding, roadmaking, drain cleaning and so on. This meant all work would finish by midday, when after work inspection everyone would set off briskly homewards, some to go and collect firewood, some to pound paddy in order to husk rice, others to the various patches of rich alluvial soil deposits down towards the rivers, where there were plantings of sweet potatoes, maize, sugarcane, and various spinaches and pulses. The tribes here were distinctly more observant of their traditional dress and customs than at Medeloabam. The Koyas and the Mundas seemed impressed and delighted when I spoke their language, even very much like the student I still was. There were many Oraons and Santhals, and small numbers of Saoras and Parjas, who like the Koyas were hunters and root gatherers, living in their own secluded clusters of huts away from the others. Vallance said he had told them the aeroplane *sahib* was coming to take his place, which had impressed them. He said one young Saora girl had asked if I flew off to live in the clouds when she had seen the Auster disappear into the distance. The estate was hard against the sudden emergence of steep, forested ridges of the foothills, beyond which the ridges went on in petrified tumult all the way to the eternal snows and the Tibetan plateau, with very, very few human inhabitants in between. The tea areas were on irregular rolling terraces, stepped gradually down to end on the edge of a tall cliff formation about a hundred feet high, below which lay the area of alluvial deposit in which giant trees grew among dense glades of tall grasses and wild bamboos: the haunt of elephant, wild pig, various deer, gaur (magnificent wild cattle) and snakes. Vallance said on Sunday mornings in the cold weather, when the sun began to reach the glades below, there was a chance of seeing the elephants or a small herd of gaur, feeding and taking the warmth. The Daflanoi enclosed the large area from the small gorge for about two miles south-east to where the Mirijuli, a far smaller river, joined it, both rivers forming the boundaries of the estate. The factory, and my bungalow, were at the point above the river confluence, well below the height of the rest of the area. It was remarkable how just before the sun went behind the purple descending ridges to the west, people and cattle disappeared into houses and byres, fearing deeply the menace of the man-eater. Vallance said the twilight killings were therefore now less, but the leery old tiger had begun moving stealthily during the day, and had killed Holaram during the early afternoon. Being chased off that kill it had taken a cow at Bankukurajan within two hours afterwards. The Koyas were absolutely convinced the tiger had not crept away unnoticed after Holaram's death. It had most probably changed back into human shape, being an undetected were-tiger, unnoticed in the crowd of people beating the thicket. He told me at Daflanoi, after a man was killed early in the morning, people went out to bring in his body, and when an old woman emerged from the scrub in the crapping area the people had beaten her to death. The police had to be brought in an estate lorry to investigate, but they failed to make the people speak, and said it was one of those cases impossible to solve, where there was no murder motive as such. Vallance had tried sitting over a kill several times, and was convinced the tiger was too clever to expose itself like a normal healthy forest killer. He told me old Johann Oraon, a famed *shikari* who in his younger days had been tracker and adviser for many a *sahib* over forty years or more, had told him the man-eater would smell a *sahib* with a gun from a hundred paces away, and change his course immediately and magically. Johann was now a solitary opium addict, grey and rather deaf, who lived on the southern edge of the Daflanoi delta described above, in a small hut by the cold weather track used by the Dafla hill tribals. It was probable Johann was a distributor of their opium in return for his own small share. Vallance said I should go to talk with him. People said he was regularly visited during the bright moonlight nights by the tiger and the odd lone elephant, something confirmed by the tracks to be seen around his hut. Vallance showed me the boundary track which ran through the forest covering the northern edge of estate land, and took me down the eastern end of the track which, after half a mile, came out at the deep cleft of the Mirijuli. On the way we saw the elephants' favourite rubbing trees, showing fresh smears of pale mud from a salt wallow deep in the hills, and there were two trees where two different tigers had raked their claws in the fibry bark very recently. On the pale sandy bed of the Mirijuli we saw their tracks, with many old and new marks of pig and deer. There were very few human tracks to be seen at all.

The Indian staff of field and factory were mostly Assamese. They were pleased enough when I tried my Assamese on them, but were quite frank in saying they preferred to improve their English by talking it with me. I had also learned by this time not to speak tribal languages in the presence of the staff. Vallance said one always had to watch the daily labour count, and check with the books at the end of the day, as in the past it had happened that field writers covertly arranged to pay extra servants without the knowledge of the management, which was exposed by jealous field workers, and he had sacked a clever writer who managed to create four labourers who never existed, and drew their pay without having to call their names at the pay table. He said the only trouble here was hockey. The Christian Oraons were keen hockey players, and years ago, after many years of an annual hockey match between Mirijuli and Bankukurajan, it had led to a bloody battle with hockey sticks, spreading to the many spectators, causing so much injury that West had cancelled any further inter-estate matches. He said the Oraon men, generally happy in their everyday life, could flare up into serious quarrelling without warning. The Oraon women were sharp tongued in a rather humorous way, but were very, very feminine and sweet, and the girls, Christian or animist, could be very attractive. He said the Oraons never pimped their girls, who seemed to look after themselves. Vallance warned me to beware, as he knew of six of his predecessors who had finished up with Oraon mistresses, who had lived with careless abandon until it was found they played to entirely different rules from those of their pale paramours. He named the men, and I recognised two, and wondered at how they had changed course to the safer and more respectable game of strict rules.

By the time Vallance left for the South Bank, I was well briefed, not only on the geography of the place, but the protocol. After Vallance's departure I was invited to tea with the Wests at their large, stilted bungalow standing next to the first tea area, with a large cattle paddock stretching for several hundred yards to the north, where beyond a dense ridge of forest the steep blue hills rose dramatically in splendid prospect against a cloudless sky. Mrs West, whose children were at boarding school in England, paid for totally by her husband, was a very quiet, pleasant lady, with pale green eyes, and a gentle manner. In the cold weather they would attend the club in North Lakhimpur every Saturday evening, meeting six other managers with wives, and a varying number of mostly unmarried assistants, a number now increasing as recruiting began to return to normal. All the time I sat enjoying the excellent home-baked cake and good tea, she sat working on her embroidery. West asked me many questions about myself, my time in the air force, why I had come to tea, and what were my hobbies. I thanked him for the stable being built near the bungalow for Rani, and he wagged a finger at me, saying the North Bank was a bad place for horses. He said they went in the back from a disease called '*comrie*'. He told me never to ride up on the estate; it would terrify the horse, as he knew from experience. He suggested I should ride down and along the river, over to Bankukurajan on the south side.

When it was time to go I thanked Mrs West and went downstairs with her husband. He walked down the drive, with me wheeling my bicycle, and said it was very disappointing to learn the Auster was not, after all, going to be stationed at Mirijuli. He asked if I knew who was going to fly it over from the South Bank, and I said it had never been discussed with me; but I told him what I had come to think over the past couple of days: which was that only Telford had a flying licence. None of the other ex-service pilots had taken a licence, and I had been able to fly as a pilot on the reserve of air force officers. I told him I had found my voluntary flying had gone on for too long, and had interfered with my training as a planter, and I had asked to be released from it last October. He asked if I had been requested to fly over here, and I said I had not; but I had in October recommended the Auster should really be kept over here for sudden emergencies, making only programmed visits to the South Bank. He patted me on the shoulder and said I had worked it out well. He asked who the Auster belonged to, and I said as far as I knew to Telford, at which he gave a broad but cynical smile, stretching both arms at me palm upwards. West was obviously once a good looking man; his features were rugged but well chiselled, and his eyes were of palest blue, deeply set under shaggy light brown brows. He was lean, broad and always 'raring to go', but seemed drawn as if worried about something which couldn't be discussed.

He said he was being very confidential in telling me Horsey had been suffering from nerves and depression, on the edge of a nervous breakdown, drinking too much and all that sort of thing. He had been sent over here for a quiet time. He said he found it a bit of a nuisance to have to look after a man like that over here, and wanted me to help him as much as possible to get back to normal. 'Don't be rough with him,' he said, which opened my eyes, making me think Delapere had probably given me such a reputation. 'He's never been in the army or anything like that; soft, if you know what I mean.' I began to feel sorry Horsey had been placed between us, and realised I was being more selfish than I had ever been about my own future.

Vallance had left me with all his servants: Nakul the cook, a flat-nosed Santhal, with a fixed cynical grin which never seemed to leave his face; Girdharilal bearer, a fit, dark-skinned Kariya, with large expressive eyes, and three youths who seemed to be trying to learn what they were supposed to do. The dialect was different over here, sounding like a mixture of Sadani and village Assamese, with quite a bit of what I called missionary Hindi thrown in. Vallance had brought in a stalwart Oraon, bigger in build than usual for them, who showed keenness to be my stable boy, his only condition being that I should teach him to ride. The stable was large, built from bamboos and mud plaster mixed with fresh cattle manure, like village houses. It was amazing how the stink of cow manure soon gave way, by virtue of its chlorophyll content, to a fresh odour, pleasant to me at least, perhaps because I was becoming more what people called '*jungli*'. Rani disliked the stable at first, and clearly missed the company of other horses. I rode her over to visit Coleman at Bankukurajan, and really enjoyed meeting him again.

Here I was, on the North Bank at last, uncertain of how the senior staff arrangement would work; dizzy with the prospect of exploring the primeval hill forest and the mountain rivers; and eager to learn to know the people, the systems, and the intricate social structure of a strange new habitat. I wondered how long I would be staying here. All I knew was that the planters over here were different.

Chapter XX

It did not take long to discover the several advantages and disadvantages of living and working at Mirijuli. What became immediately apparent was how West, having been manager for many years with only one assistant to do his will, could not easily readjust to the transfer of his authority to Horsey. He was a thorough and energetic man whose attention to detail was at first impressive, but with time became irritating. Although he had approved I would write out the work plan in detail every afternoon for the following day after discussion with the manager, it began to happen that after I had made my early inspection of all work, starting it as planned before returning to breakfast, West would intercept Horsey, on his way up to the estate after his office work and breakfast, and tell him to change the work plans. This entailed Horsey having to move the labour '*challans*' (teams or gangs) to different places, often to different tasks. This led to what I thought was reasonable disgruntlement amongst the labour and the *sirdars*, found by me mostly without having met Horsey who might have explained why orders had been changed. After nearly a month in which we had five instances of such changes, I suggested he should somehow get West to approve the work plans on the previous day, so that we could get it right and avoid waste of time as well as misleading the labour. I said it didn't do the new manager and the new assistant any good to be thought by the labour as incompetent. What Horsey actually said to West I could only guess, and my guesses were the result of an interview I had when West beckoned me to wade out through the tea where work was going on to where he stood beside his car. He was not only annoyed, but gave me little opportunity to respond to what he was saying in a rapid and impatient torrent of words.

'What the hell have you been doing to Horsey? I told you very clearly we had to do our best to help the unfortunate man, and here you are already turning him into a bag of nerves and anxiety, shaking like a case of shell-shock.' Ignoring my puzzled request to know what Horsey had said, he shook a finger at me and went on. 'You mustn't take advantage of a man who is a nervous wreck; that's bullying, pure and simple. I would have thought you a better man than that; and you've started frightening him about the labour, telling him the labour thinks he's incompetent. Disgraceful!' He went on thus for some time, and I could but stare at him in disbelief. Eventually he stopped, having said he warned me he would not put up with this kind of thing, and made to enter his car. I went forward and said I felt as a fellow ex-officer he would understand it was only fair to hear what I had to say in defence of the criticisms he had made. This brought him to a halt, and he raised a finger. 'Go ahead! Say your piece, but watch what you say.' I told him what I had said to Horsey, saying I had noted he was beginning to become unsettled and wanted to help him, and I repeated what I had actually said to him.

When I had finished he obviously realised there was a probable conflict of reports, and came close to a Telford-style digression. 'Listen, MacStorm! I am not the manager. It is simply not right that I should approve of the work plan every day; that's the manager's responsibility, and I've got four estates to look after. You must see what you're suggesting is impossible. But if I see something going wrong I can't let it just happen, can I?' I tried to say Horsey and I must learn as much as possible not only about how to manage Mirijuli, but about how he, with all his experience, wanted us to do it. I told him I had several times found *challans* working in different places and on different tasks from those I had seen them start, not having met Horsey, and had to listen to *sirdars* politely expressing worried concern about late changes of orders; and since I found it was likely to undermine my standing as assistant manager I would either have to discuss it with my manager or change our chain of command so that it would not appear as if the management team was in confusion.

He stared at me before saying, in a softer tone, I was asking him to believe Horsey was twisting the truth, and he didn't quite like that, to which I said I had already made up my mind I would henceforth write down anything I thought I should bring to Horsey's notice and hope he would, if it merited further discussion with the superintendent, show it to him. 'That's very much a sea-lawyer tactic,' he said, with a smile that showed mockery, 'I don't like it.' I said in that case there wasn't much chance of me ever earning a fair appraisal from him; but I wanted him to know I would do my best to help Horsey as much as possible, if he would let me.

Not long after this West gave me a long lecture. 'I've been hearing you are good at languages. You'll have to be careful not to do yourself harm, you know.' He then repeated mostly what I had already heard on the South Bank. 'When I told my wife of your talent for languages,' he said, 'she raised her eyebrows and looked at me sideways. You know what that means? Most linguist planters learn their languages from sleeping dictionaries.' To this I smiled and said I had not heard of anyone having kept a Munda, Koya or Assamese mistress, which just happened to be the languages I was learning. He raised his eyebrows and nodded in agreement, but went on. 'If you can't learn Oraon, Saora, Parja, and so on they will always be jealous, and you can't afford that, you know. The Assamese staff say they have asked you not to speak Assamese to them.' I said this was right, and reasonable, especially as I had found some of the Assamese staff speaking a kind of patois with many Hindustani and Sadani words mixed with basic Assamese. I wanted to learn it properly because of the advice I had from B.P. Kentwell in 1947. This interested West, who said B.P. was a remarkable man, and a fine speaker. He said had it not been for him things in Assam could have gone wrong for the tea industry. He drew a note from his breast pocket and waved it at me. 'Ration issues!' he said, 'Your note. The reason we have it every week on Saturday afternoons is that if we have it after payday on Fridays more than half the labour force is absent on Saturday, and when the estate is roaring away with leaf we can't afford that kind of thing. Your idea of switching it to Fridays after pay is a non-starter; but Horsey says he will wait for you and take you to the club after you've had a shower. You should go to the club, you know; you mustn't go *jungli*.' This was a disappointment, on an essentially selfish subject, as I had hoped to be able, especially for the remaining three months of the cold weather, to disappear before three-thirty every Saturday with some food, a kukri, rifle and camera, to penetrate the hills up the many small rivers; to spend the night in a shelter made after the style shown me by Gerella; ascend further until midday; and return on Sunday evening having learned more and more about the forest and its denizens: furred, feathered, and pachydermatous. Now I was stuck with ration issues every second Saturday, except at puja festivals, with a frustratingly shorter radius of action.

Whereas at Medeloabam ration issues had been several tables and tarpaulins, each with a staff clerk entering issues and payments, all running smoothly and swiftly, with me strolling around watching the book entries and the scale loadings, here the whole thing was burdened on me, aided by the stores clerk and twelve men. We would begin at three-thirty after a quick cup of tea, to control the issue of lentils, salt, mustard oil, lamp oil and paddy. Each employee's family had a four inch square of plywood with a piece of stout paper stuck to it under varnish which showed in clear handwriting the total weights of each item to which the family was entitled, for workers and non-workers (children, grandparents, and sometimes cripples or idiots), provided there had been no more than one day of absence in the week. The system demanded I should take the card, the stores clerk would call out the amount to be paid, and I would call out the weights and volumes of the various items, and watch the scales accordingly. People brought beer, gin or whisky bottles for their cooking and lamp oil, usually the empties from planters' bungalows. They would collect their lentils in cloths, and their salt they would wrap in banana leaf. The paddy was what caused me most of my discomfort as the issue went on. It was bought from local suppliers who had collected it from local farmers in old sacks, and most of it had been insufficiently winnowed, scraped from a dusty floor straight into the sack on an ancient beam scale. When it was poured into a pile for the ration issue the fibre and dust billowed in thick clouds which settled everywhere. Later in the season it would settle on my sweaty arms, face and legs, so thickly that I managed to raise my low morale by looking at myself in the mirror before having my shower: it was a truly amusing sight, made more impressive by artificial light. It seldom happened that we finished by sunset, and we always needed half a dozen hurricane lamps, which brought all manner of flying insects to irritate us all. I declined the invitation of Horsey to take me to the club, much to his relief, as it was always late enough to spoil his only social outing. West would drive out with his wife about seven-fifteen, past the rations operation some forty yards away, waving vigorously from the window of his newish Studebaker saloon; and he was followed fifteen minutes later by Horsey in his small Ford Anglia. Horsey once stopped to see how things were going, but as I was having trouble from a drunken woman who said her husband had gone away fishing, taking the ration card and the money with him, Horsey said he thought he would leave me to fix it, and drove off. He never stopped again. At the end of each issue I had to count all the money taken, all of it grubby, and record it in the issue register. The remaining stocks of each item were weighed and locked away; and the poor stores clerk took the issue register after I signed the money total, knowing that before Monday morning he would have to reconcile issued weights with the money, and check his stocks with me on the Monday afternoon.

There were some decided advantages for me, the greatest being proximity to the real primeval wilderness. One really welcome material improvement was the arrival of refrigerators, provided by the company for its employees. They had been able to buy these from large stocks of American materials once meant for support of the war effort in Burma. A huge Servel refrigerator was carried into my bungalow, and I set it in the dining room. It was a kerosene-burning model and big enough to walk into. West immediately ordered a supply of sealed tins of clean oil which was fortunately available in Assam. The first trials proved the impressive efficiency of this 'fridge', which had probably been designed for somewhere like the Gulf, or Lower Sudan. It froze like the arctic permafrost, and it took time before I was able to establish a level which enabled us to remove chickens and fish without the aid of an ice axe. It meant I could keep milk, butter, and fruit without any problem, and it made a big difference to my diet. I soon discovered the servants were covertly producing ice in large quantities for the office staff and others, and had to warn them to desist, knowing the dangers of laryngitis if one drank iced water to slake a thirst caused by the dusty roads, where the pulverised surfaces sent up clouds of finest powder which were bound to include dried cattle manure and other unmentionable detritus. I gradually made myself comfortable in my bungalow. It was not large, but was strongly built with a certain amount of mosquito wire, which helped a lot. As soon as I had arrived I found the evenings and nights were much colder than on the South Bank. I welcomed the remarkable breeze which began as soon as the eastern sides of the hills lost the sun. The shaded faces of the valleys radiated heat into the clear sky, and after sunset the wind increased. If there was cloud over the mountains the katabatic wind never happened, but that was more likely towards the middle of the year, when the wind would have been more welcome to cool things down. Because of the katabatic wind there was never any mist at night or in the morning, within about ten miles of the foothills.

I found Horsey had been an engineer before he joined tea, and his knowledge of engines was good. After the estate work was finished, and I had written the work plan for the next day, I would visit the factory to see how the cold weather overhaul of factory machinery and vehicles was proceeding, and gained plenty of knowledge to add to my meagre experience of studying and watching engine maintenance in the air force. The factory had a good collection of engineering manuals which I studied frequently depending on whether the work was diesels, petrol engines, water pumps or turbines. Talking engineering was the only time Horsey spoke with confidence and a light in his eye. It became clearer as time went on he had never spent long in the field, and it seemed likely he was good enough as an engineer for managers to put him where he was most effective, especially during the war for which he was too old. He took me once a month into North Lakhimpur to the only 'European'-type store, run by an Indian gentleman with the honourable title of Rai *Sahib* Gangaram Chowdhuri. There one could buy New Zealand butter; British and Italian cheeses; British and Dutch beers; Chianti, claret and French white wines; dried yeast, tinned biscuits, tinned ham, tinned cream, evaporated milk, and packets of dried raisins. The only Indian items available were tins of Lipton's South Indian and Darjeeling tea. The latter I tried, and it became my one real luxury for a long time. The Mirijuli spring tea was good, and Bankukurajan was very good; but like most of Assam the high cropping mid-rains liquors were rather plain, and the teas didn't keep well in the high humidity of Assam. The shop once had rounds of Bel Paese cheese of which, despite vivid memories of MacFortune, I bought two. For several weeks I had cheese omelettes and all other manner of cheese dishes every day, enjoying the excellent pungency and flavour. In all the years since I have never again found as good a Bel Paese. My great appetite for this cheese reminded me of Ben Gunn in Stevenson's *Treasure Island*, and I realised the lack of calcium in Assam which, according to the books I had read on its wildlife, caused the deer antlers and elephant tusks to be significantly smaller than in other parts of India, was probably affecting me, especially over here where the abundant monsoon rain came straight off the mountains with little chance of absorbing iodine from forest vegetation, and mineral calcium from the rocky soil.

I made a visit to old Johann *shikari*'s hut, which was tucked away on a slight ridge, hidden amongst trees and wild bananas which showed signs of elephant feeding. He was indeed very deaf, but during the day I was able to speak loudly enough for him to understand and respond. His hair was like a helmet of pewter, and his face was like a carving in mahogany, marked by the sun and the autochthonous way of life. His eyes showed the pale ring of age, but their sight was remarkably good. Once he was set in a flow of speech by one of my questions, he seemed to focus his eyes on the scenes he described, and I often wondered if this had something to do with his opium. Simply by sitting often on a tree stump beside him I learned so much, not only about the wilderness and its creatures, but about many of the planters for whom he had worked first as an estate employee, and later as a tracker and hunter. I asked him to tell me about Hamish Breck, famed amongst planters as an intrepid elephant and tiger hunter of many kills. To my surprise he cackled about the 'Berrek *sahib*', saying he was not a real lover of the wild forests. He said he just liked killing these creatures, and would ride on the back of an elephant to kill an elephant or a tiger. He only killed one real rogue elephant, but it took him twelve shots and twelve hours to drop it, which gave him the name of 'Bara Kartush (twelve cartridge) Berrek *Sahib*'. He said he was a *pukka sahib* and paid him well, but he didn't like sitting and waiting, and just liked killing things, which was against the law of life. I told him I would normally only kill things to eat, but felt obliged to kill animals which killed people. This seemed to meet with his approval. I had gathered he was a Christian, but knew he didn't attend the chapel on the estate or go to church. I asked him about the man-eating tiger and the rogue killer-elephant, wanting to know what could be done about them. He told me he was too old to guide me or teach me about the local country, but recommended Rondey *sirdar*, a Munda, who would within a month or so show me all the tracks and trails which would help me to find my way about within easy reach of the estate boundaries. I knew Rondey, who was a tall, well built man with a quiet manner and a good sense of humour, who had already been helpful in improving my Munda vocabulary. As for the man-eater he said it was old and lame; he had seen it often by day and by moonlight. He said it was struggling to keep itself alive, and finding it difficult to find food. The rogue elephant was different. It was most likely an elephant which had been caught young, trained by men to deal with timber, and was easily thirty years old. It probably had a bad *mahout*, an ageing *mahout* who relied more and more on opium to keep him in his job; 'Like me!' Johann said, grinning. An old *mahout*, being afraid, begins to be cruel, thinking that will keep him safe from the mighty power of his elephant. He said he had seen this tuskless rogue often, 'Right here', he said, pointing to a spot not more than fifteen feet away. In the moonlight he had seen the holes in the rogue's ears, holes made by the owners during training. He said this rogue had probably killed his mahout after rebelling against too much of hard steel drawing blood from his head, after which he had not far to go to reach the wild herds in the foothills. Although rogues could find mates fairly easily, they seldom had more than a very distant relationship to the herds, and moved mostly on their own once their mates rejoined their own herd with their year-old young. He warned me this rogue had a reputation as a ghost. Many *shikari sahibs* had tried to shoot him without success, the rogue being capable of disappearing like a ghost when being encircled by guns on trained elephants. He said he used to work for the *sahib* who once came out from England to catch elephants over at Bandarjili, who only wanted to know from him where the rogue was moving. He said such escaped elephants knew more about human behaviour and movements than humans knew about each other, and this one was the most dangerous animal he had ever come across. He only left the hill forests to enter men's habitat by night. No-one would ever get near him by riding on another elephant. It was interesting to hear most of the rogue's victims had been either drunks or people accidentally blundering into his path in the dark. After many visits and further talks with Rondey, I had built up notes on the behaviour of the man-eater and the rogue. Johann said the man-eater would be very unlikely to kill a buffalo calf tethered for bait. He told me to carry my rifle everywhere at work or play. The old tiger had been seen so often during the day, which was the best time to use a rifle from up to a hundred yards. He pointed to where his neck met his body, saying from the front quarter to hit at the base of the neck, and from the rear quarter behind the top of the foreleg; but never in the head. He moved around his vegetable patch and brought a *brinjal* (aubergine) slightly larger than a tennis ball, and said this was the size of the brain even of the biggest tiger: never in the head. He told me to ask Brijlal Singh, the factory head fitter, to ask one of his men to make clips for me on my bicycle to hold the rifle safely. He should also make wood and metal clamps to hold a large torch parallel to the barrel of the rifle, so that the switch could be switched on and off easily by the forward left hand. He said it was possible to keep switching on and off when waiting for a tiger to make up its mind to come to its kill, without the tiger becoming suspicious, provided one was high up or downwind of it. I had with Horsey's permission given my rifle, minus bolt, for the cycle clips and the torch brackets to be made, and was driving the Austin three tonner up to the estate with a load of cement, sand and stone for the repair of a concrete bridge. The mason was sitting on the seat next to me, and the driver was standing on the running board outside, holding on to the door. I heard one of the labourers riding behind give an urgent shout, and looking forward saw the head and shoulders of a large tiger behind a clump of shrub, twenty-five yards away. I jammed on the brakes, and the driver, seeing the beast watching us with a head made broad with a ruff of straggly hair, opened the door and jumped in, on to the lap of the portly mason, clashing on to the tools he was holding. He wound up the window, and told me to do the same. I kept the engine running and watched. The great, rangy beast lolloped down the verge, and paced easily across the shingle road, and went up the other side, raising a cloud of dust, and disappeared into the scrub and tall grass. I drove up to the crossing place and got out to examine any footprints. One of the mason's helpers who was a Munda crouched down and scanned the clear prints in the soft dust. 'Look!' he said, 'look at this hind paw: five toes. A were-tiger! That's him.' The driver, doubtless because he was the owner of several cattle and immediately saw their danger, said we should drive fast up through the tea, some 300 yards ahead, near West's bungalow, and run left to the edge of the high plateau, where we would be able to see the cattle grazing eighty feet below, and we should shout for the cowherds to round up the cattle before the tiger got down to them. This we did. The angle of the sun, the level green of the grazing ground with clumps of shrub and several beautiful trees casting deep shadows, and about thirty brown and white cattle cropping the grass, all presented an ideal rural scene, viewed from above. Hearing the shouts the cowherds began swishing their staffs, shouting at the cattle, not fully decided what they were to do. From our grandstand view we saw our tiger suddenly emerge in a stiff and floppy canter, making surprising speed. The cattle galloped in all directions, except for a cow which had borne a calf probably twelve hours ago. The oldish cow, with good horns, still receiving the strong signals from her brain of the need to protect her calf, put down her head and charged the tiger, which like a lazy old cat performed a switch of course and a steep turn back as the cow swung away, lunging in to grasp the cow's shoulders with his claws, trying to sink his teeth in her spine near the neck. The cow managed to buck free, and galloped off followed by her calf at amazing speed. The tiger carried on cantering, and we saw another two attacks, the last dropping an old black cow, before the rather brave cowherds charged with their staffs, chasing it to spring into the undergrowth below the plateau. I ran back to the road just in time to see him cross it about 200 yards away, safely hidden in cover which would shield him all the way to the forest. Johann was right. Two days later we heard the tiger had killed a man on Daflanoi estate.

Two weeks later, having previously explored the area between the northern boundary and the Mirijuli river, I cycled early on Sunday morning, taking my rifle, to visit an area where some old abandoned tea grew amongst the giant forest trees. There always seemed to be tracks of small deer and wild pig, and Rondey had pointed out that where the many-stemmed abandoned tea had grown tall with its canopy fairly high below that of the larger trees, visibility between the old tea rows was excellent when compared with the often profuse forest undergrowth. I went in treading carefully and slowly as Gerella had taught me, listening and seeking for movement. The sun was on the trees above, but would not penetrate the gloom of the forest for another hour. There were not only fresh deer tracks, but what seemed to be fresh tiger tracks on the soft earth turned up by wild pig feeding on roots; they were not of the old man-eater. I went through the old tea area without sight or sound of interest, into the small forested valleys which extended towards the river, and hearing birdsong from many small birds I sat on a fallen tree, propping my rifle a few feet away from me. The birds arrived, many different kinds of them, some prospecting high, some low, moving in some kind of stacked formation as if it was a kind of instinctive defence arrangement. There were at least twenty different kinds, flycatchers, ground thrushes, babblers, tits, wrens, flower peckers and sunbirds. I enjoyed what I can only call a blessed experience when two small olive green birds with white crescents at the outer rim of each eye, making them look comically cross-eyed, perched one on my right knee, and the other on my left shoulder, totally unafraid, interested in looking for small insects. They moved on with the others, leaving me with a feeling of precious privilege and trust. This was where there was no fear of strangers, and had to be a special place. I tried to remember as many of the birds as possible in order to identify them later in my books. After a while they had moved almost out of sight, and I heard the gobbling goblin calls of the white headed laughing thrushes, the watchmen of the jungle. I thought they had sounded off because of me, but they seemed to be on the hillside opposite, at a fair height. It was a beautiful cold weather morning, and I absorbed the scene with delight, letting my gaze wander, drinking in the strange plants, large and small; the seeds on the ground; the scratchings on the forest floor. It was a new world, with a multitude of signs and shapes to be learned. It was primeval forest, belonging to a host of wild creatures, yet it was magically quiet and peaceful, where only an occasional tiny movement would catch my eye and show me a green snake, a large, hairy brown spider, sitting two feet from me on the same fallen tree with all the patience in the world.

There was a clump of rusty and green ferns about twenty yards away amongst profuse undergrowth, and my eyes were caught by an arrangement which looked curiously like the face of a tiger. I stared, intrigued and very slightly excited; but it remained as still as inanimate ferns always did. Grinning at my imagination, tickled by the fresh tiger tracks and building hopes for something to stir my blood in this edge of my new wilderness, I carried on scanning, intent on absorbing the forest scene. There came a low, hoarse sound from a long way behind me, and something sent my gaze to search for the tiger's face in the ferns. There was no trace, and feeling my blood stir I moved over to pick up my rifle, and smiling at my dramatic view of the strange noise I thumbed the safety catch off and quietly opened the breech to confirm there was a cartridge ready in place. Now Gerella and Johann had both said all wild animals are basically shy, and never dangerous unless they are afraid of being driven into a position of no escape. I looked at my watch, and feeling the pangs of hunger for my delayed Sunday breakfast, decided it were better to make a speedy and not too furtive return to the edge of the estate where my cycle waited. I moved scarcely five yards into the undergrowth towards the estate, when I was shaken by my first experience of the full-throated roar of a tiger at very close range. My heart started thumping strongly and rapidly, and aiming on a curve away from the sound I strode carefully but swiftly westwards. There came a shorter but more urgent sounding roar, followed by a kind of interrogative moan. I felt it came from behind, and quickened my pace, shouting 'Push off you damfool, push off.' To my horror I heard another explosive roar, and heard the rush and swish of the tiger coming in my direction. I could see nothing; he seemed to have stopped not far away, and after a brief wait I decided to move on quickly. He charged a second time, yet seemed to diverge before closing with me, falling quiet again. I started again, seeing I was not far from the abandoned tea; but the tiger roared, and this time I saw the colour of him, coming straight towards me in the undergrowth. When he was about five yards away I shot, not seeing him clearly enough, aiming at what I thought was just past his head, into the bulk of his shoulder. He coughed and seemed to fall, but I couldn't see him. For a second or two I had the crazy urge to stride quickly, close enough to see him and place a positive lethal shot; but I had enough instinctive sense to turn and make for the clear aisle in the abandoned tea, clear of undergrowth and only a few yards away. I went ten yards into it, and turned to listen over the deafening sound of my pulse for any kind of sound. I remember thinking it was all rather unfair; tigers aren't supposed to do this sort of thing. It couldn't be the man-eater according to all I had heard and read; Johann would no doubt explain this. I waited for about five minutes before I heard what I was sure was the death rattle, and desperately hoped it was. I waited for another ten minutes for any kind of a sound. The laughing thrushes cackled from more than fifty yards away behind me. With the stupidity of inexperienced youth I presumed victory. I walked slowly about five yards towards the fallen tiger between the rows of old tea, listening hard, beginning to feel I had managed to come out of this dangerous encounter well, considering it had not been in accordance with my recent education. For whatever reason I remained still, some small but insistent voice from nowhere whispering urgently: beware! Eventually, for the lack of a taught procedure or a developed instinct I tightened my sweaty grip on the rifle and rattled the bolt. The tiger launched himself suddenly, uttering no sound, bursting from the undergrowth as full of life as a charging bull. His face was like a Chinese mask, almost without expression. He sprang when he was ten feet away, almost like a rugby tackle, twisting and spreading his huge forepaws, one above the other; but he had aimed too high, and seemed to struggle on his hind legs to reach me. I heard Gerella, and Johann: 'never in the head', and in the split seconds granted me by a strange lop-sided dance in which the somehow impeded tiger struggled to reach me with extended paws, I fired up into his gaping mouth at close range with complete conviction it was the only way to survive. He dropped with a thump which shook the earth at my feet. I waited with another round ready, but he was dead. His left leg kicked for a few seconds, then he was still. Looking at this beautiful dead creature, muscled and coloured in perfect condition I felt a terrible crush of guilt. This surely was not a man-eater. I knelt to examine his great claws, when suddenly I leapt, seizing the rifle, heart thudding: a tiger moaned not more than twenty-five yards away. It was a sweet, plaintive but terrifying moan, and my feelings being what they were, I seemed to let some ancient instinct rise so that I roared abuse as loud as I could. 'Don't be so damned stupid for God's sake! Push off! Jao! He

145

didn't know what he was doing, the idiot.' There was dead silence, and I decided I should make haste back to the estate, making plenty of noise and keeping eyes and ears open. When I reached my cycle I saw five Saoras trotting up along the boundary fence. When they reached me they said with broad grins they were ready to carry it back: a deer? or a boar? When I told them what had happened they put their hands together and said it must have been the man-eater. I was very much in doubt about that, but took them back so they could cut a strong sapling and carry the tiger to the lorry track, and wait for me to come with a lorry to take it down to my bungalow for skinning.

After the bloody business of skinning I found my first shot had in fact entered the beast's back beside its spine, and hit the upper end of the femur. One of the vertebrae had been grazed, probably paralysing the hind leg for a short while; and the injured femur caused the error in his final spring. It was a serious lesson on the dangers of snap-shooting at a mostly hidden, fast moving target; but it was West who said he thought this was probably one of a family group of man-eaters: a three-year-old son, probably with the mate I had heard, who had learned to kill and eat humans and cattle as well as jungle game. He told me there were several tins of salt and alum in the stores, left by previous *shikaris*, which I could use for rubbing the skin before sending it to Calcutta for curing and mounting. He told me to be very careful about going after tigers on foot, and I said it was something I hadn't contemplated doing until I had learned much more about tigers and the jungle in general.

It was scarcely a month later that I had the strange fortune to meet another striped creature of 'fearful symmetry'. It was not far from the previous encounter, actually on the estate's forest boundary which ended down on the bank of the Daflanoi. The boundary patrol watchmen, Koyas armed with bows and arrows, who walked all the perimeter boundaries once a month, told me they had that morning found fresh wild pig rootings leading into the estate forest, and were sure I would find them if I went there in the afternoon. I arrived there at about three-thirty after finishing office work, and crept stealthily along the boundary, seeing the rootings, and listening carefully for the soft, intermittent noises of the wild pig feeding. Every now and then I followed Gerella's advice and put my rifle between my knees, cupped my hands behind my ears, and able to hear like a deer, rotated my head in search of tiny sounds. The amplification of noise was impressive. After about a hundred yards and fifteen minutes I registered a noise I could not identify, but attributed it to wild pig feeding. The sound seemed to come from beyond a huge tree, about three feet in diameter, which stood about twenty yards away on the southern side of the boundary. I advanced as silently as a cat, and began to pick up the occasional noise without cupping my hands. Although the undergrowth beyond the tree was not dense, I saw no sign of dark grey pig, and moved to hide behind the tree in order to see further. The noise had stopped, and still unable to see any shapes or movement I moved slowly round the tree, peering intently beyond. There came a sound almost like a sneeze, at very close range, making me catch my breath and tighten my grip on the rifle; it was a strange and urgent sound, and seemed to come from somewhere round the tree, higher than my head. The whole of my inner vitals and brain jolted violently when I found I was staring into the face of a large tiger, about two and a half feet away. It was frozen, wide-eyed, with both forepaws up before him on the trunk, where he had been dragging his claws down through the fibry bark, making the noises I had misinterpreted. Within a second and a half he threw himself in a leap rather like an Immelman turn, curving over backwards and sideways, bounding in great arcs away, down and off the boundary. He swung, up to his back in undergrowth, ears cupped at me, and an expression of outrage on his handsome face. He turned his ears back, threw his chin up, and roared, which had the effect nature or creation had intended, and paralysed me with sheer naked noise; and by that I mean: with no bars between us. I stood rooted, remembering Gerella's advice to keep staring if I ever met a tiger's eyes, and I held the rifle ready, safety catch off, in case there was another failure to play to the rules. I felt I was on the edge of proving to myself that Gerella and Johann were right, and felt exhilarated that this powerful great cat was interested only in whether he was threatened or not. I felt as if I would burst out laughing at him; tell him what a helluva fright he had given me, and I him: a happy exultant feeling. He turned and strode away up the slope of the hill to the north, where he once again roared, not a long angry roar, but a short puzzled one that seemed to come down his nose. Thereafter he disappeared silently, leaving me delighted with our brief and close acquaintance, embarrassing as it was before parting so promptly, but without a quarrel. After another ten minutes I moved into the estate forest, following the pig rootings without much attempt to do so stealthily, thinking his majesty's roar would have sent all sensible pig and deer at quiet speed as far away as possible in the opposite direction. I stopped, hearing a kind of deep crooning from low down ahead. I stooped to peer into the dark undergrowth, and at that moment three Kalij pheasants erupted into flight with a strange cry, making me jump with surprise. There followed a crashing stampede of what sounded like a large sounder of wild pig, which taught me never to misread the signs and sounds of the forest, but to develop patience enough to wait for hidden and silent creatures to begin moving again when there is no more dubious sound. The most inanimate scene could, if one had patience enough, turn out to be full of potential movement, leading the hungry hunter on to sustenance, be he a powerful moving shadow, or a motionless and invisible python. It was Johann who put it well in his Sadani: if you want to kill something good to eat in the forest, or just to find and watch the wild creatures, you must learn to become like one of them: silent, careful, watchful, and as patient as a python. One very pleasant effect of the close encounter was that after one bad dream in which I found the rifle would not fire, and the dancing tiger swung closer with his cruel claws, a few nights later I had a happy and humorous dream of the tree-scratching episode; it happened several times thereafter over the rest of the year, and like other perhaps symbolic dreams always left me with a feeling of deep and confident happiness.

Shortly after this episode I managed to win West's approval to let me have my annual fortnight's leave. When I told him I wanted to explore the east bank of the Subansiri, possibly with a Miri guide, he tried to dissuade me, saying I needed a proper holiday: somewhere like Shillong. In the end I won, and he said I could take one week first, and another week later, this because he was going on local leave with his wife, to stay with planter friends on the South Bank. He would take me to Bogahilonia on his next weekly visit, and bring me back the week after that, which was his last visit before going on holiday. I thought it was wise to accept this arrangement, and West confirmed this when he said he didn't want to leave Horsey on his own. I sent a letter by our estate *dakwalla* (postman), asking him to see it was given to his counterpart from Bogahilonia, for the Jonson *sahib*. I asked him kindly to arrange a Miri *shikari* who could give me advice on the Bergua river, the first tributary joining the Subansiri from the east after leaving the gorge. I had seen it from the air, and noted the many tracks of elephant, gaur, and smaller animals of several kinds. I said I would spend three days on my own exploring as far as time allowed, and thereafter cross to the Dulung, further down on the western side, in the hope of seeing gaur, sambar, and who knows what else.

There is no doubt that many human beings, mainly young males, tend to become addicted to the adrenaline produced in their own bodies by what the air force humorously called 'dicing with death', which in the piping days of peace leads them to dangerous sports in which there is always a high chance of a thrill, strongly laced with fear; the after effects were always good. My wanderings and explorations were seldom undertaken purely for such a reason, as there was so much to learn of all kinds: birds, animals, insects, snakes, strange tracks, and very often simply strange noises, some of which were still unknown to people like Rondey, and took me several years to solve. There were occasionally times when I would become depressed and frustrated when Horsey, lacking in field knowledge and experience, left things to me to organise, which I did on the basis of what I had learned from MacFortune, Foyle and Telford. Too often West would find something was not being done in his way, and would alter things either himself, or make Horsey alter them. It was obvious he would never order me to change things, as I knew he was meticulous in using the proper chain of command. From the *sirdars*, who seemed to understand, I learned Vallance suffered a lot from West changing things without doing it through him, often explaining it was because he couldn't find him soon enough. I found it hard on the labour, for whom it was a waste of their time, yet were surprisingly tolerant, accepting the strange whims of a *sahib* they had known for many years. After one of these annoying instances, not long after the adrenaline seemed to have cleared the windscreen of my morale, I found no amount of recollection of the series of tiger incidents lulled me to happy sleep. Eventually, one evening when the moon was nearly full, and visibility was extraordinarily clear, either the moonlight or my state of mind convinced me on such a night as this I would not sleep easily. The nightjars were jugging like ghostly spirits, and in the distance I could hear the bewitching call of the barking deer, being passed along the forested Himalayan mountains. It was otherwise a silent night except for the wind, and when it was ten-thirty p.m., I set off in shorts, canvas shoes, and a woollen pullover, with a sharp Gurkha kukri, and rode my bicycle up the long slope to the estate. I aimed for the view from the north-eastern corner, wondering if I would see either elephants or gaur 100 feet below in the feeding glade. When 200 yards from the vantage point I heard a loud crack, and dismounted. I was warm from my exertion on the bicycle, breathing heavily, and waited for another crack. It soon came, but instead of coming from down below the plateau, it came from somewhere north, and I swung to scan the level stretch of tea to the north-west. I was thrilled to see there were seven elephants, one with gleaming, thick white tusks, and one young one, half the size of the others, feeding in the tea on the lower branches of the many shade trees (albizzia chinensis or stipulata). I found it hard to believe they hadn't seen or heard me, but realised the wind was blowing from them to me. They seemed almost luminous in the moonlight, and I surmised they had wallowed in the pale mud I had heard of, now dry and ghostly on their huge bodies. They were about 150 yards from me. Remembering West having said they were a damned nuisance the way they damaged the trees, I thought I should warn them off, and clattered the kukri against the crossbar of the cycle for a few seconds, watching them. There was a small, sibilant suggestion of a trumpet, and the elephants looked as if someone had opened a valve and let air out of them. Almost as if commanded they swung about, and like silver balloons they moved, with no sound I could hear, to the northern edge of the tea. I heard a very low-pitched rumble, and they moved east in close line astern until they came to a game track in the forest's edge, and disappeared with dignity and silence. I had a very wistful feeling they had disappeared too soon, and rebuked myself for not waiting a while before disturbing them. Having looked from the vantage point and found nothing, I rode through the tea up to the other end, the tiger end. From there I could see Venus in the west, over the forested ridge beyond the Daflanoi. The wind rustled the trees high up, and there was no other noise except some small insect which seemed to say 'Up the navy!' time after time. In one of those strange fits of self-challenge which come to lone young males, I made up my mind I would walk, carefully and not too quietly but fairly fast, summoning up the adrenaline, along the boundary, through the tall forest and down to the Mirijuli river. I left the cycle against the wire fencing, took the kukri, and set off. The moonlight was very bright, the shadows inky black, so black I found it difficult to tread carefully over the various gnarled roots on the annually cut boundary track. I passed the tiger's tree quite confident there was not the slightest risk of him being around here in the dark; but a combination of adrenaline and subliminal wisdom from that mysterious and protective core of the brain accelerated my pulse. I froze at the sight of a pale form crouched in a patch of moonlight ahead, and after a few minutes realised it was a new termite castle. I imagined hearing odd noises, heard an owl call eerily, and began to feel it was a ridiculous thing I had done. I had enough adrenaline to keep me awake all night, simply by being afraid of what I couldn't see. A sudden swish of foliage in the treetops, and a fleeting glimpse of a huge, silent-winged creature gave me an uncanny thrill: an eagle owl, as I later found in my book. At last I saw at the end of the slope downwards the gleam of the white sand and boulders of the river bed. The streamlets trickled pleasantly in a friendly way as I walked on to the sand. The moonlit landscape was wonderful, almost like a snow scene, and I moved into the shadow of the bank to sit in obscurity on a tree root and enjoy the impulsive desire simply to watch, and listen, for whatever the moonlight would bring forth. After about fifteen minutes I congratulated myself on having done what I had dared, but made up my mind not to go back for my bicycle, the way I had come. I chose the long walk back, down the river and round to my bungalow. I would have to rise at four-thirty to walk all the way to bring my cycle back. In the moonlight my watch showed it was nearly half-past midnight. I walked with long strides along the river bed, putting a red-wattled lapwing to wing with its silly call of 'did 'e do it!' repeated several times until he winged over the bank into the scrub. Several pintail snipe rose petching when I began walking on the bank after the trees ended. After half a mile I heard the faint sound of strange, distant music. As I drew nearer, walking on the flat grassy ground below the terraced rice fields I made out what sounded like elfin music, on a scale reminiscent of pan pipes, or bagpipes. In the moonlight it was the only sound of life in the area where people were indoors, well battened against the lurking man-eater. Ahead I could see the faint glint of a fire, near the cluster of huts where our Koyas lived. There was something like the hypnotic notes of the snake charmer in the music, but with more attractive melodies, hinting at tiny lightfooted dancers in some moonlit glade, like swirls of dead leaves in the wind. A hundred yards away from the Koyas' fire I stood against the trunk of a large mango tree, entranced by the bewitching sounds. Sitting with blankets over their shoulders before their rosy glow were three Koyas with their backs to me; one playing a large bamboo flute, and the other two playing fiddles. They seemed totally involved, and reluctantly I moved away, listening on to a music which in the way of Mozart and Chopin sent one's spirit questing memories or dreams of wonderful times long ages ago. It made me feel wistfully lonely, missing something or someone I had never met, and I thought this was close to a religious feeling, or some kind of spell woven by this trio of primeval hunters. I was quite weary when I climbed up from the river to the bungalow, and heard the snores of my night watchman coming from the gardeners' store room on the ground floor. I was glad he was well protected by his noise and stout doors from the man-eater, wherever he might be. I slept deeply and rolled out of bed at four-twenty, early enough to stride off the two miles to where I had left my cycle without attracting attention in the dark. I rode back to organise a cup of tea before going to the office, and spent the rest of the day in smug satisfaction that the nocturnal peregrinations of a damfool were my own secret. When eventually I returned to breakfast, Nakul the cook appeared after sending in my chupattis and fried eggs (small, yolks almost vermilion, with a delicious flavour), and he said with his odd grin that I had been seen coming down the Mirijuli without my *bundook* (rifle or gun) in the moonlight; and the polish boy said the cycle was very wet when he cleaned it whilst I was in the office. It was a kind of accusation, but I was happy to think no-one would have followed me along the forest boundary, and no-one, including myself, would be able to fathom why on earth I had done such a thing. I felt better for having done it.

The following night I had a vivid dream of being stalked by a tiger, and awoke in a sweat some time after midnight. I put a towel round my waist, took my rifle down from its place above the mantelpiece, loaded it, and went downstairs in my bare feet, wondering if I was awake or sleepwalking. I heard a loud whinny from Rani, and moved across the lawn to the bamboo bridge across the deep nullah, making comforting noises until I reached her. She was in a state of fright, very tense, with a sweat on her neck in spite of the cold breeze. She kept swinging her head with ears pricked up the river, and after another ten minutes I thought she was calm enough for me to return to bed. After office in the morning I went to the bungalow for breakfast, and was beckoned by Nakul who stood on the bamboo bridge. When I went over he pointed into the soft bottom of the nullah. There, very clearly, were the deep prints of the rangy old man-eater, with the dropped dew claw on one paw. Over breakfast I thought seriously: I needed to be more careful, in every way.

Chapter XXI

It took me a longer time on Mirijuli to come to know the people as well as on Medeloabam, and it was possibly a lot to do with the very early start in the morning, with everyone going to work long before the office opened. I think it was also a lot to do with most of the labour force being very much involved in their own separate tribal disciplines, living in distinct groups of houses in exclusive areas. There was a smaller nucleus of settled workers, who were happy to mix with others of various tribes in the area between the hospital and the factory. Whereas the Christian Mundas and Oraons tended, not always but often, to take their moral affairs to the missionary priests who ran the Salesian mission church on the road to North Lakhimpur, the tribal community regarded it as a point of honour to deal with transgressions of and within their own people according to tribal custom. Only on rare occasions where misdemeanours overlapped with other tribes, or pertained to such things as land disputes, would matters be raised by appeal for settlement by management. There were far fewer elopements or premarital misdemeanours amongst the tribal people, including the Christians and, as I was to discover, there were very serious measures taken in cases of marital infidelity, the severity varying depending on the tribe. Most of the tribal people seemed to be remarkably loyal to each other, and strongly bound to their tribal systems, and it was clear that although the most important rules on marriage were closely similar, other moral laws tended to vary slightly from tribe to tribe. As far as I could understand from speaking to them about their customs and rules, they were emphatic that their moral laws were evolved by their own tribe, with the aim of saving themselves from suffering; forestalling violence from jealousy, envy and uncontrolled lust; protecting women and children from abandonment through irresponsible infidelity; avoiding disease; and preservation of the sources of their sustenance in their remote and ancient habitat. If those who have been able to study such subjects in this present age feel inclined to despise or denounce the woolly preoccupations of a damfool in his own wonderland, it has to be said it took time in that wonderland, so far from the bookshops where works of people like Verrier Elwin and Fuhrer von Haimendorf could be bought, for damfools to discover such treasures. I spent a great deal of time trying to understand how these people managed to regulate their lives and communities so remarkably well, in contrast to other castes and communities in India which had been drawn into systems of morals said either to have been revealed by divinities, or imposed by conquerors interested in subjugation of their captive peoples. There was already no doubt in my mind that the nearer one approached to highly populated areas, the more one came across crime and social misbehaviour. The tribals I met had no priests, only elders who handed on the forms of ceremonies and the ancient wisdom from a past which – who knows? – reached back into the early dawn of human intelligence. There is no doubt they were superstitious folk, but hardly more than some of the country folk in Britain and Europe, and probably less than contemporary mariners and aviators in the 1940s.

I noticed the women and girls were not at all prudish on the North Bank, and although they observed graceful modesty, they were neither ashamed nor self-conscious about displaying their breasts whilst bathing in the river. The Koya women, although not in the upper standards of beauty, like several of the other tribes, never covered their breasts in their home lands, and had to learn to cover them whilst in Assam, where prudery and perhaps excessive male voyeurism prevailed. They were delightful in their charm, gentleness, and humour. Their Hindustani and Sadani were poor, but they spoke their own language like cooing doves, and could laugh until tears came. The Koyas particularly had their own names for most birds, in which they had a 'consuming' interest. When I asked them to tell me about a bird I hadn't seen before, they would first describe how much oil it contained, then give details of the colour, male and female, and fitted the bird calls to sayings in their own language. The black-headed golden oriole, a splendid bird with a scarlet beak and brilliant yellow body, had a melodious yodelling song, and a delightful habit in springtime of chasing each other, swooping, diving and calling in small clusters of trees, never shy of people. The Koyas' traditional words to fit their call amount to 'I can see your "pudeh"'; this last word meaning pudenda, which seems an intriguing connection with Latin for a language relatively strange amongst thousands of tongues in India. The Parja language was vaguely similar to the Koyas; and the Koya language, spoken with intonation and expression very similar to Italian, was quite remote from the Sanskrit derived tongues, except for fairly clear cases of borrowing. Their first five numerals came from the South Indian Telegu, and the remainder from Hindustani, using for numbers beyond the teens a system similar to the old English, of such as three score years and ten. It was interesting to find Koyari having two verbs where most other languages have one: one for to go, and another for not to go; and so on for most of the verbs I managed to learn. The only other of the few languages I tried to learn which had this system was Assamese which, despite its close similarity to Bengali, had many separate negative verbs of a given action which were quite different from the positive.

Late one night in spring, the factory watchmen had taken refuge in the higher levels of the leaf withering sheds from a brazen intrusion by the shabby man-eater, under the electric lights between the factory buildings where he walked blatantly unafraid for several minutes. I was summoned, and went with my rifle, torch attached, to investigate, drawing a complete blank. After returning to my bungalow I prepared to go to bed but was disturbed by another call. It was a young Koya in distress. I dressed and went down to hear him. He wanted protection, but would not tell me why. My night watchman was asleep, his snores just audible, and we spoke quietly in Koyari with reasonable understanding. He would not respond to my questioning as to why he needed protection, but eventually he told me how during the time of the Vallance *sahib* one Pande Arma had disappeared, completely. The manager reported it to the police who came and interrogated the Koyas, without any kind of success; Arma had simply disappeared. He told me he knew what had happened, and there seemed to be an implication such might happen to him. The wife of one of the more senior Koyas was very attractive, and after several years she had still not produced a child. Arma, being a bachelor of about twenty, was suspected of playing sick too often, and of meeting the good-looking woman secretly once or twice. One Koya was detailed to return unnoticed from the road to work, to conceal himself and follow Arma if he moved. It was thus established the two were committing adultery, and plans were made to deal with Arma. Strangely, a final proof was considered necessary, and one night when all the Koya men were said to be out hunting pig in the moonlight, Arma was at home, having been 'sick' that day. The woman, under serious instruction from her husband who had left with the others, placed a hurricane lamp outside her house door, and called for Arma, whose house was not far away. When he appeared she told him he should come quickly, before the others returned. Arma went, and as he entered the light of the lamp about twenty arrows were fired into him from twelve to twenty feet. He died immediately. His body was wrapped in a cloth and taken into the forest by a route which would show no tracks, and left where it would never be found. They returned silently and invisibly in the way of born hunters; nobody except the Koyas knew what had been done or how it was done; Arma had simply disappeared. We stood in the dark shadow below the bungalow, avoiding the single light bulb which remained on at night, taking care we would not be seen talking. I felt a cold prickle run up my spine, and realised Poyami Bima, silhouetted against the light cast on the ground behind him, was trembling with the fear of a similar fate. I asked if he had his belongings, money, and any idea where he would be able to take refuge. He had nothing except his bow and three arrows. He said if he could find a rope he would hang himself; he could never live as a Koya any more. I said he should go to the police for protection and he laughed with a bitter gasp, saying that would not work. In desperation I said I would give him fifty rupees. With it he should take a bus to Tezpur, and there have his head shaved, so that he could not be recognised as a Koya. He should throw away his bow and arrows, then find work on a tea estate somewhere down beyond Tezpur where there were no Koyas, start a new life. He was convinced he was under sentence of death, and the only way he could save himself was to report to the police what had happened to Arma; but this would lead to severe action of the police against the Mirijuli Koyas, his tribal brothers; the police would find out from the others that he had shot one of the arrows which killed Arma, and a score of them would be hung. I told him to wait whilst I brought the money, and went upstairs. When I came down he had gone, and no more was ever heard of him. Questioning the Koyas produced nothing, neither innocent amazement nor furtive denial. The estate *sirdars* were as ignorant as I was as to what had happened to Poyami Bima, and Harriya, one of the older, settled *sirdars*, said if the Koyas didn't know what had happened to one of their own, nobody had a hope of knowing. It was to be some years before I acquired some anthropological books on tribals, and came across not only special studies of the high rate of suicide amongst Murias and Marias, the tribal groups to which the Koyas belonged, but had actual suicides amongst Koyas who worked for me, mainly resulting from cases of infidelity, perhaps exacerbated by abnormal drinking.

There was a striking case of a misdemeanour amongst Catholic Oraons which was brought to the Mirijuli office for settlement. It concerned a girl whose Christian name was Hanna, but 'paybook' name was Bara Mangri. This latter kind of name was used by immigrant labour from tribal areas in order to shelter their real names from curses by people of evil or jealous intent, and was very common. Let us use the name which gives her anonymity: Hanna. Vallance had proudly showed me the top beauties of the labour force, of which Hanna was one of the best. Compared with Medeloabam the Mirijuli women and girls were mostly far below in standards of beautiful appearance; but although they were generally smaller, perhaps leaner, they had more natural humour, and their tribal dress gave them a special and admirable appearance which was less sexually charged than what I had seen on the South Bank. There were Hindu Bilaspuria Gonds here who had a similar humour to those at Medeloabam, full of innuendo and Rabelasian rawness; but the other tribals had a refreshing style of treating sexual matters as part of life just as food, hunting, fishing, work and so on were treated, with no smutty humour and no mockery. They would nickname people by their physical characteristics such as 'Lame', 'Pale', 'Crouchback', 'One-eye' and so on, without any suggestion of derogation or taunt. Hanna was slim, well built, with a skin colour of tan with the glow of red blood below it. Her nose was slightly flat with mobile nostrils which, working with her extraordinary eyes, combined with minimal movement to produce expressions of which any leading actress would be proud. Her dark brown eyes, although heavily lidded, were large enough to show the pupils fully, giving her a bright smile, further enhanced by splendid teeth. Her lips were well cut, and she enjoyed protruding her lower lip after giving greeting. The Christians over here took a delight whenever an assistant or manager came near them early in the day, going in knots to shake hands and say 'Jai Jesu' (more or less like 'Greet Jesus'); and when Hanna did this to me with her sparkling smile it made me just a little dizzy. Her hair was drawn back and plaited behind her neck, and then wound into a chignon, neatly pinned. She must have been about seventeen or eighteen. Vallance said she sometimes behaved like a leopard, with eyes flashing and lips writhing, arguing with someone over something like being too proud to marry until some rich man came along with lots of gold bangles for her. Round about Fagua Puja she

157

was married in the Salesian mission to one Birsha (another 'paybook' name), a good-looking Catholic youth of about twenty. He had some education, and worked in the factory, mainly on stencilling the tea chests with information in English, and serial numbers correctly given to each one. It was a responsible job, and he would also paint lorries, signposts, and room designations at the hospital. His only fault was in being 'meek and mild' to an excessive degree, although he was well built and said to be a good hockey player. To me he always spoke painstakingly in the Hindi taught by the mission school, embarrassing me because it was a manner of speech used very little in Assam in those days. They were given a house in the Christian area, and it seemed we would now wait to see how soon she became pregnant. They had been married little more than a month when there was serious trouble. Birsha arrived at the office one afternoon when West, Horsey and I were discussing weather possibilities and fertiliser application. He was obviously in a very disturbed state, and had a sad tale to tell. It took a long time before we were able to understand what had happened. His story was that after the first couple of weeks his wife refused to allow him to lie with her. Early that day, before the sun rose, he asserted himself, and insisted she cooperated in conjugation. She screamed at him, insulted him with bad names, and many people making ready for work came out of their houses and went to see what the distressing noise was about. A woman went to the door of their house and called to them to come out and talk about their trouble, whereupon Hanna came out backwards, bare to the waist, pulling the unfortunate Birsha by a tight and obviously painful grip on his genitals. She dragged him around amongst the shocked people for several minutes, jeering at him, denouncing him, and calling him unmentionable names, paying no attention to anyone's remonstrances. His morale was extremely low, and for the devout Christian that he was it must have been a terrible trial for him. He said it was a matter of great sin (*Bara paap ka bat*), and she had returned to her parents' house, refusing to have anything more to do with him. The *sirdars* and *chowkidars*, and the inevitable gathering of curious bystanders, showed by their mixture of counterfeited concern and ill-concealed smirks that despite being amazed at the violent assault by one of the bonny darlings of the estate on her new husband, they found little sympathy for Birsha, who had obviously bungled his great privilege of marriage to one of the choicest and most vivacious beauties of Mirijuli and its surrounds. West said to us he was mystified as to whether the girl was frightened at the thought of the loss of her virginity, or he was hopelessly incompetent in making married love as enjoyable as it ought to be; but he said he didn't want to question him in front of all these people. Eventually he told the bystanders to go home, and sent the *sirdars* off. He told the *chowkidars* to tell Hanna she must come to the office at seven-thirty tomorrow morning, to explain the reason for the shameful behaviour. One of the Oraon *chowkidars* said Birsha had told her to come with him to the office for a settlement of their problem, but she refused, and went to work. West said if she didn't come tomorrow her work would be stopped until she did come; and turning to me he said I should make sure tomorrow when I went up to see the work starting that she wasn't allowed to take up work, until she appeared at the office to explain her conduct. When everyone had gone he said whatever we found out he felt strongly, remembering the marriage was a Catholic one, he would in the end have to tell Birsha to be a man and dam' well go to it and make his marriage work properly.

Next morning I went to the area where the Oraon women were plucking, and noticed straight away they were all silent, intent on plucking, a few yards into the tea. I saw Hanna well ahead of the others, arms moving quickly as she plucked in the style of an expert. I called the Oraon *sirdar*, a grizzled non-Christian called Etowa, and asked why Hanna had been given work in spite of the Supritan *sahib*'s orders (Superintendent). He said, '*Sahib*, Hanna is very irascible these days; won't listen to anyone.' I called Hanna to come out, and she turned to face me, eyes wide open and brows down. The sun was rising over the eastern hills, and the reflected light from the pale green tea foliage softened the shadows of her face, giving her a dramatic appearance. She thrust her way out and came to me with eyes sparkling and hand held forward. I had to remember my duty and my dignity, and cast away the wayward admiration of beauty and spirit as well as the colloquial Sadani tongue.

'How can I take the hand which has committed such a shameful act? Tell me!' She took a step forward, holding her left hand out sideways, eyes still sparkling with a fierce and challenging smile.

'This was the hand for such things, not the hand I offer.' We shook right hands and exchanged the 'Jai Jesu' greeting; but I wrenched myself back to the position of disapproving authority, beginning to be aware not only were the usually ebullient and vocal Oraon women silent, but they were coming out of the tea to place themselves behind Hanna, who now stood regarding me with her chin up and her lower lip protruding through her smile, not so much in defiance as in an appeal for sympathy. I told her she was to appear at the office to explain why she had performed a disgraceful act. Her husband had come without her, which was no way to achieve a settlement. She broke in to say the husband must tell what led to the disgraceful act, for he was to blame.

'I did my best. I was patient. I gave him every chance, I helped him. I did what I did to force him to admit what is not for me to tell.' At this the Oraon women burst into a babble of passionate explaining, so mixed up and garbled that I raised my hands, motioning them to be quiet. One of the older Oraon women stepped forward and spoke quietly, waving one finger as she spoke, looking from me to Hanna and back.

'*Sahib*, she can't tell you this shameful and unhappy thing. What is a beautiful girl like this to do when she finds she is married to a man,' her voice rose in emphasis, 'who copulates like a bird?' The women's voices rose in shrill support for the awful truth now told, all of them with marked conviction and strength of feeling. It struck me this poor man Birsha suffered for some reason from a distressing over-sensitivity which was a bad enough discovery, but surely didn't deserve such degradation as he suffered in addition to his handicap. A sudden wave of doubt swirled over me, an ignorant and inexperienced damfool – there but for the grace of God...! I felt my blood rise and put up my hand.

'I understand it is a big problem in a marriage, but the man has enough to bear with that, and the loss of his wife's affections, without the disgraceful public shame inflicted on him by this girl.' Hanna glared at me fiercely, and looked as if tears would break through the wild mask; and the women raised their voices again, in Oraon and Sadani. I raised my voice in loud denunciation. 'If any woman had ever done that sort of thing to me I would have chopped her hand off; do you hear me? A good woman could have dealt with her blameless husband with kind words; sent him away and left him to live with his burden without unfair shame shouted to the world.' That produced silence, and Etowa *sirdar* came forward, his wrinkled features serious and one hand held up.

'*Sahib*, you are also a Christian. Please forgive me for what I say. We Oraons who are not Christians always make sure our youths and girls who are betrothed to be married sleep with each other until the girl becomes pregnant; we make sure they are suited to each other before they marry,

160

because then we know they will be loyal to each other forever. Christians have a different way. Now look at this girl! She can't change her husband, and...' His speech was drowned by impassioned arguments between the Christian and non-Christian women, and making half-hearted gestures of restraint I only succeeded in reducing the number of speakers until one Christian lady and one non-Christian lady held the attention of us all. For me it was a most enlightening discussion, such as would never be heard in the west except in some kind of very modern marriage guidance clinic, if such things existed at that time. The non-Christian lady spoke with impressive frankness, saying many young men had to learn not to behave like a cock, or a bull, but to use their brains, and carry on soon a second time when it takes longer, long enough for his woman's lightning strike. One pretty young woman, a Christian, started everyone laughing by saying she had three children before the lightning struck her, and she advised Hanna to be patient because everything would come right. Hanna, who had been staring miserably at the ground, lifted her chin at the laughter and said she knew all about that; she had tried and tried to start him again but he just couldn't for nearly a week, and then – just like a bird again. There was much sympathetic and expert advice given in terms which to me were so deep into the arts of erotic love that I felt myself getting out of my depth, as well as feeling cracks beginning to appear in my post-Medeloabam resolute defences. I will never forget the obvious feeling and sincere encouragement which was given by older women, long past the bloom of youth, praising the beautiful parts of marriage, and despite the strains of producing seven or eight children, proud of their lives and loves; and this from Christians and non-Christians alike. One jovial, silver-haired lady, with several teeth missing, said most men drank too much rice beer now and then but, as if she knew Shakespeare's *Macbeth*, recommended the increase of desire and, what Hanna should learn, the much longer delay of the man's final satisfaction after a few *chungis* (bamboo mugs) of *hariya* (rice beer). At that point I said everyone should get back to work before I got into trouble for delaying them. I told Hanna I would tell the Supritan *sahib* she would be at the office after work, and I would tell him what the problem actually was. That afternoon, following my report on what had transpired and what the problems were, West spoke to Hanna and Birsha in a very subdued and kindly way, and told them to go to the mission to discuss their troubles with the padre *sahibs*. Hanna never rejoined Birsha, and her parents repaid Birsha the bride price he had given before the marriage. Within eighteen months, Hanna not having conceived from her marriage, was said to have married a non-Christian Oraon who ran his own small-holding in a village near Bankukurajan. That incident made me humble and ashamed of my ignorance and incompetence in matters more important than all the education I had ever had; but I consoled myself that I was beginning to learn, for my own good.

My week at the Subansiri was a very impressive experience. MacDonald was by now at Medeloabam; Jonson was on home leave, and his acting manager was an ex-air force officer who had been in tea for a few years before the war: John Morse, who had his English wife with him at Bogahilonia. He kindly sent me in one of his lorries which needed to collect stone and sand, which dropped me off at Dulung Mukh. He invited me to call in for a meal in a week's time, warning me their two children made as much noise as a pack of hounds. I had a pack with food, kettle, powdered milk, a throwing net needing stones as weights, camera and rifle. I took a diary and a pencil, ready to record what animals and birds I saw, and any interesting experience. Morse told me to watch for a Miri boat which would come out of the islands which lay before the gorge, in which would be the Miri guide I sought. I walked north along the west bank of the Subansiri, keeping to the sandy shore below the forest. It was about nine a.m., and opposite the southern end of the first island I took off my pack and sat in the brilliant sunshine, waiting for the Miri dugout canoe. These beautiful islands I had admired from the air, and seen from the Dulung: tall with forest giants, and standing in the maze of four or five streams into which the main river divided after leaving the gorge. Where I sat I saw several tracks parallel to the river, some of a very large tiger, fairly new tracks of gaur (Indian bison) probably made about sunrise, and many tracks from the forest straight out to the water and back, of various deer, wild pig, and one of a large elephant which led into the water but not back again.

After about half an hour I saw the dugout appear, moving downstream at speed from between the nearest two islands, two people standing with long oars which they used as oars in deep water, and as poles in the shallows. A third person was crouching amidships. All three waved, and it seemed to me those with the oars were women. They rounded the south of the near island, and began to move northwards on its shore shallows. Seeing this I hoisted my pack and began to move upriver, but the midships figure raised both arms at me, signing I should stay where I was. The near stream was easily 300 yards wide, running fast in the middle where the water was deep. They went up about 400 yards before suddenly thrusting vigorously with the oars on a course aiming forty-five degrees across the current. They held way for about fifty yards before the deep water began to carry them downstream. The energy of the women was impressive, in fact as they drew nearer I saw they were damsels – a name they seemed to justify from a romantic and admiring witness – broad and bare-shouldered, with their calf-length homespun cloth wound from their armpits round and round, and tucked in at their waists. Reaching the slower shallows after losing about 300 yards from where they had begun to cross, they carefully drifted down until they beached below where I was waiting. The third person was a mature woman, who waded on to the beach, smiling broadly. The two damsels, apparently no worse for their exertions, greeted me with broad, whitetoothed smiles and laughter. Our Assamese was more or less well-matched, and I was told Paniram Miri was expecting me, but had not returned from Baligaon whither he had gone yesterday to meet some friends. I was to embark, and they would take me across four streams to their village where Paniram should be arriving any minute. The girls were delighted to examine my blond hair and blue eyes; they asked if I was married, and shrieked with laughter when I said I had not yet found a girl beautiful enough. They all questioned me about being the *sahib* who came in the aeroplane, and who had come through the forest from the Jiya Dhol last year. Their own language was described by experts as being one of the Sino-Tibetan tongues, and it sounded like it. I asked what they ate, and they said mostly fish and their own wholemeal rice. The trip in the boat was idyllic. The next stream was easier to cross being slower, and when we rounded the top end of the second island I pointed with excitement at a portly Himalayan bear, not fifty yards away from us, standing peacefully, watching us drift by. The girls shrieked with mirth, and began singing together a chorus with trills, dissolving into laughter. The black bear stood once, displaying his white crescent on his chest, and went slowly on all fours up the boulders into the forest. My camera was tucked away in my pack, and the gunwale was about three inches above water. The mature woman was well built but lean; the girls were in magnificent condition, with the powerful beauty of bloom, that has more strength than all the ancient and modern cosmetic sophistication in the world. They were indeed strongly attractive, bubbling with marvellous good humour. When we arrived at their village, which was built on piles in a crescent glade under the tall forest, the whole population of women and children, and a few old men, came to the water's edge to wave greeting and examine the pale stranger who could fly in the air like an eagle.

Paniram had not returned; all the men were away, fishing, looking for turtles' eggs, examining their fishing traps, hacking out new dugout canoes from trees down the river; and there was no sign of Paniram on the two miles of river downstream which one could see. I was invited to sit on a deerskin under a tree with the old men, one of whom could speak Assamese. A woman brought some rice beer with brass bowls. It was something I had never tasted, but I thought I should honour their hospitality, and took about a teacupful whilst talking to the men. They were very interested in my Mauser rifle, which I handed to them to examine. One of them brought an ancient muzzle loading shotgun, the stock and butt of which was of ancient wood like yellow ivory, carved with vaguely Islamic patterns. They were clearly disappointed I had no shotgun cartridges, which they might have been able to empty for their ancient weapon. The old spokesman told me the Miris' real home was in the mountains on the western side of the Subansiri, in the area roughly bounded by the Kamla river on the north, and the high ridge to the south of that river, a small enclave in the territory of the Daflas (in later years known as the Nisei). The hill Miris wore helmets similar to the Daflas, but wore their totem on the frontal peak, which could be a patch of skin from a leopard, a leopard cat, a clouded leopard, a Himalayan bear, or a red tree panda. They never wore tiger fur as the Daflas claimed to be descended from the tiger. The plains Miris lived anywhere on the North Bank of Assam which was miles away from anyone else, preferably where there was fish and game. They kept buffaloes for milk and ploughing, pigs for food and 'hygiene', and had many small watchdogs, some of which were good for hunting. By midday there was no sign of Paniram, of whom I had learned he was an intrepid hunter, and an expert boatman on the rapids and boulder shoals of the Subansiri. I learned a lot of the Bergua river, and told the old men I would have to go off on my own, happy to have learned from them what it was like, and what to look for, and would come back to the gorge, near the mouth of the Bergua, by midday on the third day hence. I said I was not going to shoot, and wanted to be on my own to see animals and birds. They asked why I was taking the rifle, and I said in case I needed to defend myself, at which they said there would be no such need. They said I would have to leave the village along the beach, but further up there would be so

164

much tangle of dead trees, large and small, I would have to go into the forest and follow elephant tracks to return to the river where it would be clear after a few hundred yards. They said when I came back down the Bergua I should wait at the gorge, and a dugout would come to take me over to the west bank and down to the Dulung. I left them, with the women and children watching me move off, and soon came to the tangle of timber. Beyond it the beach was clear all the way. There were no tracks of men; they had told me there were no shallows where one could throw nets for fish, but there were tracks of many animals and birds. I saw a Pallas fishing eagle, a large bird with a white band on its dark tail feathers, and a wild call like a squealing pulley in the rigging of an old ship. I saw an osprey, small by comparison, lungeing talons first into the rapids after fish. Out of the gorge came occasional formations of goosander and smew, and on the beach were sandpipers and sanderlings, concentrating on finding food on the wet sand, not flying ahead until I was within a few feet of them. There were otter tracks and elephant tracks, but no marks of any humans.

I had the feeling I was about to enter the world as it was before Eden, and should remove the cloak of latter day civilised man in the way men removed their hats on entering church. I reached the small sandy delta of the Bergua, where two small streams of crystal water meandered to the last slope of the beach and trickled over shingle and boulders into the Subansiri. The experience of following that small river up through the great forest was impressive and rewarding. The absence of human tracks or signs made me feel I should somehow seek permission, or forgiveness, for trespassing on an ancient sanctuary where men did not belong. The nearest I came to drama was being startled by what sounded like a leopard, high in a tree. I crept quietly, gazing upwards trying to see where it had managed to climb so high, and jumped with shock when a flock of raucous winged white-tailed hornbills launched into flight with shattering noise. Their broad, serrated wings made much more noise than swans as they thrust and climbed before a pause in which they glided for a few seconds before thrashing into a climb again. The rest of those days was sheer pleasure, and would fill a hundred pages without effort; but such nostalgic pleasure, of which there is probably too much in these pages already, must be kept to a minimum as a background which affected such damfools as fell in love with it, and might explain why they went on in the way this one did. The birdlife was fabulous: hill mynahs mimicking other birds and small mammals; birds of strange plumage I had

165

never seen before, and now saw them from close range, marvelling at their tameness and colours. The third time I sat and watched the stacked flocks of birds, I saw my first Sultan tit: a lively and acrobatic bird, mainly black with a cap and crest of brilliant yellow, and a yellow lower abdomen; it was so, so handsome I hoped it would not become so popular it would be kept in the cages of the west. When that swarm of alert and happy birds moved on, I noticed a single bird, larger than all the others, sitting still, tail down. Its breast and belly were rich crimson, its wing primaries leaden grey, and its head was furry, with large, dark eyes, and short, thick bill. The head moved very slowly, scanning from back-left to back-right, each time changing the angle, slightly more down, slightly more up. It gave a rather weird impression, its motionless body suggesting it was a mechanical toy, with artificial clockwork movements of the head. When I moved closer to inspect it in the shadow, it flew off soundlessly. I saw several barking deer and, late on the first evening, a large sambar stag with good antlers. There was a sound which I heard through the day which mystified me, like the moan of a bull or a stag without the rasp or roar; it seemed always to be on a nearby ridge, always high up, a sad, deep sound. Another sound suggested a small goat, with a bleat repeated at intervals late in the evenings; it was to be several years before I discovered what it was, because even the experienced *shikaris* were unable to tell me. That evening I managed to net some small fry in the river which were very tasty when fried in oil. The water was crystal clear, and made good tea. At night the wind made gentle noises in the treetops, and I slept well, waking every two hours or so. Once I heard the horned fishing owl, making a noise like a huge deep-voiced Zulu muttering threats or incantations, an uncanny noise I had learned under Gerella. On the third day, after more fish, chupattis and tea, I reached the gorge to find the elusive Paniram and his friend Jadurai, dugout beached, sitting in the sun, waiting for me. I greeted him and asked what had happened three days ago. He said in the village where he had eaten, a house had burnt down, and as the house was a long one it took a long time to build a new one. Several families would live in one long comparted house of timber piles and pillars, with bamboo-plaster walls and thatched roof. He explained in village Assamese how, when such a thing happened, everyone would immediately combine to collect materials and build a house, not stopping except for meals until it was completed. They took me in the dugout up to the great, rock jaws of the gorge, so steep there was no hope of entering on foot except by ascending for several hundred feet into the steep forest at the side, out of sight of the river. They crossed the river rowing with impressive energy, and gained the shallows on the other side showing little sign of heavy breathing or exertion. As we went Paniram said he could not believe I didn't want to shoot anything, laughing incredulously. He said his people were always happy to have fresh meat as a change from fish, and as I wasn't going to need it I should lend him the rifle and two bullets so that he would be able to kill either a sambar or a boar down the river where there was a swamp where he was sure to find something. I had to say I wasn't allowed to let anyone else use my rifle unless I had the written permission of the Sub-divisional Officer (SDO). He laughed and said the SDO would never know about it; no government people ever came here. I said this time I wanted to explore, see animals and birds; some other time I would go hunting with him, when I knew more about everything. He gave me very good advice on the lie of the land along the Dulung. After a mile or two the forest closed in towards the river, with rising hills and ridges on the north, and flatter, smaller forest with more elephant grass and small marshes on the south. To see animals and birds I should find the Lata Poong, a salt lick up a small, clefted tributary of the Dulung on the north side. He told me how to find this place, and to camp well away from it, so that woodsmoke and the smell of food would not give hints of strange intrusions. I thanked him, and gave them a packet of tea which I was not going to need, which seemed to please them. I asked what I owed them, producing some rupee notes, and Paniram laughed, said he didn't need any money, and didn't want to be thought a thief. I waved as they thrust their vertical oars into the water, aiming upriver again, and watched until they reached the stream between the first islands. Their stamina was admirable, and having tried to propel a smaller dugout solo my admiration was indeed sincere.

By this time I was moving preferably barefoot, not only for silence but for the enjoyment of treading the riverbeds, where stretches of shingle were easily avoided or soon crossed. The tracks were far more than on the Bergua, and were to be seen on the first wide stretch of the Dulung delta in such profusion it made me wonder when, and in what numbers, the animals actually moved. By the time I reached what I took to be the Lata Poong cleft, I had decided on a campsite, and went back to where a great grey tree lay with its buttressed roots rising skywards on one side, the lower roots being buried deep in the sand. There was a sheltered angle between trunk and root, the trunk well sunk into the sand, and I saw plenty of dry firewood lodged against the roots by the Dulung's swift monsoon floods. On the way I had seen the tracks of a giant tiger, and of two other different tigers, one medium and one small, presuming there must be a family territory. For some reason there were no tracks within fifty yards of my tree, and I managed to build a good shelter with enough sweet smelling reed grasses to keep any rain off. The sky was more hazy now, but there was no sign of any kind of heavy cloud. I made some tea and ate some chupattis and tinned Australian cheese. I decided I had to be more positive about the idea of clearing my mind of everything except what I was going to see and hear; I needed to think like a wild creature, perhaps like man before he became civilised and literate: I would absorb what I saw, what I heard, what I smelt, and what I sensed in any other way. I would not use my memory of anything except my present close environment; no tea, no West, no Horsey, no Telford, no aeroplanes, no beautiful girls, no imagining of any kind; I wanted to know how it would work, if it would eventually allow the re-emergence of thought processes which must have helped to sustain man before he began to develop language and literacy. Remembering these ideas, I admire the starry-eyed enthusiasm but cannot recapture how or why they germinated. Hiding my rifle in the roots, I set off with my kukri to make a discreet reconnaissance of the salt lick. There were few tracks in the small stream bed, and between the high sides of the cleft there were many boulders, some over six feet high. At one place I found a strange, continuous track, with long curves, and guessed it was a large snake, perhaps a python. I went slowly, and took about forty-five minutes to come upon the salt lick, where I saw from about twenty yards there were three porcupines, one of them huge, snuffling and licking at the rock and paste at the foot of a tall outcrop. The stream was scarcely five feet wide, shallow and trickling musically. Without moving I noted the rocky ledge at the top of a sloping face opposite and about twenty feet above the lick. I waited about twenty minutes for the porcupines to disappear, which they did upstream, and slowly made my way up through creepers and plants like begonias until I found the way to the warm and fairly comfortable ledge. It must have been around two p.m. when I reached there, and it was five p.m. when I left. In that time I saw half a dozen green Imperial pigeon descend to take their cure: back, wings and tail burnished green with blue and bronze sheens, the head and breast being pale grey-white, with a faint pink blush where the wings joined below the neck; under the tail the vent was a rich

168

blend of magenta and sepia. I saw a red tree panda, with a kittenish head and long ringed tail. A boar and two sows came and wallowed in the sandy mud for fifteen minutes. Returning down the cleft I came upon what I recognised as a python, lying across a narrow part of the stream showing eight feet of itself, but no tail or head visible. It took me time to work out where the head was, but as the beach was fairly clear of trammel I crept slowly up to it, then leapt and ran until the huge boulders slowed me down; I laughed at my small-deer timidity. I made tea and ate again, and collected some good logs for a fire, to be lit about sundown. I wandered round the next bend in the after glow. The sky was luminous pink, and the sand was like mauve icing. I moved slowly and quietly, scanning the expanse of sand which was in places about seventy yards broad. In the gloaming, just as I was about to turn back, I saw ahead of me, silhouetted purple against the pale sand and the misty hill forest, a small herd of gaur, several cows close together and the bull a few yards separate, head up and his horns, reminiscent of an African buffalo, thick and hooked, like threatening weapons. I raised a hand in a kind of slow, friendly salute, and the bull stamped both hind feet powerfully, swinging away, and they all galloped in a long curve from west to south, their hooves making a sound like distant thunder. The bull let the herd enter the forest, turned to look again, then followed into the dark obscurity with hardly a sound. That bull must have stood six feet at his arched shoulder: tremendously powerful, but shy.

The dry logs burned brightly and without smoke. It was difficult as the night deepened to prevent habitual recall whilst exposing oneself to the potent stimulus of a smouldering campfire; but I made it into a challenging mental exercise, staring into the glowing red caverns and flickering blue flames. Venus was becoming bright as the afterglow faded, incredibly bright; and weaving to prevent my mind from embracing memories, I found, although I twisted away from them, Venus was focussing that molten silver light unerringly on whatever generates yearning in a human being. I listened until Venus slipped below the far ridge, heard the soft wind in the treetops, heard a night jar, the barking deer; and pushing the radial logs into the embers to stay red until dawn, I slept deeply. Next morning I found tiger tracks in a wide arc, thirty yards away, round my camp. I felt strangely enlightened, watching the sun rise, and having my chupattis and cheese I concentrated my mind on watching the scene. I made my way to the Lata Poong, and settled in the sun as patient as a heron, listening, watching, and relaxing. That day I saw a monitor lizard; a bear with its half-size cub; a strange bearish creature with short, untidy fur and tattered ears, with a poor but definite small white crescent on its breast (an Assam binturong, as I later discovered); two palm civets, marked vaguely like a Siamese cat, moving like small ballet dancers with their long tails balancing their dainty movements, like giant squirrels.

In the days that followed I saw two female elephants with two-year-old calves. They took the salt and wallowed for some time until suddenly one of the mothers swung away from the wallow, trunk high, questing scent. She uttered a muffled trumpet sound, and all four moved quickly and amazingly quietly, into the forest. Once, hearing a rustle in the creepers on my left, just behind my feet, I slowly moved my head round, and saw a large civet regarding me with its large dark eyes, quite dispassionately and slightly myopically. I heard white-headed laughing thrushes gobbling and screeching several times in unmistakable outrage at some unwelcome intruder, far enough away for me to be sure it was not me, and later saw an old leopard, lean and brown, take a few licks and move wearily away. I saw a large mongoose, suspicious and nervous, which began to ascend towards my hiding place before turning and fleeing, probably scenting me. Concentrating on my aim of keeping my mind free of sophisticated thoughts was difficult, but with practice it began to work, and I found I was often sensing the approach of creatures, without any indication of sound or scent; some other wavelength was beginning to work, but I could not identify how. Eventually I felt as if I was somehow becoming able to anticipate the reactions of wild creatures, and felt the strange trancelike euphoria I had sometimes arrived at when attempting to develop the art of meditation. There was no doubt that after these several days of wilful brainwashing, something extraordinary was happening. I thought I heard a voice say my name: Hamish, and I turned on one elbow, trying to work out what kind of call it could have been; some unusual bird or beast which perhaps my subconscious suggested was my name. It came again. I was unable to locate where it came from: it wasn't below, or above; and what is more, to me it was the voice of Johnny, who had baled out of his burning aircraft four, or was it five, years ago. I had not thought of Johnny since I stayed with Nicky MacFortune, and that was over two years ago. I told myself this was a psychological thing; I had done what Freud used to do by clearing the present from people's minds, to let the subconscious emerge: that was it. I

170

stood with my shirt and kukri in my hand, took a deep breath, and decided I must wake up. I began to smile at having hypnotised myself when, loud and clear, his voice came again, saying my name, now with a note of query in it. I came down the steep face and bounded fast all the way back to the open sands of the Dulung, no longer trying to work out what or why, and only sure I had no desire to enter the mists of anything like spiritualism, communing with the dead, or anything else. There was not only a kind of fear, but a feeling that Johnny's voice was somehow not genuine, as if he had been hypnotised, or suddenly disturbed from a deep sleep. I took tea and food again, killed the fire, and with pack on my back I went as far west as I could in order to explore the upper Dulung, returning to my camp by sunset. I saw a pair of sambar in full sunlight, and came across a monitor lizard nearly six feet long, dead and covered with flies. Its skin was banded with four-inch bands of grey-black and muddy ochre, and I could see no sign of any wound. I reached my campsite by five in the evening, and made tea, kneaded more chupattis, and ate them with handfuls of raisins. I then decided I was going to return to thinking normally, and wrote notes on all I had seen, until the light died. Then I made a good campfire to stimulate my free-ranging cogitations, and sat with my back to Venus with an open mind. My mind spun from one thing to another, first of all thinking of the strange long wait without company at Lata Poong that day. Had I actually been renouncing my human self? I found myself thinking of the similarity of what I had read in Banerjee's *Vivekananda*, what the New Testament said, and the self-renouncing way the Miris seemed to live. Renounce oneself! Self renunciation was evident in the way the tribals lived, but that was in those early years before malaria was eliminated, before the rising tide of population began to flow in Upper Assam. There was much to think of, and I needed to read more. I began to ponder my aim of marriage, and thought of the quiet, patient Mrs West, separated from her children for two or perhaps three years between costly home visits, visiting the club once a week, and having four dinner parties a year out, four at Mirijuli; knitting, embroidering, wandering in her large flower and vegetable garden with her *malis* (gardeners), and looking after her milking cattle. It seemed an unrewarding life for a woman unless, well – unless I was ever to find a girl who would enjoy the wilderness as I did, and lead a full and satisfying life. I counted again: I would be due for six months' fully paid home leave in 1951; a long time to wait.

Chapter XXII

I remembered West arrived at eight-thirty when he delivered me, and told me he would leave at twelve to visit Bor Deorigaon estate, having a picnic lunch on the way. He said I should be on the road at Chauldhoa, where he would come off the Subansiri 'punted' ferry at about four-thirty. Before starting to walk south I had a swim at the pool where the Dulung met the Subansiri, and after drying in the warm sun, set off on foot at eleven towards Bogahilonia. Morse met me on the track not far out of the estate, and took me in his battered pre-war Morris Oxford to his bungalow; West had apparently left at twenty to twelve. Mrs Morse was a merry girl from Lancashire, who all the while tried to discipline her two small hyperactive sons. They kept escaping from their elderly Khasi *ayah* (nanny), and were apt to disappear without trace, which at three and four years old was worrying. The man-eater had not so far visited this area, probably because the territory was ruled by the huge tiger whose tracks I had been seeing up the Dulung. Morse and I talked a lot about the air force and the Middle East. At tiffin his wife said she loved the North Bank, but people in the club warned her it was very different in the rains, and when the rivers flooded as they so often did it would be very difficult for her to visit the store in North Lakhimpur. She was delighted to have the extra fridge, and hoped by next weekend to be able to buy enough extra stores of food to carry her through the worst of the floods. She asked what I had done to be sentenced to the penal settlement over here, and her husband, albeit with a ham imitation of a curmudgeon, told her one did not ask that kind of thing, especially of young bachelors. I told them of my offer in 1947 to swap with MacDonald, who doubted if this would be a good place to start a happy married life, and how this surfaced on my file two years later when I was posted here. Morse said MacDonald had told him I was said to be posted because I was the company pilot, and the company wanted me to fly from Mirijuli. To this I had to say I was never told they wanted me to fly from the North Bank. Mrs Morse said in a conspiratorial tone that it looked as if MacDonald was likely to be engaged to Jock Gordon's daughter soon. Morse, seeing my raised brow, said she was a tall, good-looking blonde girl, who came out last cold weather and was obviously intercepted by Mac. I remembered seeing her, and admired Mac's choice and initiative; I thought he was at least two years older than me. Morse reverted to what 'one didn't ask', and said he had run into trouble with his manager, an ex-non-commissioned officer in the army during the first war. Morse, who was clearly a meticulous man, had found suspicious transactions in the accounts, and had composed a letter to the head clerk asking for his explanation of several irregularities in connection with contract labour and purchases of paddy. He handed this to his very senior manager, a tall portly man with a beer-belly, who apparently never rode a horse but attended morning office in riding breeches and highly polished boots, with spurs! In tea estate offices there were no confidential secretaries; one had to type such letters oneself, borrowing one of the office's ancient typewriters. To borrow a typewriter was to hoist a red flag at the office which everyone could see, and the head clerk having been cross-examined by Morse was ready for action. When Morse presented his letter to Leary at morning office, his manager lit a Dutch cigar, grinning with eyebrows down like a poker player about to show four aces.

'Good at this sort of thing, eh? Learn it in the airworks?' Morse described his diction as polished cockney. 'Head clerk! We'll see what he has to say for himself, eh?' The head clerk came in looking down his nose at the letter, knowing what Morse would have written after their unhappy session of inquiry. 'Head clerk, you have been working for the company for twenty-five years, eh? You have never made a mistake in the accounts in the twelve years you have worked for me, have you? Right! You know well I am a very strict man? You know if you are ever found guilty of fiddling the accounts, or letting others fiddle the accounts, that I will give you the sack. Eh?' The head clerk looked at him with an appealing expression of wounded pride, confirming his understanding, upon which Leary picked up the letter, tore it into pieces, and handed it to Morse, telling the head clerk to get back to work, and to be careful. He told Morse to leave these things to him; he knew these people through and through. 'As long as they are loyal, you can trust them completely. If they think you don't trust them you can expect trouble, big trouble.' When Morse protested, in low tones which would not carry to the main office, that here was a clear case of corruption, and enough evidence for dismissal, Leary stood and told Morse to go with him out of the office. Once away from hearing range Leary told Morse he didn't want him poking his nose into the monthly accounts and upsetting the staff. 'You've been here for eighteen months, only your second billet in tea. You know next to nothing, understand? Get it straight or I'll have you posted, somewhere you might not like. Get it?' To his great credit Morse said he would, in view of what had just happened, like to be posted, by personal request; and that was why he was here.

His wife turned to me with large eyes. 'I'm really proud of Dotty, and I'm very happy we are living here, far away from that dreadful man.' When she said Dotty I looked at him, and said 'Dotty?'

'Oh! That's the nick-name he brought with him from the air force. Morse code, you know: dots and dashes.' I laughed. 'But the way people talk about that awful man, everyone knows what he is up to. His wife isn't back from their last home leave, and he's keeping a labour woman: his old girlfriend, borrowed from her husband on payment of rent. He's—'. Her husband stopped her, saying it was best to forget Leary, and let others do the talking.

On the way back with West that afternoon he told me he had made a mistake: he should have arranged for me to go down to Bor Deorigaon with him, to spy out a place for a landing strip. Before the war there used to be two Europeans there; now, since 1941, he had promoted the only Assamese, in fact the only Indian manager in the company, to run the place. He was managing well enough, having been promoted from the post of head clerk, to which he had risen from joining as a field writer; but during the rains it was sometimes very difficult not only getting there, but getting back. He said the Subansiri in flood was quite frightening; the water level went up incredibly fast, and came down almost as fast. He gestured at the mountains and said if we measured 140 inches in five months just in front of the hills, one can imagine it must be nearer 200 inches in amongst the mountains. Reverting to Bor Deorigaon he told me the tale of an assistant at that place in the early thirties. He was always getting into trouble with his crazy behaviour: a typical immature public schoolboy, aged about thirty-five, butterfly bachelor, always thinking up what he called 'wizard japes'. In those days a small paddle steamer used to ply up to the estate once a fortnight, bringing things which had been ordered three or four weeks previously, and had come by rail to Tezpur, then by steamer up the Subansiri. Late in the cold weather the steamer often had to offload at Luhit, because the river was by then too shallow. This wag had heard the steamer was not coming any more until the rains, and decided on one of his japes. He took an old furnace chimney from the factory down to the river, and painted it like the steamer chimney. He propped it up with bamboos so that it showed above the trees to anyone sitting on the manager's bungalow verandah. The manager's wife, once a violinist in a well-known London orchestra, and related to a Liberal peer, used always to dress formally, wear a large decorated Victorian-style hat, and with her floral parasol she would walk, attended behind by one of her bearers and her personal *ayah*, every fortnight, to meet the steamer. Being delighted to see the smoking chimney of the steamer, unexpectedly arriving with much needed supplies of all kinds, she made ready, and after breakfast walked in state down to the jetty on the river. The poor lady was both disappointed and hurt at the way she was made to feel stupid in front of many grinning estate people, who took it for granted this was the kind of strange play the *sahib*-log often got up to. When she told her husband, requiring him to issue a serious reprimand and an order to apologise, he burst out laughing and said he would have been taken in himself. When he told his wife he thought it was a brilliant jape she spent the rest of the day with a headache in her room, her Khasi *ayah* consoling her by telling tales of the '*chota sahib*'s' bad behaviour. The assistant was very popular with the labour force, and could get them to do anything, up to a point. Fraser was the superintendent at that time, and when a further area of forest was being cleared for the planting of tea, he said the large pipul tree, previously on the border, was a dam' nuisance, positioned as it was exactly where the main leaf recovery road should be extended. He said it should be removed if possible, but advised care in going about it as pipul trees tended to be regarded as sacred. He suggested trying the Santhals, or Mundas, who were not Hindus. The assistant tried every idea he had, but no-one wanted to have a hand in the removal of the large tree. Eventually one of the staff confided he should try asking some Abors from the mountains, who often passed near the estate.

One day a *sirdar* brought an Abor to the office, and it was agreed by the other *sirdars* that if the Abor made the first five cuts into the pipul's roots, all the other estate workers would do the rest, without fear. The Abor demanded a bottle of rum and fifty rupees – a large sum in those days –

before he began. Next day the Abor took the bottle of rum to the tree, and began drinking, with about forty labourers standing around with axe and daos waiting for the first strokes, after which they would begin the felling. The Abor became so drunk, being unaccustomed to drinking so much rum, that the assistant had to remonstrate with him and demand quick action. The Abor, with his large, cruel bushknife, swaggered uncertainly to the tree, declaiming in his own Tibeto-Sinese language and brandishing his dao. He made a huge swipe at a large root, but was so drunk he barely scratched the bark, and cut himself deeply on his left shin. Everyone laughed, with one old *sirdar* thrusting his finger into the air, crying that the gods' justice was done. The assistant took a man's axe, and saying it needed only four more cuts, slashed them fiercely in the roots, and waved the men to start hacking it all to bits. The Abor, feeling little pain with the anaesthetic effect of the rum, was taken with blood streaming from his leg, to the dispensary for disinfecting and bandaging. He never walked again. The bushknife had been used to cut all kinds of things, and whatever the poison was, it caused frightful swelling of his leg. Ten days later he died. People all said that was the way the gods cursed anyone who initiated the death of a pipul tree. A year later the assistant was posted to Medeloabam as acting manager. One beautiful cold weather afternoon he drove out to the trunk road on his way to play tennis at the club in Dibrugarh. He had a Morris open sports car, and on that beautiful day of blue sky and golden sunshine, without the slightest breath of wind, a very tall simul (bombax – silk cotton) tree began to fall, and made perfect interception with the man in his car, killing him immediately as if it had been aimed precisely. In the amazing way before such things as telephones made it easier, the story soon spread in planters' clubs, small towns, and villages around Bor Deorigaon and Medeloabam about the *sahib* and the pipul tree over on the Subansiri, and Hindu priests for many miles around probably tell the story, sixty years or more after it happened.

West asked about my explorations, and I told him what I had seen of birds and beasts. The six-foot monitor lizard and the binturong surprised him, and I guessed many of the birds were quite unknown to him. He said I was not having enough contact with people of my own kind, and should consider taking my remaining week when he returned, to go to the South Bank, before the big rains arrived. I said I would think about it, and mentioned Constable who had said he would fly over 'once I was settled'. I would write straight away to see if he would fly me over and back.

176

During West's two weeks away I had a call after midnight from people who lived in a double row below the plateau where I had seen the man-eater attack their cattle. It was not the man-eater causing trouble, but a lone '*mukhna*' (tuskless) elephant. It had been feeding on planted bananas, and went to one house where it tore away a wall from the top, and was feeding on the paddy stacked in huge woven and plastered baskets, scooping the grain into its mouth, impervious to the shouts and screams of the people, who eventually ran for fear of their lives. I fixed the torch to the rifle, and dressed in dark jungle green shirt and shorts. It was cloudy, with no stars or moon. The people from the eight houses, mainly Parjas, had taken refuge in the hospital waiting bay. It took about twenty minutes to reach the scene of the depredation, and by that time my night vision was as good as it was likely to be. The men came with me only far enough to explain how to find the house being raided, and they then retired, saying they would go to shelter at the hospital. One of them said this was the big rogue, and I should beware of his guile. The lack of light was distressing, and the cloud had made the night warm. I went over the open grazing land until I drew near to the houses, and began aiming short flashes of the torch in the hope of seeing the huge robber. Nothing showed, and I went slowly and quietly into the road between the houses. Flashes revealed nothing, and as I reached the northern end I heard the faintest swish of water, and of grass. I switched the torch on and saw, entering the tall kaguri grass from a stream some twenty yards away, a large tusker, with thick tusks slightly skewed, one further ahead than the other, followed by three smaller elephants, striding away for the forest. I shouted abusively at them, and feeling the Parjas must have made a mistake, began to return along the track which would lead me through the high scrub to the back of the hospital, where I would tell them it was safe to go back. The track wound, and I kept flashing the torch to ensure I was on the track. Without warning I heard a hoarse roar ascending into a trumpet, with a crashing of twigs and branches. Aiming the torch in the direction of the sound, I saw over the solid tangle of lantana and eupatorium, about ten yards away, a tumult made by what had to be the rogue, charging straight for me, with no sight possible until four or five feet from where I stood, if I waited for him to break cover. In the frantic seconds of registering all this, I decided I must run, torch on, as fast as I could along the path, hoping he would not be able to twist and turn as fast as I did, with a red-hot incentive to escape. To my horror it sounded as if he was chasing me with amazing speed, and seeing a straight stretch ahead I switched off the torch and ran like a cat out of hell, not knowing there was a two foot dip in the path. I went down with a crash on the path, and instinctively rolled quickly to one side, sitting with my back against the lantana, torch and rifle ready for a desperate attempt to escape the rotten perversion of fate. All sound had ceased, except for the pounding of my heart, and the throttling of my breathing, in the hope he would not hear. I waited for about ten minutes, without any kind of sound, and rose carefully to my feet. I did not very much like the kind of close cover I found myself in, and not knowing where the brute could possibly be I was unsure if I should use the torch to start a final sprint to safety, praying I was not very far from the hospital. Wanting to be careful before switching on, I tried to feel my way with my feet, hoping to ascertain I was actually on the right starting line before anything else. I stood on a twig, which snapped like a pistol shot, and I heard the beast move from a location more or less abreast of me. I put the torch on and began to run. Hearing a loud trumpeting and crashing I fired in the air, shouting all the war cries I could think of, some not repeatable, and ran like a wing three-quarter in fear of the Kiwis until I reached the open ground and saw the lanterns burning round the hospital. I sat on the low wall and told the menfolk what had happened, not having come up against the *badmash* until I was coming through the tall scrub. They said he was a dangerous one; only a *badmash* would come through scrub like that, meaning mischief. The other elephants I had seen were no problem; they always disappeared when people shouted. I offered to take them back to their houses before going back for my own sleep, but they said they would rather sleep where they were until it was light enough to go home safely; the *badmash* would never show himself by daylight, and seldom by a full moon. On my way back in the dark I realised just how difficult this business was, trying to compete with a vicious enemy of human beings by dead of night. It was three o' clock before I went to bed, and I thought I had so much adrenaline – of the bitter kind – in my bloodstream that I could not easily fall asleep. Next day in the afternoon I went to see Johann *shikari*, and spent an hour going over what had happened. He told me the shot was something it understood, and it would probably not intrude here again until the paddy began to ripen in October. He said it was very dangerous to go after him on nights when there was no starlight, no moon, and too much close cover.

About this time I was waiting for some communication from Constable, and decided I would explore the Mirijuli, spending two nights out. It was not a popular place. About three-quarters of a mile upriver there was a confluence of two streams. The one on the west was where the Daflas would strike off to a village several miles into the hills, on the slopes of the Daflanoi valley. The one to the north was the one which rose about 2,000 feet up, below the prominent mountain formation known locally as Parboty's breasts. The formation sloped steeply down to the Daflanoi, on the other side of which it rose again, not so high, in another well known as the Maiki, Mota, Lora, Sowali (woman, man, son, daughter) on account of the descending series of peaks, covered with thick forest. I had permission to borrow a tarpaulin which we would rig as a tent at the end of the easily traversable terrain, for shelter in case it rained, and managed to attract Rondey and Ram, a younger Munda *sirdar*, to come with me, carrying the heavy tarpaulin. We went on Friday afternoon, and spent the first night without the tent, the sky being clear, and the night being pleasantly mild. Next morning after we had taken tea and chupattis, I said they should give me half an hour's start, as there were plenty of wild pig marks on the river bed. Sure enough, I had made my first ascent of a small waterfall with huge, slippery boulders, and had sat to take a rest whilst surveying a good view, when I saw a beautiful large boar coming down the river bed towards me. I saw him through a cleft in the large boulders, and carefully, without showing myself, lay on a flat boulder above the bed, guessing he would keep coming and walk into view about fifty yards away. I aimed well downwards between shoulder and neck, and knocked him rolling and kicking, sure I had found his heart. By the time I climbed over the boulders and down onto the river bed, he had moved several yards, and was still kicking with his hind legs. Just as I had thought to give a coup de grace, he stopped kicking. His tusks were frightening, seven and a half inches when extracted, and as sharp as a steel knife. Hung from a beam below my bungalow he was six and a half feet; a very heavy brute. Rondey and Ram, hearing the shot, came loping up the difficult boulders until they saw me, back where I had fired. I told them they should forget about coming any further. Ram, being the younger, would make haste back to the estate and gather another three or four men, and be back within four hours. They were to cut the haunches and shoulders separately, and put one haunch in my fridge, another to West, to be cut between him and Horsey, and the rest they could divide with my servants and their families, with some for the hospital. To my surprise they said they would take the boar down themselves. I could see they could drag it down the slope without much difficulty, but warned them it was too heavy on the lesser slope back to the estate. They said they would either come themselves to collect the tarpaulin on Sunday midday, or send some fellows to do so. I wished them luck. They said it would warm up and the pork would go off if they left it too long. I wished them well, and left them smoking bidi cheroots, not so much for enjoyment, but to use them to burn the huge ticks, marked like miniature crabs, which were crawling all over the boar, having abandoned their safe haven in the hairy mane over his shoulders. I learned many years later from Rajastani friends that the flesh under that mane was prized, claimed by the hunter as the meat which contained the incredible courage of the wild boar.

I continued on my own, first along a gentle slope where the very small river tinkled down the amber shingle bed with the sound of merry elfin laughter, a veritable Minnehaha which had me smiling for the rest of that day. I began to see different birds: a Daurian redstart, blue rock thrush, and a beautiful and vocal spotted forktail which kept ahead of me, flashing its black and white plumage with great panache and shrill protest. Overhead I had a fleeting glimpse of three giant grey woodpeckers, the first I had seen. The gentle slope ended, and the steep little waterfalls began, and I was soon ascending through the giant terraces and steps of huge boulders with exertions which surprised me. After I had gone for about four hours, I had a long look at the sky. I decided there would be no rain for another twenty-four hours, and carried on, remembering I should be careful not to exceed my daylight radius of action for the following day. I was annoyed I hadn't brought any kind of cleaning gear for my rifle, but felt glad I had been able to give Rondey and Ram some good meat, something most of the locals needed every now and then. I was soon at a height, and on such steep terrain that I could see for miles. It was too hazy to see the Brahmaputra; the cold weather clarity had disappeared. I had one dangerous climb up a very steep wall of slimy, algae-covered boulders, and slipped badly through using one hand only. My leg went into a cleft which fortunately narrowed enough to hold me secure without any bruise or sprain, and I remained so held for a minute or two, sweating with the realisation that to break an ankle or worse would put me in a very difficult position. On this occasion Rondey and Ram would certainly find me before I starved; but it was a lesson, a pointed one, to a damfool seeking pleasure from solo adventures like this. I decided I would leave my rifle below the steep slimy wall so that I could climb more safely, but was shaken to find the descent more difficult than the climb. I left the rifle in a prominent place, without ammunition, with a freshly stripped branch of white wood to attract attention. I climbed with the kukri in my belt and my food haversack over my shoulder, taking plenty of time and using the friction of my bare skin against boulders in the difficult stages. There were not many places which could show tracks, and I was fascinated with the curious geology now visible. At last I managed to climb over a steep wall of pale dry boulders, to find a delightful terrace about sixty feet wide, with trees and creepers round its upper rim. Above it the mountain rose so steeply it seemed impossible to climb. A small waterfall fell from about fifty feet, bouncing off boulders until the last ten feet, when it poured into a splendid deep bowl of palest rock, thirty feet wide, and something like fifteen feet deep, full of perfectly clear water, pale green and so cool that it brought the temperature down in the amazing terrace. The surrounds were steep, and the water dribbled over the edge into the boulders below with a friendly gurgle. I stripped and went carefully down the rough, dry slope. The water was cold enough to be inviting, but cold enough to advise when I had swum enough. I came out and found a comfortable place to lie in the sun, drying off in great pleasure. Looking at the steep rise above, I thought this perhaps was far enough. I couldn't have risen more than about 1,200 feet, and wondered how people knew the source was 2,000 feet. I was about to move to the western side of the terrace in the hope of seeing the twin peaks of the breasts, a forlorn hope with my experiences of summit seeking, when I was surprised by a sudden plopping splash at the foot of the waterfall. As I stared, there was another splash, followed immediately after by a third. I sat still, watching, and saw three otters chasing each other in the lucid depths of the pool. Soon they surfaced, showing silver-white throats, and what seemed like broad grins. They swam with heads up in line astern, and came to my side of the pool where they trod water and looked at me. I was seven or eight feet from the edge, entranced with their beauty and their curiosity. They dived and chased each other in the depths again for a few minutes, and suddenly broke surface below me, with one coming to stand, dripping with water, beaming at me as if to say, 'I don't know who you are or what you are, but it's nice to see you!' A second one came out on all fours, more nervously. The first one approached me on a wide curve, unsure but very curious. He came close enough almost to touch my foot with his nose, seeking a clue as to my identity. The third otter came out, and began chasing the second round the rock rim, and was joined by the first who, giving up his investigations, followed them until they all had one more underwater tail-chase before drifting with the downstream water on to the boulders below. I genuinely felt I should address my thanks to the Creator for that enormous privilege, and sat in a glow of strange fulfilment, telling myself this, if nothing else, made the whole of my damfool programme wonderfully worthwhile.

My efforts to find a possible way upwards found nothing which looked feasible, and I hoped when Constable came we would be able to locate this beautiful pool from the air. I remember clearly thinking how much I would enjoy bringing my eventual mate to this pool, and how I made it a requirement she would have to be able to climb to reach it. It would never become a popular resort with such difficult terrain and arduous exertion. I spent the daylight hours watching, and waiting at that pool, and found a good place where, with a little kukri work, I could spend the night. The only creatures I saw were several birds: a white-capped redstart with splendid plumage and bearing; two large Himalayan squirrels, dark backs and tails, with white fronts, drinking a little and disappearing without curiosity; a pied kingfisher which spent two minutes hovering over the pool before flying downwards with a shrill cackle. Just before sunset I heard the delightful call of green pigeons, recognising the sound from bird books and descriptions by planters of how they sounded like the melodious whistling of a schoolboy (in the days when they still whistled). I also heard the deep moan of some mysterious creature which I had heard up the Bergua, thinking again it had to be a large deer. I slept as usual, waking at regular intervals, and felt cold towards dawn. There was little wind, and when I peered out of my leafy hide I saw there was a thick mist over the pool, and as the sun rose it seemed thicker. I rolled on to my elbows, and caught my breath as I found myself staring at what appeared to be, believe it or not, a dinosaur! Standing opposite, in the mist against the sun, it looked about twelve feet tall, and my heart thudded with excitement. It dropped slowly on to its front legs, which I could see were equipped with huge talons; but the movement shattered the illusion: it was not on the other side of the pool, but a mere four feet away from me: a scaly pangolin, now in focus in the weird mist. I laughed at my over fertile imagination, and watched the shy creature creep into the undergrowth, probably wondering what on earth kind of a creature I was.

When I eventually descended, I found Ram and another Munda waiting at the tarpaulin. They reported Rondey was in hospital with a fever, probably from a tick bite, but also perhaps the carrying of the boar was too much for them. Ram, being younger and fitter, had come to take the tarpaulin back with his friend. The boar had been divided and delivered as required, and everyone seemed pleased. I thanked them, gave them some tea to drink with plenty of sugar, and set off back with some haste to visit Rondey in hospital, where I found Dr Dutta very worried about him. He said the tick fever was bad enough, and he would normally be expected to recover; but he had found bad sounds from Rondey's lungs, and suspected tuberculosis. When West returned from his holiday, he told me I was to blame for Rondey's condition, made me feel guilty about Rondey's wife and family, and although I told him I had warned the men not to try carrying such a weight themselves, West seemed to think I had done Mirijuli down by bringing this misfortune on Rondey. He had brought plenty of news from the South Bank. Fraser said the company had recruited new assistants, and one of them was learning to fly in England so that he could fly the company plane; should arrive in the cold weather. On the South Bank there was deep concern about the spread of communist unions. It had spread from the Dooars in Bengal. The Assam Branch of the Indian Tea Association has been speaking with the Congress people in Assam, and the latter say they must galvanise their unions into action to prevent the communists from misleading tea labour. Everyone is saying this spells big trouble; so far the Congress unions have been very reasonable, and the Tea Association has been cooperating on such things as housing standards, medical services, and wage levels. Now the communists are using all kinds of wild promises to win the attention of labour everywhere. They are already provoking strikes in the Assam and Bengal railways, and many businesses in Calcutta, including the docks, are running into more and more strikes. There have been many cases of violence against staff in Calcutta and the Dooars, and morale on the South Bank is sinking. The Assam ITA is working on a manual with standard procedures for dealing with labour discipline, legal processes, definitions of offences by employees, with explanations of such things as misconduct, gross misconduct, excessive absenteeism, workers councils, and the possibilities of organising staff and labour provident funds etc., etc. West was emphatic that it was only a matter of time before the communists took hold of the vast numbers of Indians who were drastically poor, and he said he was more worried about this than he had been with the coming of Independence. It was a sobering, if not depressing, basket of news, made all the more significant by the arrival at last of an air letter from Jackie Moss. He said how glad he was to be in touch again, and said he had very much enjoyed the life in rubber, where the surroundings and the people were very much to his taste. The only trouble was the creeping infiltration of Chinese communists, hell bent on taking over Malaya. They had already murdered several planters, but were able to disappear into the vast hill forests without trace. It was hoped the British army would build up a strong force of jungle-trained troops to deal with these murdering b————s before they paralyse the country. He said we ought to meet one of these days, and asked if I had any ideas. Looking at an atlas and finding just how far Johore was from Calcutta, I wrote back and asked him when his first home leave would be. Maybe we might manage to travel home on the same ship?

When the rains arrived I was impressed, if not shaken, with the dramatic arrival of the first monsoon deluge. Temperatures had risen steeply, although the North Bank had many cooling showers well before the middle of June. It was debilitating, hot and humid in the three weeks before the rain arrived, and when it did arrive it did so with the sound of 1,000 armoured tanks advancing into battle slowly and menacingly from the Assam plains. The dark grey wall of heavy rain obscured all it overtook, and a swirling pale mist rose as the fusillade of fat drops struck the hot and thirsty earth. The people had watched, and heard the approach for at least half an hour, their voices increasing and rising half in a spirit of celebration, half in an uncertainty bordering on fear. Through the areas of tea which lay on the plateau there ran many small, deep valleys with boulder and shingle beds, long dry since November; but now they suddenly ran full with tumultuous bouncing floods of rainwater. The roads became shallow rivers; and every one of us, sweetly relieved with the drenching cool rain, began to feel a gradual chill through the soaked garments. The rain gauge at the office opposite my bungalow showed four inches of rain in the first twenty-four hours of the monsoon, against six inches measured at West's bungalow up on the tea area. Roads, drains, bridges and many a thatched roof showed immediate need for attention and action, and we were kept busy dealing with reports, all urgent, beginning with West and then coming from different places on the estate. The turbine flume, which had demanded many man-days throughout the cold weather for removal of the silt which a succession of very heavy downpours had deposited in floods thick with eroded soil, now needed immediate measures to clear what were always the worst early transports of whatever the mountain landslides had dislodged, miles above where the flume began to carry water from the Daflanoi. There was a lot for me to do, and I enjoyed the fight against the elements, soaked most of the day, and by eight-thirty in the evening so exhausted I mostly fell asleep over my book after supper.

For the first week the rain hardly abated, and there were many people reporting sick with chills and flu. One day I went to see how the plucking was progressing, and found the *sirdar* sending a small Saora woman, little more than eighteen, off to the hospital in the pouring rain. The hospital was over a mile away, and this young woman was swollen with pregnancy. I asked what – apart from her obvious condition – was wrong with her. I had learned women who were pregnant preferred to work until the very last moment, so to speak, and was told she was beginning to have her birth pains. I asked the Saora *sirdar* to tell her to walk the 300 yards to the lorry road, and sit on the concrete bridge parapet to wait for the leaf lorry which I would send to take her to the hospital. The *sirdar*, after an exchange with the woman, told me she would rather go home. I told him she would be allowed home after the doctor had seen her, but go to hospital she must. I rode off in the rain, rough-riding on the paths and roads already scoured into runnels and pits by the heavy rain, and put all my energy into reaching the factory soon enough to find an empty one straight off. I was lucky, and with my cycle on the back of the lorry drove all the way up to bring the woman back again to the hospital. She was not on the bridge as expected, and I told the driver to wait whilst I found out from the *sirdar* where she might be. I met him halfway, and he told me she said she was going to the hospital, but she went 'that way' down a better path. I went back and told the lorry to go right whilst I went left, and to bear round until we met where both roads joined, being sure she had to be on one road or the other. I found her, sitting on the parapet of a bridge on the road, a long way from where she should have been; but there she was, halfway through the delivery of her child. She gave me a sheepish smile, and sat there holding her wizened child which had half emerged head first. Having been a Boy Scout and learned St John's first aid, I helped to deliver the child on to my sodden shirt, spread on the concrete floor of the bridge, using my pocket knife to cut the cord, which I tied with one of my tennis shoe laces. She sat smiling at the tiny child, trying to encourage it to suck her breast. I told her not to move, and cycled fast to

185

intercept the lorry. Riding to pick her up with the lorry, we found her walking towards us a couple of hundred yards from where I had left her, smiling but clearly weak. I put her into the cab and told the driver to drive carefully to the hospital, hand her over, then be on time for the leaf weighment. I cycled back all the way to my bungalow to change into shoes with laces, and went back with the next lorry for the weighment. The Saora child and mother flourished admirably.

The difficulty of keeping up with the plucking round was something I had encountered at Medeloabam, where we had fairly level terrain, less violent rainstorms, and a factory conveniently situated in the middle of the estate, which meant less dependence on lorries for collecting leaf. By contrast, the tea areas at Mirijuli were far from most of the workers' houses, and too far from the factory for the pluckers to carry even the last baskets of the day to be weighed. By the time the monsoon rain arrived the tea began to grow very fast, and tea shoots of the right size and tenderness had to be plucked every seventh day; that meant the whole tea area was divided into six roughly equal areas, so that one-sixth was plucked each day excepting Sundays. Chills, flu, and malaria, often exacerbated by heavy rain and persistently wet clothes, retarded the plucking effort, and even after putting the whole labour force – except the factory people – on to plucking operations, it was very difficult to recover lost ground. The worst of the problem was the way growth of tea shoots continued to accelerate exponentially, so that if they were left to grow without plucking on the seventh day, they would increase their length rapidly and begin to harden their stems, forming tough large leaf which would simply not give the colour, strength, and character of the seven day growth. In addition to this, the longer the shoots, the more difficult it became to pluck the tough, woody stems, and the slower the plucking became. No planter liked taking the only possible action to keep up with plucking of good small leaf, which was the only way to sell good tea; but it meant 'skiffing' the tough leaf off with sharp pruning knives, which led to some loss of crop. If one delayed this action the pluckers, eager to earn the bigger remuneration of the plucking season, simply plucked the tender leaf, leaving sometimes two or three leaves on woody stems all over the bush. This in turn led to a loss of crop because of future difficulties in plucking tender leaf from amongst the hard stems sticking up from what ought to have been a level plucking surface. We were well into the middle of the plucking season when eight days of unrelenting heavy rain laid many people low with flu, chills and malaria. The number of people turning out to work fell to a level which was insufficient to cope with the plucking programme. The Mirijuli work force was remarkably hard working, and most of them aimed to save money either for children's education or to take back to their country to buy cattle for their family farms.

Having fallen behind more than a whole day's area, I suggested to Horsey we should put men on with knives to skiff the leaf, which was already woody and long, and because of low turnouts and slower plucking we were hardly likely to catch up. He said we should wait until the following day, which was the day West would be inspecting Mirijuli, to take his opinion on skiffing as I had suggested. Next day West and Horsey arrived at the plucking when the rain was deluging heavily. I was beckoned out, and went to where they stood. We were all under umbrellas, and I was drenched from my solar plexus down. West asked how many pluckers there were, and I told him the not very impressive totals of men and women, saying there was a lot of sickness. I saw West was, like Horsey and myself, worried about how things were going. He said with such a poor turnout we would have to keep the pluckers out late. I began to say these were the hard triers; they had been out at six in the morning with their wet clothes, and were plucking until two in the afternoon; it didn't seem fair to load the people who were doing their best already.

At this West turned to Horsey and told him, 'There you are, you see! He's soft with them.' He turned to me. 'You spend all your time learning their languages and going shooting with them. They've got you in their pockets. I came past the hospital with Horsey on the way up, and there weren't half the people there that are absent. You should take a stick and go and turn them out of their houses. Get them out to work, that's what you're paid for. You young chaps are all the same.' He plucked a leaf from a nearby bush and brandished it at me. 'That's where the money comes from: yours, mine, theirs. D'ye get it? If you can't get it off we'll all be out on our arses.'

I was shocked, finding it hard to believe West meant what he said. 'I spoke to the doctor on the way up, sir' (when I said that, he should have known I was on my high horse) 'and he told me he was giving most cases two aspirins and sending them to rest at home, which was the best way to get them back to work in the shortest possible time.' West stepped towards me, raising a finger, I presumed about to admonish me. 'I can't believe, sir, that you are serious: that I should take a stick and flog so many willing horses.'

187

He tried to stop me, but I went on, fuming with indignation. 'These folk here work much harder than those at Medeloabam, under far worse conditions. These people want to save money, and I can't believe there are more than half a dozen slackers in the whole bunch. I beg you, please do not ask me to do something which would force me to hand in my—'. He interrupted me, raising his voice.

'Be careful what you are saying, MacStorm. You haven't been in tea long enough to know what you are doing; you must know that. I won't have it, I tell you.' Turning to Horsey he pointed at me and said, 'Let him deal with it the way he wants,' and turning to me, 'He said you wanted to skiff. Do you know how to skiff? Who told you about skiffing? D'ye realise we'll lose crop if we skiff?'

'I've learned about it from Telford, from Foyle. We'll need about fifty men with sharp slashing knives, they'll skiff to one and a half inches above the prune. I'll do my best. It'll keep us plucking the tender leaf ahead instead of being slowed down by the long stuff.'

It was thus left to me, and the only problem I had was that the men didn't want to skiff, saying they would lose on their plucking. I gave them a big task rate, and told them they could, if they finished early enough and skiffed well, they could either help their wives or pluck for an hour or so before leaf weighment. It was my luck that on the next day the weather cleared, and stayed clear for over a week, with rain showers at night. I found the skiffing men with cloth plucking sacks on their back, plucking the tender leaf off before skiffing every sixty bushes. Horsey nearly wept when he found what they were doing, but I told him they had used their heads, and we were not skiffing the tender leaf off with the tough stuff. Within a few days the plucking force was back up to strength, and the pluckers worked wonders; I felt greatly relieved. The weather made it possible for us to surge ahead in crop against the previous year, and remembering the scourge of dysentery or enteritis at Medeloabam I thanked my luck and gratefully counted my blessings, as well as those of Mirijuli. This euphoria was very much the kind one enjoyed only for a brief spell, knowing that to have done well almost by accident in response to a challenge was surely less rewarding than giving in to outraged authority. From that incident on, relations with West deteriorated. When Rondey *sirdar* died later in the year, my sorrow was darkened even further when West blamed me for having over-strained him, letting him and Ram carry the huge boar down the river bed.

Then there was the episode where I went out to sit over, or more literally, by, a bullock which had been killed by the old man-eater. It was killed in the scrub not far from the airfield, on a grazing path. The only tree was a wild plum, in whose branches I sat, only seven feet from the ground, with a narrow path cut down to the kill ten yards away. It was pouring with rain, and I sat under my umbrella from six in the evening, unable to hear any furtive attempts by the tiger to eat or move the kill. I had no other way but to flash the torch briefly on the kill every half minute, hoping to see the old beast on the carcase. After more than an hour of this, I pressed the torch button after counting thirty for countless times, and saw to my fury the bullock was no longer there. I immediately dismounted, wet, frustrated, and angry, and making plenty of noise walked fifty yards each way with torch on, but drew a blank. I called at the hospital to tell the compounder (dispenser), whose bullock it had been, his bullock had been taken from under my nose in the rain. He was very upset, and I told him so was I. The sheer indignity of having the kill whipped from under one's nose was hard to swallow. Next day Horsey, salivating over a wet cigarette and leering with amusement, said he had heard I had fallen asleep and let the tiger steal the bullock from under my nose. I managed to tell him what had actually happened, and that I doubted if anyone could sit in a plum tree festooned with thorny creeper – fine for protection but dreadful for comfort – in heavy rain under a leaking umbrella and go to sleep, at about seven-fifteen in the evening. I had to explain the same thing to West who, without any humour at all, asked what had happened. His comment was briefly that I needed more experience for that kind of thing, with which I agreed. He said he had heard from his servants how many people were keen to try to plant their rice fields again in the areas lying in the very fertile flats between the sinuous ridges and hills which were covered with dense jungle and joined to the primeval forest. All these areas had been abandoned for years because of elephant damage to their hard-worked crops. He said many people had gone after the man-killer rogue, and the forest department had tried all tricks to find and destroy him, without success. I said I could but try; but I couldn't guarantee I would get him, especially after hearing Johann *shikari*'s stories. West said Johann was past his day, now only an opium dealer. He told me sometimes he bought opium from Johann in the past to get the factory furnace stokers to work; they were all opium addicts. I told him I had ordered more Mauser ammunition, and would do my best as soon as there was a sign of the rogue

189

moving again in the district. West said it would be a fine thing to be able to rely on the fat yields of those areas, and even if I could keep frightening them off it would be well worth while. I told him Johann had said if the rogue were to be killed, the men would be able to keep watch in shifts and scare the ordinary wild elephants away. In mid-September the rogue emerged near Bankukurajan, and a drunk went to cut off his trunk with a bushknife. The rogue charged him, knocked him over, and trampled him to death. It made me resolve to develop as much cunning as would be needed to avoid such a fate.

In late September I was out on the delta near the Daflanoi when I heard a great commotion in the area covered with about three acres of giant kaguri grass. I could identify what might be a boar, and probably an angry tiger. Hastening to Johann's shack in the moonlight I asked if he would come to listen to the very loud fight going on. He came reluctantly, but it took no time at all for him to confirm it was indeed a fight to the death between a huge boar and a full-grown tiger. He said I should come early in the morning, for there would be a body to find. I went on my return from seeing the work started and Johann, who had been up since before dawn, took me to see the tiger which the boar had killed. It was ripped, disembowelled, and completely ruined; not the man-eater nor even of his family. Looking around I found the boar's tracks in a trail of blood, leading into a dense thicket. Johann told me to come after breakfast again, and perhaps there would be a good pair of tusks for me. It nearly was: one tusk eight inches, the other broken near the jaw. The old boar was raked by the claws of the tiger with one small slash through an artery in its neck. Johann told me to oil my rifle: the dhan (paddy rice) was fattening, with milk in the grain; the elephants would soon begin to appear.

Chapter XXIII

Bobby Constable had flown over whilst West was on holiday on the South Bank, fortunately on a Saturday afternoon which was not ration day. Horsey met him, and brought him down to see me at the office, where I was just finishing the plans for Monday's work. Constable said he met West at a dinner party, and West had told him he could take me off for the weekend leaving Horsey in charge. I noticed Constable spoke gently to Horsey, with no trace of his terse candour; they knew each other well. Within ten minutes, delighted to fly again without knowing where, I bundled some clothes and shoes together, told Nakul and Girilal (short for Girdharilal) I would return on Sunday an hour before sunset, and off we went to the airstrip. Constable suggested to Horsey he might like to see his estate from the air, and MacStorm could fly him all round it inside fifteen minutes. Horsey nearly swallowed his day's fortysomethingth cigarette, and declined straight away. He said he wasn't at all keen on flying, and in any case he wouldn't risk it with a crazy bastard like MacStorm. This he followed with his throaty laugh, more like the gurgle of someone choking, hunching his shoulders rhythmically to accentuate his humour. 'And I certainly don't want you to scare the life out of me again, Bobby! Not after the way you terrified my Bobby and me in that blarry speedboat o' yours; in the first week she came out to Assam.' He turned to me. 'He scared the livin' daylights out of us on the Dibru, with all those blarry great crocodiles. Twenty-five horse Johnson clamped on to a speedboat. Strewth! You're welcome to your speed and all the rest of it, you chaps. I must say I like my engines bolted to the face of the earth, running smoothly, same speed all the time. You know what I mean?' We were soon airborne, and Bobby suggested we flew north-east along the North Bank to look for game from about 800 feet, coming lower when we saw something interesting. We saw herds of buffalo, one small herd

191

of elephant, including one bull with unusually large tusks. There were deer of all sizes, and many wild pig, all in the fairly open glades of wild ginger, easy to see from the air, but completely hidden to men on the ground. At Kobo Chapri, about 500 acres of thatch grass, we saw a herd of buffalo, the bulls of which had huge horns, not the straightish ones with a curl at the ends, but the circular ones. I kept thinking of the famous seven and a half feet single buffalo horn found on a shore of the Dihang. This river, which flowed for hundreds of miles from west to east in Tibet as the Tsangpo, turned south into the North East Frontier tract as the Dihang, which turned in the Assam plains to flow west as the Brahmaputra, having been joined from the north-east by the Dibang and from the east by the Luhit. It was a fascinating trip, and we landed back just before sunset. Over a cup of tea in Constable's bungalow he said he had been hearing odd tales about me from the North Bank. To me it seemed certain West had been talking, and I smiled with an eyebrow raised. Constable was a man whose straight talk I admired, with its complete absence of innuendo, circumlocution, and nonsense. If he had a fault it was that he affected severity as a kind of camouflage, something I had noticed of many planters, and found amusing; it was ham histrionics and as transparent as gin. He began to talk.

'Tell me how you get on with West. I've known him for a long time, and I don't think he's a bad type.' I told him of the various difficulties I had, but saw the problem was Horsey, and was sure if I worked directly under West we would get on well together. 'Your company does some very strange things at times. Horsey: a simple man, good engineer, hopeless as a manager. Had his stunning wife stolen by a handsome army hero. She was so good looking no-one could understand how the hell Horsey had managed to marry her. He's a very uncouth man whose unattractive appearance would have had to be supported by a strikingly strong character, like me.' He gave a wry grin. 'He is soft, and completely devoid of strong will. He was always a happy drinker, but after losing his wife he went on the booze, and I can tell even now he is scared of his own shadow. Everyone knows he is on the verge of a nervous breakdown, and what have they done? Sent him to the North Bank, the last place on earth even for people with no threat of nervous breakdowns. The number of people who resign from the North Bank is high. Are they trying to push him over the edge? It just isn't usual for Assam Lothian to do things like that; but I can't believe you bullied him.' I explained why I thought West might have said I did; I said I pitied Horsey, mainly for his fear

192

of doing anything at all without West's approval. We spoke for a long time, with me admitting charges of seeming to be anti-social, mainly because I preferred to explore the wonderful primeval hill forest, with all it held. I didn't despise people unless they forced me to despise them. He listened attentively to everything I had to say, and at the end, when it drew near the time for us to have a shower and a change for dinner, he said, 'You've complained bitterly about things like ration issues on Saturday afternoons, West's annoying tendency to change work orders, and his extraordinary business of telling you to take a stick to turn sick labour out to work. I'd complain too; but I have to point out: although you are reputedly becoming a very accomplished *shikari* in quite a short time, you are stalking your prey in your career like a Sherman tank. Your target is success, promotion for excellence at your work; to make and save money by working for your company, and I don't doubt it is well within your capabilities; but if you go roaring and clattering at your prey you will frighten it away. You must study how to achieve what you believe to be the best results, without annoying the Wests, the Telfords, and whoever else is the boss in your arena. Bad reputations have a habit of growing in this country; it must be the fertile land and the climate, or maybe just club gossip. The people most criticised are those who seldom appear at the club. You must know all that already. I want to warn you, very confidentially, that West told me, and will no doubt tell your group head office, although you have the potential to become one of the best assistants he has ever seen in his career, he says you spoil it, because if things are not done your way, or the way you learned elsewhere, you lose interest in it completely, and work to rule, as our fellow workers in Britain are now so keen on doing. I hope what I say makes sense to you, because I don't intend to waste any time arguing with someone of your abilities. You have been an excellent teacher to me of the finer arts of flying, which I appreciate very much. I return the compliment by teaching you something I know a lot about; I am sure you will chew over what I have said, and I think you know I never waste time on idle chatter. Right? Now let's have a quick shower.' He looked at his watch. 'Slacks and long sleeves, no ties, twenty minutes from now.' With that I thanked him, and said with a smile I couldn't have put it better myself. Whilst dressing after my shower I heard him play the piano: a crashing polonaise by Chopin at a speed which led him into trouble. I drifted into the sitting room, enjoying the pleasant scent of his Dutch cigar, and witnessed his furious replaying of the difficult passage several times before thumping down the lid with a curse. 'Practice makes perfect, they say; but what they don't say is that for people like me on pianos it takes a thousand times as long as Backhaus. There's some fresh lime for you.' He questioned me in detail about flying, all through dinner and up to nine p.m., when we listened to Vivaldi's 'Four Seasons' before going to bed.

The following day the sky was cloudless and the weather warm. We flew over the hills to the north, probably illegally but benignly, to the nearest snow range we could see, ascending to 13,000 feet. Being well clothed with slacks and sweaters we didn't suffer too much from the cold. We had breathtaking views of the snows from a mile away, and regretted we had brought no camera, partly because of a sense of honour, but also because we thought it would be stupidly embarrassing to be found out acting like spies on a forbidden frontier. The flight was longer than we had thought, and turning for home we put the nose down, using half throttle to keep the plugs from oiling up. At 8,000 feet the engine began to run rough, and we decided to make a forced landing where we knew an airstrip was being prepared by the political officer of the Abor area, easily reached in our descent to the Assam plain. We opened the throttle in the downward flight and were delighted to find the trouble cleared. We landed anyway, hoping to see Paul Jackson, and wanting to check the engine before crossing the Brahmaputra. Paul was out on tour, and Bobby wrote a message saying why we landed. There were large trees and branches lying all over what looked from the air like a landing strip, and we were lucky not to have put a wheel in some of the holes hidden by the long grass. Whilst we opened the engine cowlings to check the magneto, carburettor and plugs, we attracted about twenty Abors: the men short but broad, with huge calf muscles, and the women of similar size, with very attractive features and colouring. One of the political officer's staff spoke good Assamese, and asked who we were, and from where we came. They all had the appearance of free and equal dwellers in a world about which they knew little except that the Indian plains and towns were badly over-crowded. They looked well fed, and wore various claws and teeth of wild animals mixed with the turquoise and other polished stones of their beads. We were back in good time for lunch, Bobby having invited the Napiers and Jeremy Corders for a curry tiffin. He said he had tried to have MacDonald over, but he is very exclusively occupied with his blonde lady friend, and will be playing tennis with her at Dibrugarh club. He also told me the polo there was beginning to founder: too few of the younger men had taken it up. It was still strong at Jorhat, but that was a bit far for weekend polo.

Wallace Napier was from Melrose, and his wife Catriona from Perth. They were a handsome couple, and struck me as ideally well-matched. Catriona, if anything, was a touch too good-looking, and after ten minutes of acute observation I suspected her not only of being aware of her effect on men in general, but of enjoying their admiration a little too obviously. I noticed her habit of looking hard at one whilst she spoke, and after evoking a reply to a question she began to turn her head away, leaving her eyes fixed until her head was facing her next interlocutor. Her husband was a quiet, no nonsense sort of Scot, and asked me various questions about the North Bank, and about the flying I had done in the air force and in Assam. He told me his wife had learned to fly in Britain, and had flown solo twice; but they had left to work abroad, and she had not flown for two years, except as a passenger with Bobby. We spoke of the Assam Lothian air service, Napier having heard from MacDonald that he and I had put up the idea of a visiting aircraft, mainly for medical emergencies. His wife said she couldn't understand why I didn't want to fly the Auster for the company, and asked if I didn't like flying. I told her I loved flying, and the best thing that had happened after I arrived in Assam was meeting Bobby, and flying with him a lot before I was sent to the North Bank. After tiffin the Napiers left, exchanging hopes of meeting again. Corders said he supposed some women were just like that: couldn't help enjoying coquetry, to which Constable said as far as he knew they were a very close couple, and that she couldn't help being beautiful. The flight back was a delight. We had time to look at the 'Ivory Pool' up the Mirijuli, as I had called it, and Constable said it looked marvellous except for the difficult climb. It looked as if in order to ascend to the breasts I would have to branch off a couple of hundred feet lower, to the east, to find a route which looked feasible. I enjoyed the weekend, and thanked Constable for his wise words. He told me he was going on home leave next year, 1950, for six months, and meanwhile was thinking of selling the 'Monster', which was a fine aeroplane, but was getting rather old. He said Napier was interested on behalf of his wife, but thought it was no good unless she could find someone to teach her in. They had asked MacDonald who had said he had no licence and couldn't fly except as a passenger. Constable said he wasn't even going to offer the 'Monster' to me, as I didn't even own a motor cycle, let alone a T model Ford, and was obviously saving up to get married. 'Correct?' After take-off Constable did a wingover at about 300 feet, and came back along the strip very low down, frightening the usual crowd, mainly of children, who had come to see the aeroplane. He was certainly a 'speed merchant' with exhibitionist tendencies, and I hoped he would remember what I had told him about the dangers of low 'beat-ups'.

In October, as Johann *shikari* had forewarned, the elephants emerged from their vast habitat of primeval forest, following their memorised and inherited custom of visiting the paddy fields interspersed with the wooded ridges and hills. I had seen myself the plump green rice grains, and had squeezed them to see the milky juice spurt, weeks before the grain hardened in the husk. The elephants enjoyed the hard grain, to be sure, but the unripe and milky heads of rice which stood in fields still wet with accumulated monsoon rain were tempting and delicious. Only where humans planted their crops could they find such concentrated areas of their favourite food, without having to seek laboriously amongst the forests and marshes for random traces of such delectable tidbits. Bamboo shoots were also prized, and they would raid the well-kept plantations of estates and villages without warning, and in one night steal acres of the lush new shoots, growing profusely close to the ground. They did this so cleverly, often travelling ten miles or more from one raid to the next to take people completely unaware. The damage was often serious, as each bamboo shoot took three years to grow before it could be cut for its many uses.

It was worrying that so much land had been reclaimed for rice planting. Much hard work was involved in ploughing, harrowing, planting. Water retention measures required complicated systems of controlled overflows involving much heavy digging and building of low, horizontal ridges, usually turfed on top to allow passage by foot. By the second week of October I realised I could not carry on responding to every call from areas where the elephants, in spite of amazing patience and stealth, had been detected by the vigilant cultivators who came hot-foot to beg me to return with them. In nearly every case we would arrive only to find they had disappeared. The cultivators took it in turn to sit up through the night, always two of them awake, with others snatching sleep. When the elephants were seen or heard, they would shout, bang drums, blow horns, and often wave burning brands from their watch-fires. I heard there was a herd of seventeen elephants roving in the district, which seemed to separate into two or three smaller groups. At first the watchers managed to frighten them away successfully, and so long as they did this, I told them I would be ready to deal with any elephants which could not be frightened away. I too had to be up every morning to begin my day's work, West had made that clear. It took a week to communicate to all the Mirijuli and Bankukurajan people, estate workers and villagers, a system which would save me from hopeless wanderings in the mud and the forest fringes at night, never sure where the sounds were coming from. I said each distinct area, depending on the shape of the forest edge, the lie of the land, the lie of the rivers and streams, would use its own call-sign. There were six main areas: Pandra Number, Coffee Palang, Mirijuli Pathar, Bankukurajan Kherbari, Ampara, Kasipathar. The call-signs were made by horns: first area long, long, interval, long, long, interval; next area horns: short and long, interval, short and long; third area horns: short rapid blasts. The other three areas used drumming, on a similar system. I said I would be out by six-thirty each evening, and would bring my supper, mosquito net, and waterproof bed strip with blanket. To begin with I would base myself in the area between the airstrip and the river, in the shelter of a thatched roof where the cultivators kept their watch. I would go to sleep after food, and the watchers would wake me as soon as they heard signals. To begin with it was all very confused. I felt I had to back the cultivators with demonstrations of initiative, and found although there were often attempts to raid as early as eight p.m., most of them took place well after midnight. I tramped with my rifle to wherever signals sounded, and only saw elephants once or twice in a week. Sometimes I had a guide to lead the way, which was often along the narrow bunds between the still muddy fields of paddy. Sometimes I had to manage alone on unknown ground, frequently sinking up to my knees in mud, and wasting time by wrong choice of routes. I was able several times to see the old skew tusker with his three companions disappear into cover, frightened off without doing much damage; and on one occasion counted seventeen elephants in the moonlight, purely by accident on the way to a signal beyond where they appeared. The shouts of the watchers were like magic, causing an immediate disappearance as silent as their debut. People came several times to early morning office to complain of very bad damage, both by feeding and by trampling on their small fields. This only happened when watchers had either gone to sleep, or when for a week no elephants had appeared in their area, and the watchers did what I would dearly have loved to do, and slept at home.

At last the phantom rogue entered the scene. The first time he identified himself was beyond Kasipathar, well east of the 'protected' areas, where he charged several watchers who had become confident from experience of frightening normal wild elephants away promptly. I had luckily slept at Ampara, not far from where this had happened, and was summoned by some Munda villagers, pleading for help. They had been badly shaken, and knew where to find me. I went with them to where they said the rogue was feeding with impunity. It surprised me to hear from them that this rogue had one tusk: a 'Ganesh' as they called it; and they had reported it to the Forest Officer in town, who said it was proscribed, and could be shot. The idea of there being two rogues rather depressed me, remembering my first brush with the tuskless one on that black night some months ago. There were six men, and I told them only two should come with me to show where he was last seen. I gave my squelching tennis shoes to one man to keep for me. The night was clear, with Orion and Sirius bright overhead, and just enough starlight to make one comfortable. The rogue had chosen a wickedly difficult plot to raid; it was a rectangle of less than an acre, bounded on three sides by high pampas-type grass, and standing four feet above the fields through which one was bound to approach. There was a 'bund' (low earth wall) about two feet wide, leading to the middle of the rogue's platform. From sixty yards away I scanned the plot in the dim starlight, but could see no sign of any movement or shape. I flashed the torch from forty yards, and we saw there was nothing there. One of the men said in a hoarse whisper it was certainly there earlier, and the other man said I should go up and look at the damage, the tracks. I put the torch on, moving forward, up to the raised plot. From the tall, plumed grass straight ahead of us the elephant charged: huge, broad and, to my amazement, tuskless. The two men behind me cried out and began to run. I heard one of them fall with a splash off the bund into the wet field below. I raised the rifle, realising it might be wiser to turn and run, as no elephant would risk that four foot drop on to the narrow ridge; but the rogue showed no sign of slowing down. In the torchlight he seemed like a pale grey cardboard cut-out of an elephant head-on, flat and featureless. I had been warned about frontal shots with the Mauser 10.75mm., and the necessity of aiming at the right point on the bulge of the forehead, depending on his height and distance. As his head was up and his eyes glowed in the beam I chose to follow the rule that the brain was sure to be between the eyes, and probably shot too high. He crashed down on his chest and trunk, and after a few seconds gave a rattling sigh; but after about twenty seconds he struggled with great effort to his feet, obviously stunned and very unsteady. I kept the torch on him as he swung to his right with a quick lurch, going down on his knees again. I thought I should run alongside him and put a bullet into his brain from the side, but strangely I thought 'this one is not proscribed, I'll have to report it'. I watched him stagger away, and heard him make a noisy retreat until he reached the large forest. One of the Mundas came up behind me as I stood waiting with the torch off, hoping for the sound of another fall. 'He'll die, *sahib*. He must die. We'll find him tomorrow.' I hoped it might be possible they would find him either dead or in a state where he needed to be finished off; but there was no such luck. There was to be good reason to regret my idiotic deference, and to curse myself for it many a time. The rogue did not appear for another eight days, but during that time the news had spread far and wide that the man-killer had returned, and might still be alive. The watchers began to lose their nerve, and the damage by harmless wild elephants increased, adding to my already heavy and depressing sense of responsibility as well as more weary nights of creeping through the mud in the darkness.

The time came when I made my bed with mosquito net in the Coffee Palang area, not far from the Saora homesteads, and the first two watchers were Hurriya and Jogi *sirdars*. We sat on logs around the fire, and I watched the fading afterglow as I ate my boiled eggs and chupattis. Before lying down to sleep I listened to them tell fascinating tales of the *sahibs* they remembered, and of earlier *sahibs* whose tales were handed down as legends. I think they had taken some rice beer, as they seemed remarkably gifted as raconteurs. The talk swung to the various girls who were mistresses to planters of the past, of how some of them bore several children who were sent off to mission schools, and how some of the women eventually joined their *sahibs* in heavy drinking. The clever ones, according to Hurriya, were the young *sahibs* who had so-called secret liaisons, well known to the deeply perceptive local population, but regarded in a way as respectably modest. This talk went on as I lay down to sleep, and I kept my ears open as the tales became more interesting, mostly of people I never knew. 'Then there was the twelve-time Chota *sahib*,' Jugi *sirdar* said; but Hurriya murmured he should not talk of that one, who was now a *bara sahib* somewhere. Jugi said I was asleep and wouldn't hear what they spoke of, and Hurriya called softly to me: '*Sahib*! Do you hear me, *sahib*?' In mischievous deceit I remained silent, and the tales went on. I recognised several of the people of whom they spoke, and was at times amused, once disgusted, and often incredulous. There was one who sat in a high post in Calcutta who, when serving as an assistant manager somewhere on the South Bank, was passionately infatuated with a beautiful girl on an estate not named, and paid a large sum of money to enter into a connubial contract with her, agreed by her family, said to be Santhals. The contract was to be terminated after three years with a good bonus if there were no children born. Early in the third year the parents had thought it would pay them handsomely if their daughter bore a child, as this would compel the liaison to continue, and the *sahib* would have to treat them as family members, which in India meant the sharing of wealth. They decided any child born must look like the child of a union with a white man, and after many botched attempts decided a certain young Assamese member of the staff, pale skinned and fond of pretty girls, would be encouraged to lie with the beautiful girl whilst the *sahib* was off playing polo at the club. Many bribes had to be paid to ensure things went according to plan. The only one who would not be bribed was the *sahib*'s head bearer, Biharilal – who later came with the *sahib* to work at Mirijuli and told the tale – who refused to betray his *sahib* in a display of honour well understood, but who was accustomed to receiving covertly a special bonus from the *sahib* for watching his successive paramours like a hawk. On the polo day the *sahib* rode off to the club, which was not far, at two-thirty, and was not expected to return until at least midnight. Biharilal kept careful watch, knowing from his spies what was planned. He saw the pale young man ride his bicycle to where a path through the tea met the bungalow drive. He saw him dismount, and watched him creep, bending low to avoid being seen, to a point not far from the rear of the bungalow, where his head bobbed up to spy out the land. Biharilal watched from a concealed position behind curtains, and seeing all was laid for the plan to proceed, walked to the rear verandah and dropped an old brass pot with a clang on to the concrete beneath. A boy leapt on a bicycle behind the cookhouse and pedalled furiously to the club, carrying with him a white towel. When he arrived he saw the *sahib* standing in conversation with others, and went to him with the neatly folded towel. The *sahib* knew of the whole plan, there being no such thing as a close secret in India, and jumped on his horse. His friends had pulled his leg about the pistol he wore on his belt that day, and were told a leopard was causing trouble on the road to his bungalow. He galloped to the bungalow where, Biharilal having locked the bedroom door from the outside, the pale young man was

200

wrestling with the door handle when the *sahib* arrived. There was a brief exchange of conversation, the waving of the pistol, and the young man shot down the stairs like a scalded cat, sprinted to the path where he had hidden his bicycle, and pedalled off furiously, scared to death at the sound of the *sahib* galloping after him on his horse. The *sahib* chased, twisted and turned along the desperately tortuous route, firing shots into the ground close behind the young man, who, when they were passing the estate office, threw himself off into the dust, and crouched on his knees, hands together, eyes closed. The *sahib* said he was shocked to find the thief was one of his own field staff, and told him he must report to the office on Monday morning to explain himself. He then rode back to the club and enjoyed his polo, and his club night.

I was about to doze off when I heard the curious nick-name of the 'twelve-time *sahib*', and listened further. It turned out this was the name given surreptitiously to a young assistant, well before the war, who sounded like someone who exceeded by far the libertine exploits of Don Juan. The two raconteurs, who were young and unmarried at the time, delighted in reminding each other of the names of the twelve girls who were 'laid' by this young assistant in one day. The times, the locations, and other embarrassing minutiae, were perhaps even more outrageous than the *One Thousand and One Nights*; but most shocking of all was the discovery of the assistant's name. All I could say was that he had in the many years elapsed since then become a paragon of virtue; for, even allowing for the literary licence of the experienced raconteurs, I would never have imagined such a thing. That night there were no signals at all, and I slept until the first cock crow, piercing the pre-dawn darkness with silver fanfares by several wild jungle fowl: *gallus gallus Linnaeus*. The lower pitched village cocks followed later as I walked back to my bungalow.

It was not long before the rogue made himself a worse menace than before. Out near Coffee Palang the Saoras had built two fires, and hoisted a pitched torch to burn on a tall bamboo, in the hope of keeping the rogue and his followers away. I was called from the Pandra Line by men who told me the rogue had knocked over the bamboo and trampled the fire out, something a wild elephant would never do. I hurried with them to the scene, moving easily in the light from a waning moon. The paddy fields in this area were of irregular shape, narrow and winding with rising terraces into the hills, where on all sides except the lowest fields there was thick forest. It was difficult even dealing with ordinary wild elephants, who would disappear first round a bend, then into the forest where they would wait until the watchers tired of shouting or blowing horns, and drift out stealthily after an hour or more. We saw the rogue feeding insolently a hundred yards from where the watchers had made their fire, and counted eight elephants behind him, with perhaps more round the hill. He was clever, and seemed to know his enemies would need to approach very close in order to place a telling shot, and kept well away from the skirt of the ridge. There was little sense in trying to aim by moonlight at a hundred yards, let alone the horror of wounding such a devilish creature. I discussed the shape of the hill beyond the herd, and learned there was a good but steep path to the ridge, where to reach the top one had to climb a very steep bouldery cleft. At the point where the shoulder of the ridge swept down there was a small, bare platform, falling away steeply on all sides. It seemed ridiculous to regard it as a safe place if I had the rogue on my tail; but I could imagine nothing worse than being kept there for a long time if the rogue decided to hide quietly on the downward path, and I confessed I would like to tempt him to assault my bald platform, where I could stun him with a head-on shot, then dash round to hit him between the ear and the eye to finish the whole pantomime. I arranged with the watchers that as soon as the rogue disappeared they should shout and beat drums as loud as possible to start the other elephants moving away. If they saw the rogue moving away from the ridge where I was bound they should sound slow, single drumbeats. If they saw the rogue actually move into my ridge they should sound the horn which one of them had, which to me would be a danger signal. I told the men I was going to walk away with my back to the herd, and when I reached the cover of scrub and small trees I would swing north and reach the ridge without being seen by the elephants. The wind was coming as usual from the north-east, and it was likely my scent would carry down towards the elephants. The ridge was hardly a hundred feet high, and I guessed the rogue would possibly pick up my scent, and perhaps a whiff of gun oil. I moved off as fast as possible, remembering the huge and ever vigilant ears of the raiders, hoping to find a place high on my way up the ridge from where I could see how the rogue might react. Bare feet were excellent for silent movement, but the undergrowth on the lower part of the ridge was thick with cruel thorn creeper, difficult to see in the dark. I found the path to the top of the shoulder, but found no place from which I could see the elephants below, and had to continue to the top. Carefully I edged forward on the small bald patch, and was rewarded by the sight of all nine elephants, black against the moonlight. There were two fairly large tuskers, and one half-size youngster, and five females. It was cold in the night wind off the high Himalayas, and I missed the warmth of the forest. After half an hour I saw the rogue turn north and raise his trunk for a few seconds. The herd stopped feeding and turned towards him. He swung from one forefoot to the other three or four times, and then gave a deep, rattling growl followed by a huge echoing exhalation of breath, like a large ship spurting steam to its horn, insufficient to sound it. The wild herd clustered, well away from the rogue, and when the rogue strode a few yards towards them they wheeled and moved away, stopping when the rogue stopped. They all began feeding again after about fifteen minutes, but the rogue pushed them slowly, very slowly, feeding all the time, into the bent, tongue-like cul-de-sac of the rice field. He raised his trunk again, by this time upwind of my ridge, and stood motionless, making me speculate wildly on his dark thoughts. He was further away now, and I thought perhaps the watchers were unable to see him. He began feeding again, and slowly pushed the wild herd to the skirt of the forest. It could well be he intended to disappear very soon. In the moonlight my watch showed it was after two a.m. I knew very little of the lie of the land along the skirt of the ridge, but the thought of the rogue leaving the tongue by the same route as the herd started my heart thumping. If I was now downwind of the rogue, and if I could descend to the skirt, I would probably find a reasonable path just within cover, all along the edge as tended to be the pattern. I began to descend, realising I would have to turn west to round the end of the ridge, and make haste to cover about 600 yards along the northern skirt, hoping to locate the herd's exit point and hide close enough to it for a side-on interception of the rogue as he followed them into the safety of the dark forest. My heart fell as I rounded the point and saw the elephants so far away there seemed no hope I would be able to reach the exit before the rogue. I kept finding leeches on my legs and in between my toes, and gasped several times at the cruel stab of thorns. Eventually the skirt path improved, and I slowed down when I saw the rogue feeding about sixty yards from the exit, with three elephants still feeding fifteen yards from the jungle. I managed with extraordinary patience to position myself in deep shadow some twenty yards from where I was sure the rogue would approach the exit, hoping the absence of a clear northerly wind through the forest meant my scent would not travel anywhere near him. I heard a muntjac bark several times in quick succession, not more than 200 yards inside the forest: a definite alarm call, not provoked by the elephants. One of the elephants in the forest gave a shrill trumpet, and my plans were smashed to smithereens. The three elephants swung about and began to lope along the skirt where I hid; the rogue roared and swung to the opposite side, crashing up the bank and into the forest; and the other five elephants came in swift single file along the skirt path, passing my hiding place five yards away with the gentle sound of a faint wind in the trees. After a few minutes I heard the watchers beat their drums, and moving fast back along the path, using the torch occasionally, I reached the ridge point in time to see the herd trampling across the tongue and disappearing into the forest on the other side. I uttered a benediction for the wild herd, having feared a violent reaction if they had stumbled on me in the dark, knowing the miserable feeling of a lone intruder out of his natural sphere of operations: a kind of shame at having taken stupid chances, and risked pointless death by accident. What caused the stampede I never knew. Johann said my scent would travel into the forest, where the warm air often rose, drawing in cold air from the edges, and he was probably right. I felt cheated of the opportunity to slay the man-slayer, and when I told the watchers how things had worked out they were despondent, for the elephants had eaten a lot, and trampled more than the cultivators could afford to lose. I began to develop a guilty conscience.

There followed a lapse of two weeks. I had more sleep, but dreamed too much of the rogue, and elephants charging in the dark. I began to feel depressed. I ate with a great appetite but began to suffer from indigestion for the first time in my life. I shot two barking deer buck and three pig in a week, glad to send joints out for the coming of Christmas. The man-eater killed the small Saora woman who had given birth with my help. Her dead body, unmarked but for claw marks on one shoulder, and the tooth marks on her neck which extinguished her life, produced an infinite sadness. Her child was a lovely bundle of joy, hardly aware of her mother's death. I tied a buffalo calf and sat all night, less in the belief I would kill the man-eater than in rendering some sign of compassion to the sad-eyed Saoras who had buried the indomitable lady that day.

The Foyles arrived to take charge of Bankukurajan, and invited me to spend Christmas with them. It was a pleasure to meet them with their small children, and we had a lot to talk about. The Christmas rain, a curious annual meteorological occurrence, arrived early in 1949. The rogue was reported as killing two more people, one near Daflanoi estate and one in a village half way to Bogahilonia. There were still areas where water and mud lay in uncut rice fields, mainly in the area between the Saoras and the Mirijuli river. I kept trying to intercept the rogue without being intercepted by him, but although I had several bad frights and false alarms I was achieving nothing. Johann told me the only way was to ask the Forestry Department for an elephant to track and find the rogue during daylight, but when I asked them they said they had been trying to do this, and the rogue always managed to disappear into the North East Frontier area, where neither they nor I would be allowed to enter.

The night came when it was completely overcast, with continuous light rain. The rogue was raiding on his own now, and although I had told the people I would not go out on overcast, dark nights, I agreed to do so in order to ease my bad conscience, and to give myself a chance to lay the rogue ghost before the rice fields became the gleaning grounds for the jungle fowl, who had already begun scratching in the deep elephant tracks where the valuable ears of paddy had been trampled in under the protection of the *badmash mukhna*. On my way out I was confident of the chances: there was a very limited area yet to be harvested, and the rogue could be expected to give them his attention; the rain helped to hide noise, both that made by the elephant, and that made by his persistent opponent. The main and nearly overwhelming drawback was the hopeless visibility under the drizzling cloud; but I had by daylight made much reconnaissance of the maze of ridges, and had convinced myself it would be possible to creep into a position on the skirt paths, most of which were a few feet above the rice field level, where using cupped hands behind ears I could determine if the rogue was moving on a line at right angles to my line of detection, so that from the sound I would have a good chance to estimate his distance. If all went according to hope, it could be a matter of raising the rifle, pressing the torch stud, and shooting between the ear and the eye without waiting, fairly safe on the raised edge. The watchers had a large fire and a thatched roof to keep the rain away. There were five of them, including Hurriya *sirdar*. They wished me well, and I set off to where they said they expected him to be. I wandered for about three hours, cold, wet, and disconsolate at drawing a blank. I found a tree on the skirt which dripped less rain than usual, and stayed beneath it for another hour, some 300 yards from the tantalising watchers' fire. There came a chorus of shouts with a tone of urgency, and I began feeling my way back along the skirt path. Before I had covered a hundred yards I heard the rogue walking fast, his feet sucking when he went through mud. He stopped not far away, and after about fifteen minutes I heard him begin to feed, pulling the bunches of stems with a squeak, waiting for a minute, beating them against his forelegs to shake off the leeches, and after another minute munching for a few seconds, listening, and repeating the routine. He was too far from me for the torch and a shot, but after another twenty minutes I gauged he was moving on a line across a kind of bay of rice, and I began to move back round the bay, praying he would continue on that line and converge to come within shot. For some reason he came suddenly straight to the forest where I was hiding, and I heard him heave up to enter cover, about thirty yards from me. The idea of trying to meet him head on in the dark and congested forest was too much for me, and I turned back, going quickly towards the watchers' fire. It was no use; he must have eaten enough, and I had failed again. I eventually came wearily within earshot of the watchers. 'He'll never be able to shoot that ghost. It moves only at night. No *shikari* shoots at night except from up a tree.' Other voices murmured in agreement. I heard Hurriya say they should not give up: the *sahib* is trying hard; he has lost much sleep but he never gives up. He will never give up. My feelings at overhearing this talk were stifled when distant shouts were heard over the other side of the ridge. 'He's in Sinki's *khet*', someone said, 'and there's no-one watching there.' I took a deep breath and crept away undetected like an unhappy ghost, driven by mixed emotions. It was the same situation in reverse, but this time my patience after another one and a half hours was rewarded when I heard the rogue converging slowly, feeding more recklessly with more noise; but he didn't come close enough. The rain had become heavier. I knew he was about forty yards away, and would not come closer before rounding the headland out of reach. Most of the fields were fairly dry, and I told myself I could descend and advance to the sound in the heavy rain, able if necessary to fire head-on to stop him, perhaps lowering my aim a little. I guessed the field level to be about three feet, and sat on the edge to lower myself carefully to stand in the rice. The weed and grass was wet, and the three feet turned out to be about five feet. I dropped with a resounding plop knee deep into a pan of very viscous mud, at which the rogue, using his huge ears, charged straight for the sound. There was no hope of extracting myself from the mud to climb fast enough to escape the attack, and feeling the chill onset of wistful hope mixed with calm fatalism, I raised the rifle, pressed the torch on, waited until he was about ten yards distant, and fired, lower than last time. The Mauser rifle had quite a kick, and the kick this time did for the torch bulb filament, consigning me to darkness. The shock of instant blindness was dispelled by the shower of glutinous mud thrown at me as the great brute hit the ground, eight yards away. I reloaded, telling myself it was the right thing to do but I hoped the infernal rogue was this time finished. I managed to climb back up the edge, and felt better above field level. I could hear slow breathing, and hoped it would terminate in the slow rattle of death, but it was not to be. He eventually rose, turned away, fell, rose again, went about fifty yards, fell again, and with five more rounds I simply could not find it wise to aim vaguely in the dark to fire again. I went back to the watchers and told them what had happened. They were disappointed but sympathetic to me, making me feel worse; it was their loss which was great, not mine. When I got back at four a.m., and had a cold shower, it stopped me shivering, but I knew I was not going to be able to win this way. I stopped going out at nights, but slept badly with dream replays of the rogue charging in the dark, and the awful paralysis of legs which couldn't carry one away from danger.

Napier arrived next day by the company plane, brought by Telford, and I bumped into him at the hospital as I was coming back from the field for my tiffin. He greeted me cordially and said straight away I wasn't looking well; West had told him at lunch I was overdoing the night patrol business. I admitted I was sleeping badly, and felt for the first time in my life my nerve was beginning to crack. He stepped forward and pulled my lower eyelid down. 'Show me your tongue,' he said, and when I did he told me I was very badly anaemic, probably because I was wandering around hunting in bare feet, picking up hookworm where people had crapped near a path. He told the doctor to dose me with the full hookworm treatment, and said it would fix me within a week, nerves and all. So it turned out. The treatment was itself revolting enough to convince me that bare foot stalking was not worth it, except deep in the forest. Johann went personally to examine whether the rogue was likely to be found dead, and came to tell me he still lived. I was sorry for the cultivators, but began sleeping well, eating well, and was almost ashamed to have earned praise from everyone, except West and Horsey.

Just before Christmas I was out early on Sunday morning, hoping to shoot a boar for the Christmas festivities. I had gone into the hills and was creeping along a ridge above a marshy wallow which lay out of sight below, listening for pig sounds. A branch cracked like a pistol shot, and after a long wait I saw a female elephant move in a gap in the trees across the small valley. From behind her came a deep rumbling growl, and I saw her return to where her bull had started a whole young tree shaking. The note of that growl seemed suspiciously familiar, and my heart began to thump at the idea of being close, in daylight, to the rogue. I waited with hands cupped at my ears, and heard them move. It was a clear morning, about eight o'clock, and I began trailing them, deeper and deeper into the hills. By two-thirty I realised I had little chance of being able to see or identify the rogue as I had hoped. I was so far away from the estate boundary I would have to turn south and go fast to reach the estate before sunset. I had not been moving long before I realised the bull was now trailing me, and felt – as one used to say in the air force – the icy hand of panic clutch at my lower bowel. This was the rogue. I used the sun angle to lay my course, and moved fast, not sure of where I would reach either the estate or the Mirijuli river. On the way I startled a sounder of pig, and cursed my luck. It took hours before I found myself on known ground, and although I frequently stopped to listen for sounds from the bull, I came to the conclusion I had lost him at last, and with a spurt came out not far from the tiger's claw-cleaning tree. With a light heart I began striding westwards for the estate; but without hearing anything, seeing anything, or smelling anything, I stopped dead in my tracks, gripping the rifle hard, wondering why the hair on the back of my neck prickled, sending a tremor down my spine. The sun was still above the ridge, and I was near home, but something was warning me with powerful urgency to beware. I looked carefully all around. All was quiet, except for a jungle cock calling from further south. At last, I nearly jumped when I saw, only fifteen yards further along the estate boundary, about three feet of something unusual lit from behind by the sinking sun; sunlit bristles on what had to be the top of an elephant's back. Its head was behind a great, thick tree. I waited, and felt my pulse begin to moderate. It was clever enough, and patient enough, to have planned this interception; but even if it was not the rogue, I was going to wait for as long as he did. Perhaps it was twenty minutes or more I had to wait, never taking my eyes from his back. The sunlight on the bristles faded, and I saw him move, like a battleship leaving its moorings. His head emerged, trunk slightly curled forward at the tip. Came his eye, and a brief stop; then he accelerated, exposing his ear, and I fired. He fell away from me on to his side, rolling momentarily on to his back, legs waving in the air, and then collapsed, his breath leaving his lungs with the final rattle. I ran to him and put another shot where his spine joined his head. On his forehead there were two bullet wounds, and in his ears were two holes, about two and a half inches diameter, one at the top of each ear. It was the killer. I was walking away, and came out on the edge of the estate when I saw five Koyas running with bows and arrows, grinning broadly, come to carry the game. I ran back and climbed up on the great beast's body, waving the rifle. They stopped, staring, and I felt the body move. I jumped down and ran, shaken and incredulous. We crept back and I stalked close. He was stone dead, and the body had simply moved because of my weight. We laughed at the false panic; it was all over. The Saoras came as we were leaving, and danced with joy.

Next day West and Horsey went with Mrs West to see the terror of the district. The Foyles took me up in their car with the children, and took photographs of various groups sitting on the elephant. Nakul, Girilal had to have their photograph taken with me, and many other people, first of all those bound for work, and later those from all along the raided fields came. They left chickens, ducks, eggs, two goats and two pairs of mud-stained old tennis shoes I had lost during the campaign. I spent time with old Johann *shikari* looking at the rogue. He confirmed it was the rogue, showing me the three-inch holes at the top of each ear, which proved it was once owned by men. The size of the lapped over skin at the tops of the ears was estimated by Johann to show the elephant was at least forty years old. He said he would send men who knew how to remove the very small stumps of tusks, and cut off the right foot. There were five toes on each forefoot, and he said the beast had been in excellent condition. He said the flesh in front of the shin was excellent eating, and I said I would take some. That evening I went before sunset to see the men he had sent, and went down for a quick gloaming sortie up the river. I shot a sambar with a good head, cut off a haunch, and sent men with lamps to skin it and bring the meat down to me. It would be good for Christmas presents to many people.

209

Chapter XXIV

It was good to have plenty of meat to share with many people, the only problem being how to distribute it without upsetting those who received nothing. The Wests, Horsey, the head clerk, head factory supervisor, the Sikh fitter, the doctor, the midwife, my servants, the Foyles, the hospital patients, were all on the list. I told my servants to send a sirloin of sambar to the Wests, with a haunch of boar. Somehow or other it turned out they were given a huge steak of elephant shin, a mistake Nakul cook discovered one day later. He sent the venison, telling the man who took it to tell the Wests' cook to return the elephant meat forthwith, keeping the mistake secret. I knew nothing of this. The Wests' cook had served steaks the night before which were praised as delicious by the Wests, who sent me a letter of appreciation with half a Christmas fruit cake. Secrets being impossible to keep, the following day West stormed into the office at six a.m., boiling with rage, accusing me of having a warped sense of humour and very bad taste in sending them elephant meat pretending it was sambar. He said his poor wife was ill, and asked me to imagine how it felt to be the butt of the labour force, who would be laughing behind every tree at the *bara sahib* eating elephant. I called my servants who explained what had happened, and I apologised; but I told him I had eaten the elephant meat and found it excellent. I have to say that although my servants saw how good it was, neither they, nor any of the staff or labour, wanted to eat it, mainly because the Hindus, who were the majority, honoured Ganesh the elephant god, and regarded such meat nearly as sacred as beef. Indeed several non-tribal Hindus shaved their heads, which is what the males do if there is a death in the family. When I asked them about this they said there was no objection, but as they were of a particular sect which worshipped Ganesh that is what they had to do. The body of the rogue was far enough away from any of the estate dwellings to avoid unpleasantness from the odour of putrefaction; but people's dogs showed disapproval and doubt when the cold winds came down from the mountains. Jackals were heard east of Mirijuli and south of Daflanoi, but they dared not trespass on tiger territory. A family of civets investigated the gamey scent. News had travelled mysteriously over long distances in the sparse tribal territories in the mountains, and six hill Miris arrived seven days after the kill, by which time the carcase was teeming with thousands of fat white maggots. The hill Miris built fires, and first scraped out several pounds of the maggots, cooked them in oil, and made a great feast of them, much to the disgust of most onlookers. They then made racks from green saplings, placed two to three feet above the fires, and began cutting the 'well hung' elephant flesh, and laid strips of it on the racks. The fires were kept burning with dead wood, on top of which non-resinous green wood produced plenty of smoke. For about another week they camped alongside the carcase, and were joined by about another ten men and women, including several girls with pink cheeks, rose-bud mouths and a bubbling laughter that sent my head spinning with appreciation of their beauty and sheer happiness. They made loads of the – well – biltong, pemmican, or whatever one might call the two foot long, hard, smoky sticks of what seemed like wrist-thick chunks of greyish mahogany timber. With what seemed to me like a weight of around sixty pounds in beautifully woven baskets, they helped each other to lift them and place an endless loop of woven cane band, holding the tapered basket round the bottom, and fitted with a cloth pad over the carrier's forehead. They would walk below the foothills for about twenty miles, and then begin their mountain trek for another six or seven miles, up and down steep ridges until they reached home in the valley of the Kamla river. They all had calf muscles and flat bellies to be proud of, and went off laughing with delight that they had food for another year from the *bhagal badmash*. Only a few of them spoke Assamese, but they seemed, for all the signs in the older people, that they lived a hard life, like people from some Shangri La that I yearned to visit.

Three days after I had killed the *bhagal badmash* (the fugitive rogue), I was called from my bed at ten-thirty p.m., by West. A messenger had arrived from Newton of Daflanoi, who had written to West saying there was much serious trouble from the elephants. There seemed to be a rogue tusker amongst them, and some villagers had just reported this tusker had taken away an eight-year-old boy. The tusker is now feeding with other elephants, on a low-lying area of late ripening rice, and he hoped MacStorm would come and help. A lorry is waiting at the river on the other side. The people are saying the MacStorm *sahib* has chased the elephants over the river to their side, and he should come and send them away westwards. I made ready and went, feeling fairly sure there was something weird about a rogue carrying off a boy and, being confident there could not be another rogue as dangerous as the one now lying on our boundary, I went with the sensible confidence of recent experience. When I had crossed the river by starlight in a dugout canoe I found the Austin lorry waiting for me. They took me about a mile to the other side of Daflanoi estate, where I met seven or eight men, waiting to tell me what had happened. The father of the boy who had disappeared was in a state of serious depression and I found it difficult to understand his disjointed speech, but there was an estate *sirdar* with them who seemed able to give a good description of what had happened. He said it sounded now as if the elephants had moved away, but if we went quietly to where the rogue had charged them he could explain everything. I told the men I wanted only the *sirdar* and the boy's father, so that if the elephants were somewhere near there would be less noise and more chance of me locating them. I showed them my torch fitted to the rifle, pointing it northwards and pressing the torch on, evoking quiet grunts of approval. They said they had been sitting by their fire some way out, and when the elephants came they waved their torches of burning pitch and yelled abuse at them, expecting their usual immediate disappearance. That was when the rogue charged, and they all fled, throwing their torches down. The boy, fast enough on his feet, was not found with them, and they had shouted, listened, and gone back halfway, believing in the end the rogue had taken him away. One of the men said the boy had been sleeping, but surely must have wakened when they began shouting. I began to think the child might be lying dead in the paddy field, out in the dark expanse of which I had no idea how the land and the clumps of trees lay. Ratna *sirdar* and Seoprasad took me to where their fire still glowed dimly, some fifty yards from the nearest grove of trees, beyond which the ground sloped in shallow terraces down to a small river hundreds of yards further south. There was plenty of soft mud. We stood still for about fifteen minutes, but heard no sound of movement or feeding. I then used the torch to examine tracks, and found those of the rogue, not as large as the *bhagal badmash*, but big enough to send a chill down my spine. I asked Seoprasad if he had called from here, and since he remained silent

Ratna told him to call, to shout loud for his son Syamlal. Seoprasad burst out sobbing, and Ratna shouted at him, whereupon he shouted his son's name, trailing into the heart-rending downward wail of a mourner. It was an atmosphere of bleak, dark depression. I was moving the torch beam further and further out, hoping we were not going to find a mangled child's body in the foot or so of churned mud. At Seoprasad's second, louder and more heartbroken cry, we all froze: there was an unmistakable small cry of a child, calling in an indistinct moan. Ratna roared 'Syamlal! Where are you? Speak! Speak!' Seoprasad went down on his knees calling on Hari for help to bring his child back from the dead. I heard the other men running and squelching towards us, and told Ratna to hold them behind us. I told everyone we must search, and showed them how to put their hands cupped behind their ears to focus on what they heard. I led the eerie line, moving the torch beam slowly, with Ratna calling loudly every minute, and the boy's weak voice becoming louder as we proceeded. It was scarcely believable that his voice had ultimately become so loud, yet the torch revealed nothing but an expanse of mud with a few tussocks of green stems. One man said he was afraid, and asked me to frighten evil spirits away with a shot from the rifle, and I was beginning to think there might be some point in trying to break the spooky web that seemed to be forming around us when suddenly, about five feet before me, I saw the boy's small face, only his face, eyes closed but nostrils and mouth clear and well formed in spite of the glistening covering of mud. Apart from the mud-covered features, no bigger than the palm of my hand, there was no other sign of body or limbs.

'Syamlal,' I spoke softly, and then repeated his name more loudly, realising his ears were in the mud, and was rewarded with a kind of happy whimper, like a puppy glad to have found his way back to safety. Ratna came quickly to my side, and seeing the small face slapped his hands together, turned his face to the sky and said 'We see him, God!' Then he roared to the men who came as rapidly as the mud allowed, eyes wide. We were all of us shaken, with a great happiness flaring like a sudden blaze. I told Ratna we must be careful, not knowing how badly he might be injured. Seoprasad, typically for a parent finding his child back from the dead, began raving with a mixture of rebuke and endearment, at which Ratna told him to shut up and get his arms under his son's shoulders. Ratna lifted Syamlal's head, and with a cloth cleaned his ears, telling the others to wait and be careful. He asked in a loud voice if he was in pain, and the boy smiled and said only a little.

Gradually the men lifted him clear of the mud, and it seemed to me his limbs were not distorted or broken. As we made our way to the higher ground I walked with the torch shining ahead, turning it to Syamlal's face to check his reactions. He had been wearing a shirt, blanket, and a pair of tattered old shorts. Seoprasad asked us to stop so that he could remove the mud-soaked blanket and replace it with his own. It was then that we saw, hanging from the inside of his thigh, a large patch of skin, thick with mud, about eight inches along the thigh, and about six inches across the hanging flap. There were signs of blood in the muddy mess. I asked how far it was to the Daflanoi Hospital, and was told by Ratna it was less than a mile if we went through the scrub to the road. I sent one of the men to run ahead and wake the doctor, and we went on. When we arrived at the hospital the doctor greeted me with wide eyes, and when I showed him Syamlal's injury he was shocked for about thirty seconds, and then sprang into action. He saw that bucket after bucket of water was poured over the shivering boy on the polished concrete verandah of the hospital, and meanwhile had water boiled on primus stoves, mixing salt with it. He made a careful search for other injuries, and found none. He then gave Syamlal a small injection of morphine, explaining he was going to try to clean the wound and the skin flap, which would give him much pain. I stayed until the boy was completely cleaned, dressed in a night shirt, and put to bed with the flap bound by a large bandage over the area it had previously covered. The doctor said Seoprasad was a good fisherman, and his son looked in good condition, which meant there was a good chance of the skin growing back where it belonged. I washed my hands and asked for some paper and a pen to write a report for Mr Newton; it was somewhere around two a.m., and as everything was under control I saw no point in waking him. I finished the report saying I would be willing to help should the fearless rogue return.

I had reported the killing of the *bhagal badmash* to the Forest Officer, and followed it up with a report on what appeared to be another dangerous rogue at Daflanoi. Syamlal's story was that he didn't know what had happened. He had been asleep, and when he awoke the men had gone. He was frightened by an elephant trumpeting almost in his ear, and ran in terror, only to fall into the mud on his face. He had turned over and shouted for his father, and something had stood on him, pressing him into the thick mud, leaving only his nose and mouth exposed. Being afraid he lay still; it must have been three hours before we found him. The Forest Officer sent me a letter from his head office saying the Forest Department wanted me to become an elephant control licence holder, and enclosed an application form for me to fill in. Within a week the Forest Officer brought me the control licence, telling me it was in order to shoot all male elephants which had become a danger to people or dwellings, or which were causing damage to crops upon which people depended for their own livelihood. I noted that the tusks of any male shot would only be made over to the licence holder if a *mukhna* (tuskless male) had been shot within a certain period of time.

It was some ten days after the finding of Syamlal that news came again from Newton of Daflanoi that the fearless rogue and twelve wild elephants were raiding the low-lying rice fields again. This time the news was brought one Sunday morning by Harvey Hunt, an ex-army lieutenant posted to Bogahilonia as assistant manager. Newton had met him at the club and told him about Daflanoi's elephant trouble, and told him to contact me if he wanted to help me deal with the rogue. He had turned up with a .405 Winchester of the kind reputed to have been used in the wholesale massacre of the bison herds in America, with jack-lever reloading under the action instead of a bolt. I gave him lunch, not telling him he was eating elephant shin steak until he had praised it. I took him to see the skeleton of the rogue, telling him all that had led to the final fortuitous kill. Eventually we had tea, and he went off on his motorcycle to Daflanoi, eighteen miles all the way compared with two miles for me across the river. We reported to Newton, who thanked me for my previous sortie and promised a lorry would be waiting at the hospital to take me back to the dugout ferry across the river. We were early enough at the place where the elephants had been coming, and I took the opportunity to have a good look at the lie of the land before it became dark. The little I saw of Daflanoi estate intrigued me a lot: it was very secluded, further from the steep foothills, with tall forest on three sides and seemed full of profuse birdlife. There was a quarter of a moon, and a clear sky. Ratna turned up and told us it would be at least midnight before the elephants showed if they were still interested in the last area of ripening rice. This disappointed Hunt, and I explained it was a matter of patience and long waiting, be it elephants, tigers, or curd-fat fish in the river, and what was more we would have to stick firmly to complete silence after ten-thirty, as huge elephant ears would pick up human sounds from half a mile away, be it an impatient whisper or a yawn; this I learned from Johann, bless him. Hunt didn't like the idea of going barefoot, and I agreed he should wear socks and tennis shoes, but not enter wet areas. I said we would move only one at a time. Hunt had no way of mounting his torch to his rifle, and I said he would have to fire when I fired, which would only be when we were able to come within fifteen to twenty yards of the tusker, with it standing sideways, showing an eye and an ear. No shots head on or backside on would be fired except in serious emergency. It must have been about one-thirty a.m. before we heard the elephants, and it meant we had to move about 300 yards south-west to gain sight of them. We had to cross a village grazing ground, where the short grass was dotted with clumps of eupatorium, many of which in the starlight looked very much like elephants. Hunt became excited and kept coming up behind me, tapping my shoulder and stabbing his finger at what he felt sure was an elephant. The quarter moon gave good light, but when we came within 150 yards of the seven feeding elephants there was not a hope of approaching any closer; there was no cover at all. I could see two tuskers, one of which was probably the *badmash*. I motioned Hunt should sit on the ground beside me behind a straggly collection of eupatorium and a damson tree. For a para-trooper he seemed inept in the business of concealed approach and observation. He kept moving and poking his head out, blowing down his nostrils with impatience, and I made slow signs to convey to him we must be quiet and remain concealed. I heard him move, and saw he was creeping to the other side of our cover. It was hopeless to use noise to warn him, and the herd suddenly froze with ears focussing on where we lay. I saw the smaller tusker raise his trunk, and heard a short trumpet note as he and the others wheeled and strode quietly but quickly for the nearest tree cover beyond them. The bigger tusker stood still, ears aiming exactly at us, and then he took about six strides towards us with his head held high. He stood still for another five minutes, and then began again to feed, all on his own. He turned across the line of the others' retreat and moved slowly, feeding every now and then, turning unerringly towards us with ears alert. After another half an hour he seemed to have lost interest in us, and began to be covered by the thicker vegetation between hunters and hunted. It was time to move on to a new tactic. I signed to Hunt he should observe our plan of him moving behind me when I stopped, and stopping when I moved, never coming closer than twenty yards and never showing himself to the rogue. The first bit was fairly easy and fast, but finding a possibility of converging with the rogue's line, I began crawling to remain hidden behind the smaller scrub. The wind was in our favour, and I thought our chances were good if we were able to move ahead of him to a place where the paddy field was no more than thirty yards wide before it opened out, hourglass fashion, into the next open stretch, where it was possible the other elephants might be feeding. Eventually we were well hidden on land three feet above the narrow neck. I was confident and happily optimistic to find such an ideal place, and finding no sign of Hunt thought it better to leave him in peace wherever he was, rather than give our position away to an elephant now slowly and, I hoped, unsuspectingly coming closer and closer to his final reckoning. Perhaps having killed the great beast which had put the fear of death into me, I had become over confident and conceited, because after fifteen minutes it became obvious that our prey had either sensed our presence, or had in the way of a war-time flier decided to make unexpected changes of course in the interests of avoiding interceptions based on his apparent heading. I could not see back along the narrowing rice field because of the overhanging vegetation, and after a further ten minutes without sight or sound of the rogue, I began to retrace my steps, peering every now and then through the screen of leaves, hoping for a sight of the grey ghost in the now descending quarter moon. Wondering what had become of Hunt I carried on back the way we had come, until at last, not far from the place where we had begun to crawl, I saw the tusker standing thirty yards away from the edge of the scrub cover with his back to me, showing one tusk in the faint moonlight as he whisked a cluster of rice stems and knocked them against his forelegs before beginning to chew. I heard a small furtive noise behind me, and had begun to turn very, very slowly without the tiniest rustle of shirt collar or sweater sleeve, when Hunt fired from behind me, six feet away, with a shattering explosion and a long purple and orange flame on a line I could have touched by extending an arm. He had shot the rogue in the backside, and I pressed the torch on to see if it would show its head, even for an oblique shot. The great pale body seemed to shrink, and then with a rattle of air, followed by a loud trumpeted complaint, the rogue began a shambling run, swerving to the left. At about fifty yards I had a clear side view of his head, and as the torch still gave a fair shape of his head, showing the eye and the laid back ear I aimed between them, something telling me at that range it would be a lethal shot at an errant beast. He wheeled away and staggered, going down on his knees, with his back to us, but was soon up again, and walked with long strides away into the dark, gasping and uttering deep rattling grumbles, heading west for the nearest tongue of dense forest. I then began cursing myself for taking a shot which was now clearly ill-judged. Hunt said the thing was so close he thought he would be sure to drop it with what he called a 'back-raking' shot. He said he hadn't seen me when he fired, and had lost me half an hour ago. I made no comment, hoping my singing ear would soon recover, but made up my mind never to go after a target with another gun present, unless under instruction of an experienced man. I sent Ratna with two Koyas, taking Newton's permission, feeling there was a strong possibility the rogue might fall, or be standing badly wounded somewhere. The following day a letter came from George of Sirisbari in the hands of Ratna, saying they had found the elephant dead about three miles from the estate. He had put two Daflas to guard it so that no-one would steal the tusks. I sent a report to the Forest Officer, who said I should extract the tusks and take them to his office pending the Chief Conservator's approval to give them to me. West permitted me to go with Horsey in his car to Sirisbari the following day to thank George and extract the tusks, but when we had walked the three miles with George into the forest, we found no Daflas, no tusks. We found the Winchester bullet in the rear left ham, and weeks later George showed me the skull, with the Mauser bullet just inside the roof of the brain. The political officer much later said he had heard of a pair of tusks being moved into the interior, but all trace was lost, and the men who had been appointed for a good sum to guard them were never identified.

Within the next week I had a note from Foyle saying the elephants had started feeding on the late rice not far from his bungalow, where water lay in an old oxbow bed of the Mirijuli. There was an archipelago maze of irregular islands in the crescent of rich silt, each covered with dense stands of elephant grass, pampas grass, wild ginger and cane thorn. These were impenetrable to man, and often held wild pig and jungle fowl. I had seen this area from the air, and it struck me how like a maze it was. Foyle's labour cultivated this area, and were pleading for me to protect their crop. It was a difficult area to watch over at night, as so little could be seen of the elephants. I was invited to dinner with the Foyles, who still had some of the sambar venison and served a delightful meal for a bachelor accustomed to a very simple diet. Foyle pleaded that I shouldn't kill an elephant in that area, as it was upwind of the bungalow, and the stench would be unbearable, and so I assured him I would try to scare as many of them as possible, using my old ammunition. I had walked round the area on my way to their bungalow before it was dark, and Foyle had posted watchers to let me know when the elephants arrived.

Their only safe approach was from the forest through the estate, where they walked 'hull down' in the little valleys where streams ran through the tea. Surprisingly, we had just finished dinner and had sat before the fire talking of our days at Medeloabam and the curious behaviour of Telford, when the head bearer announced the arrival of the watchers below the bungalow. The elephants had arrived, and had crossed the road which ran north past the bungalow. They were now out of sight amongst the islands, making quite a noise at feeding. There were twelve of them, three of which were small ones, and there were three tuskers. I changed into my outfit, which amused the elegant Dierdre, but wore mudstained tennis shoes for safety, not needing to creep closely to deal with a rogue. I said I would try to frighten them off with shots into the water very close to them, and after three shots I would go back to bed, which I hoped wouldn't be very late.

I told the three watchers to go round to the other side of the area, which was hardly four acres, where they would be able to gather river boulders of cricket ball size which, after coming as close to the rice area as possible, they should lob over the islands in the direction of the feeding noises, and keep on doing this until they heard a shot, when they could go home to bed, like me. I went north along the track, and had a good look in the bright half-moonlight at the possible escape routes. I found fresh warm droppings about 150 yards from the bungalow, and thought this was the place I should watch. The watchers did very well, and were joined by a handful of cultivators, who joined in the lobbing, and began a lot of shouting as well. The elephants emitted several trumpet blasts, and I heard them begin to move fast, audibly in a fairly tight scrum. My calculation of where they would cross the track was wrong, and I had to lope on tiptoe towards the bungalow. On the other side of the dip in the track I thought I saw someone with a bright white turban. The tree shadows made it difficult to see detail. However, it was clear the herd was going to emerge and go through the dip. I hid close against the fence and waited. First to cross was a huge female who went for ten yards and blew, rumbled deeply, turning to see the others. Three females with three youngsters, all close together, went through at speed. Behind me I heard noise, and turning I saw one tusker and two females crossing into the estate. I turned back to see the last tusker emerge. When he was head and shoulders out he stopped, and turned a little towards where I had seen the white turban. I aimed the rifle about two feet behind where his tail would be, downwards into the water, and fired. The tusker swung round, raising his trunk to trumpet, and beginning to move fast, not to follow the herd, but along the track where I stood. I had little time to think, and although it flashed through my brain that he was charging the source of the shot, the fact that he was beginning his run not at me on the side but at the middle of the track kept me from firing at him, and he was past me going at speed within a couple of seconds. I fired two shots past his ears, and heard a long, shrill trumpet blast from the herd, now receding fast towards the primeval forest. I had heard cries, and saw the white turban and three other figures running to the bungalow. The following day Foyle sent a note thanking me for my sortie, explaining they had not known I was actually on the other side of the elephants which were crossing the track on their way home until I started firing, when they ran like startled rabbits back to the bungalow. I quote: 'It was difficult for Dierdre in her long evening gown, but if the elephants were half as shaken as we were they won't be back for a hell of a long time.' The only sour note was the next day when West, sweeping past me to drive home for breakfast, said with a frosty smile it was a good job I had missed with my three shots; it would have been a terrible stench for months if I had killed an elephant next to Foyle's bungalow at Bankukurajan. I thought it most unlikely Foyle would have said any more than that he had asked me not to shoot any elephants so close to his bungalow, and I had in any case begun to wonder if some of these older planters depended upon the reports of their spies, because I had decided after the episode involving the mistaken delivery of elephant steaks it was not worth while trying, even with a polite little note, to set the record right; better to see the funny side of such convinced misinterpretations – privately, of course. It was but human for me to bask in the good regard of the people who were grateful for the successful efforts of a young *sahib*, who not only flew aeroplanes but killed dangerous rogue elephants and tigers. As so often happens in life, legends are woven around most good deeds exaggerating and embellishing the reputation of the perpetrator with outrageous hyperbole. The doers of good deeds or the performers of dangerous expeditions are the worst affected as a result of this, protesting at the incorrectness of people's claims yet glowing with a certain amount of forgivable vanity from the heavy wine of such praise.

By mid-January I felt life was beginning to be simpler, and I was learning more to relax and take things less seriously. Looking back and feeling embarrassment at the behaviour of a twenty-six-year-old bachelor whose only ambition was to explore the vast wilderness of primeval mountain forest, it is easy to suggest he was suffering from a combination of an isolation which he mistakenly preferred, and a suppression of sexual activity in spite of and in response to the raw attractions and opportunities of his fecund environment. It was a case of him having missed the normal programme of adult development that had only begun to reappear when the war had been ended for at least a year, so that the business of growing up was forgotten in the strange new life of the Assam 'out-back'.

The more I enjoyed the 'cold weather' wanderings in that beautiful forest, the more I began to enjoy proving what Gerella and Johann had told me: that creatures like tigers and elephants were, like humans, dangerous only when they were threatened. I had begun to discover I was a changed creature, with a part of my brain which knew what was required of me in the wilderness, and gave me messages, although I had hardly known I was storing such information. It seemed I was beginning to develop a deep love for the world as it was before humans began to colonise it. It was old Johann who, when I sat over his fire talking with him in the twilight, said I was learning a lot about the jungle and its creatures. He said I had quicker than most become able to receive messages from the spirits of animals; it was this that had probably saved me from being killed by the *bhagal badmash*; but I was a young man, and young men should not become completely dedicated *shikaris*. He laughed when he said my exploits with the elephants frightened the girls; they admired it just as they admired me for flying aeroplanes; but it frightened them. He said the older *shikaris* saw nothing in women and girls, but the girls are always telling each other, and their mothers, that you look at them as if you wanted them, but nothing happens. 'They SAY they are afraid, *sahib*, but that is most likely not true. It is not good for you to live without a wife or a mistress, not good for your health, and not good for people to wonder what kind of man you really are.' When he smoked his opium all kinds of frank analysis and philosophy would flow, and I was grateful for it, but I always told him I would only marry when I found the right girl. I said it was true there were many very attractive girls, but it would not be a good thing for anyone if I made a girl pregnant, and might ruin her chances of making a good marriage. He laughed, and said I thought far too much. 'God is only concerned to people the earth with plenty of children,' he said, 'and it's only people who make all the difficulties.' He was a wise man, and it was true animals had no fear or suspicion of him. When I left him after that talk I had no idea I would never see him again.

The following day was a black one, and was to remain so. West took me into his office and asked me to sit, handing me a letter from the Calcutta agents. I was to pack and depart for the South Bank, to take the post of assistant manager in charge of Baorijan, the first place in which I had lived when I first arrived in Assam, three long years ago. My first instinct was to ask why I was being posted, but West, seeing the signs of protest in my expression, told me with my three years of experience it was necessary to use me on a bigger job. New recruits were being taken on, but they all needed training. He said I had spent six weeks at Baorijan, and wouldn't find it strange. George Fraser would visit me weekly once I had found my feet. The letter said I was to arrive at Baorijan not later than the 15th of February, which shook me, as I had hoped to stay until June 1951, when I would be due for my first home leave of six months, having served four and a half years. West went on to tell me how he had reported on me. He said he thought I was my own worst enemy, because I had all one needed to make a success of a career in tea, but spoiled it by being too critical, and too contrary. In fact for an air force officer I seemed to have lost my sense of team spirit and service discipline. He said I would have to be patient and put up with the people ahead of me, absorbing experience as much as possible in view of the fact that if I won recognition for achievement, I would be promoted as manager within five or six years. Having said this he stabbed his chest with a stiff finger: 'I had to wait twelve years for my promotion, and took a cut in pay when the thirties slump hit us. I joined the company in 1920, two years after having been demobbed as a lieutenant. I've had to pay for the education of my two children in England. I didn't see my wife at all during the war, and have only been able to save for the past six years. When I retire in three years' time at fifty-five I hope I can get a job to keep me going until my policies mature. I don't want you to repeat this, but I made the stupid mistake of doing what you've been doing: venting my scorn on my manager, whose reports were sent to London without me knowing what he had said. He was a deadbeat boozer, but could write marvellous reports in splendid English; they were all rubbish, but went down well. Those bad reports hung round my neck and spoiled my chances of promotion, even after I became a manager. I hope by telling you this it will help to put you on the right road.'

That, poured on top of the depressing news of my posting, was a further assault on my morale. I stood, almost dizzy with guilt and compassion, and saddened at what he had told me. 'Thank you, sir! I know I've been difficult and apologise for it. It makes me very angry to hear what you have had to suffer, and I shall never forget what you have just told me.' I held out my hand, and he stood, scowling with moist eyes as we shook hands. As I left the office I told myself I had to grow up. Ringing in my ears was what the colonel in Allahbad had said: 'You can't carry on flying Spitfires all your life. You'll have to start growing up.' I saw I hadn't really broken away from the similar adrenaline thrills of creeping after elephants in darkness, wandering through the wonderful wilderness, having random encounters with beautiful wild creatures. True, I was being sent away from all that, and that it hurt suddenly seemed like being operated on for something like a growth that wasn't in fact all that good for me. West's message made me feel small, selfish, and lacking in understanding. It was simple enough to be compassionate for the estate workers, the villagers, and their precarious existence; but I had to realise my focus was too narrow. People like West and Horsey, I realised, not only suffered, but needed compassion and support, and I would have to think more of my religion, to explore ways to do more good, not for glory, but by stealth. Although I had been reading less, I felt ashamed to have read so much of spiritual improvement, Christian and Hindu, and enjoyed the readings almost like poetry or music, and yet felt like a selfish oaf when West, whom I had written off as hopelessly hidebound by weird protocol, presented me with the undeserved gift of wise advice, drawn from his own unfortunate experience. I saw I had a long way to go. I owed a lot to Constable, and would have to tell him so.

My journey to Baorijan remains in my mind as painful and nostalgic, almost as bad as leaving the air force. The details are lost in those fortunate mists of memory which by some benign concern of our Creator drift across many of the miserable experiences in one's life. What I do remember well was the crystal clarity of the landscape of the North Bank on the day of my departure. I watched it as it receded: the blue ridges, the dense mountain forests, and the luminosity of colours, all of which made me swear never to rest until I managed to graduate with the confidence of the company, competent not only to run an estate well, but to convince the board that I would be highly successful working on the North Bank. Not much of an ambition, to be sure, but a positive aim. I had left early in the morning, and when I told Nakul and Girilal I would return in a year or two, they grinned awkwardly, and told me not to leave it too long.

223

By the time I arrived at Baorijan I had made up my mind to begin anew, do my best, and not eat my heart out at having to live in a place which had nearly destroyed my dreams of what life in Assam would be like. I had a good welcome from MacFortune's old servants, who had elected to remain with their own families. I remembered the names of Porakeet the cook, Kobi the head bearer, and Ganesh the kitchen scullion, and was glad they remembered me. Since MacFortune had left, Baorijan had seen four different assistant managers, one of whom had been stoned and chased off by the workers. The present incumbent, another over-age retired planter, wanted to hand over as soon as possible, being no longer interested in dealing with such a labour force which, he said, was being stirred up by competing unions determined to influence their voting in the huge new democracy of India. The day after I arrived I reported to George Fraser in his office at Hiloibhanga. At first he depressed me by telling of the development of frequent labour trouble. He said things had deteriorated at Baorijan, mainly because of a clash of unions, and a certain amount of ineptitude by the assistant before last who had a filthy temper, and used too much derogatory abuse. The result was the people were now not so much lazy but deliberately inefficient. They were being affected by the communist agitators who had caused the recent trouble at the railway workshops near Dibrugarh. He told me how when a magistrate and a Deputy Superintendent of Police went to meet the raging mob of railway strikers, mainly to warn them if they did not vacate the workshops they would suffer a lathi (long baton) charge. When this was announced the mob became inflamed, and amongst them were at least two people with guns. The Deputy Superintendent was shot, and died. It had become so bad that last season people from Hiloibhanga had to be sent to pluck at Baorijan on Fridays and Saturdays, because the pluckers were going slow, absenteeism was rife, and the leaf was tending to grow coarse by the time it was plucked. They needed a keen man who would, with circumspection and good discipline, bring them back to what they used to be. Fraser said it would be difficult, a very tough assignment, but he had a hunch I would take it carefully and succeed in time. He said he would send my cycle back and take me for a drive round the estate. I noticed only the *sirdars* greeted by saluting, and some of those did so in the way of surly, disgruntled men. I recognised Siria *sirdar*, the only Munda *sirdar* on the estate. Fraser stopped to speak to him, telling me he was one of the only decent *sirdars* they had. He raised his hand and smiled shyly, but when I

224

spoke to him in Mundari he gave a broad grin and replied robustly, saying I had learned well, as he remembered when I first arrived I could hardly speak at all. We drove to a place where there were no people working, and Fraser got out, saying it was a good place to talk. He filled his pipe, and began delivering his inaugurative message.

'I am disappointed at your performance on the North Bank, MacStorm. This business of losing interest if your own idea of doing something isn't accepted is certainly not the way I work, and not the way you would like people who work under you to behave. Here we have a bunch of truculent bastards who are behaving just that way. What West found most annoying was that he found you knowledgeable, hard-working, good at the language – in fact the languages – but he couldn't understand why you were so difficult for Horsey to handle.'

'We discussed it all just before I left, sir, but without Horsey. I apologised for not understanding Horsey's problems more. I learned a lot from West, unfortunately just too late to do anything during my spell there. He filled me in on what he had been through in his time, and I felt I would have behaved differently had I known it before.'

'Good, MacStorm! I want you to understand clearly that I agree with what Telford, Foyle, MacFortune and West have said about your potential. I tell you now you will have a very tough assignment on this place, and you will run it yourself with guidance and enthusiasm from me. Ask plenty of questions and keep me completely in touch with what you are doing, and what you aim to do. My reading of your temperamental problems tells me you will do better without a long chain of command above you; if you don't you will deserve no more chances like this.' He stared through his spectacles with the well-remembered magnification of his large black pupils, his lips pursed tightly with the trace of a smile, and said, 'Now let's look at the grazing ground down yonder; it's a bit near the main road, but I want you to let me have a report on the possibility of making an airstrip there. I'm fed up with the idea of having to drive fifteen miles to Medeloabam if I want to fly to the North Bank, or down to Tocklai. Let me know what the estimated cost will be to level it, fill in the holes, and change the positioning of the stiles so that no-one crosses the strip to get over the fence.' People tended to make fun of George Fraser's dramatic diction, but despite the distinct warning's impact on me, I blessed the concise briefing on what was expected of me, and thanked him for describing the shortened chain of command, without any reference to the frustrations of Mirijuli except for what must have been an irrepressible expression of relief on my face.

As we walked the 220 yards of hard grazing ground, noting how much levelling would have to be done, Fraser told me there was the first of three new assistants due to arrive in this year of 1950, each of whom was qualifying as a private pilot in England at the company's expense before sailing for India. 'The first should arrive at Medeloabam within two to three weeks, to work under MacDonald when Telford goes off on his home leave. His name is Bracknell, and the Board wants you to fly with him, first of all to report on his suitability for flying out here, and next to introduce him to all airstrips he will need to use when he begins his flying duties. How do you feel about that?'

My first question was, 'I presume Mr Telford will be happy with this arrangement?'

'I think he is fully in the picture, MacStorm, and advice has been taken from an ex-air force wing commander who is an aviation consultant, recommended by you to Telford. He gave a lot of good advice on how to be careful about ensuring valid insurance in case of accidents et cetera, and how to manage the air scheme using young, not very experienced pilots who certainly may not fly for hire or reward. I have already put it to the Board, through Calcutta, that as you will be running Baorijan yourself, and since you disliked being taken off your estate duties to fly so often, you will be trusted to arrange your flying with new pilot-assistants to suit – how did one say it in the services – to suit the exigencies of Baorijan. How's that?'

I thanked him for explaining everything so clearly, and said I was glad to be able to fly again, particularly as Constable was going on home leave this year, and I would lose my flying with him. This pleased Fraser immensely, and he said he was glad to have me confirm I was still very keen to fly. 'Someone had told the Board you said you had lost interest in flying,' he raised his hand and shook his head when I began to expostulate indignantly. 'People sometimes really get it wrong you know,' he said, 'and some of them tend to say what suits them. Now! What matters is you have confirmed you are very keen to serve in the capacity required by the Board. I told them you would fly for the love of it. Right?' He looked at his watch and said he must go. 'My visits to see you won't be previously arranged. I've so much on my plate it can't work that way. I'm not going to try to catch you out; but if I have not been to see you at least once a week, you come and see me.' With that he entered his car, waving. 'Fix this bloody place, MacStorm. You'll have a lot of trouble, but fix it! Take ten days to study and make notes before you start to put things right.' He burst out laughing and drove off in his sports Riley. I began making my notes. It was difficult to believe there had been so much left undone, and so much wrongly done, except when one remembered what the *jemadar babu* kept saying: that there had been so many different assistant managers, all with different ideas, and one or two very slack.

Within the first week I had my first unusual incident. Attending office in the thick and chilling South Bank mists was a depressing change from the fresh, cold breezes and the bright sun at Mirijuli, and even when the mist cleared and gave way to the sun there was no brightness in the faces of the workers, in stark contrast to Mirijuli and Medeloabam, even to Baorijan when MacFortune was here. The thought of working with people who were sullen made me yearn to find out how to cure this, and I was not optimistic. Within a week of taking charge, at about three in the morning, a house had caught fire and had burnt to the ground. Shivering without blankets or warm garments, a couple with four children appeared at the office, to report their misfortune. Everything had been burnt, except for a few pots and tools. They had nothing left of their food rations, and all of their meagre clothes and blankets had been burnt to ashes. I gave orders for the cutting of bamboos, and the rebuilding of the house, putting the sufferer in the building team to ensure everything was done properly. I remembered there was a 'welfare fund', started by MacFortune, which was where fines, paid by villagers or estate labourers for letting their cattle, goats or pigs trespass on the estate, or any employees' fruit or vegetable gardens, were kept in a special account for charitable grants. I discussed with the J.B. (*jemadar babu*) how much the unfortunate people would need for food until next pay day, and how much they would need to purchase clothes and blankets on a reasonable scale. He was totally opposed to any kind of payment, saying if they lived in a village and were silly enough to get drunk and allow their house to burn down, who would pay them? 'NO, sir! It will only bring trouble to interfere with what everyone naturally accepts is a situation they themselves have to deal with. If you are kind to these nasty drunken people they will take more advantage from it.' I thought this man lacked compassion, and said such accidents sometimes happened, and we could not let them go without food and clothing. I was not being soft and over-compassionate, rather thinking if we depended upon these people for their work we must support them thus. I ordered they should receive sixty rupees for food and clothes, which the J.B. and staff reluctantly arranged. When Fraser appeared three days later it was one of the things I reported to him. He was clearly surprised at what I had done, but laughed, and said it was better for me to discover for myself what was likely to happen when one disbursed charity with a heart of gold. We went through the list of notes, and he made comments such as 'stall that one for a bit', 'go ahead hard with that', and so on. Within the next three weeks two more houses were burned to the ground, and *chowkidars* and *sirdars* came whispering to me that in each case the contents of the houses had been safely removed before a torch was applied. I gave no more grants for such cases, and issued letters to the claimants warning I would call the police to investigate what were rumoured to be cases of arson. I was learning life in the proximity of a town was different. I soon found the cost of food 50 per cent more than it was on the North Bank. Another threat to economy was the easy availability not only of food, but of clothing, bedding, curtains etc., which made me realise that I could no longer save so much; but I was delighted to find how, with yearly increases in salary, I had saved a good sum.

Very soon I was meeting people. Steve MacDonald drove from Medeloabam to see me; and Bhupendra Sarma cycled along to renew our acquaintance. At Hiloibhanga I met a new Indian assistant called Rabin Bhattacharjee, trained as an engineer in England. My jungle life was shelved, and the social life edged nearer, whether I liked it or not. About ten days later I met many other people when we were called to the Frasers' bungalow one day for a reception with drinks and snacks to meet the London Chairman on his visit to Assam.